BRENI

A BEAUTIFUL MESS

"Anderson delivers an impactful story about the power of faith within flawed, complicated people. . . . Readers who enjoy the work of Karen Kingsbury should check this out."

—PUBLISHER'S WEEKLY/BOOKLIFE

If you like realistic stories about flawed people learning to follow Jesus, then this is a book for you . . . well-written story with excellent characterisation.

—CHRISTINE DILLON, Award-winning author of *Grace in Strange Disguise*

A Beautiful Mess is a powerful, realistic read about the love and faithfulness of God to repair and restore the pieces of our broken lives. I loved it. I always adore all of Brenda Anderson's novels.

—JULIA WILSON, ChristianBookaholic.com

This book drew me in from the very beginning. I laughed, cried, mourned, and cheered throughout the story for the different characters. Brenda Anderson has given us a truly beautiful story of how God can take the broken pieces of human's life mistakes and sins and create a truly wonderful mosaic.

—MARGARET LAWTON, avid reader

What an incredible work of art. This story is amazing, a true forgiveness story, bringing out how God loves us and is waiting for our repentance.

—CHERYL KRAUSS, avid reader

BROKEN TOGETHER

A NOVEL

BRENDA S. ANDERSON
& Sarah S. Anderson

Vivant Press
Broken Together

ISBN-13: 978-1-951664-05-3

Cover Design by Marion Ueckermann and George Weis
Cover Photos from Depositphotos

Printed in the United States of America

19 20 21 22 23 24 25 7 6 5 4 3 2 1

Welcome to

THE MOSAIC COLLECTION

We are sisters, a beautiful mosaic united by the love of God through the blood of Christ

Each month The Mosaic Collection releases one faith-based novel or anthology exploring our theme, Family by His Design. We share stories that feature diverse, God-designed families. These stories range from mystery and women's fiction to humorous and literary fiction. We hope you'll join our Mosaic family as we learn together what truly defines a family.

Subscribe to *Grace & Glory*, the official newsletter of The Mosaic Collection, to receive monthly encouragement from Mosaic authors as well as timely updates about events, new releases, and giveaways.

Subscribe:
www.mosaiccollectionbooks.com/grace-glory/

Learn more about The Mosaic Collection at:
www.mosaiccollectionbooks.com/

Join our Reader Community, too!
www.facebook.com/groups/theMosaiccollection

For those who’ve been wrongly incarcerated,
and for the families who fight for their freedom.

Know you are seen,
you are not forgotten,
and you are loved!

"You had to be free in your heart. Guilt, fear, anger—
they were all their own kinds of prison.
You could be out in the world and still be doing time."

– Ronald Cotton –

Picking Cotton: Our Memoir of Injustice and Redemption

Summer of '98

"How can I help you?" Chad Taylor grinned at the young woman with the Courtney Cox-like hairstyle. Seemed like everyone their age was mimicking that popular *Friends* series.

She squinted at the menu, frowned even, as if nothing looked good. If he made it, it would taste good. "Do you have anything other than coffee?"

Other than coffee? He stepped back as if she'd shoved him but maintained his smile. "You come into a coffee shop but don't want coffee?"

"That's correct." She returned a smile, clearly confident in her reply, and continued surveying the menu. "I'll have a hot cocoa."

Hot cocoa? Cuppa Truth served the best coffee ever, made by the best barista ever (him!), and she wanted hot cocoa?

"Um, have you checked the weather?" He nodded toward the windows, which showcased people walking the sidewalks, all wearing as little as legally possible it seemed. "Not exactly a hot cocoa type of day."

"Yet, people order hot coffee. How is that different?"

"How is that different?" He planted his hands on the counter in front of himself and bent toward her as the door to the shop opened, ushering in a river of hot air. "Does hot cocoa wake you from your morning stupor? Give you energy? Does it help you think better? Make the sun look brighter? Coffee soothes the soul! On top of that, it's healthy. It's full of antioxidants, helps your memory. It's good for your heart. Word has it, it might even cure cancer. Best of all, it gives you the good sense not to murder those close to you."

She chuckled at his slight exaggeration.

"I'm winning you over." He always did. "So, tell me, what do you wanna try?" No doubt, she'd love anything he made.

"I'll have a hot cocoa, please."

You've got to be kidding me. He sighed and dramatically splayed his hand over his heart. "You have no idea what you're missing."

"And I'll take whipped cream on top of my drink."

"As you wish." Shaking his head, he rang up her drink and told her the cost.

She handed him a five. "Keep the change."

"'Preciate it. And your name?"

"Jennifer."

Jennifer? Nah, he'd call her Cocoa.

PLANNING THE ESCAPE

"Bring me out of prison, that I may give thanks to your name!"

Psalm 142:7

Chapter One

Present Day

Today was the perfect day to plot her prison break.

At least that was what Jennifer Taylor called her intent to break free from her parents' home. Six years and four months of being under her mother's over-watchful eye was six-plus years too long. But with her husband in a real prison, she'd had little choice.

Until now.

She hummed with her car radio as she drove along the winding country road, her teens blessedly silent and not arguing, for once. The air conditioning blasted cold air to combat Minnesota's August heat and humidity that made many in the state long for winter. But for her, it was a reminder that school would be starting soon, and she'd be teaching third graders for the sixth year in a row. She did love the age. Young enough to be eager to learn and not old enough to have developed the disrespect that was frequently exhibited, even now, among fourth graders.

Maybe farther out of the Twin Cities, respect was more commonplace.

That was what she hoped. In one year, the twins would be in college, and she could move on. Live on the opposite side of the Twin Cities metro area from Mom and Dad. Close enough for the occasional visit, yet far enough away to avoid the helicoptering Mom excelled at.

Close enough to easily make the drive to visit her husband.

She shot a glimpse at Jason beside her in the passenger seat, then in the mirror at Chloe. No surprise, the twins were occupied with their phones.

Ah, bliss!

The Mississippi periodically peeked through the trees that would be donning their fall coats in another month or so. Oh, Chad would love it once he served the last half of his sentence. A long seventy-four months for a crime he didn't commit. Having a home—owning a coffee shop—by the Mississippi had always been his dream. For now, a house would have to suffice.

A steeple rose above the trees, then a thirty-mile-an-hour sign informed her the town of Donaldson lay just ahead. A good friend, a realtor, had recommended she look in this area for affordable homes. The town was small, with a population of less than five thousand residents. If she could secure a job at Donaldson Elementary a year from now, that would be perfect.

The area was also three-plus hours away from where Chad had been convicted, so no one here would be aware of her past. Once she found a teaching position and a home, she would be starting anew. She'd not only be breaking free of her parents' home, but she would finally be free from the stigma of being a prison wife.

Oh, she'd like to give a good tongue-lashing to whoever coined that term.

She banished the label from her mind and focused on the scenery, still a luscious green.

Older but well-kept homes now clustered on the sides of the winding road. It took a big S-curve around the church and past a fire station, then spilled onto a main street that was nothing to brag about. A post office—that was barely bigger than a postage stamp—and a dumpy looking bar occupied one side of the road. The other side might have been a retail area at one time, but what had likely once been storefronts were all vacant.

This main street definitely needed some love and attention. Maybe that was why homes were more affordable in this Minneapolis suburb.

"Mom, stop!" Chloe screeched behind her.

Jenn slammed on the brakes. Her heart pumping faster than the car had been moving, she glanced around to see what had caused Chloe to yell.

Behind her, an impatient driver honked, so Jenn pulled off on the side of the road. Then she turned to her daughter, who opened the door, letting steamy air inside.

"Didn't you see it, Mom? Jase?" Chloe reached up to the front passenger seat and tugged an earbud from her brother's ear. She pointed down the street. "Look!"

Both Jenn and Jason followed where Chloe pointed. A handful of empty brick storefronts. The main drag through town, albeit a small town, was not exactly where she wanted to live, but she'd humor her dramatic daughter.

"What's your problem?" Jason tugged out his other earbud, obviously in no mood to humor his sister. "There's nothing here but a bunch of dumpy buildings."

"You have no imagination." Chloe stepped out of the car and slammed the door.

"Come on, Jason. You know she won't leave us alone until we see what she's excited about."

He groaned. "You don't want to live here, do you?"

"Right here? No. But it wouldn't hurt to check out the town."

"What town? There's not even a coffee shop. Dad'd hate it."

She couldn't argue with that. Still, she nodded toward his twin, who was already halfway down the block. Impulsive, like her father.

"We're exploring today, that's all." Jenn put an arm around his shoulder, but he shrugged it off.

Teenagers . . .

She got out of the car and jogged to catch up to Chloe, who'd stopped in front of the brick building on the corner.

"Mom, look!" She gestured to the window. "It's for sale!"

"I'm not really ready to buy—" A glance through the window stopped her, drew her in closer as if she were metal and the window a magnet.

She removed a napkin from her purse and wiped dirt from the window. Peered inside. Saw mounds of dirt. Even more junk.

And a long wood bar. "Your father's dream," she said, barely above a whisper.

"And yours." Chloe had rubbed her own spot clean.

"Yes, but your father isn't here." Jenn retreated a step, forcing reality to banish the dream.

"And it's probably way expensive." This from Jason, who kept Chloe grounded.

"That too. But your father would remind us that it's always good to dream." With a sigh, Jenn headed to her car. Someday she and Chad would realize their dream of opening a coffee and cocoa shop, but first he had to be released from prison. Her immediate dream—her daily prayer—was that evidence would come forward proving his innocence.

No way did her husband murder his former mentor.

"Mom, can't we at least check it out?" Chloe grabbed her arm then thrust a note into Jenn's hand. "Here's the realtor's number. Give her a call, please?"

Jenn stared at the number, wanting to call, more out of curiosity than anything, but they'd be wasting the realtor's time. Chad wouldn't have hesitated. "We probably wouldn't see it today."

"We can always return. It's not that far from Gran and Pop's place. Please?" Chloe looked at her with those puppy dog eyes that Chad had always succumbed to. Jenn was less prone to giving in, but admittedly, she wanted to see this place, too.

"Okay, fine. I'll call, but she'll most likely say *no*."

"Thank you." Chloe kissed Jenn on the cheek then hurried to the storefront.

Jason harrumphed. "She's just gonna be disappointed, and then she'll pout for the next month." Her too-mature-for-his-age son was always the voice of reason.

"You do realize"—Jenn's finger hovered over her phone's keypad—"that if I don't call the realtor, Chloe will spend the next month sulking anyway."

"There is that."

"So, why not? That's what today is about. We're breaking free, remember?"

"I s'pose." He kicked at the concrete sidewalk that had more weeds growing through it than concrete.

"I'll call the realtor, we'll drive around a bit more, check out a house or two on the Open House Tour, then grab some ice cream."

He snorted. "Not from this town."

Too true. Jenn swept an arm over her forehead, wiping away perspiration as she looked up and down the street. A constant stream of cars whizzed past going much faster than the thirty-mile-an-hour sign instructed. Children played in a park across the road. Maybe there were no stores or cafés, but it was a growing area. It would benefit from a coffee shop, wouldn't it?

She dialed the realtor's number and waited through only two rings.

"Kimberly Midge, Star Realty."

"Yes, Kimberly. This is Jenn Taylor. I'm looking at one of your properties in Donaldson. It's right on the main drag."

"Oh, yes, the old Lawton Bar. It was once a bustling place."

Well, not anymore. "Would it be possible to look at it, or do I have to fill out paperwork first?"

"Are you there right now?"

"Yes, we are."

"Hmmm. Usually, I'd require seeing a pre-approval letter, but I'm free at the moment, so why not? I can be there in five minutes."

"Really?"

"What?" Chloe looked expectantly at Jenn, who put a finger to her lips.

"I live a mile away in a new subdivision. See you soon."

Jenn hung up and grinned at her daughter. "Guess we're looking at a bar."

"Brother." Jason shook his head and trudged to the car.

"He's such a party pooper all the time." Chloe returned to the window and stared inside.

Yeah, Jenn agreed, he might be a killjoy sometimes, but then so was she. Six years without her helpmate had molded that in her. She had to live—to parent—in this harsh reality, not in Chloe's dream world.

But for one day, visiting that dream world wasn't a bad idea. It was healthy even.

Minutes later, a bright blue Jeep pulled to the curb and a woman who looked like she'd stepped right from a salon got out. No doubt, she was always ready for calls to come in.

Jenn walked toward her. "Kimberly?"

"You must be Jenn." Kimberly extended her hand. "Nice to meet you. And you are?" She held out her hand to Chloe.

"Her daughter, Chloe. And that guy"—she pointed her thumb toward Jason, who plodded toward them—"is my brother, Jason. Don't mind him."

"Aw, I understand brothers. I have four of them." Kimberly opened the lockbox on the door of the bar and inserted the key into the lock. With a little struggle, she finally got the door to budge. She shoved it open and spread her arms. "Ta da! Welcome to your new business."

Jenn nearly choked from the stench coming from this grand "new" business. Heat rushed out as if the store had been strangled and needed fresh air.

"That's nasty." Jason gagged and backed away, fingers pinching his nose.

But Chloe, her eyes big as quarters, stepped inside. "Wow," she whispered in awe, seemingly oblivious to the stench and the heat.

This is a bad idea. Jenn buried her nose in her shirt and stepped inside the building. Saunas were cooler than this. What she did for her kids. It took a moment for her eyes to adjust to the darkness. *Wow is right.* She examined the layers of garbage on the floor. Fast food bags and wrappers. Beer bottles. Other items she wouldn't touch with five pairs of gloves on.

"It's a dump." Jason remained in the doorway, still pinching his nose.

"You have no imagination." Chloe waded through the garbage to the bar. They were all going to need a tetanus shot after this. "Mom, feel this. It's real wood."

"That it is." Kimberly smartly remained in the doorway. Apparently, she didn't want to be infected with whatever might be lying among the garbage either. "The ceilings are the original tin. The floors, if you can find them, are original oak hardwood."

"Hmm," Jenn said, trying not to sound too interested, though inexplicably, she was. Too much so. Keeping her nose buried in her shirt, she gingerly stepped through the junk to the bar. She pulled a tissue from her purse and wiped a spot so she wouldn't have to touch whatever animal's feces polka-dotted the top. They'd all need a shower after they left here.

She touched the wood, then knelt to examine it. Two inches thick. Someone who knew how to restore wood could make it shine. She walked around the bar and took in all the storage beneath the wood top. Like the floors, all the shelves were filled with junk, but junk could easily be tossed.

There was plenty of room to move around behind the bar as well. She closed her eyes and envisioned Chad standing there, chatting with customers like Sam Malone did on *Cheers*, though Chad would be serving coffee instead of booze. He'd be in his element.

The seating area would have plenty of space for guest tables. Below the window, they could create a free library. Maybe even a food shelf, so the hungry could help themselves to groceries.

"We could display local artists' work on the walls." Chloe's outward enthusiasm echoed Jenn's internal excitement. "And invite local musicians on the weekends. I'll bet we could find a local baker to provide pastries."

"I know just the person." Kimberly searched through her purse and removed a business card. She gingerly made her way from the door to the bar and handed Jenn the card. "Paula is phenomenal and currently works out of her home. I'm sure she'd love to have a physical store to sell her products."

Jenn pocketed the business card with a quiet, "Thank you." She didn't want to show how excited she was about this place already.

"Mom." To no one's surprise, Jason didn't share their enthusiasm. He remained in the doorway, his arms crossed, looking so much like a younger version of his father. "Seen enough yet?"

Yes, she had, because like Chloe, she was already drooling over the place. Cleaned up, this former bar was Chad's dream come to life.

"Well, this isn't all." Kimberly sounded like one of those TV commercials that kept saying, "And there's more!"

If Jenn were smart, she'd grab Chloe and turn around right now, but curiosity compelled her to follow the realtor. Window shopping never hurt, right?

Kimberly picked her way across the room to a hallway. "Here you'll find a restroom that needs a little renovation."

Jenn peeked into the room and laughed. It needed a gut, not a little reno.

"If you want, you could put a second powder room here." Kimberly opened the door to a good-sized closet. "Or it would make a good storage room."

Or maybe an employee breakroom . . .

Kimberly pointed out what likely had once been an office, with a heavy desk taking up a third of the space.

"But this is the cherry on top." Kimberly led to the end of the hall. She pointed to a door straight ahead. "That will lead you outside. I'd show you, but the doorknob is broken. You do have your own driveway."

"Asphalt?" Jenn could hope.

"Gravel."

"Garage?"

Kimberly laughed. "There is plenty of space to build one. That's all nice, but this is what I can't wait to show you." She inserted a key into a door perpendicular to the one leading outdoors, opened it, releasing more hot air, and gestured upward. "Your own apartment."

An apartment? Jenn tried tamping down her enthusiasm. Really, she did. But, in spite of the heat, she hurried up the solid wood steps to find an apartment that had been renovated in the sixties or thereabout, complete with avocado-green appliances. Layers of dust covered everything, but at least it didn't have the squatter garbage that filled the retail area.

"Open concept." Kimberly spread her arms and did a three-sixty in the center of the room. "Perfect for modern-day living."

Jason harrumphed again. "If the 1960s is modern."

"But she's right." Chloe stood beside the realtor. "You could put a wheeled island in the kitchen that could serve as a table, too." She gestured to the side of the room across from the kitchen. "A sectional would fit there nicely, don't you—" She gasped. "Mom, you have to see this." Chloe hurried to a cracked window that offered a blotchy view of outside.

Jenn joined her and released her own gasp. Chad would probably cry at the view of the Mississippi River, slightly obstructed by trees. In between the trees sat a neglected swing set with two swings dangling from the metal pole above. Perhaps it had been a park at one time? Chad would be adamant about checking it out, probably pushing her high to get an aerial view of the river. Then he'd insist she push him.

She couldn't help but sigh at the moments they'd missed together.

Come fall, the view from this window would be magnificent. Jenn hadn't asked the price, but this location informed her that she couldn't afford it. She needed to leave now before she and Chloe fell more in love with the place, and the realtor had to break their hearts.

She aimed for the door, and Jason looked relieved.

"You're leaving?" Kimberly asked. "But you haven't seen everything."

"I've seen enough to know it's not in my budget, and I'm sorry for wasting your time." She gestured for Jason to take the lead down the steps.

"But it's only—" Kimberly named the list price.

Jenn jerked to a stop at the top of the stairway. "How much?" She'd heard an unbelievably low number, one that was definitely within her budget, even considering the work that would have to be done.

She had to have heard wrong.

Kimberly named the price again. "It's been on the market for over a year, and the seller is very motivated. Most people see a major fixer-upper in a poor location, but I can tell you see its potential. I know a man who lives right here in Donaldson, who could help you fix up this place in months." Once again, she reached into her purse and pulled out a business card. "Caleb Johnson is the best you'll find."

Jenn stared at the card, but it was all a blur. For the price of a single home, she could purchase a business and a place to live. If Chad were here, he'd shout, "Sold."

"Mo-om."

Jenn ignored Jason. Would it be possible? Could she finally open the coffee and cocoa shop of their dreams?

What would Chad say about her moving on without him?

That was the real question. Still, her curiosity needed to be sated before reality quashed their dreams. "Show me the rest."

The realtor grinned. "I knew you'd say that." They toured a nice-sized bathroom that was also stuck in the sixties, but a gallon of paint would do wonders to refresh it. The bedroom was even large enough for a king bed, but the closet wouldn't fit half her wardrobe.

"And finally . . ." Kimberly gestured to a door between the bedroom and the bathroom that Jenn hoped would be a closet. The realtor tugged it open to reveal more stairs and even more heat. "A third floor that could be finished off someday."

Chloe squealed and Jason mumbled something under his breath, but Jenn had to take the creaking steps. She got to the top and looked around. Solid floor. Raftered ceiling. Windows at both ends of the room. And scat from some wild animal she definitely wouldn't want as a roommate. Still, if the room was finished off, it would be huge. They easily could add a couple of bedrooms and a game room. Maybe another bathroom.

Or maybe a master bedroom someday.

For now, it would suffice as storage area. Once it was cleaned, disinfected, and fumigated, that is.

A lot of elbow grease and TLC would make this apartment habitable, the bar welcoming.

Saying nothing more, she climbed down the steps, then walked through the hallway and café area and outside, where the air was breathable. Funny how it didn't feel sweltering anymore. She took in a huge cleansing breath and slowly let it out. The air was still August hot, but compared to suffocating inside, it was springlike.

"You could put patio tables out here." Kimberly locked the store. "Decorate it with planters."

Jenn looked up and down the sidewalk at the other neglected storefronts. One of the few negatives she'd found. "But we'd be the only business here." Not counting the dive bar across the street.

"Someone has to be the first." Chloe retreated a step and examined the row of empty buildings. "That would be the perfect location for a pizza shop."

Jason crossed his arms. "Then let someone else open a pizza place."

"I disagree." Chloe mimicked her brother, crossing her arms while glaring at him. "Why shouldn't we be the first to open? This is what we've always wanted."

We've always wanted . . . Jenn stared at the cracked sidewalk, tuning out the kids' argument. Until today, she had no clue that Chloe had adopted the dream as well. Jason was too serious to dream. Or to speak those dreams out loud. Both kids had witnessed the fallout of dreaming big, but that never deterred Chloe.

Perhaps it was time for Jenn to dream again. She jogged across the street, weaving among the too-fast traffic, for a different perspective. The building's brick exterior was inviting and didn't appear to require a lot of work. The front windows were filthy, but intact. Painting the front door azure, Chad's favorite color, would help it stand out from the rest. After that, all it needed was a sign—a name—something snappy that easily identified the place as a coffee and cocoa shop.

Yet, the storefronts to the left were all empty. Would a single coffee shop be enough of a draw to entice people to stop?

A lone coffee shop on a main drag through a town beginning to bloom with subdivisions? With the closest Starbucks miles away, people were probably begging for a coffee shop. Why shouldn't she be the one to open one?

This bar was Chad's dream, and she could make it come true.

But he wasn't due for release for years yet. Even if evidence was found proving his innocence, early release wasn't a guarantee.

Still . . .

Maybe this was God pushing them in a new direction.

"What do you think?" Kimberly and the kids joined her, breaking up Jenn's internal debate.

"I don't know." This was just a daydream, right?

"You're approved for a *home* loan, right Mom, not a business loan?" Naturally, Jason would bring up reality.

"That's true." She shook her head. A business loan would likely be completely different, and probably more difficult to obtain. After declaring bankruptcy when Chad went to prison, she'd worked hard on reestablishing her credit score to where she could get a decent mortgage rate, but was that enough for a business loan?

Kimberly handed her a card. "Talk with Howard Dayton at First National in Elk Run. Tell him I recommended you. He lives here in Donaldson and would love to see the downtown revitalized. A family-run business would be an excellent beginning."

"Is there anyone you don't know?" Jenn added that card to the others Kimberly had handed her. A realtor, carpenter, pastry chef, and now a loan officer.

"You don't get far in this business if you don't have connections, and I've been selling real estate for years." Kimberly aimed a remote at her car. "Go home. Think about it."

Jenn stared at the cards in her hands. Were these legitimate? For all she knew, this Kimberly Midge was a fraud. Before Jenn made any kind of decision, she needed to do a whole lot of research.

And even more praying, although, in the years since Chad's arrest, "No" had been the frequent reply to those prayers.

Knowing the obstacles placed in front of her right now, she was certain that "No" would be the answer again, but that didn't mean she was giving up hope. It only meant she was going to pray harder.

Chapter Two

"Are you sure?" Phone in hand, Jenn stared out a small opening in the snow-plastered window at the drifts piling high in her parents' backyard. She'd prayed for a white Christmas and was answered with, "How about a blizzard?" As long as she didn't have to drive anywhere, she was perfectly fine with it.

She wasn't certain whether she was fine with this phone call on Christmas Eve, of all days. Why were people even working today?

"Without question." Mr. Dayton's strong bass gave her no doubts that he was being truthful.

"Okay." She tore her gaze from the blizzard as a storm brewed inside her. "I'm going to have to think about it. Pray about it. I'll get back to you next week." She had been praying about it for months, during the entire loan approval process, and this was the answer? It could upend her life. Again. And she was tired of pulling herself and the kids upright.

"Jennifer, are you coming?" Mom yelled from the bottom of the steps. "Supper is ready, and we're all waiting."

"Be right there." This was going to be one heckuva Christmas Eve—a day that was never easy to make it through. Yesterday marked six years since Chad had been sentenced to 150 months for second-degree murder. She blew out a breath, recomposing herself. What did it mean that the holiday was still difficult, but it no longer summoned tears?

Guess she'd become too used to pressing through all the difficulties, as she would do now.

She grabbed the notebook she'd written notes in from the phone call and set her phone on her dresser. No electronics were allowed at the kitchen table. A rule Jenn had no problem with. Truthfully, most of Mom's rules were born of common sense and respect. Even kindness. It was the lack of being treated as a mature adult that irked Jenn and the kids.

She followed the delectable scent of slow cooker roast beef to the dining room. When Jenn moved out, she'd miss Mom's cooking and cleaning, but not the mothering.

Chloe, Jason, and Dad already sat at the table. The food would not arrive until Jenn sat. Another Mom rule. She didn't let Jenn or the kids help—which was a life skill Jenn had wanted to instill in her kids, but that was difficult when Mom insisted on being in control.

"It's about time." Mom hustled into the dining room with a platter of beef in one hand and a bowl of steamed veggies in the other.

"I'm sorry. I received an important phone call."

"On Christmas Eve?"

"Businesses don't stop for Christmas Eve."

Mom hmphed. "Well, they should. Your father's does."

"That's because he's the owner." Jenn spread a napkin across her lap. Having extended holidays off was one advantage of being a teacher. "But you won't receive an argument from me."

"You will from me." Chloe reached for the beef platter. "Customers were so rude this morning." She forked a small portion of meat. "I lost count of how many people complained about how slow we were. But when you have fifteen specific directions to how you want your coffee made, it takes more than a minute."

"And then they don't tip." Jason took the platter from Chloe.

Both kids worked at the local coffee-shop chain, and, like the customers, they'd done nothing but complain.

Maybe that provided her answer to Mr. Dayton's news. One more thing to add to her growing prayer list.

Mom brought in a basket of rolls and a bowl of mashed potatoes. All comfort food, which was exactly what she needed today.

Finally, Mom sat beside Dad and extended her hands. "Jennifer, will you say grace please?"

Mom would expect her to say their rote prayer, but Jenn couldn't. Not on Christmas Eve, and especially not with the discussion they were about to have.

"Lord, 'thank You' seems so inadequate when I think about Your gift of Jesus." Jenn could feel the heat of her mother's glare, but it didn't matter. If praying from the heart was breaking one of Mom's rules, then Christmas was the best time to be a rebel. "You saw beyond the cradle to the cross. You saw more than a child in the manger. You saw Your Son, innocent of any wrongdoing, take the punishment for all of us. But we do thank You. For Jesus. For this time of celebration. For my family seated around this table, and for the food You've blessed us with."

Beside her, Jenn heard her father whisper his own thank You.

"Please remind Chad that he isn't alone. That he is dearly loved and missed. I ask again that the truth will be revealed, and that Chad will be able to come home soon." She blinked away a tear. Celebrating never felt right without him. "And also, I ask for wisdom regarding the information given to me earlier. Please guide our discussion. In Your holy name, amen."

Amens were muttered around the table. She dared peek at her mom out of the corners of her eyes. Hmm. No pinched lips. No furrowed brows. Maybe Mom was finally getting used to Jenn's rebellion.

Ha! Some rebellion.

Small talk accompanied the food being passed around the table. And then no talk happened as the meal was devoured. Somehow, Mom's meals always tasted better than Jenn's, though they followed the same recipes. One of those mysteries of life, she supposed.

Another mystery would be solved soon, in between her last bite of potatoes and gravy and serving dessert. She ate slowly, both savoring the food and delaying the inevitable.

"Children," Mom said to the twins who, at seventeen, didn't appreciate the label. But Jenn had taught them well. They zipped their lips and smiled at their grandmother. "Why don't you clear off the table, fill the dishwasher?"

"Gladly." Jason jumped up and began gathering dishes. He'd do anything to avoid conflict, claiming that was how his dad got into trouble.

Well, Jason wasn't wrong. Trouble did seem to follow Chad and, by extension, it also followed Jenn and the twins.

Jenn watched her kids hurry from the dining room, their hands full.

"Careful, now. That was your great-grandmother's china."

"Yes, ma'am," Chloe said from the kitchen.

Jenn nibbled on her final spoonful, trying to make the potatoes last.

"Jenny, dear."

Dad? Oh boy. Only he was allowed to call her Jenny. To Mom, she was Jennifer. Chad called her Jenn or Cocoa. She still loved the pet name.

"Yes, Dad."

Typically, he only spoke as part of the good cop, bad cop routine. He'd soften her up, so she'd give in to Mom faster. Not that it was strategic, but that was the way it always played out.

"You've left us with quite a mystery. The phone call, your lovely prayer."

She gulped down the potatoes. Why did she feel like a child?

She glanced toward the kitchen. "Jason and Chloe need to be part of this discussion, so it can wait."

"Children." As strict as Jenn's mom was with manners, one would think she'd forgo yelling, but that was wishful thinking. "Please rejoin us. Dishes can wait."

The kids slouched into the dining room and slumped in their chairs.

"What'd we do wrong now?" Jason picked at some imaginary lint on the tablecloth.

"Apparently, your mother has some words," Mom said through pinched lips.

Darn right, she had words—that Mom wouldn't allow in the house, much less at the dining room table. Though Dad might get a kick out of it.

Well, here goes nothing. Jenn sat up straight. Folded her hands on the table, trying to look far more confident than she felt. "Back in August, the kids and I looked at a business."

"A business?" Dad held his coffee cup in midair. "You going to take after your father?"

She shrugged. "It's not a machine shop."

"'Course not." He set down his mug. "Tell us about it."

Tell *us* . . .

She might tell them both, but eye contact would belong to Dad alone. "In the town of Donaldson. West of Minneapolis. Skirts the Mississippi."

"Ah yes, I've done some business out there."

No surprise. He'd done business all around the state.

"It's quite a little ghost town," he added.

"Not exactly." She squeezed her hands together. "New subdivisions are being built all around the area. This might be the perfect time to buy."

The creases between Dad's eyes deepened. "You haven't said what kind of business."

Oh, he was bleeding it out of her slowly.

She cleared her throat. "It was a bar—"

"A bar?" Mom practically screeched.

"Mother." Dad lifted his right hand barely off the table, enough to calm her mother. "I don't believe our teetotaling daughter plans to open a bar."

"No." She licked dry lips. "But your non-coffee-drinking daughter would like to open a coffee and cocoa shop."

Mom's sigh was loud enough to wake the baby Jesus. "This again?"

"Tell us about it." Dad saved Jenn from saying something she'd regret.

"It's so cool." Chloe broke in, apparently unable to rein in her excitement any longer. "It's this beautiful old building with a wood bar and tin ceilings and hardwood floors and an apartment. It's everything we've ever wanted."

"We?" Mom glanced from Jenn to Chloe.

"Yes, we." Jason? He was for it all of a sudden? "I've worked on the books for Pops' business the last couple years. I think I can handle it."

"And I've got Dad's dream book with all his plans, vendors, and recipes."

Chloe had it? Jenn had wondered where that notebook had

disappeared to.

“And a zillion more ideas and a marketing plan.” Chloe waved her hands, emphasizing her excitement. “And I’ve designed a logo.”

“A logo?” Jenn jerked toward her daughter. “How can you have a logo when we don’t have a shop name? When we don’t even own a shop?”

“Don’t you think it’s good to plan in advance? As soon as we got home that night after looking at the bar, I couldn’t help myself. The idea practically burst from me.” Chloe reached beneath the table and pulled out her phone. The little sneak. She scrolled through the phone, then shoved the screen toward Jenn. “See?”

Jenn released a soft gasp. Chad’s Choco-Latte Corner. It was perfect, with chocolate colored-lettering, the font reminiscent of *Cheers*, but not an exact replica.

“You like it?” Chloe nibbled on her lower lip, a sign of her insecurity.

“It will make your father cry.”

“See.” Jason jabbed a finger toward his sister. “I told you Mom’d like it.”

“Let me get this straight.” Jenn glanced between her scheming children. “You two have been planning this since August?”

“Gave us something to dream about when we think of Dad.” Jason stared at the table. Her stoic son was never one for a teary display, but clearly, he wanted this dream to become a reality more than she’d imagined.

“If you’re doing all that work, how do you expect to finish college?” Mom’s words quickly extinguished the light she’d seen in her children’s eyes.

But then Jason looked directly at his grandma. “We appreciate you offering to pay for our last two years of college, but we’d like to take a gap year—help Mom out in the business.”

“Wait a moment.” Jenn held up her hands like a stop sign. They were all getting way ahead of her—she hadn’t told them the best news yet. Now she knew what answer she planned to give the banker when she called next week. “The reason I was late for supper was because I had a phone call from Mr. Dayton, the business lender in Elk Run.”

"And?" Both kids leaned toward her.

"We got the loan!" She practically jumped from her chair when making the announcement. Chloe did leap up, then high-fived her still-seated brother.

"You got a business loan?" Mom sounded incredulous.

Now came the biggest challenge. Placating her mom. "Yes, thanks to you and Dad." She glanced from one parent to the other. "If you hadn't taken us in six years ago,"—after she'd spent every penny they had on Chad's defense, then had to file bankruptcy anyway—"I would have spent all my salary on rent and childcare. You letting us live here allowed me to save and to restore my credit."

"Hmph." Mom crossed her arms. "So you can make another mistake."

"If I make a mistake, it's mine to make."

"Last time, as you deftly said, your father and I had to pick up the pieces."

Jenn had nothing to say, but she silently counted down from ten, a method she often used to calm herself when teaching.

"You tend to make bad life choices, Jennifer. You broke off an engagement with an attorney—who's doing very well now. And you married a barista—who's in prison. Your father and I would wish to rescue you from another terrible decision."

"Uh-uh." Dad threw his napkin on the table. "If Jenn and the kids want to open a business, that's their doing."

Mom's lips grew so tight, wrinkles crowded around them like weeds in the grass. "But we told Chloe and Jason that we'd pay for their final two years of college."

"*If* we took college-level courses in high school, which we both did." Jason had found some *chutzpah* today. Good for him. "And both of us have two years in."

"Statistics show that those who quit college don't return."

No surprise, Mom was well-learned when it came to those statistics.

"We're not quitting, Gran, just taking a break to help Mom." Jason reached his hands to Chloe then Jenn, uniting them. "This is our dream."

Our dream. Oh, Chad would love to hear that. She'd have to write that in her next letter to him.

Mom drummed her fingernails on the table until the clacking gave Jenn a headache. Then she shook her head. "No. If you two wish to have your final years of school paid for, you need to go this fall. And . . ." she looked directly at Chloe ". . . you need to choose a worthwhile major. If you insist on studying art, you need to add teaching to that."

"But—"

"Those are our conditions."

Dad just grunted. In Mom terms, *our conditions* meant *hers.*

"I'm going to do dishes." Chloe pushed away from the table and stomped to the kitchen like she used to as a small child. Jason was right behind her.

If the kids weren't in the next room, Jenn might have released a volley of words that would tell her mother what she really felt.

But her kids were there.

And this was Christmas.

And she was supposed to model Christlike behavior to them.

What did that look like when someone was being unjust?

With Chad's conviction, Jenn had learned what comes from rash decisions and wrong deductions. The best thing she could do, at the moment, was to remain silent, because whatever she said could—no, make that *would*—be used against her in the court of Mom.

Starting today, she was beginning her countdown to freedom. Five months until this school year ended, and then she'd resign. Which meant it was five months until she'd move into her new apartment. It would be another two or three until Chad's Choco-Latte Corner opened.

Assuming that was what God wanted.

But wasn't the loan approval confirmation of God's plan? If God said "yes" to this, maybe Chad's release from prison wasn't far behind.

Tonight, she'd get down on her knees, as she'd done nearly every day since Chad was first arrested, and have a talk with God. Hopefully, for once, her plans would align with His.

BREAKING FREE

"I want you to know, brothers, that what has happened to me has really served to advance the gospel, so that it has become known throughout the whole imperial guard and to all the rest that my imprisonment is for Christ. And most of the brothers, having become confident in the Lord by my imprisonment, are much more bold to speak the word without fear."

Philippians 1:12-14

Chapter Three

Today she was going to break out of prison.

With August's morning heat bearing down on her, Jenn slowly took in a breath. From the swing near the river, she glanced across the grass-bare yard fronting a brick wall scarred by years and weather. For the first time in over seven years, hope, like a lilac-scented spring promising new life, filled her and compelled her to take those first dangerous steps toward the wall barricading her figurative prison.

Not like the one that confined her husband.

A tall figure emerged from a door on the back of the building housing Chad's Choco-Latte Corner, and her heart stilled. Chad? No. Couldn't be. She shook her head and her husband's mirage became their son who more and more looked like the man she'd met twenty-plus years ago when they'd feuded over whether coffee or cocoa was better.

She laughed at the memory, then sadness crept in like a prowling cat, as it always did when reminiscing transported her to simpler times. If only she'd had an inkling of their future—or lack thereof—together, perhaps she could have prepared her heart.

"There you are," Jason called out, his voice also too much like his father's, another reminder of the betrayal she was committing.

Eight months after she'd signed the loan papers, three months after she'd moved into the store's upstairs apartment, and she still hadn't told Chad about the shop. She'd had multiple excuses, naturally, but none of them seemed right anymore, and that little demon named Guilt kept whispering in her ear. The truth was, she couldn't bring herself to tell him she was moving on while he faced another five-plus years in prison.

No, she would not jail her hope again. Chad wouldn't want that, but he would want the truth. Next week when she visited, she'd tell him and hope he'd forgive her.

"Just needed fresh air." She gestured to the empty swing beside her that Chad would occupy someday, and together they'd watch the Mississippi flow.

"Looks like everything's ready. Cash is in the till. I've tested the POS system, and it's working."

"You know, back in the day, we called the point-of-sale system a cash register."

"This is easier."

"Depends upon your perspective." How you looked at life in general depended upon perspective. Like her breaking out of her self-imposed emotional prison while her husband sat barred inside the real thing for the past seven-plus years for a crime he didn't commit. His best friend had been the key witness, testifying of Chad's guilt. The judge and jury shared the same perspective.

Then the public and her church had deemed Jenn and the twins guilty by association, and she'd worn that guilt like shackles since Chad's conviction.

Yes, it was time to break her chains and free herself from this prison.

"Let's get to work." Work she was ill suited for. What non-coffee drinker opens a coffee shop? And who gives up a tenured teaching career for a business that offered no guarantees? Her mom's words clanged in her brain as she stood and strode toward the coffee and cocoa shop, Jason at her side. Hopefully, distance would soon mute the discouragement.

Busyness would help, too. In an hour, they'd be hosting the first day of soft launches, this for the most forgiving of clientele: family and friends. A dream come true for her, even if Chad wasn't by her side. He'd applaud her for moving on.

Wouldn't he?

"How many RSVPs for today?" she asked her analytical son.

"Last check was seventy-six."

"Huh. Didn't know I had that many friends." Which was the truth.

Nearly every so-called friend, and much of her family, had abandoned her when Chad was arrested. More left once he was convicted.

"Probably your promised discounts." Jason grinned, another reminder of his father.

"Probably." She threw open the back door to her business and walked the narrow hallway, over restored hardwood floors, past the unisex bathroom to the café.

No surprise, Chloe was still at work at the top of a ladder, tweaking the shop's décor, paintings by local artists that the coffee shop retained a small commission for. A win for both the shop owner and the artists. Chloe was as meticulous about artsy things as Jason was about numbers and facts.

Already, the dining area made Jenn want to sit with a friend and while away the afternoon. She prayed their clientele would have the same inclination.

Hopefully, this was what Chad imagined for their shop.

"Chloe, come on down." If Jenn didn't say anything, Chloe would keep tweaking. "It looks fabulous already, you don't—"

Chloe turned too fast and wobbled.

In a flash, Jason was below her, steadying the ladder, and she regained her balance.

"Thanks, bro." She climbed down then stood back, looking up. "What do you think?"

"Better than I ever imagined." Jenn hugged her daughter while surveying the former dump heap of a bar. Its redbrick walls and copper tile ceilings had required a lot of elbow grease to clean. Thankfully, the only cost for those had been a little soap and water plus a whole bunch of sore muscles.

The black walnut bar top, which spanned a good twenty feet, had been sanded, but not enough to erase all the dings and cracks and cup circles. Caleb Johnson, the carpenter the realtor had recommended, had epoxied that history into the wood so all patrons could appreciate it.

Chad would probably come up with stories about each of those imperfections.

She imagined the shop looked much like it had a hundred years ago when this place had first opened. Well, except for the employee space behind the bar that had all the modern conveniences required for a coffee and cocoa shop.

"Mom, you have got to try this." Jason held out half of a chocolate croissant he'd removed from the below-counter display.

She nibbled a corner of it and moaned with delight. Paula's Pastries were going to be a hit.

They'd built this place, but would people come? If Chad were here, she would have no doubts.

A knock on the front door drew her out of her rumination. Lately, she excelled at hiding in her contemplation.

One of the new hires stood at the door, arriving early. That boded well for her.

Jenn hurried to the door and flung it open to the jingle of bells. "Welcome, Sally." The stay-at-home mother, whose kids would be in school full time come September, would be a perfect fit for the café's eleven-to-four shift, plus every other Saturday morning.

The woman bustled in, a grin on her face as wide as the Mississippi. "Good morning! I can't tell you how wonderful it feels to ditch the title 'Mom' for a few hours."

"Oh, I know exactly how you feel." Though Chad had been the full-time dad while working part time at the Cuppa Truth coffee shop, she'd spent twenty-plus years teaching elementary kids who frequently called her "Mom." Starting today, she added new titles—business owner and barista—to mom and wife.

Too often she wondered how applicable "wife" was when she'd seen her husband sparingly, she hadn't made love to him since he'd been arrested, and their communication was limited to letters, O-mails—the prison form of e-mail—and once-a-week phone calls and visits.

Regardless, she refused to give up the fight to have him exonerated. Fight Until He's Free had become her mantra. Someday that would happen, and their married life would return to normal, whatever that was.

"Mom?" Chloe's voice broke through her musing.

"Yes, dear?" As a business owner, she couldn't let that keep happening. Why today of all days, when she needed to be sharp?

"You're off in your happy place again."

"Sorry." Or not-so-happy place. She couldn't imagine truly being happy until she and Chad were reunited. "Trying to wrap my heart around doing this without your father."

"Yeah. I know. But he'll love it."

Sally came out of the tiny employee room wearing her apron with "Chad's Choco-Latte Corner" embroidered on the front. Chloe's logo design really popped on all the materials for the shop.

Minutes later, two more employees arrived, both high school students working their first job. The question with them was, would Jenn be the one molding them, or were work habits already ingrained? Both seemed responsible and had done well during the training, but the truth would bear out while on the job.

Time would be the decider.

Jenn assigned each employee their station for the short shift. This first week, during the soft opening, the café would only be open three to four hours per day. Today it was four to seven p.m., so her out-of-town friends and family could check out the place. Tomorrow they'd test the lunch hours from ten to two, having invited local business owners and their staff, local organizations and charities, and local government leaders.

Then Wednesday would be their first test for the early morning shift, six-thirty a.m.—yuck!—to ten. They'd find out then whether that opening time would be too early or too late for locals. Some coffee stores near the Twin Cities opened even earlier.

Beginning next week, she planned to keep the shop open until four in the afternoon, but she'd researched many independent coffee shops that closed at two.

Whatever it took to be successful, she'd do.

With ten minutes to go, Jenn called the staff and her kids together, and jitters exploded over her body. Getting up in front of a classroom of elementary kids was one thing, but leading adults was an entirely different challenge.

She took a sip of water, cleared her throat, and looked out at those who would help make the opening victorious. "Thank you all for being here for our opening day at Chad's. If he were here, I'm sure he'd give a memorable and humorous speech. My hope and prayer is that this will someday happen. I can't wait for you all to meet the man behind the inspiration for this coffee and cocoa café."

For a moment, she paused, reined in her emotions, and clutched her hands together, transferring her feelings there. "In a few minutes, we'll open the doors to Chad's for the first time."

She gestured toward a wrapped gift box on the bar top near checkout. "As I mentioned during training, our goal during this soft opening, today through Friday, is to determine what works and what doesn't, and we need feedback for that. Please encourage everyone who enters to fill out the survey found on all the tables and at checkout and place them in the gift box. If they fill out a survey, they're eligible to enter the drawing for a gift card to Chad's."

Sally raised her hand, like an obedient third grader. "Are the surveys anonymous? Or do you want people to sign them?"

"Good question." Oh, she was still sounding like a teacher. "If they wish to be entered in the drawing, they have to include their name and number, but that information isn't mandatory."

Another employee raised her hand. "Can employees enter?"

Not a surprise question from Paige, whose family faced money struggles after her father was laid off. "Sorry, Paige, but employees are not eligible to enter. Remember that you do get a free beverage and pastry for every four hours of work." That was the best she could offer for benefits right now.

"Any other questions?" She studied the small group. Elaine and Sally looked eager to go. Paige seemed nervous, but she'd get over that quickly. As for Jason and Chloe, both had zoned out minutes ago. They'd likely inherited that trait from their mother.

"Very good." Jenn clapped her hands together. "Today, you'll be serving my family and friends. While the common theory among business owners is that they're less likely to offer constructive criticism, you'll find this crowd today more than willing to share negative critiques. But it's all useful. In addition, I highly value your critique. If you see something's not working well, please let me know. I am open to listening to whatever you have to say."

Snickers came from the direction of her children, so she pinned them with her don't-you-dare-cross-me mom gaze. "That means I'll listen to you two as well. Promise."

Jason smirked and Chloe rolled her eyes. Not unexpected responses from her kids, but if that was the worst of their behavior, after all they'd been through, she was more than grateful.

She caught movement out of the corner of her eye and saw a slew of familiar faces at the door, then she checked the time. Five minutes to go.

Before speaking her next words, she breathed in deeply. This may turn her employees off, but she couldn't open her business without giving thanks first. "I'd like to say a prayer. If you're uncomfortable, feel free to step away, but I'd love for you to stay."

No one moved, so Jenn bowed her head and closed her eyes. She listened to the shuffling feet of a few leaving. Hopefully in the future, they'd stick around, but that would be up to God to work in their hearts.

"Heavenly Father, I never imagined that You'd lead me to open this place without Chad, but I'm so grateful You pointed me in this direction. Thank You for the freedom You've offered through this new journey. And thank You for all those who've stood beside me. Jason, Chloe, Mom and Dad, and now our new employees. I pray that working here may be more than a job to them, that it will be a blessing. Help us to always shine Your light to staff and to customers. Give us wisdom as we go forward. In Your precious name, amen."

Refreshed and emboldened, Jenn opened her eyes. To her surprise, the staff had all stayed.

But the twins had not.

"Thanks for stopping. I look forward to seeing you again." Jenn held the door for a friend she'd become reacquainted with via social media—someone she'd known in college then lost touch with. It amazed her how many of those friends lived in the area and showed up for the opening. Likewise, the number of her current "friends" who'd failed to acknowledge the invitation, much less visit the shop, didn't surprise her at all.

She turned toward the bar and couldn't hold in a grin. After two hours of being open, all the tables were full. Granted, they only had four actual tables with four chairs around each, plus a corner booth their carpenter had salvaged from another place. They'd also set up a couple tables on the front sidewalk. Each was occupied with guests who looked as comfortable there as they would at home.

Everything was going off without a hitch.

At the bar, each of the four stools was occupied, and Chloe fulfilled the "bartender" role well, giving each customer a listening ear as she kept the beverages coming. Where Jason had inherited his father's physical genes, Chloe had been gifted with Chad's way with people. Jenn was sure going to miss her and Jason during the week, but classes began on Monday already.

Jenn had planned around this obstacle, knowing her mom's strings that were attached to the free-college offer.

"Mom!" Chloe screeched, standing by one of the two used espresso machines they'd purchased from a local coffee chain. "It's not working."

"What?" Jenn raced to the back of the bar.

Chloe jabbed a cup filled with coffee her way, splattering the beverage over the floor and counter. "Taste this." Her nose wrinkled. "It's burnt."

To Jenn, all coffee was gross. Running this business would be a lot easier if she liked coffee, but at least her staff members were all self-proclaimed coffee addicts.

Jenn passed the cup on to Jason. "Try this."

He sipped it, and his nose wrinkled, like his sister's. "Yep. Burnt."

Burnt flavor. Jenn ran through her mind what she'd learned about the used machines. Could be a number of problems. Bad beans, but they tasted fine (or so the customers said) with the other machine. Could even be one bad bean tainting the batch. She tabled that. For now. The machine could be running warm, or it could be that the hot water was moving through the grounds too quickly.

Regardless, this was the perfect time to teach a lesson to one of her new employees.

First, she turned to the waiting customer, someone she'd met on her walks around town, and donned her best Chloe-like smile. "Sorry about the wait. Working out some bugs."

"Not a problem. Take all the time you need."

"Thank you." She pointed Chloe toward the second espresso machine. "Use that one until this one's fixed." This was exactly why she'd purchased two espresso machines, and also why she'd taken small-repairs community ed classes over the last year. The cost of hiring a repair person every time a machine broke would be exorbitant.

"Fine," Chloe mumbled.

Jenn chose to ignore Chloe's attitude and studied the broken machine. "Having an attitude like Chloe?" As if the machine could answer.

Hopefully this problem would be an easy fix and something she could use to teach her staff. She searched the room for Sally, who was wiping a table. "Sally, would you mind coming here please?"

Sally hustled to the bar. "How can I help?"

"Our coffee's tasting burnt, and we need to figure out why."

"I'm here to learn."

As Jenn thought she would be. "It could be a bad batch of beans, or even a single bad bean. We'll test that last. It could be that the machine is running hot, so we'd need to adjust its temperature, but I have a gut feeling the calibration's off. This is the first time we've used the machines this much, so it's probably adjusting." Or so she hoped. "And that's a pretty easy fix."

Jenn gestured to the top. “Remove the lid.”

Sally did so.

“Now, to recalibrate the timing, crank the lever inside—” Jenn stood on her tippy toes and looked inside the machine. “Crank it counterclockwise. That should change the grinder to the right setting.”

Sally’s height gave her the perfect view as she turned the lever.

“Okay.” Jenn held up her hand. “That’s good.” *I think*. “Want to be the guinea pig, give it a try?”

“Gladly.” Sally pulled a new shot, tested it, raised a thumb. “Perfect.”

Yay. Jenn audibly sighed her relief and laid a hand on the side of the machine. “Good girl.” First problem solved easily, though she wasn’t naïve enough to believe that all issues would be taken care of this swiftly.

“Talking to machines now?” a familiar voice said behind her. No, couldn’t be. Thomas lived on the east coast and was very busy with the Guilt-Free Project and his teenage daughter.

She spun around and couldn’t stop the grin from taking over her face. “It is you.” Alongside her mom and dad, but she’d expected them. She hurried around the counter and wrapped the friend she hadn’t seen for several years in a hug, then she stepped back, keeping her hands on his arms. She had to ask the question, though she already knew the answer. It was the same every time she spoke with him.

“Have you—”

“Not even a hello-thank-you-for-coming for your parents?” Did everything that came from her mom’s mouth have to be critical?

Jenn sighed. Oh, she loved her mom, was grateful for all she and Dad had done for her and the kids. But couldn’t Mom, for once, show she was proud of her daughter?

“I’m sorry.” She backed away from Thomas. “It’s very good to see you.” She hugged both parents. “You know I appreciate your support very much,” she said, instead of sassing like she wanted to. What was it about her relationship with her mom that always reverted her to childhood? She prayed constantly that the same wouldn’t be true for her relationship with Jason and Chloe, although being a single parent certainly didn’t help any.

"Gran! Pops!" Chloe took over, thankfully.

Now the question was, why was Thomas here with her parents? That realization sent off warning signals, which meant she needed a few minutes alone with Thomas.

With Chloe occupying her grandparents, Jenn took Thomas's arm and practically dragged him toward the hallway leading to her apartment. "Can I show you the place? Catch up on what's going on in your life?" She caught Sally's eye, giving her the message to watch the shop.

"I'd love that." He took a quick glance at her folks. "Won't they want to see it?"

"They've gotten the tour already." And Mom had no problem expressing how foolish Jenn was for opening the shop.

She pointed out the bathroom, the breakroom, and her tiny office before aiming for the apartment.

"Is this safe?" He tried the door leading out to the backyard, and it opened.

"During business hours, you can get out, but not in. At night, it's locked up tight." She gestured to the camera directed at the door. "We have them all over, in and out. Living alone, I didn't want to skimp on security."

"That makes me feel better."

"My dad was happy about that, too. And Jason." She shook her head. "That boy is as bad as my father."

"Protective?"

"Sometimes overly."

"Not an uncommon trait in boys who don't have their father in the household."

True. Naturally, she'd considered that Jason felt the need to take his father's place and had tried to avoid putting that pressure on him. Still, Jason had taken much of it on himself and refused to release it. Refused to see a counselor for it. Told her she'd spent enough time in the counselor's office for all of them. That probably wasn't far from the truth.

"And how are you doing?" she asked, while unlocking her apartment.

"Getting better all the time."

"Oh really? Ready to date again?"

He snickered behind her as she climbed the steps.

"Your mother asked that as well."

That certainly didn't surprise Jenn. Mom still held onto irrational hope that Jenn and Thomas would get together. "And did you inform her that bigamy is illegal in the United States?" She reached the top of the stairs and unlocked another door. As she'd said, she had plenty of security.

"That didn't seem to deter her."

"No surprise." She directed him into her cozy home that she'd fixed up to be her own oasis. Carpet instead of hardwood floors. She'd painted the walls a soft purple, leaving only one wall with the exposed brick. The kitchen and living room were basically one large room, which was all she needed. She added a deeper, restful purple to the bedroom. The cast iron tub in the bathroom had already gotten a lot of use and she was certain it would be used a lot more once the store opened for its regular hours.

She showed Thomas the attic space she was eager to work on, where the kids hung out when they were home. Then she settled with him on the couch. For her, this was more than a I-haven't-seen-you-for-years tour—it was meant for info gathering. They'd both learned long ago that being truthful was the best way to maintain their friendship. Still, she planned to save the tough question for last.

"So tell me." She folded her hands in her lap. "What brings you to Minnesota. And don't tell me it was my soft opening, because I'll know that's not true."

He grinned. "Things haven't changed, have they?"

"Not one bit."

He stared out the window overlooking the Mississippi River. "Noelle decided to go to St. Olaf."

"St. Olaf? But isn't she barely sixteen?"

"Sixteen and a half, already. She took college courses for high school credit on top of graduating early."

"Smart like her dad."

"Or her mom." His countenance faded. Eight years had passed since his wife died from cancer. The two had been so perfect together. Like Jenn and Chad, Thomas and Lacy had been the introvert-extrovert couple. Lacy's skill with people had complemented Thomas's quiet, studious nature. "I still miss her."

"I know."

"And now Noelle will be gone, so guess I'm an empty nester."

"I'm sorry about that."

He nodded. "Me too. I don't blame Noelle. She needed a connection to extended family, and my folks live in Northfield, so St. Olaf was an obvious choice for her. She can stay with them—which pleases me—while going to school."

"And what will you do?"

He shrugged. "Keep working."

"Sounds lonely."

"As you already know."

True. And that was the perfect segue to her last question, one he knew was coming, one she asked on those rare occasions when he happened to venture to Minnesota. One she periodically called and asked, so she'd feel as if she were doing something other than waiting for her husband.

"Any news?"

She waited through two whole beats before he answered. A whole beat longer than he usually took, which gave her hope.

"No."

And then squashed it.

"I'm sorry."

Always his answer. He'd worked on a hundred-plus cases over the years, freeing prisoners who had been wrongly convicted, but couldn't get a break with Chad's. Sometimes—and this hurt her to the core of her soul—she almost believed that the jury had gotten it right. That Chad belonged in prison. That he really had murdered his mentor.

After hearing the evidence, if she'd been a jury member, she would have said, "Guilty" as well.

Chapter Four

With visions of a warm bubble bath enticing her to keep going, Jenn escorted the final, yet very important, customer of this last soft-opening day to the door and opened it for her. "Thank you for checking us out. I've really enjoyed talking with you."

"My pleasure." The town mayor offered her available hand. The other one carried a bag of pastries left over from the day. "The entire town is grateful to have its first coffee shop." She raised the bag of goodies. "My office will be happy for these treats, and I'm thankful for the cocoa offerings as well. That iced version was exactly what I needed to press on through the afternoon."

"That was something my husband created special for me. He'd be pleased you like it."

"I look forward to meeting Chad someday. You keep up the fight."

"Until he's freed." Opening this shop hadn't lessened her drive.

"Until he's free." Mayor Barbara Webster gave a sharp nod then strode down the sidewalk leading toward city hall, which shared a building with the fire department and police department.

Jenn closed and locked the door. How wonderful to not only impress the town leaders, but more importantly, to make friends with them. Somehow, Mayor Webster had gotten Jenn to spill her life story—Chad's story. Not something easily done. She'd learned from past experiences that telling others your husband is in jail for murder did not make for lasting relationships.

But Barbara, she was different. In her, Jenn felt she'd gained an ally, someone who would help in the fight.

Chad needed all the help he could get.

Right now, Jenn's feet needed all the help they could get.

With each step across the hardwoods, her toes and arches screamed, "Ouch," even though it had been another short day. How would they survive a full day?

Buy nurse shoes, she mentally added to her to-do list, which was a mile long already. This soft opening had provided solid feedback, most of which they'd already put into practice.

They'd learned what drinks sold the best and what customers felt they were missing. Some were disappointed they didn't have a food menu, as the only eateries in town were the American Legion and the dive bar. But those guests would have to remain disappointed. Making drinks was enough for now, and with Paula providing fresh pastries every morning, that was all they needed.

For tomorrow's grand opening, they'd ordered enough pastries to feed the town. That was what Jenn hoped anyway. It would not only be their first full day of work, but the first day the shop would be open to the public. Hopefully, those who'd visited during this past week had spread the word. A good word, at that.

Guess she'd find out tomorrow.

But for now, it was time to close. She hurried behind the bar and grabbed a clean wash rag and cleaning solution to wipe off the tables and chairs and anything else hands could touch. Sally had already begun washing dishes, and Paige was cleaning the espresso machines. Jason instructed Elaine on how to count and balance the drawers. If Jason changed his mind about going into business, he would make an excellent teacher.

And Chloe? Jenn glanced around while scrubbing where little hands had likely played with a cocoa splatter. No surprise, her daughter had disappeared. Work was a four-letter word to her, unless it involved art in some shape or form.

No, that wasn't fair. Chloe had not only created all the marketing materials for the shop, but she'd gone door-to-door throughout the town dropping off those materials and chatting up the shop, making friends with half the town in the process. That was her gift.

So why Jenn's mom insisted Chloe go into teaching if she wanted her school paid for, Jenn could never understand.

Perhaps she didn't trust Chloe to make her own decisions, like she didn't trust Jenn to make hers.

Jenn scrubbed where a child's handprint had been added to the wall, a mistake easily wiped away. Jenn marrying Chad hadn't been a mistake, even with his imprisonment. Someday they'd be together again.

Fight Until He's Freed.

With the help of the staff, the shop sparkled within an hour and looked ready to greet new customers in the way-too-early morning.

Jenn called the staff together for one last pep talk before their big day.

"Thanks, everyone, for your hard work this week. We've learned a lot and are ready for tomorrow." She hoped. Prayed. "Tomorrow's our grand opening, our first all-day opening. Make sure you've checked your schedule. Get plenty of rest. And remember, if you have any issues, anything at all, come to me first."

Everyone nodded or smiled. Jason smirked, of course.

"Very good." She clapped her hands, envisioning her much needed bubble bath. "Clock out, and I'll see you tomorrow."

Tomorrow.

Oh boy. It was really happening. Tomorrow, Chad's Choco-Latte Corner would open, and the only thing missing was him.

After locking the front and back doors, she hurried to her apartment, where Jason and Chloe were already camped out in the living room, riveted to their phones. They barely noticed her as she whisked through to her bedroom.

She'd take her bath, then pen her weekly letter to Chad, share the week's successes, the difficulties too.

If only the judge and jury had known Chad.

She started the water and returned to her bedroom to get ready.

Heated, unintelligible words came through the closed door. The twins were fighting again. She swore they were worse than before they moved out of Mom and Dad's home. But they were adults now. She had no plans to helicopter over them and tell them how to solve their problems. They needed to work it out themselves.

Besides, after five days of running a business, she really didn't want to do any more training or teaching.

Knock, knock, knock.

She groaned. Couldn't she have two minutes to herself?

Jenn threw on a bathrobe and opened the door.

Chloe stood there, all red in the face. She never could disguise when she was upset. Which meant Jenn had to don the nurturing mother role.

"What's the matter, sweetheart?"

"Don't listen to her, Mom," came from Jason in the living room.

"You're a jerk."

"Takes one to know one."

"Kids!" Jenn raised her voice more than intended, and they stopped their bickering. At least for now. She cleared her throat while listening to the water fill the tub. Guess it would have to wait. She stabbed a finger toward the bed, and Chloe, her chin pressed to her chest, shuffled over and plopped down.

"Stay there. I'll be right back." Jenn shut off the water then strode the three steps to the living room and glared at her son. "I'll deal with you in a minute."

He rolled his eyes nearly as well as Chloe could.

Made her thankful that both would be leaving for school on Sunday afternoon. Then she'd finally have some peace.

She returned to the bedroom, closed the door, and sat beside her daughter. "Talk to me."

Chloe mumbled.

"I'm sorry." Jenn really wanted to respond like Mother Gothel had in *Tangled*, to stop the mumbling, but she resisted. "I didn't understand that."

Chloe heaved a sigh then looked up enough so Jenn could barely see her eyes. "When did you and Dad know you were in love?"

In love? Jenn didn't even know Chloe was dating. Again.

She held in her surprise and answered as best as she could. "If you ask your father, he fell in love with me when I walked into the coffee shop in the middle of summer and insisted on ordering hot cocoa."

That made her daughter smile. That story always did.

"But that's when Dad fell in love. What about you?"

That was harder to discern. When she'd first met Chad, she'd been dating Thomas. Then they'd gotten engaged, though they weren't in love with each other. Getting engaged had been the "practical" thing to do, and Mom had been overjoyed.

But all along, Chad had been the one who'd made her heart flutter.

She picked up their wedding photo from her dresser and studied it. His smile still made her heart beat quicker. She ran a finger over his jaw line, longing to feel his tender kisses again. "I guess the first inklings of love were there when he gave me grief for ordering hot cocoa. I'd go to the coffee shop just to see him, get teased by him, see his smile. Maybe I didn't *fall* in love, but took a slow slide instead."

Jenn placed the photo in its resting spot, then turned to her daughter. "Tell me about this young man you've fallen in love with."

"But I—" Chloe's cheeks turned crimson, and she looked away. "When I was on campus for orientation, I was walking to the dining hall with my future roommate. We were laughing hysterically about something, so I didn't see the broken sidewalk. Being the klutz that I am, I stumbled, but this guy caught my arm and saved me from falling all the way."

"I like him already."

"I know, right?" Chloe fiddled with the edge of the comforter, a sign that she was nervous. "And then I looked at him and he smiled and . . ." Her face donned a lovesick smile. Oh boy, she really was smitten.

"He's a fellow student, I presume."

Chloe nibbled on her lower lip. "He's actually a professor."

"I see." Now the heated words between Jason and Chloe made sense.

"You don't approve." A hint of defiance colored her voice.

"I didn't say that." Jenn held up her hands. The trick here was getting Chloe to realize herself that a student dating a professor was a bad idea.

Forbidding it was a sure way to send Chloe in the opposite direction. "I need more information first. What else do you know about him?"

"He teaches political science, so I'll never have him for a prof. I mean, can you think of anything more boring than politics?"

What did they have in common, then? "Has he asked you out?"

More lip nibbling and blanket wringing. "We went out that night and the next. Tomorrow night, too."

Uh-oh. "And you're in love." Jenn forced out, her fingernails digging into her palms.

Chloe sighed.

Oh, that wasn't a good sign.

"He's such a gentleman. Not like the kids I used to date."

So, her old boyfriends—of which there were many—were *kids* now. Jenn's fingernails dug deeper. If they weren't stubbly from working on the store the last several months, she'd probably draw blood.

"He's smart and kind and gorgeous and he talks about these expensive places he wants to take me."

In other words, he was trouble with a capital T. "What's Jason's objection?"

Chloe sighed with her entire body as only an overdramatic artist would. "Says it's stupid to date a professor. That he's using me."

Yep. Jason was right, but Jenn couldn't say that aloud. "What do you think about that? Does the university have a policy about professors dating students?"

"No." Chloe avoided eye contact. "It's discouraged, but not forbidden."

Which made it all the more enticing to her daughter. "How old is this . . . man?"

"Twenty-eight, but that makes him so much more mature."

Jenn clenched her teeth. A twenty-eight-year-old professor dating an eighteen-year-old freshman was looking for one thing. But forbidding the relationship would backfire. If only Chad was here to talk sense into their daughter. The trick here was getting Chloe to determine for herself that this professor wasn't to be trusted.

"He's single?"

"Mom! Do you think I'd date a married man?"

"Not intentionally, no." Jenn draped an arm around her daughter's shoulders and pulled her tight to her side. Combed her fingers through Chloe's long blonde hair. "I'm going to caution you to take it slowly. I'm wary about a man that age being interested in a teenager. What are his motives?"

Chloe pulled away and skewered Jenn with her gaze. "You don't trust me."

"I . . ." Jenn slowly puffed out a breath to avoid affirming that to be true. Chloe's choices in boyfriends had been dismal so far, no doubt a product of not having a father in the home. Was this professor a substitute for her dad?

"Sweetheart, I do trust you." Jenn shifted to face Chloe directly. Her daughter was eighteen, officially an adult, which meant Jenn had to tread carefully to avoid pushing Chloe right into the jerk's arms. "But to be honest, I don't trust *him*. Do a lot more sliding into love, and less stumbling. Get to know him well, and pay attention to what your gut is saying." Jenn's was screaming, *Drop the scumbag!* "It won't always agree with your heart. You're an intelligent young woman, so don't let your heart do all the thinking for you. Be wise. Always remember that you are a child of God, and that's where your worth lies."

"I knew you wouldn't like him," Chloe said, barely above a whisper. "But he's a good man. I'll prove it to you."

Exactly what Jenn was afraid of.

Jenn kissed her daughter's forehead. "Just be careful. Please."

"I promise."

All Chloe's previous relationships had lasted no longer than a month. Jenn prayed that would be the case here as well. "Go make up with your brother. I'm going to take a bath."

"I do have one more question."

Oh, she wanted to sigh. Guess the bathtub could wait another minute.

"Um, it's sort of personal."

"I'll do my best to answer."

There went the lip chewing and blanket wrangling again. "How have you done it? You know, stay celibate all these years?"

Whoa. That question made Jenn want to do some blanket fiddling herself. It didn't take a rocket scientist to determine why Chloe was asking this question now. Oh, she wished Chad were here.

When faced with a tough question, though, the best answer was always the truth. "To be honest, it hasn't been difficult. I'm married and I dearly love your father. Other men aren't on my radar."

"But what about Uncle Thomas? You two were engaged once. When you see him, aren't you . . . tempted?"

Absolutely not, she wanted to shout, but held it in. Her daughter was asking a serious question, and Jenn's response could determine Chloe's actions going forward. As awkward as it was, Jenn would be truthful. She cleared her throat to churn out the answer. "Thomas and I were never intimate. We planned to wait until marriage."

Chloe's eyes grew as round and large as the donuts Paula made for the store. "But you were engaged."

Oh, Jenn hated this shift in cultural mores. How did a parent teach their children something was wrong when society had normalized it? Guess it was time to be bold with her daughter.

"Your father and I waited as well."

"Uh-uh. You told us Dad wasn't a virgin when you gave us the birds and bees talk."

"But your father wasn't a Christian until after I met him."

"Oh."

Jenn glanced upward. *Lord, please give me the words.* Then she focused on Chloe. "Nowadays people think that waiting for marriage is strange, but as with anything God-honoring, there's a reason for it. If there's one thing being apart from your father has taught me, it's that our reserving sex for marriage has made our relationship stronger. I've never been tempted."

"Never?"

"Never."

"Okay." But the worry in her voice said Chloe was anything but okay.

She hugged her daughter tighter, wanting to her stay young and innocent forever, fearing it was already too late. "Is there anything else you want to tell me?" *God, please give me strength not to erupt at the answer if it's something I don't like.*

"I, uh . . ." Chloe looked toward the door, then at her lap. "Nope. Nothing else."

Hmm. Oh there was something else, all right, but until Chloe wanted to share it, Jenn wouldn't push.

Instead, she kissed her daughter's forehead. "Please know that you can come to me anytime, okay?"

"I know that."

"And you know that I love you always and without condition."

"I do. Thanks for listening."

"Always."

Chloe left the room.

And Jenn hurried to the bathroom to fill the tub once again. Her need for a good soak had elevated. But now it would come with a chat with God.

She added bubble bath to the water, enough to allow her to lose herself.

Knock, knock.

Oh brother. Jenn twisted toward the open bathroom door and peeked out, hoping her frustration didn't show on her face.

Jason this time. "Got a moment?"

She forced a smile. "Always." She pointed toward her bedroom. Or should she call it her counseling chamber? Why today of all times when she had the stress of the grand opening tomorrow morning? Probably because they'd be living away from home—from her—for the first time in their lives.

"Thanks."

She turned off the water, tightened her robe, and followed him to her bedroom where he slumped on the edge of the bed. Jenn closed the door and sat beside her son, who was no doubt going to complain about his twin.

He drummed his fingers on his knees. “How does Chloe do it? Go from one guy to the next when I can’t get a single girl to look at me?”

Oh, Chad, I really need you.

As with Chloe, she wrapped an arm around her son’s broadening shoulders and drew him to her. “The best answer I can give is that you’re a lot like me. More reserved. Cautious. You’re not a flirt.”

“Like Chloe.”

“And she inherited that from her father.”

He sat quiet, as usual, processing what she’d said before speaking out. Like Chloe, his fingers fiddled in his lap, but without the blanket. “I feel . . .”

She waited through a few silent beats before prompting, “You feel?”

“I feel . . .” He stood. Paced the room. Looked out the window, his hands secure in his front pockets. “Invisible . . .” His voice was barely perceptible. “It doesn’t seem like God even sees me.” He whipped toward her, and worried eyes met hers. “Sometimes I feel that the only way to get attention is to do something wrong. Like Chloe does.”

Oh, Lord. Where had she failed as a mother for her children to be wrestling with these issues? Hadn’t she and Chad taught the kids, from the day they were born, that God had carefully knitted them together? That they were loved and cherished by their Creator? That He called each of them by name? She could blame social media and the hold it had on young people. Add that to the court system that labeled their father Guilty. Or their former church family who’d turned their backs.

Too often Jenn wished she were invisible.

How do I answer him, Lord, without sounding trite? How do I convince him to believe when I have so many questions myself?

She closed her eyes, listening for an answer. None came, but that didn’t mean God wouldn’t speak through her. Sometimes all it took was opening her mouth, and God would provide the words.

Oh boy, did she need those words now.

She patted the space beside her on the bed.

He trudged over the carpet and plopped beside her, his head and shoulders nearly parallel with the floor.

"First of all, I love you. Your dad loves you. And God adores you more than both of us, but I can understand why you have questions."

"You do?"

"All you have to do is look at our messed-up lives. It's not unreasonable to ask, 'Where is God?'"

He gave a slow nod, but still didn't look at her.

"Know that you can boldly approach Him and ask those hard questions."

Was that a copout for an answer? Jenn wasn't sure, but it was all she had.

"What if I don't believe in God anymore?"

Jenn felt her heart shatter but refused to cry, refused to hammer her beliefs home to him. But she would have a bunch to hash out with God when she bathed, starting with, how did He expect her to raise God-fearing children with her husband in prison for a crime he didn't commit?

She pulled her son closer and rubbed her hand up and down his arm. "Many believers go through seasons of doubt. Even Jesus' disciples did. Through it all, Jesus never stopped loving them. Believing in them. If you have doubts, bring those to God too. I do all the time."

"But you're such a strong believer."

"I don't know about that, but I give my prayer muscles a workout every day." She flexed an arm and frowned at the growing flab. She patted it and grinned. "Looks like my muscles are taking a nap."

That got him to laugh.

Whew.

She gave him one more hug. "Remember, no matter what, I love you. Your father loves you. And God loves you far more than any of us."

"I know." He got up and aimed for the door. Looked back. "Thanks."

"Always."

He left the room and she collapsed onto the bed, her gaze riveted toward the ceiling. "Seriously? The night before our grand opening, and this is what You give me?" Her prayer muscle was going to get a workout tonight.

In the tub.

She hurried out of the room and started the water again, then peeked into the living room. Her kids were talking. Smiling. Sharing like they used to when they were younger. Much better. One problem solved, but bickering siblings was the easy one. The other issues her children had dropped in her lap made her want to hibernate until Chad was released. He could deal with this mess.

Fight until he's freed . . .

While waiting for the tub to fill, she grabbed her phone and found a relaxing playlist. Then she escaped to the bathroom and hoped for no more interruptions. She disrobed and slid into the almost too-warm, sudsy water that came up past her chin. Awww, now this was Heaven.

She closed her eyes, held her breath, and glided beneath the water, letting it drown out the voices in her head telling her she'd failed as a mom. Instead, she listened to the silence, for any word God wanted to give her before she brought her litany of concerns to Him.

Blub, blub, blub.

Was someone at the door? She raised her head out of the water.

Knock, knock, knock.

You've got to be kidding me. "Go away. It can wait an hour."

"No it can't," Jason yelled. "Uncle Thomas is here. Says he needs to talk to you. It's about Dad."

Chapter Five

Thomas was here about Chad?

“Give me five minutes.” Jenn grabbed her towel and stepped out of the tub. Was Chad all right? In a prison for hardened criminals, she believed his life to be in constant danger.

Or was this finally the visit she’d been waiting on for over seven years?

Oh, Lord, please let it be so.

She wrapped a towel around her hair, put on her robe, then stepped from the bathroom right into the living room. Thomas—dressed in a suit and tie, which meant he was here on business—sat on the edge of a chair. His face was unreadable, a technique he’d mastered for the courtroom. The kids were both fidgeting, which indicated Thomas hadn’t yet shared what he knew.

“I’ll be right with you.” She hurried into the bedroom, threw on a long T and some joggers, and ran a brush through her hair, enough to be presentable. Then she joined her family in the living room. Someone—probably Chloe—had set a pitcher of water and glasses on the coffee table, plus a tray of pastries left over from the shop two days ago.

She sat on the couch in between her children, with Thomas across from them. Almost felt like they were in a classroom, and he was about to deliver a lecture.

She gulped, hoping he’d be delivering good news, because she didn’t know if she could handle the opposite.

Still, she had to exhibit strength and confidence for her kids. “Are you ready?” She glanced at each child and grasped their hands.

Jason nodded.

"I don't know." Chloe squeezed hard enough to turn Jenn's fingers white.

"Whenever you're ready."

Chloe snuggled in closer like she used to as a preteen. "Okay." But her shaking voice belied that statement.

Then Jenn nodded to Thomas.

His features remained deadpan. "I received a call two weeks ago that—"

"Two weeks!" Jenn shot off the couch. "Why are we—"

He held up his hands like a stop sign.

She stopped, all right, and sat, but beneath the surface, her blood simmered.

"To preface what I'm going to tell you, two weeks ago they didn't know all the facts, and it would have been unwise to speak with you then."

"Fine." Boy, she sounded petulant, like one of her kids.

Thomas leaned toward them, his hands open as if making a peace offering. "As I was saying, two weeks ago I received a call from the Minnesota Guilt-Free Project that evidence had come forth that could possibly free Chad."

He used the word "free" not "exonerate." Two completely different meanings.

Still, Jenn slapped a hand to her mouth, and tears threatened, but she held them in. For now. "That's why you hesitated a week ago when I asked if you knew anything more."

Thomas nodded.

"And?" Jason scooted to the edge of the couch.

"And further investigation shows we might have enough evidence to exonerate him."

Might have . . . Oh, Thomas was careful with his words. Others who didn't know him as well probably wouldn't catch on.

Chloe gasped. "He's gonna be free?" Clearly, she hadn't heard Thomas's disclaimer.

"Not yet, honey." Jenn patted her daughter's hand. "There's a process he has to go through." A crazy-long process that offered no guarantees, but her kids didn't know that. They needed hope, so until now, that was information she'd kept to herself.

"A process?" This from Jason. Naturally, he'd want to know the facts.

She should have prepared them for this moment. They were adults now, not pre-teens needing to be sheltered.

Perhaps she hadn't told them because she had believed this time would never arrive.

"What does that mean?" Chloe's voice pitched. "How long does this process take? What's involved? When can we see him? Will he receive—"

Again, Thomas held up his hand and looked to Jenn. "Would you like to explain?"

She shook her head. Yes, Thomas had told her what would happen if this day ever arrived, but it was all so convoluted to this non-expert.

"First, I have to file a petition for a new trial—"

"Wait." Jason jumped up. "I thought you said the evidence proved his innocence."

Jenn tugged her son's arm, trying to get him to sit, but he refused. "Jason, Thomas said 'might' exonerate him."

"Correct," Thomas said, his tone and face still remaining neutral. Oh to have that kind of control. "To be proven innocent requires a new trial."

"That's bogus." Jason pulled his arm away from Jenn. "Let's get it going. File your petition, or whatever, and start this new trial."

"It doesn't happen that quickly."

"Of course, it doesn't." Jason plopped down beside her and let loose a phrase she didn't allow in the house. Problem was, those same words had filtered through her mind.

"How long will it all take?" Chloe huddled closer to Jenn, as if she sensed the doom coming from Thomas.

He looked directly at her. "Three months at the minimum, to prepare the petition, and probably longer to file it with the court."

"Three months to write a single petition?" Jason jumped up again. "That's crazy!"

Jenn had never seen her son so riled. Not that she blamed him. Those had been her exact thoughts when Thomas had relayed the process to her years ago. There was nothing swift about the law, despite the Constitution's claim that the accused should enjoy a speedy trial. Ha!

"Jason," Thomas said, in a way that showed he respected her son as an adult, not a child, and that seemed to pacify Jason. "For the legal process to work justly, it takes time, and to the outsider, that can seem infinite. But trust me, if we want your father's name cleared, it's best not to be hasty."

Jason snorted. "Serving over seven years for a crime he didn't commit doesn't sound hasty to me."

"You're right. It doesn't." Thomas offered a sad smile. "And I'm afraid you'll like the rest of my information even less."

So true. Jenn knew it got worse from here, so she regrasped her children's hands. Jason bucked for a second then sat and returned the grip.

Thomas took a sip of his water then looked directly at Jason, then Chloe. "A month or so after the petition's filed, we'll appear in court for a post-conviction hearing in front of the judge to present our proof."

"And then Dad'll be released." Chloe steepled her hands in front of her mouth. "That would be about Christmas!"

Once again, Thomas shook his head. "The judge will look at the evidence. If they believe it's strong enough, they can vacate the original conviction and give your father a new trial."

"If . . ." Now Jason was catching on to Thomas's qualifiers.

"Correct. *If* the judge doesn't believe the evidence is strong enough, there will be no new trial."

Jason spewed another phrase she normally wouldn't allow. She couldn't disagree with him.

"But," Chloe said, "if the judge believes the evidence is strong, there will be a new trial." Leave it to her daughter to find hope in the situation.

"That's correct."

Jason huffed. "But there are still no guarantees Dad'll get off."

"Also correct."

"That's bogus." Jason wiped a hand across his face. "That'll take another year."

"It could." Thomas kept his voice on an even keel. "It could take much longer than a year."

"But he only has five more years to serve." Chloe's voice came out in a whine.

"That's one more thing to take into consideration." In spite of her whine, Thomas treated her as an adult. "But there are a couple other possibilities that could happen to free your father earlier."

"Really?" Chloe moved to the edge of the couch. "Then do it."

"Those options aren't something I can control. The prosecutor could look at the new evidence and dismiss the charges, but that rarely occurs, even with the strongest of evidence, and I believe our evidence is strong. Don't build your hopes on that."

"There is one more possibility." Jenn finally pitched in. She didn't like this option either, though it would bring her husband home prior to the end of his sentence. "The judge could let your father out of prison early for time served, and the petition for trial would be withdrawn. The problem with that is that the conviction stays on your dad's record. In the eyes of the public, he'd still be guilty and there'd be no compensation for wrongful imprisonment."

In Minnesota, compensation could be $50,000 per year served. Monetarily, that would barely make up for what they'd lost when Chad went to trial.

But she'd forgo any money to have him home again.

The kids went quiet. The hope that had filled the apartment moments earlier had been smashed like a coffee mug slammed to the floor.

"So, we wait," Chloe spoke so softly, Jenn wasn't certain Thomas had heard.

But he nodded again, then raised his chin. "You have my promise that the Minnesota Guilt-Free Project and I will do our absolute best for him. I've believed all along in your father's innocence, and this new evidence, to me, affirms it. Now I plan to convince the courts to believe the same."

Silence again took over, which was Jenn's cue to let the kids talk this out between themselves. She caught Thomas's attention and motioned toward the door. "Go for a walk?"

"That would be good."

A minute later, they were outside where the sunlight belied the length of the day. How could it only be six at night? It seemed hours ago that she'd sent home the staff with eagerness for tomorrow's grand opening.

Now she wondered how she'd make it through tonight much less tomorrow.

She aimed toward the river, toward the swing that always helped calm her nerves. Whenever she felt stressed, she'd swing lightly, talk with God, and release the stresses into the waters that carried it away to a place from where it could never return. Always, the difficulty was in releasing the problems she liked to hold close.

Thomas had arrived bringing news of more hope, but the legal system did its best to squash it. She needed to give up that concern and cling to hope instead.

If anyone could get her husband home, it would be Thomas. He'd already had much success in his years working with the Guilt-Free Project. She had to believe he'd come through for her and Chad as well.

They sat side by side on the swings, him in the spot she'd imagined Chad being, where she'd spent hours talking with her husband as if he sat beside her. Someday. Maybe sooner than the sixty-two months he had yet to serve.

Thomas removed his jacket and his tie, then laid them on the grass. His way of banishing the lawyer role and donning the friend.

But she still needed the attorney's information. "What evidence was found?"

"A few things." He looked out across the river. "There was a signed suicide note in which someone made a murder confession."

"That's strong evidence, right?" Maybe there was hope for Chad.

"Not really."

No? “Why not?”

“You never know what prompted the note. If they confessed under duress. Wanted to leave life with a splash. The judge would laugh me out of court if that was the only evidence I brought.”

“Oh.” She pushed back on the swing and held there. “Then what else?”

“The important evidence is what the note directed detectives to.” He held up one finger. “A blood-stained glove.” He displayed a second finger. “Blood on some dollar bills.” A third finger. “And a blood-splattered, uncashed check from a Cuppa Truth customer dated the day of Garrett’s death.”

“That ties all these things to the day and place Garrett died.”

“Correct.”

Now that did sound much more hopeful and concrete than a suicide note. “Does the DNA connect those items with the person who committed suicide?”

“It does.”

She barely hoped to ask the next question. “And to Garrett?”

He nodded.

Chad is innocent.

The thought flowed through her like fresh blood being pumped into her veins, as if she’d doubted, and that suspicion was being flushed out. All those hours seated in that courtroom, listening to the witnesses—especially from Chad’s former best friend—delivering convicting replies to the prosecutor’s questions. Watching damning evidence being displayed. Seeing the accusing looks on the jurors’ faces.

If not for her knowing Chad could never kill someone, much less his former mentor, the man who’d been a father to him, when his own dad dealt with his personal demons. The trial had nearly convinced her of his guilt. A fact that the devil’s minions whispered in her ear, reminded her of her doubt which she’d fought all these years to deny.

Relief, mingled with guilt, flooded through her, stinging her heart. How could she ever have doubted Chad’s innocence?

She didn’t have to fight that uncertainty anymore, and that was nearly as freeing as opening the business had been. Perhaps more.

"How are you doing?" Thomas asked, another sign that he'd developed great empathy over the years. When they'd dated, that hadn't been his strong suit.

She breathed in, trying to sort her jumbled thoughts and feelings. The doubts and guilt, she'd keep to herself. "I'm cautiously excited. This is the first hope we've had since that jury found Chad guilty. But when I consider the obstacles we still have to overcome, it makes me want to cry. For Chad. The kids. Me. Is going through all this again worth it? Especially if it could take years?"

"Chad thinks so."

"You've spoken with him." Well, of course he had. Chad was his client. Sort of. Since Thomas lived in Massachusetts, he was licensed there and could only practice criminal law in Minnesota alongside another attorney licensed here, via some legal term she didn't understand. Regardless, to her and Chad, Thomas was Chad's legal representative, and all information was delivered to Chad first.

She needed to visit him on Thursday. "Why can't there be visiting hours on Sunday?"

Thomas respectfully didn't answer her rhetorical question.

Jenn pushed off the ground, and lightly swung back and forth, trying to wrap her brain around talking with Chad about the good news and telling him about the coffee shop. Maybe the good would soften what she'd hidden from him.

If only she could visit tomorrow, but Saturday was the shop's grand opening day, and visitors weren't allowed at the prison on Sundays. The limited visiting hours had been one of her concerns with opening the shop. She feared she'd be too busy on the few days that visiting was allowed, only Thursday through Saturday, so her hires had to be available those days.

She could phone him or do a video visit, but Thomas's news was something she needed to talk with Chad about in person. Besides, those other options were limited in time and were pricy. In person was definitely better, even if she'd have to wait almost a week to see him.

"I'm sorry." Thomas looked down, folded his hands. Praying? That would be just like Thomas.

She nudged the tip of his dress shoe with her sneaker. "You have nothing to be sorry for. You don't make the rotten rules." All created to punish the offender. Problem was, the family was punished right along with him.

She swung higher, mulling this conversation over in her mind, all the hurdles they had to leap over to get before a judge while Chad labored in prison. What was it Thomas had said about his visit with Chad?

Oh, she remembered. That Chad believed getting out early would be worth it, even if he wasn't found not guilty. But if he was released early, still guilty in the eyes of everyone but her and the kids, what kind of a life would he have?

"I don't know that I agree with Chad about getting out early being better than waiting." She got off the swing and walked closer to the river's edge. She bent and plucked a weed and threw it toward the rushing water.

"It's a tough call." Thomas joined her. "There is no right or wrong in this."

She hugged herself, feeling a chill despite the warm evening. Oh, how she wished she had someone to wrap an arm around her and tell her everything would be all right. That had never been Mom or Dad. Yes, they loved her, but they'd never offered the physical touch she required. Her old friends had abandoned her, and new ones she'd kept at arm's length, avoiding attachment.

Chloe's difficult questions from earlier in the evening about dating and love and attraction came back to her. To be honest, she hadn't been completely truthful with her daughter because right now, she really wanted Thomas's arm around her, even if as a friend.

She might like it too much.

Yet he was returning to Boston. Maybe they could bend that line a little bit for the night.

"When are you—"

"By the way—"

They talked over each other.

"Go ahead." She grasped at another weed.

"I thought you should know that I've decided to stay in Minnesota, join the bar here."

That was surprising news. "For your daughter?"

He grinned. "That—although she's not terribly happy with me hovering over her—and being closer to my folks as they get older. As a bonus, it will be easier to work on Chad's case from here, and I'll be closer if anything happens."

"You're a kind man, Thomas Nordberg."

"Could you tell that to all the prosecutors I work with?"

She laughed, and it felt good. Just as it felt good to talk one on one with another adult. With Thomas in particular. He'd been out east since the beginning of his career and had only worked with her and Chad through the Guilt-Free Project. She'd often pondered, if Thomas had lived here, had defended Chad, would her husband have been found guilty? He was certainly a better defender than the one the government had assigned.

But life didn't allow "what ifs," like her *what if* she'd told Chad earlier about the coffee shop? "When you saw Chad, did you happen to mention the coffee shop?"

"It didn't come up."

Oh good. "Please don't say anything until I've had a chance to visit him on Thursday."

Thomas scratched the edge of his lip, a tell that he was upset. "You haven't told him." And now he was a mind reader. A skill he'd probably honed in his practice.

"I couldn't." She picked up a stick and threw it into the river where it disappeared from her sight, likely floating toward the gulf. "Our visits were always too short, and when I'd try to bring it up, I'd get tongue-tied. I'd see him sitting in his drab prisoner uniform, so skinny, his hair turning gray, too many lines creasing his face. How could I tell him that I was moving on without him? That I was following the dream that we'd established together? It seemed cruel. But now . . ."

Truth had always been a big part of her life with Chad, and now she'd thrown that away. She hugged herself tighter. "I should have told him."

Thomas set a hand on her shoulder, providing little comfort. "You'll tell him on Thursday."

"He'll be so disappointed in me."

"And he'll forgive you."

"For the lie or for moving on?"

"He'll forgive you for the lie, and he'll applaud you for moving on."

"I wish I could be as confident as you."

"I have faith." His arm came around her shoulders, and she leaned into him. Two longtime friends sharing a blend of joy and grief.

"How am I going to make it through tomorrow?" She wiped her moist eyes and stepped away from Thomas. Looked into his grayish eyes that read people so well. "How will I put on a happy face and welcome new customers when I should be visiting my husband?"

"You'll be lifted in prayer. That's how."

She believed that Thomas would be praying. Problem was, they'd both prayed seven-plus years ago when Chad was arrested. They'd prayed during the trial. During the sentencing, and every day since then. God hadn't listened to those prayers. Why would He start listening now?

"Angel, got a moment?"

The deep, gravelly voice pulled Chad from his Bible reading, and he glanced toward his open cell door at the hulk of a man who had a heart equally as big. But like the Grinch, his heart hadn't grown until after he'd committed the crime that had placed him here for life.

Unlike Chad, 'Tomic wasn't innocent.

Chad set aside his Bible and gestured beside himself on the two-inch padding of what the prison called a mattress. "For you, 'Tomic, I always have a moment."

The tattooed man sat beside him, and even though the mattress spread over concrete, not a box spring, Chad swore he felt the bed dip. Imagination was a powerful thing.

"What's up?" Atomic—nicknamed for both his temper and his size—often required prompting to speak up, whereas other inmates couldn't be silenced.

The man clutched his massive hands to his knees and looked out the door into a vanilla hallway. "Rumor has it you leaving us."

Chad shook his head. Gossip spread faster here than at a church potluck. In this case, Chad prayed the rumor would come true. "My lawyer's working on it. Says there's new evidence that I didn't do it."

Nearly every prisoner in this maximum-security prison told a tale that they were innocent, but in Chad's case, his story was true. Though few believed him.

"Won't be da same 'round here. Who gonna lead our study?"

"There is a chaplain."

The man huffed, shaking the air. "Lotta good he does. You da one who understand us."

"I'm not out yet."

"I pray yer freed."

"Thank you, my friend." Chad cuffed a hand on the man's thick shoulder. "Your prayers are heard." Though Chad often wondered if his own were heard or if they simply bounced off the prison ceiling. His head knew that wasn't true, but the longer he stayed in here, away from Jenn and his kids, the more his heart needed convincing.

He feared that completing his hundred-and-fifty-month sentence would steal his faith completely, which was why he was now hunkered in his cinder block cell, alone with God and his Bible.

"Why you sit alone? Why you not outside? Sunlight is good for you."

Chad turned and looked out the long narrow window overlooking the yard, where many inmates played ball. That ball game could quickly become a brawl. All it took was one misinterpreted glance . . . Something Chad knew personally.

"I need to keep my nose clean. I don't want anything to stand in the way of being released early."

"As always, you da wise one." The man stood, taking up much of the space in the cell. He was a good man for Chad to have on his side, but it was wise to not trust him too much. "I will always protect you, Angel."

With that, the man lumbered from the room. Chad would never forget meeting—or rather, running into—the man for the first time. Right after he'd been transferred here, Atomic was the first inmate he'd seen. In that moment, he believed he'd be meeting Jesus within a few minutes. But then Atomic showed off his gap-toothed smile and offered his baseball-mitt-size hand. Said he was the peacekeeper in this block. All Chad had to do was behave.

Or else.

Chad shivered. Too often in those early days here he had witnessed what "Or else" meant.

And then Atomic became a believer. The man was still a protector, but now he did it without the threat. Still, Chad had to remind him often that threatening inmates to believe wasn't the best way to make converts.

Chad picked up his Bible, and said a prayer for protection over 'Tomic. He'd miss the big guy, but nowhere near like how his heart still broke over not being with Jenn—Cocoa—and the kids.

He stood and, as he often did, studied the pictures on the three-foot-by-three-foot square above the counter that spanned the length of his cell, with a steel sink in the middle. He ran his hand over Cocoa's face on an unposed picture Chloe had sent him, and his heart ached with missing her.

She'd missed her visit this week, which happened infrequently, and that made his heart hurt more. The O-mail she'd sent, explaining her absence as work-related, couldn't compare to the real thing.

The square on the wall also had Chloe's and Jase's graduation pictures. Chad's jaw always tightened at the fact that he hadn't been there for that important moment.

Like he'd missed their confirmations. School plays, concerts, ball games, parent-teacher conferences. Chloe's first date and her first broken heart. Jase was too busy trying to take Chad's place to date.

"Lord, please let this new evidence be my road out of here. Keep me out of trouble until—"

A crash and yelling broke into his prayer. More yelling. A whole bunch of cursing—words he hadn't known existed until he'd been incarcerated—and then another crash-bang.

Stay put, Chad. Don't need to be a peacemaker here. Be a peacekeeper. Let the guards handle it.

He hurried to the doorway to close out the chaos, but curiosity won out and he checked to see what was happening.

Oh no. The new little guy was being initiated with introductions to another small guy's fists and feet.

Chad stepped into the hallway and stopped. The guards would be here any second. Atomic too. They'd stop it before it went too far.

But his rebel feet pushed him forward. How could he remain silent if someone was getting beat up?

"Leave him alone." Chad stood as tall as he could, which, at five foot eleven, was about five inches taller than the guy doing the smackdown. The man, nicknamed Iron for the toughness of his fists, glared at Chad, his eyes black and his fists poised for another knockdown. That was what evil looked like, and it made Chad's blood turn cold.

"Mind your own business," Iron said, his voice deeper than Atomic's.

Chad braced his feet shoulder-width apart and squeezed his hands into fists at his sides, his insides quaking like Jell-O. "Can't do that, Iron."

The man smirked, and suddenly Chad's arms were cuffed in another inmate's hands. Something hard jolted the back of his knees, and he fell, his forehead smacking the concrete right before his chin landed. Someone gripped his hair and yanked up his head.

Iron.

"This is what you get for sticking your nose into where it doesn't belong." The convict displayed his fist then rammed it into Chad's face.

And the world went dark.

Chapter Six

"You've got this." Jenn strode through the hallway from her office to the shop, the cash envelope for the till in hand. Today, she had to compartmentalize and place Thomas's news in the "deal with later" file. She'd smile and chat with her customers—hopefully, they'd have customers!—and show everyone why they couldn't wait to return.

She flicked on the lights in the shop and glanced around. The staff had done an excellent job cleaning the day before, so she just had the morning prep.

"I'll take the till." From behind her, Jason grabbed the envelope.

She screeched and jumped, then skewered her son with her best Mom look. "Planning on a career in espionage?"

He laughed at that, which was a beautiful sound to begin her day.

"Sorry. Still thinking about Dad's news."

"It's hard not to, but for today I have to prioritize the shop." She gestured toward the register. "You get that set up and I'll start the rest. Is your sister up?"

He huffed. "Sure, but she's hogging the bathroom. I had to come down here to get ready."

"So we'll see her when we see her." She checked the clock above the front door. Almost six. "Staff should start arriving in a few minutes." For today, everyone was scheduled for six-hour shifts as they'd be open from six thirty a.m. to four p.m. Once the place became established, she hoped to be open Saturday evenings as well, to showcase local musical talent.

But one thing at a time.

Jenn turned on and pieced together the espresso machine and made sure the shots were timed correctly. Sally practically bounced through the front door, ready for the day, and moments later, Paige staggered in. So, she wasn't used to the early mornings either. Welcome to the club, kiddo. No surprise, Sally went right to work on her checklist: empty and rinse the commercial-sized coffee airpots from their overnight cleaning, grind and brew coffee. Paige needed a little prompting on her list—put pumps in the house-made syrup and scoops in the toppings—but this was her first job, and Jenn would have the privilege of molding her.

Hopefully, training young folk would fill that teacher hole in her heart.

Jenn emptied fresh cold brew from the five-gallon tub it was brewed in into smaller jugs, and someone knocked on the door. Paula was here to drop off the pastries.

"Jason, can you give her a hand?"

He was on the way before the words had left her mouth. A self-starter, like her and Chad.

And then there was Chloe. Speaking of whom, where was she? Jenn looked around the shop. No sign of her daughter—not that Chloe would make a quiet appearance. Even if she didn't show up for the prep work, which seemed to be covered—lesson learned for future scheduling—Jenn still needed her to play hostess today. She was the extrovert this place needed, especially this first weekend.

"Sally, would you mind creating the pastry display? I need to check on something." Or someone.

"On it."

"Thanks." Jenn hurried down the hallway, unlocked the apartment door, and clomped up the stairs so Chloe wouldn't be taken unawares.

The bathroom door opened as Jenn stepped into the apartment. "Are you just coming out now?" She made a point of looking at her watch.

"I have to look good, don't I?"

"Did it have to take all morning?" Jenn jabbed a finger toward the stairs. "We're opening in ten minutes, and I need you today."

The drama queen groaned as if she were being asked to run the entire shop by herself. "I'll be there. I promise. It's so early and Jase and I talked 'til midnight. Then I couldn't sleep 'cause all I could think of was Dad still stuck in that rotten prison."

Jenn sighed. Oh, she knew the feeling. "Come here." Jenn opened her arms and Chloe melted into a hug. "It stinks. If they've found evidence, he should be freed, now, but that's not how the *justice* system works. Still, we are very grateful to have Thomas on our side. We'll keep on fighting until Dad is free."

Chloe sniffled.

Oh boy. Now was not the time for this.

"How can you work after hearing the news?"

It wasn't easy, that was for sure. "By getting out of bed and then putting one foot forward and then the next. Like we've been doing these past seven years."

"I'm tired of doing that. I want our lives to be normal again."

Jenn hugged her daughter closer. "Me too, Chlo, me too." How did she tell Chloe that "normal" wasn't ever going to happen? That even once Chad was released, he would be changed? They'd all changed.

And that scared the dickens out of her. Too often she ruminated on the fact that the Chad she'd fallen in love with was no longer the same man. She was no longer the same woman. But Christ was still their center, and that was what she had to rely on.

"We have to keep praying for God to keep us strong. Look how far we've come." She pointed to the doorway. "When your father was arrested . . . convicted, who would have believed that only seven years later we'd be opening our coffee shop? I owe so much of that to you and Jason. So we can either feel sorry for ourselves, or we can get to work and make Chad's Choco-Latte Corner the place everyone wants to come to for their coffee and cocoa fix. When your father does come home, he'll be so proud of us." But first she had to tell him about the shop.

Now, it was time to get to work.

She gripped Chloe's hand and practically pulled her toward the door, then down the steps. Chloe tugged away once they reached the main floor, and Jenn hoped she continued to follow. Didn't matter from this point on, really. The shop was opening with or without Chloe.

Outside the shop window, a couple of people had already lined up. Customers! Praise God!

Oh my gosh, it was happening.

Adrenaline pushed Chad to the back of her mind. Her heart suddenly pumping madly, she focused on the store. The place was clean. The employees had done all the morning prep work. The pastry display was filled with treats no one would be able to say no to.

The clock read six twenty-four, six minutes before go time.

She gestured for everyone to gather round her. "How's everyone feeling?"

Lots of mumbled "goods" and "okays" and a yawn from Chloe.

"Any questions?"

Some head shakes, and otherwise silence.

"I'd like to begin the day with a prayer. As I've said before, you're not required to participate." She bowed her head, but not before she observed Chloe and Jason retreating from the circle. As she did with Chad, she gave them up to God every day, so they were in His hands, though it broke her heart.

"Heavenly Father, it's hard to believe this day is finally here. Thank You for blessing this idea, this dream, and making it a reality. Thank You for bringing each of these employees to me. Help me to be the kind of employer who sees them. Hears them. And I pray that You will use each of us to bless each customer who crosses the threshold, that this shop may be here for Your glory, not for ours. In Your precious name, amen."

A smattering of "Amens" were spoken as Jenn opened her eyes.

She glanced at the door. More people—strangers—lined up outside. Time to let them in.

On shaky legs, she crossed to the glass door, forced a smile through her nervousness, and flung the door open. "Welcome to Chad's Choco-Latte Corner," she said over the jingle of the door's bell.

Three of the customers mumbled as they passed her—clearly, they needed their morning coffee before they could summon manners.

"Good morning, and welcome to Donaldson." A flannel-wearing man offered his hand as he stepped over the threshold. "Precisely what our little town needs."

At last, a sunshine-filled face.

"Thank you." This time, Jenn's smile was unforced. "We're excited to be here." She gestured around the room. "You can order at the bar. We have regular coffee or specialty drinks that can be made with or without coffee, plus tea and smoothies. You're welcome to stay as long as you wish. Our Wi-Fi password is on the chalkboard." Jenn motioned above the bar to the menu written on chalkboards.

"I'll stay another time. The little woman is expecting me home with her coffee. Mornings don't like her as much as they like me. But I'll bring Delores over another time to say hi."

"I'd like that, Mr. . . . ?"

"Henry. Just call me Henry, but what can I call you?"

"I'm Jenn."

The door jingled behind them.

"I s'pose I should get outta your way, Jenn." Henry nodded. "Hope you have a grand day."

"Thank you."

Henry sauntered toward the bar, and Jenn greeted the next guest.

Nine and a half hours later, her feet achy from standing, her voice crackly from talking, and her cheeks sore from smiling, Jenn slumped onto one of the mismatched chairs by the mismatched tables. Customers had appreciated the eclectic furnishings and cup ware she'd purchased at secondhand stores, more out of being budget-conscious than going for a trendy look. If a mug broke, it could be replaced for minimal cost.

Fifteen minutes to closing, and the store was now empty, but she could already proclaim that Chad's grand opening was a success. Sure, the internet had tanked earlier, rendering their register useless, right in the midst of a rush, but most of the guests had been understanding. Thankfully, that had lasted only a few minutes. And it gave them something to brainstorm. In the future, how would they deal with outages? So much of their business was dependent upon Wi-Fi and electricity. But nowadays, no business could run without them.

She took out her phone and wrote "generator" under her Store Notes file. She'd keep an eye out for a good used one. That would put a bandage on an electricity outage, but what about internet? Something to ponder.

The door's bell jingled, and she jumped up. A nice-looking young man, probably about the same age as the twins, entered the store. She aimed for the back of the bar, but Chloe cut her off with a hotly whispered, "I've got this."

"Welcome to Chad's Choco-Latte Corner." Chloe's smile alone could light up the store. Whatever happened to her being so in love? No doubt, Jason—who stood at the register eyeing the newcomer—would razz his sister later on.

She offered her hand. "I'm Chloe."

"Carlos," he said with a slight accent. His returned smile was equally bright.

Oh brother.

Chloe pointed out the menu as she walked behind the bar. "We've got coffee and cocoa drinks, including flights, which I highly recommend. Then you can sample several of our drinks at once."

"Perhaps another time." Carlos studied the menu. "I'm in a hurry tonight."

"Fuel for the road?" Chloe shoved her brother away from the register with a scorching glance. She stood across from the customer, leaning slightly toward him, smudging the edge of propriety. Jenn would have to have a talk with her daughter about proper behavior. Again.

"Exactly." Carlos took out his wallet. "I'll have an expresso, please."

Chloe blinked and backed away. "You'd like an *es*presso?" She emphasized the "es."

"Yes, please." His upbeat tone indicated he hadn't caught on to Chloe's hint.

Jenn couldn't stop herself from grinning. The handsome young man had committed the cardinal sin of coffee ordering. In Chloe's book, that would likely remove him from the "potential boyfriend" list.

Chloe rang up the drink and named the price.

The young man paid with a ten then stuffed the seven-plus dollars in change into the tip jar. That upped him on Jenn's list for suitors for her daughter. Not that she was trying to set Chloe up or anything, but anyone would be better for her daughter than a college professor.

"You gonna make it or you want me to?" Jason stood by the espresso machine, smartly waiting for instructions from his sister. Often, he could read her mind, but he'd learned it was better to ask.

"I've got it." She shot a smile to the customer and a look to her brother that said *Outta my way*.

Yep, Jenn would definitely be chatting with her daughter about appropriate on-the-job behavior, even if she would only be working weekends from now on. Maybe Jenn should schedule her kids every other weekend so they wouldn't have to work together.

She made that notation in her phone as well, then focused on the drama at the bar.

"*Es*presso for Carlos." Chloe called out his name, even though he was standing right in front of her, and handed him his drink. "It's the best *es*presso you'll ever have."

He took a sip and grinned. "Definitely the best expresso. Gracias." He bowed his head and aimed for the door.

Chloe rolled her eyes so dramatically, Jenn swore the store swayed too.

"By the way." Carlos turned toward Chloe and gestured to the free library shelf and food pantry shelf. "Thanks for offering these services to the community. It is much needed."

"I agree." Chloe grinned, going from annoyed to flirting so quickly Jenn practically felt a breeze blow through the store.

The bell jingled, signaling the young man's exit, and Jenn burst out laughing. Apparently, Chloe's being in love with the professor had lasted a mere evening, thank goodness.

"Something funny?"

Thomas?

Jenn got whiplash turning toward the door. There stood Thomas in his suit, which meant this wasn't a casual visit. He must have entered when Carlos left.

Any joy remaining from Chloe's antics and the successful grand opening evaporated. She cleared her throat and tried to summon some of that happiness. "Just Chloe flirting with a customer."

"Mo-om."

The tease worked. Chuckling, Jenn stood and met Thomas with a hug, which he stiffly returned.

Yep, he was here on business, and it obviously wasn't happy news he'd be delivering.

All-too-familiar stress tightened her muscles. She looked to the bar where Jason now stood alone. Had Chloe fled when Jenn teased her? She'd always been sensitive and dramatic, but those were the very traits that helped her create the shop's marketing plan. Jenn owed her daughter an apology, but that would come after she'd spoken with Thomas.

"Jason, can you make me an iced cocoa and Thomas a . . ." She looked to her friend.

"An Americano." Espresso and hot water meant he needed a jolt to stay awake. Must have been a long day for him, which didn't bode well for her or Chad.

"On the house," she instructed Jason.

"I'm paying." Thomas took out a ten—more than twice the cost of the drink—and handed it to Jason. "Keep the change."

Jason looked to Jenn, who nodded, reluctantly.

She sighed. "Won't you let me do something for you once?" She gestured toward the corner booth. It was the farthest table from the bar and the sidewalk window and offered the most privacy.

"Next time." He gestured for her to sit first, then he sat across from her. He unbuttoned his jacket and folded his hands on the table, his expression far too serious.

Jenn swallowed as her stomach whipped like Lake Superior in a November gale. "What's going on?"

He looked toward the bar, where Jason was creating the drinks, a hint that Thomas wanted to wait until they'd have no interruptions.

Making her stomach churn even more. She clutched her arms around it, hoping to still it. Didn't help. Obviously, something had gone wrong with their case. Was the new evidence not as strong as Thomas had insinuated? Or did it somehow implicate Chad rather than exonerate him?

No. She wouldn't, couldn't think that. Her husband was innocent.

Wasn't he?

Oh, there went that demon, doubt, again, spooning lies through her ears into her heart.

"Here you go."

Jenn startled as Jason placed the drinks on the table. She let Thomas take a sip before she interrogated him further. She took a small drink, but the whipped cream topping only made her stomach rage more.

She set the cocoa aside, folded her shaky hands on the wood tabletop, and made eye contact with Thomas. "Talk to me."

He puffed out a breath, not something he'd do in front of a jury or judge, but a friend? "Chad was beaten up, and he's in the infirmary."

Chapter Seven

Jenn gasped. "What?" she said much louder than intended, drawing Jason's attention, but she needed the facts before she shared with her children. She bent toward Thomas and hushed her tone. "Is he going to be okay?"

"He will." Thomas took a sip of his coffee, probably needing a pick-me-up after delivering his news. "But they want to keep him one more night to watch him."

"Oh, thank God."

"Amen."

Part of her wanted to retract her praise. God hadn't protected Chad from getting beaten up. "How did it happen? Where were the guards?"

"They were reacting to another incident. A diversion."

"So the attack was planned." Her stomach still churned, but with anger.

"Yes, but not against your husband."

She pressed a hand to her forehead. Though she wasn't prone to having headaches, she felt one coming on. "I'm confused."

"Chad wasn't the target, but he tried to defend the person who was. The gang leader didn't appreciate Chad's interference, so he sicced his gang on Chad instead. The guards saw most of it, so they know Chad's role, but weren't able to prevent it. The security cameras confirmed what the guards saw."

Jenn clenched her fists and closed her eyes, directing her rage to her hands. Problem was, her anger wasn't aimed at the gang.

"Why does God allow this?" she said between gritted teeth.

"I—"

"That's what I want to know," Jason growled

Oh, Jason. She sighed, opened her eyes.

Her son stood behind Thomas, his arms crossed and his normally indigo eyes black as a starless midnight with his own fury.

"What did you hear?" She clasped both hands around her cocoa mug.

Jason recounted everything that Thomas had told her. Wonderful.

"Then you may as well sit." She gestured toward another chair by the table. She kept forgetting that the twins were adults, that they were old enough, mature enough, to handle whatever Thomas told them. And by including them, less weight would press on her shoulders.

Steeling herself for the details, she gripped the mug with both hands and nodded to Thomas. "You said he would be okay, but I don't know what that means. Any broken bones?"

"Yes. His nose."

She sucked in a quick breath. By now she should be prepared for this kind of news, but she never got used to it.

Honestly, she didn't want to get used to it. The sooner he got out of that hell hole, the better. But would it be worth it if the world still saw him as guilty? If he received no monetary compensation for the years the prison had stolen from him? From them. From the kids.

No, getting beaten up, their fearing for his life, was much worse.

"Will I be able to visit on Thursday, or is he in trouble?"

Thomas managed a small smile. "I made sure they understood that he would not be punished."

She sighed again, but this time out of relief. What a blessing it was to have an attorney on their side.

Jason slammed his fist on the table, and both she and Thomas jumped. "That doesn't answer my question."

What question? She paged through their conversation to where Jason joined in.

Oh.

Why does God allow this?

Both she and Jason looked to Thomas. She certainly didn't have an answer.

But Thomas shook his head. "That's a question all my clients ask, but there isn't a pat answer. I could tell you God will use this somehow for His good—"

"But not my good or Chloe's or Mom's or Dad's."

"Often, that's what it looks like."

"If it walks like a duck . . ." Jason crossed his arms.

"That's a good argument, Jason. My daughter has made comparable comebacks."

Her son smirked.

And Jenn almost laughed out loud. She pictured Thomas's daughter using a similar phrase, with the same cocky attitude, which probably irritated the heck out of Thomas.

But he maintained his cool demeanor, treating Jason as an adult. "The best I can say is that I have faith. When God told Abraham to sacrifice his only son, imagine what Isaac's response would have been. His father followed a God who claimed He loved him and Abraham. I'm sure that situation waddled and quacked like a duck to Isaac."

Score one for Thomas. Jenn still wasn't sold, but she didn't want her son to lose faith. What other Bible story would he be familiar enough with to fill in the blanks?

Ah, she knew the perfect one. A favorite of Jason's. "What about Joseph when his brothers threw him in the pit? God had been speaking to him in his dreams, showed him he'd be a leader, but instead, he was going to—"

"Die. Yeah, I know all that stuff, but those guys were important to God. Dad's just important to us."

"That's where you're wrong, Jason." Thomas pulled out his phone and scrolled through it.

"If you're gonna quote verses at me, I'll stop you right there." Jason held out his hand. "Mom's drilled it all into us."

He said that as if it were a bad thing. Jenn took a sip of her iced cocoa. She and Chad had taken the twins' spiritual education seriously, and that hadn't stopped after Chad was imprisoned. Maybe even more so, afterwards. But as a teacher, had she made it too much about bookwork, and not enough about relationship? That was something she'd have to talk with God about.

Another knock against the "Why does God allow this?" question. If she and Chad had been coparenting instead of her parenting alone, the twins' spiritual life would be much healthier. They wouldn't have these doubts.

She wouldn't be having these doubts.

"I'm sorry." Thomas's words broke through her doubting. "I know this isn't what you needed to hear today."

"What?" Her sarcasm filter had long worn out. "I love ending good days with news that my husband's been beaten up. Again."

"Then let's change the subject." Thomas pulled off his suit jacket and loosened his tie. "Tell me about your day."

She gladly recounted the grand opening, from her anxiety to begin the day, to Chloe's flip-flopping over the handsome young man who didn't know how to say "espresso."

"I counted the till." Jason quoted a number that made Jenn's brows rise. "If every day is anything like this one, we'll be in the black in no time."

"You've got a good head for business."

Jason beamed at Thomas's compliment. "That's what I'm studying."

"You'll do well."

"Thanks." Jason got up, his attitude much brighter than a few minutes ago. The entire room's attitude had shifted to a better place. "And thanks for helping Dad. I know I'm struggling with trusting God with this, but I do trust you."

Jason offered his hand, and Thomas stood and shook it as if the two were equals.

"I need to check on Chlo." Jason nodded upward. "Catch you later."

Then Jason hustled down the hallway, leaving them in silence. Jenn waited for the click of the apartment door closing before speaking again.

"How did you do that?" Jenn asked.

"What?"

"Jason. He came over here all upset and left as if he could conquer the world."

"Maybe he can." Thomas grinned and gestured toward the business that had only been a dream, even a year ago. "Looks to me like you can, too."

Jenn strode toward the prison with a hop in her step she couldn't hide. There was little that built up your psyche like having someone believe in and affirm your dreams. Last week's soft opening, followed by Saturday's grand opening, and then the continued steady business Monday through today had her believing Thomas was right. She could conquer the world.

But not before Chad knew about the world she was conquering. Why hadn't she tried harder to let him know she was fulfilling their dream?

Without him . . .

Funny how a wayward thought can change your attitude and perspective. The ominous brick building suddenly loomed over her, taunting her for arriving, threatening not to release her, should she enter.

Regardless, she stepped through the doors of the prison where the COs—Correctional Officers—regarded even the visitors as guilty. Before visiting the first time, she'd had to fill out an application, then was subjected to a criminal check and had to wait for approval as if she were guilty as well.

She gave the CO her driver's license and signed in. The woman who'd probably seen more bad in people than good, assessed Jenn's wardrobe. Nothing titillating could be worn. Jeans had to come up to the waist. Skirts and dresses had to cover the knees when sitting. Shorts had to be mid-thigh when seated. Also, no hooded garments were allowed. No jackets, vests, shawls. No sunglasses.

After receiving approval for her simple jeans and T-shirt outfit with laceless tennis shoes—she didn't want the lace grommets to set off the metal detectors again—she deposited her keys and pocket-sized wallet in a locker. All jewelry she'd left at home.

She held her breath as she passed through a metal detector. One time she'd entered wearing a bra with underwires and had been subjected to a pat search. That still gave her the shimmies. That was a mistake she wouldn't make twice.

The first time she visited Chad without her ring, she'd felt as if she'd betrayed him. So, the next visit she was ready with three woven lines circling her ring finger in a permanent tattoo. That had made her husband cry. He knew how she despised tattoos.

She rubbed a finger over that tattoo as the guard led her through a brick-walled hallway with gray concrete floors. No color or artwork, nothing to give the place character or a sense of hominess. She supposed that was the point. Prison wasn't supposed to become your home, yet too many in this prison would spend far more time here than with family.

The guard led her into a room filled with half-circle tables with three seats by the oval part, and one on the straight. Saying nothing—Jenn had learned quickly that small talk wasn't welcome—the guard pointed Jenn to her assigned table.

She sat on the round side on a seat that was connected to the table with a black metal bar. Nothing could be moved or rotated.

Now began the wait. Sometimes, he was escorted in promptly, other times she waited for what seemed an hour. But then with nothing to look at, no book or TV to distract her, no clock, phone, or watch to inform her, time did drag.

The prison-side door opened, and she sucked in a breath as the guard held it for the prisoner.

Not Chad.

A good thing, too.

After being beaten up last Friday, he would certainly look tough. Gasping or staring would only remind him of the incident. She closed her eyes, prayed that God would prepare her, that He would give her words to build up, not tear down.

The prison-side door opened, and once again she found herself holding her breath.

Chad!

The tears that were always present upon seeing him threatened, and as before, she blinked them away.

He crossed over to her, an attempted smile on his face, but the bruising, redness, and puffiness masked his smile.

"Cocoa," he said through those puffy lips. "Missed you."

She couldn't get the words out that she'd missed him too, as that would bring on the avalanche of tears. She stood and held out her hand for the too short, too platonic handshake. His hands were coarse, needing lotion. If only she could rub moisture into them.

Then he drew her into the too-quick hug she didn't want to release.

Lastly, they gave each other a peck on the cheek as if they were distant relatives. If only she could really touch him, kiss away those bruises and wounds, but prison protocol allowed nothing more than hasty, cool touches.

And then they sat across from each other on those unforgiving stools, their hands on the table in front of them where the guards could see them at all times.

"Like my look?" His question came out muffled.

Of course he'd joke about it. Life had always been a joke for Chad Taylor, until the joke was on him. Still, she forced a grin and played along. "It's colorful." If she didn't go along, anger and unforgiveness for those who did this to him this would eat at her.

"And I know how you like color."

"I do. It has a lot of purple." Her favorite. She rubbed one hand across the other, a simple way to tell him that she longed to take his hand and never let go. A prelude to what she had to tell him that would likely hurt him worse than the wounds on his face.

She laid her palms open on the table, a sign they'd developed to relay that she was going to lay open her heart on something. Over the years, they'd developed many signals to enhance their short time together, a way to speak that didn't take time or words. Each of the sixty minutes they shared had to be spent wisely.

"There's something I haven't told you, that I should have long ago." Dang, why did every moment of this visit want to induce tears? She sniffled and wiped a hand across her nose for lack of a tissue.

His eyes narrowed, but then he also spread his palms open up on the table, letting her know he was listening and would hear with his heart and without judgment of whatever she had to tell him.

Here goes nothing . . .

Her throat suddenly dry, she forced out the words, "We opened a coffee and cocoa shop a week ago."

He withdrew his hands and looked away from her. Not a planned signal, but she knew this meant he was disappointed.

"I'm sorry I didn't tell you." She inhaled. "I'm sorry for hurting you."

He responded with silence.

New worry lines accented her eyes, but Chad was unable to reply and ease her anxiety. His silence had little to do with the swelling around his mouth. Honesty had been at the core of their relationship from the beginning. After all, Jesus is Truth.

Jesus is also about forgiveness. That voice in his head nagged at him.

No, that wasn't true. God never nagged. What did niggle at Chad were the secrets that he'd kept from her. But some things were meant to stay locked away forever.

He swallowed the little bit of pride this prison hadn't already stripped away and laid his hands open on the table, a signal to her that he longed to hold her. "I understand." Which was true, even if it bothered him. "And I forgive you."

"Thank you." Her worry lines didn't completely vanish with her thin smile—they were probably a permanent fixture there now. How he'd love to kiss them and somehow ease the burden she was forced to carry, but that would get him in trouble. After his beatdown this past week, Thomas had stressed to him how crucial it was to stay out of trouble. Well, it wasn't like Chad went looking to get beat up.

But he was wasting precious time, feeling sorry for himself. Rule of thumb for visiting was that you don't lay your problems out to your loved ones. They had enough to deal with because he wasn't at home, so he plied a pain-filled smile. "Tell me about the shop."

Aw, there was the smile he'd fallen in love with.

"I was looking for a house, not a place to open shop."

"That's what you'd told me." And he couldn't have been more excited about her moving out of her parents' home once the twins graduated.

"I'd been scouting different areas outside the metro that were affordable, that had a school system where I could potentially work. The kids were with me when we drove through downtown"—she made air quotes—"Donaldson, and Chloe yelled at me to stop. I practically pushed the brake pedal through the floor of the car."

He laughed at that. "Sounds like Chloe."

"Doesn't it?" She shook her head. "Anyway, Chloe pointed out this old brick building on the corner of Main Street that had a For Sale sign in the window." Her eyes bore into his as if looking for affirmation. "I couldn't not look at it."

"I don't blame you." He nodded and smiled, hoping to convey he wasn't upset and to hide the envy sprouting inside him.

She sighed. "You were all I could see when our realtor showed us the place. It has an old bar, brick walls, tin ceiling. I could see you resting on your arms on the bar, giving rapt attention to whoever needed a listening ear, while convincing them to try your latest concoction."

He closed his eyes as she described the scene. He could see it too, smell it. His mouth watered as he imagined the flavors he'd invent. Someday. Someday he'd have real coffee again. The sludge served in here didn't count, though working in the kitchen had allowed him time to tweak the coffee they did serve to make it somewhat drinkable.

Someday.

But today, he had an important question to ask. "What's your favorite?"

She blinked. "My favorite?"

"New coffee flavor." He couldn't hold in his smirk.

Her nose wrinkled, as he'd expected. That wrinkle was still adorable.

"*None* is my favorite."

"What?" He slapped a hand to his heart, faking surprise. "You can't be a barista and not drink coffee. It's in the barista code."

"Well, you know me." She shrugged one shoulder and mimicked his smirk. "I gotta be a rebel."

He laughed, and oh did that feel good. "Yeah, you've always been a bad influence on me."

"I know. I'll try harder to behave." Her worry lines had completely disappeared.

If only he could keep them away. "Tell me more." He closed his eyes again as she described the downstairs and then her apartment plus an attic that could be renovated for living space. She raved about the logo Chloe had designed and bragged about how the twins each used their gifts to make this dream a reality.

The place sounded like Heaven, exactly what he'd envisioned in his dreams. Jenn was rarely impulsive—that was his department—but he was glad she'd broken character for this, even if he couldn't be by her side to enjoy it.

He opened his eyes. "I can't wait to see it."

"I can't wait to show it to you." Pride glowed from her face. She'd overcome so much to make their dream a reality. "I'll mail pictures."

"Thanks." Hopefully soon, he'd physically share that dream, which led him to the news his attorney had shared. "Thomas spoke with you, right? About the new evidence?"

A little worry line reappeared. "I don't like all the *what ifs*."

"Yeah, but what about the *what is*?"

"I'm not following."

"The proof. That's what is. The letter, the bloody glove, and money. I can practically smell my freedom."

She looked beyond his shoulder, probably at the CO standing there. "But Thomas said there'd likely be another trial. It could take months. Or years." She shook her head. "And you have only five years left to serve."

Unless he did something stupid, or was accused of something he didn't do, that would add to his sentence. He certainly planned on behaving, but this was prison, and little was in his control.

He had to offer her hope, though. "There might not be a trial."

"Thomas said that's extremely rare."

"But nothing God can't handle."

She huffed at that, which bothered him. No surprise, her faith had taken a hit with him incarcerated.

He laid his hands flat on the table, palms up. "There's also a good chance that the judge will release me for time served."

"You wouldn't be exonerated."

"But I'd be with you and the kids."

"Is that enough?"

"That's all I want. Besides, in God's book, I'm innocent. That's what matters."

She nodded, but he could tell it was more from wanting this conversation to end than agreement.

"The judge will listen. He'll look at my record in here. I've kept myself out of trouble."

Her brows jutted up as her gaze went to his bruised mouth.

"Okay, mostly out of trouble, but I couldn't stand by and let them beat up the kid."

"No. I suppose you couldn't." Her lips pinched, creating new worry creases around her mouth.

If only he could kiss them away.

"Cocoa," he said softly, so she'd be forced to look directly at him. "I'll behave. I promise. I'll stay in my cell except to work and eat. I'll ignore calls for help. I need to get home. I need to be with you."

She heaved a sigh. "And I need you. The kids need you."

"Tell me about them." He'd wasted too much time sulking and not catching up on family. What an idiot. "How is college going?"

"It only started this past week." She filled him in on what she knew about their classes. "I'm trying not to be a helicopter parent. Give them their space to make choices. And mistakes." She grimaced at that, which meant they'd already made their share.

"Care to talk about it?"

The simple question stole her smile, and that made his stomach knot up.

"Well . . ." She sighed and told him about Chloe's new boyfriend and Jason's worry about feeling invisible and the twins' avoidance of prayer. Her head seemed to be on a constant swivel, yet her gaze remained fixed on the table where her hands clenched together. "I feel like a failure as a parent. My most important job is to show them Jesus, but too often I've shown them how to nail his hands to the cross."

The five-minute warning buzzer went off, which meant he couldn't waste any more time.

"My dear Cocoa." She certainly wasn't to blame. He was the one who hadn't been there for his kids, and there was only so much spiritual leadership someone can show from prison. "Our kids are amazing, and that's *because* of you. They're searching right now, like I had to, but God won't let them get lost."

That was what he prayed anyway.

"I hope so."

"Hope." He smiled at the word the prison chaplain had talked about this past week. "Did you know that most people say the word 'hope' with crossed fingers?"

She shrugged. "Me included."

"I did too." Oh, he wished he had his Bible on him right now to turn to the notes he'd taken. He'd do the best he could to repeat what he'd learned. "When the Bible talks about hope, it means a certainty. A confident expectation. God is faithful."

"Yes," she sighed. "Yes, He is."

But he could tell she was saying it out loud more to convince herself.

He'd done his own share of that in his early days here.

Not wanting to spend the last few minutes on a downer, he changed the subject. "Let's talk coffee and cocoa."

Her eyes lit up and she gave a relieved sigh. "Chloe came up with this new espresso drink that's to die for, or so customers say."

For the next few minutes, she talked coffee, cocoa, and customers, and she seemed happier than she'd been in years.

Soon, he'd join her. No matter what it took.

The alarm blared, telling everyone in the room that their time was up. Oh, he hated that sound. Hated every time it rang during the day, ordering him and every other inmate around.

Mostly, he hated not being able to say a proper goodbye.

They both stood and rounded the table toward each other, arms open. They hugged, and he drew her closer, taking in the coconut scent of her hair, the—

"Taylor," CO Bulldog barked.

With clenched fists, Chad released his wife. He gave her a kiss on her soft cheek, a kiss meant for an aunt, not a wife. Their hands slid together for a brief shake, then he pulled away, not wanting to give this prison any reason to keep him longer than his sentence ordained.

"I love you more than coffee." He stepped back and showed her the American Sign Language sign for love.

She grinned through the tears that were always present when they parted. "I love you more than cocoa." She blew him a kiss then turned, drawing a hand to her face.

His fists and his teeth clenched as he followed other inmates out of the room. He put on his prison face, one that showed no emotion. One never knew what would rile up a prisoner. Sometimes a word said with the wrong inflection. Other times, a raised eyebrow would be all the reason for someone to start a fight. He'd learned early on to show no emotion, which had been difficult, but you did what you had to do.

Walking the sterile brick halls, going through several sets of locked doors, he blocked out obscene banter going on around him as best he could. But after so many years here, racial slurs and vulgar words had implanted themselves in his brain, in his dreams, and too often exited his own mouth.

He could easily let loose a slew of them right now. It would feel good for a second, but then he'd feel worse.

They reached their module and he aimed for his cell, ignoring someone calling, "Angel." Dinner call would be soon, but saying "goodbye" always stole his appetite.

And his good attitude. If ever he would start a fight, it would no doubt happen after a visit, so it was best he minded his own business.

He reached his cell and slammed the door shut behind himself. That didn't cut out the noise from behind the doors. Never did. This place was never silent.

Only one thing would dull the sound. He ripped a seam at the top of his mattress and dug out a pack of cigarettes—a popular prison currency—he kept on hand for times like these. He grabbed a mug and strode out of his cell, aiming for the last cell on the floor in this module. The stench of Moonie's stash punched Chad's nostrils and made him want to throw up. He must be making a fresh batch.

But still Chad pressed on until he stood at Moonie's open door.

The man whose face had seen the business end of a fist more often than Minnesota had snowstorms still showed surprise at seeing Chad.

"Got some buck?" Chad held out the cigarettes.

The man's eyes flitted from side to side as if searching Chad's mind. Then he grinned, displaying a mostly toothless mouth, probably from drinking far too much of his own product.

He snatched the pack from Chad, then tugged his bed away from the wall, unscrewed the vent, and pulled out a garbage bag. "Fresh. Just for you, Angel." He poured prison wine into Chad's mug. "Go have yourself some communion."

"I'll do that." Chad raised his mug in salute and strode to his cell, his nostrils burning from the stench of the drink. He reached his cell and closed the door. Of course, that didn't mean no one could see him. Cameras were everywhere. He couldn't even pee in private.

Still, he sat on the mattress, pinched his nose, and brought that buck to his lips. He took one sip. It burned its way over his tongue, down his throat, and threatened to heave up. Which was always worse than swallowing, so he forced it down.

Prison wine might taste like liquid manure, but it gave a good, hard buzz, and for a few hours he'd forget he was in prison, away from Chloe and Jason. Away from Jenn. For a few hours, he could be gloriously numb.

Chapter Eight

Chad raised the mug to his lips again, and his gaze rested on the picture wall across from him. His wedding photo. The newborn twins. One of his dad fishing with Jason. A photo Chloe had sent of Jenn laughing at something.

Oh, she'd be disappointed to see him now. Dad would be too.

The man had been sober for twenty years and fully knew the siren call of alcohol's numbing effect. It had been years, but there'd been a time in Chad's life when he'd been on the road to alcoholism as well.

Meeting Jenn had been a saving grace.

Chad's gaze rose to the paper cross Chloe had drawn for him shortly after he'd been convicted. She'd told him it was a reminder that prison walls couldn't keep God away.

God is faithful. The words he'd spoken to Cocoa flitted through his brain.

Something Chad had to remind himself of daily. Especially right now, because Jenn wasn't the only one blaming herself for the kids' faltering faith. If he'd been there for them, they wouldn't be doubting.

The mug felt heavy in his hand. He stared at the rancid brew and gagged. If he drank it fast, his senses would be dulled in minutes. He lifted the cup to his lips.

What about tomorrow?

There went his conscience again. He looked upward at the concrete ceiling. "You said Yourself not to worry about tomorrow."

Oh, brilliant, Chad. Being snarky with God was absolutely brilliant.

Which was exactly what drinking this muck was.

He pushed off the mattress, took two strides to his toilet, and poured it in while looking up at the prison camera. He flushed it, then retrieved mints from his drawer, anything to cover the nauseating flavor lingering in his mouth.

Not only from the buck, but from what he had almost done. Getting drunk today would make it all the easier to drink again. And again. And pretty soon he'd be like his dad had been and ruin any chance for getting out of prison early.

Oh, the devil loved messing with him.

"Not today, Satan," he said out loud. "I'm covered by the blood of the lamb."

He washed out his mug with soap and water and filled it with fresh water. Then he took a bag of chips from his drawer, ripped it open, and removed one chip. This might not be official bread and wine, but it would suffice.

He knelt by his bed and opened his Bible to 1 Corinthians 11:24. Then he held the water and the chip and said the words aloud. "This is my body, given for you. Do this in remembrance of me."

"Do this, as often as you drink it, in remembrance of me."

Kneeling, Jenn sipped from the goblet Thomas held in front of her, then bowed her head, laying her many sins at Jesus' broken body and feet, feeling the freedom and peace from His forgiveness. Then she sat on her chair as those around her sang along with Sidewalk Prophets' "Come to the Table," to close out this first home service.

And what a wonderful service it had been. Chloe and Jason both showed up, for which she gave thanks. Okay, she'd practically bribed them to be there for her first Sunday evening service at Chad's. Besides Thomas, she'd had no clue if anyone would attend, but shortly before six p.m., the mayor of Donaldson had arrived with her husband. Minutes later, Caleb Johnson, her carpenter, entered with his family. Carlos, the cute *ex*presso guy, followed in right behind them, which brought out Chloe's smile. And just as Chloe turned on opening music, Elaine, the high school senior Chad's had hired, showed up.

Yes, they were an eclectic group befitting of the song playing, that invited all to the table. All the broken and weary and hungry. She was certain Jesus was smiling on them.

If only Chad could be here, he'd be relishing this moment.

Maybe soon.

Her stomach clenched at the thought. Why did his coming home fill her with dread?

As others sang around her, she tried shaking off the feeling, hoping joy would fill her, as it should, but it didn't. Perhaps she should visit the counselor again and learn what that meant. It had been a while.

The song ended and the room grew quiet. She glanced up, and everyone was looking to her. Oh, yes, she was the leader, wasn't she?

"Uh, let's pray." She closed her eyes and folded her hands. "Father, thank You for joining us today, for directing those here to come and worship. We don't want this shop to be just a place to get a beverage. We want it to be a welcoming place for anyone to gather. A place where someone who needs to vent will find an ear to listen. A place where people feel safe. Where they can be fed and nourished physically, mentally, and spiritually, and that can only happen if You are Lord of this place. Help us to keep You at the forefront of our days and nights, our work and play. In Your holy name, amen."

The others echoed her amen, as she pondered the words that had somehow seeped from her mouth. Was that God's purpose for this shop?

People stood around her. Caleb's family excused themselves right away to tuck their girls into bed. Elaine and Carlos left at the same time. Were they a couple? If so, they'd be awfully cute together. Jason and Chloe hurried upstairs to pack for school. At least they'd stayed for tonight.

Mayor Barbara and her husband volunteered to help straighten the room.

"That's not necessary, but I appreciate the offer." It would take a minute to put the chairs away. Jenn and Thomas could easily handle that.

"Then we'll see you next Sunday." Barbara extended her hand. "That was a lovely service and a beautiful way to begin the week."

"I appreciate you coming."

The couple walked out the front door, and Jenn locked it behind them.

Which left her and Thomas. That he'd come so far for this made no sense, but she'd been grateful for his steady presence.

"I suppose I should head out, too." He picked up a dog-eared Bible from his chair, then slid that chair beneath a table.

"Do you have a moment before you leave?" She gestured to that table.

"Sure." He held a chair out for her.

But she wasn't ready yet. "Need another coffee?"

"Not if I want any sleep tonight. What was that flavor? I'm not one for fancy coffees, but I did like that."

"Another Chloe concoction." She retrieved a couple glasses of water and sat. "I think she added hot cocoa to regular coffee, but I'll have to ask her."

"Somehow Chloe's ordinary coffee and cocoa tastes better than others." Thomas took the seat across from her. "She really takes after Chad, doesn't she?"

"Oh, in so many ways. Some I wish she didn't, and others I'm very thankful for."

"Like all the artwork and marketing?"

"She's been invaluable."

He looked toward the hallway that led to their apartment door, then at her. "And while Jason clearly looks like his father, he's got your temperament."

"Is that good or bad?" She winced, thinking of Jason's peppering Thomas with questions over a week ago.

"All good, I assure you. He's inquisitive. Protective. Organized. Do you think he'd like to be a teacher, too?"

She shrugged. "I see him more as a behind-the-scenes businessman, making sure everything is precisely done."

"That makes sense."

"And your daughter, do you see her becoming a lawyer?" Thomas's wife had been a prosecuting attorney.

He laughed at that then sobered. "Noelle has no desire to study law. She wants to discover the cure for cancer."

Jenn could only nod. Thomas's wife had died from lung cancer when Noelle was only eight, so she'd been without a mom for half of her life.

"Speaking of which, I should get home to see her." He stood and picked up his Bible.

"You're a good dad." She walked beside him toward the door.

"I try, but being a single parent isn't easy, as you well know."

"I'm not technically a single parent." They stopped at the door. "Chad helps where he can. The kids each received letters from him after our talk last week. He does what parenting he can through the mail, and when they visit him, the last thing he wants to do is lecture."

"You don't have an easy life, Jenn, but you're doing well with what you've been given."

Was she really? "If only you knew what the kids talked to me about last week, you'd rescind that comment."

"Bumps in the road mean you're normal. It's how you navigate those hurdles that makes you unique. Like opening this coffee shop. You encountered an obstacle and created an opportunity. You persevere where others would quit."

She opened her mouth to object to what he had said.

"Before you say a word." He held up a finger. "Know that I would testify in a court of law, with my hand firmly planted on the Bible, that you are a good mom. An amazing woman. Your only response should be, 'Thank you.'"

She bowed her head, and said softly, "Thank you." My, this man was good for her ego. Too good, for that matter. It was time for him to go. She opened the door for him. "I'll lock up behind you."

He headed out then turned back. "Take care of yourself. What you're doing isn't easy."

"When have I ever done things the easy way?" She laughed it off, but oh for once she would like to take things easy.

"True." He nodded. "I'll be in touch."

She closed the door behind him then watched until he was in his car, like she would do for her children. "For heaven's sake, Jenn, he's not a child." She rolled down the drapes and shook her head as she checked the doors and then made a final inspection of the machines and the kitchen area. Everything was off, clean, and ready to go for tomorrow morning. Jason's doing, no doubt.

Yeah, he was her son, and that was what worried her. Like her, would he continue to choose the most obstacle-filled road in life?

She looked out the window and watched Thomas drive off.

What would life have been like if she'd made other choices twenty years ago?

Uh-uh. She couldn't go there. That was her mom speaking. That was too many years spent relying on Mom and Dad for help and having to listen to her berate Chad.

"Mom," she said out loud to convince herself, "Chad's coming home soon, and he'll be the husband and father he promised to be. And God's going to use this bad time. Somehow. Don't ask me how, but He will."

He will . . .

Oh, Jenn prayed He would, but from all the things she'd been reading lately about spouses coming home from prison, she already knew the road ahead was only going to become bumpier.

Chapter Nine

How could it be October already? Her and Chad's anniversary month.

Twentieth anniversary at that.

But how did they "celebrate" when they'd been apart? Usually, everyone ignored it, as Jenn would do now.

She scrubbed the bar top as she watched orange, red, yellow, and brown leaves dance through the air outside the shop window. Normally at this time of year, she'd be preparing for the last half of the first trimester at school. Oh, she did miss the kids. Maybe she should start a tutoring program here after school . . . Hmm, something to noodle on.

But not right now. She couldn't add one more thing to her to-do list.

Chad's Choco-Latte Corner had been open for over a month already, and they'd developed a good rhythm, figuring out which days she needed more help, days where it needed only her. Saturdays usually started out quickly, then died down. Her pocketbook wished it would speed up, but her burning legs hoped for a break.

"Hot caramel apple cider for Gina," Sally called out as the door bells jingled, announcing the arrival of more customers.

A young woman bopped to the pickup counter to the beat of more jingles, then hurried to a table she shared with friends. This store was already becoming a destination for people in this town, thanks to employees like Sally and pastry chefs like Paula. To be honest, all her employees deserved a raise.

If only that were possible. Jenn sighed and joined Sally behind the bar to assist her with the sudden rush. "I'll take the register."

"All yours." Sally stepped away and went to work on the order she'd taken. They were both in their happy place. Jenn would always prefer to take orders over making the beverages, though she wished she had some of Chad's and Chloe's flair for chatting with the customers.

Would Chad be joining them soon? If Chad could be home for Christmas, that would be the best Christmas ever. She needed to talk with Thomas and see how things were moving along.

Speaking of moving along, the line in front of her had suddenly grown while she was daydreaming.

She turned on her smile to the middle-aged man wearing overalls that reeked as if he'd come from flinging manure. This was farm country, so the idea wasn't farfetched. She held her breath and said, "Welcome to Chad's Choco-Latte Corner. What can I make for you today?"

"Just a regular coffee. No fancy stuff."

"We do have the best regular coffee, and you get free refills today."

"I 'preciate that, ma'am." And she'd appreciate it if he'd take his beverage outside and drink it at one of the tables they'd set up. The weather couldn't be nicer.

She rang up his order and, no surprise, he paid with cash and tossed the change into the tip jar. Many of the local farm folk did, which she appreciated, because that saved on credit card fees.

She rang up a few more orders and watched the line for picking up beverages grow long. Where was Chloe? She was supposed to be the backup. While ringing up the next order, she finally spotted her daughter.

By the little food pantry, sitting on the window seat, and talking with a man who, no doubt, was homeless. No surprise, Chloe treated him with the same respect she treated all the customers. Maybe Thomas was right, maybe Jenn wasn't a complete failure as a parent.

Still, Sally needed help creating the drinks, and Jason was working on the books, so she called Chloe over.

"Mom," she whispered angrily when she arrived at the counter. "Can't you see I'm helping that man?"

"Yes, I can, and I appreciate it, but Sally would also appreciate help behind the counter."

"But—"

"Chloe."

Her daughter huffed and shook her head. "One second." She filled a cup with coffee, grabbed a chocolate croissant from the pastry display, and hurried to the man. She directed him to an empty table and handed him the food, drink, and a napkin before joining Sally behind the counter.

Jenn took the next order, then turned to her daughter. "Thank you. That was very kind."

"Mom, if you only knew what—"

"We'll talk about it when we get a break." She nodded toward the now-longer line of people waiting to place their order.

Chloe looked at the line, and her eyes grew wide. "I've got this one." And she practically shoved Jenn out of the way.

Ah, Carlos the *ex*presso guy. Why Chloe wanted to wait on him was beyond Jenn, especially since she was still dating that professor. Whom Jenn had yet to meet, and didn't really want to, for that matter. If Jenn could, she'd set Chloe up with Carlos and say adios to that shady professor forever. Whenever the young man came in, he annoyed Chloe in some way with his order. Personally, Jenn thought it was cute. Reminded her of her first flirty encounters with Chad.

She eavesdropped to see if Carlos would mess up again today.

"Um, I'd like a grande berry mocha."

Uh-oh.

Sally snickered. So, Jenn wasn't the only one enjoying the drama.

"You mean a *medium*?" Chloe couldn't hide the annoyance from her voice. "That's our sixteen-ounce drink."

Clearly flustered, Carlos blinked and looked around the room, settling on Jason in the corner booth, who shook his head.

What was that all about?

"I . . . uh. Sorry." Carlos cleared his throat. "Yes, I'll take a *medium* strawberry mocha."

"Would you like that hot or iced? We could also blend it, but I wouldn't recommend that for our berry mocha."

"Um," Carlos's eyes took on that deer-in-the-headlights look. Clearly, he hadn't expected so many questions about his coffee order. "Hot?"

"Excellent choice." Chloe turned on her syrupy sweetness. "Will be my pleasure." She spun around, practically knocking the hot cocoa from Jenn's hand.

"Careful," Jenn whispered and headed to the pickup counter. "Hot cocoa for Stacy." A woman hurried to the counter and thanked Jenn for her drink.

On to the next—

"I've got this drink, Mom." Chloe pointed toward the screen detailing the orders. "You take orders."

"Yes, ma'am." Jenn grinned and then greeted the next person in line. "Welcome to Chad's Choco-Latte Corner, what can I begin for you today?"

She took two additional orders before Chloe called Carlos to the counter. Her daughter was all smiles for the young man, who thanked her and left a generous tip.

But then once again, Carlos glanced around to find Jason, who simply nodded before Carlos left the shop.

What were those two up to?

"Mom?"

Jenn's gaze jerked from Carlos to Jason, who now stood in front of her.

"Mind if I take a break?" Jason handed her his laptop. "I'm all caught up with the books."

She grimaced first and had to consciously pry her lips upward. "Go ahead."

"Thanks." Jason threw on a hoodie and hurried outside. Across the road to the park. To a bench where Carlos sat.

"It looks like your son has found a friend." Sally whisked past Jenn with a drink.

Could it be that one of her prayers had been answered the way she wanted? Did that mean others would be answered soon, as well?

"You okay, Mom?" Chloe whizzed past her with another completed beverage.

Jenn smiled. "Just thinking."

"You've been doing that a lot this morning."

"Guess I'm missing your dad." That was certainly the truth. She'd love to share good news about their son.

"Speaking of Dad, when it's quieter, will you have a moment to talk?"

"Absolutely." Jenn and the other baristas buzzed about, greeting customers and making drinks until the line was down to none.

Releasing a tired breath, Jenn surveyed the bar area. The tables inside and out were filled with customers chatting. She should be happy instead of exhausted trying to run a business, trying to parent her grown children, working on keeping her marriage alive when they were physically apart. Teaching was so much easier.

"Chloe." Jenn tapped her daughter on the shoulder as Chloe made herself a drink. "I have time to talk now." Though all she really wanted was a moment to herself to have a one-on-one with God. "Sally? Can you handle the counter?"

"Not a problem. You two go ahead." Sally waved her hands in a shooing motion. "Besides, Kayla will be coming in soon, won't she?"

"Oh, that's right." Kayla was her new hire replacing Paige, who'd already quit. Kayla was a first-year trade school student studying plumbing, of all things. Apparently, it was a family business. Regardless, good for her. And really, her work ethic proved she'd make it in whatever field she worked in. No doubt she'd last longer than Paige had.

Chloe led Jenn to the corner booth, the one Jason had vacated, the one he usually occupied to work on the books. He liked to be near in case Jenn needed him for anything. He'd always been that way. Well, maybe not always, just since Chad went to prison.

That was the way her life was defined, it seemed. Before prison and during prison. No doubt whatever Chloe wanted to talk about was a "during prison" dilemma. But before the conversation started, Jenn needed to acknowledge what Chloe had done earlier.

Jenn leaned over the table, keeping the conversation to themselves.

"I saw what you did for that man earlier. That was very kind."

"That's what I wanted to talk to you about." Chloe's brows drew together, a sign that she was worried or concerned.

Which in turn made Jenn worried, but she wouldn't let Chloe know. "I'm listening."

Chloe glanced over at the man, still sipping at his drink, nibbling at his pastry. "That's all he's had to eat today."

"I saw you two by the food shelf." The town of Donaldson had turned out mightily, donating food for the hungry.

"But that doesn't work for him. It's mostly canned goods, and he doesn't have a can opener. He doesn't have a stove to cook things on. Or milk. Or butter."

"What are you suggesting?" If Chloe was going to suggest they open a soup kitchen, Jenn would give an emphatic *No*. She couldn't take on one more thing.

"I don't know . . ." She took another glance at the man. "Maybe instead of selling day-old pastries, give them to the homeless shelter near here. Or maybe your mayor friend, Barbara, could work with churches to open a soup kitchen. Just because we're not in the cities, doesn't mean there aren't homeless and hungry."

Oh, Chloe, you have the biggest heart. "Your father would be very proud of you." More good news to share with him.

"You think so?"

"You share his heart, Chloe."

Her daughter looked away, but not before Jenn caught a smile. Perhaps this was also a teaching moment.

"Instead of me speaking with the mayor, I think you should talk with her."

"Me?" Her voice squeaked out.

"I can't think of anyone better. You have the passion and drive and heart to get something going. Barbara will certainly listen to you."

Chloe nibbled on her lower lip, something she did when deep in thought. "I suppose I could do that."

"I know you can." Jenn started to get up.

"But that's not all I need to talk about."

Okay, here came the bombshell. "I'm still listening."

Again, Chloe glanced at the homeless man. "His name is Adam. He got out of jail a year ago."

Jenn hiked in a breath. So, that was where this was going. She remained silent as Chloe went on.

"No one will hire him."

"Chloe, I can't hire another—"

"No, that's not the point." She raised her hands above the table. Her eyes were glossy with reined-in tears. "His family doesn't want him anymore. No one will give him a place to stay. All people see is his record. What if that happens to Dad? If he gets out for time served, everyone will still think he's guilty. Before, I wanted Dad home. But not at that price. He needs to have a trial—I don't care how long it takes—and be acquitted so the world—not just us—knows he's innocent."

Jenn closed her eyes and absorbed Chloe's words. Never would she have figured that Chloe, Daddy's little sweetheart, would want her father to remain in prison.

The thing was, Jenn agreed with her for many of the same reasons, and for some of her own. But those weren't things she could share with her daughter. Instead, she simply let Chloe know she'd been heard.

"I understand."

Chloe looked up. "You do?"

Jenn reached across the table and laid her hand on Chloe's. "How do you choose between freedom that's not really free and incarceration that may never lead to true freedom? Truth is, we may not have any choice at all."

"So, I'm not awful for thinking that."

"Not at all. It shows how much you really love your father because you don't want him to go through what Adam has gone through. Granted, your dad will have a home to stay in."

"And a job." Chloe looked around the shop.

And that was part of Jenn's concern. Yes, Chad would work at the coffee shop, but no way did the store make enough to support one adult, much less two. That meant she'd have to find a job to support both of them. And considering that, if he got off, it would be in the middle of the school year, she likely wouldn't find a full-time job as a teacher, but as a substitute, and subs didn't make benefits. How would she afford insurance for two? Then there would be the driving issue . . .

Lord, help me to stop borrowing trouble. "Have you spoken to your brother about this?" Jenn looked outside toward the bench he'd shared with Carlos. Jason sat alone now. Did that mean anything? Was she borrowing trouble there as well?

Probably.

"Jase disagrees with me. He thinks Dad should be home doing his share around here, but he hasn't met Adam."

Not that that would matter.

"I'll talk to him, and then with your father. I need to feel them both out. But in the meantime . . ." Jenn nodded toward Adam. ". . . you have an assignment to speak with the mayor. And know you have my support a hundred percent."

Chloe beamed the smile that had captured so many hearts. "Thanks, Mom." She got up, rounded the table, and gave Jenn a hug. "You're the best."

"Oh, I try."

And trying now meant having the hard, heartbreaking talk with Chad to let him know that they believed he should choose a trial, if it came to that, and not time served.

Chad knew he should be wearing his prison face, but making the walk to Jenn, he couldn't contain a smile. Not only was he going to see the woman who still made his heart leap, not only had they made it to their twenty-year anniversary, by some miracle, but he couldn't wait to tell her more good news. On top of that, the letters he'd received from the kids had brightened his week. Nothing could discourage him. Not even Jenn leaving after the visit. Nope. He wasn't going to make that mistake of letting prison wine tempt him again. Last time, he'd come too close to giving in.

He arrived at the door with CO Wilson. A decent enough guy. Prisoners were never friends with the COs, but most Chad had respect for. Regardless, you treated all COs with respect. That was part of the prison code if you didn't want to do more time.

He bounced on the balls of his feet, waiting for the door to open, but then he tamped down his excitement because that could get him into trouble. Being overly excited led to bending the rules, and that also led to longer prison time. But oh, he wanted to give Jenn a proper kiss. Someday soon, hopefully. He couldn't think of a better Christmas present than to make love to his wife.

But for now, a brief kiss on the cheek, a grandmother-like hug, and a shaking of hands would have to suffice.

"It's time." CO Wilson opened the door then stretched his hand in front of the opening. "Remember to cool your jets, Taylor."

Chad rubbed his hands on his pants. "Working on it, but it's our anniversary and . . ." He nodded to his wife who always looked sexy and beautiful. "You see what I'm dealing with here."

"Yeah." Wilson smiled. "Keep up your good behavior."

"I promise."

Wilson removed his arm and Chad hurried to the table. He kissed Jenn's velvet-like cheek, hugged her slender body against his, then shook her soft hand, taking care not to linger at any of the allowed touches. Then he sat across from her, his hands stretched out where Wilson could see them. Jenn placed her hands palms down, her signal that she was holding his in her imagination.

"Happy anniversary." Even though he couldn't give her a proper kiss, he couldn't stop grinning. "It's so good to see you."

"It's only been a week."

"Nope. It's been forever. Some weeks seem to last longer than others."

"So true." Her gaze broke away from his. He couldn't ignore that she hadn't acknowledged their anniversary, not that he blamed her. The only thing to be celebrated was that they hadn't divorced, which was a rarity for the incarcerated. Still, it was clear to him that her long week was due to hardship. Maybe soon he'd be able to free her from that.

"What's wrong, Cocoa?"

She half grinned at the endearment. It always worked.

"Tell me what's going on."

She shook her head. "The usual. Chloe's still dating the professor, although she's crushing on this boy who comes into the shop." Her eyes did that narrow-crinkly thing they did when she was concerned.

"Doesn't the professor have a name?"

She raised her chin, peered over her nose, and said in a snooty voice, "Nicholas Christopher the third."

"You've gotta be kidding me." Laughter burst from him. "Have you met him yet?"

"No, but I haven't exactly been welcoming either. I . . ."

"Don't like him."

"How can you not like someone you've never met? Never spoken with. Chloe doesn't even talk about him other than to tell me she went out with him. It's more of a gut feeling."

"I get that. Guess I feel the same way, which makes me feel bad for judging." Time to change the subject to something that would make her smile. "How's the shop going?"

She shrugged. Why was she being such a downer today? "Pretty much the same as last week. I revised the hours now that I have a feel for when customers stop in, and that gives me a bit more freedom at night."

"Good plan."

"But I would like to talk with you about the menu and hours going into the holiday season. And special promos we can do for Thanksgiving and Christmas. We'll be closed both days, of course."

"Of course. I'll think about menu items and O-mail it. Does Chloe have any ideas for the holidays?"

"Oh, she has plenty of decorating ideas. You should see her Pinterest board."

Pinterest? "I have no clue what that is."

"Oh." Her mouth twisted as she thought. That was as cute as ever. "It's this social media platform that allows people to save pictures and ideas online."

He shook his head. The world was passing him by as he sat in here. All the more reason to get out as soon as he could, regardless of the consequences.

"That leads to something else we should discuss." He sat up straight, excited to share the news. "Thomas visited this week, had some news."

Her face brightened. There was the smile he adored. "What was it?"

"He said there's a good chance my hearing will be set before Christmas. Cocoa, I might be home for Christmas!" He practically cried as he said those words. "And life can return to normal."

"Normal?"

He'd been so excited, he'd missed the anguish on her face.

"What's wrong now?"

Her head seemed to move in a never-ending shake. "The only way you're coming home is if the judge grants you time served. You'd still be guilty in the eyes of the law."

"There's also a chance the prosecuting attorney or the judge will look at the evidence and say I'm innocent."

"Sure. A very slim chance for either. Thomas said that rarely happens."

"I'm not going through a trial again. If the judge lets me walk for time served, I'm taking it."

Her face turned grim. "Do you think that's wise?"

"I thought you'd be happy."

"It's not that." Her hands moved farther from him, close to the edge of the table.

He was pushing her away but didn't know why. "Help me understand."

"The kids and I have talked . . . Do you know what it's like for ex-cons?"

He grunted. "Better than you."

"People won't give them jobs or homes. Communities turn against them and their families. My store might suffer. The kids—"

"So that's it." His breathing accelerated. "It's not about me getting off, but the stain I'll put on you and *your* store."

"You're putting words in my mouth."

He cursed and didn't care who heard it.

"Taylor," CO Wilson barked.

Fine. He'd curb his language for now, but his temper couldn't be contained. Something prison had taught him.

He glared at his wife, who he had always thought loved him. But hadn't she hidden the coffee shop from him until she thought he might come home? Had her plan, all along, been for her to move on without him? His heart splintered at the very idea. Most marriages didn't last the first year of a spouse being imprisoned, but he'd always believed their marriage would survive.

Many prison wives moved on to someone else. He had to ask the question, whether he wanted to hear the answer or not, but he looked at the table instead of her face. Hearing her reply was one thing, but watching her expression as she admitted it . . . "Is there someone else?" He practically whispered.

"No!" She answered too quickly, almost. Too forcefully. Or was his messed-up mind reading into things?

"But you don't want me to come home." He dared look up.

Anguish showed tight and red on her face. "Of course, I do." She sighed, backed away, her hands clinging to the edge of the table as if she was hanging on to their relationship by her fingernails. "It's more nuanced than that."

So, the survival of their twenty-year marriage was down to nuance. She hadn't said the words, but he'd clearly heard her cry for freedom. It all added up. Her moving farther away from the prison. Starting a coffee shop. Missing more and more visiting times. The kids hadn't been to see him in months. And now them not wanting him to get out early.

Well, if his family wanted their freedom, he'd give them good reason to escape, as much as it would hurt him.

He stood and forced out the words, adding as much venom as he could. "I'll give you nuance. Happy anniversary, Jenn." He flipped her the bird. It pained him to do it. He knew she'd be appalled, and that might be all she needed to loosen her grip on their marriage. She deserved to be free.

His heart shredding, he strode away from the table, trying to shut out Jenn's pleas for him to come back. But if he turned around, she'd still be chained to him, and he wouldn't do that anymore. She deserved better.

Guess it was time he acclimated to the prison culture. But he couldn't do that without help, at least for the night. He made his way to his cell, grabbed his mug and several packs of cigarettes, and strode to Moonie's cell.

"Fill me up." He handed over a pack and extended his mug.

Moonie tucked the pack under his mattress. "Gonna drink it this time?"

How the heck did Moonie know Chad had flushed the mug-full away last time?

The man laughed. "I have eyes, Angel. But it's your money that's wasting." He dug out his bag of buck and filled the mug.

The buck stank like a pig farm, but today Chad didn't care. He needed this to get over what he'd done. Tonight he didn't want to feel a thing. He plugged his nose and chugged the sludge. "Hit me again." He handed over a second pack and extended the mug.

"Got some bad news, eh?"

"None o' your business."

"As long as you can pay." Moonie grabbed the cigarettes and refilled his cup. "Now get outta here afore someone catches you."

Chad raised his cup toward the cell camera. "Not like it matters." Then he scuffled to his cell and collapsed onto his bed, where he slowly downed the rest of the drink. In no time, nothing at all would matter.

Chapter Ten

Jenn sat unmoving where Chad had left her, her hand covering her mouth and tears pleading to be released. That would happen. But not here. Numb, she got up and trudged toward the CO guarding the visitor door. Neither said a word as the CO opened the door, then Jenn walked through a maze of hallways and passed through cages designed to close off access should there ever be a riot or prison break.

Nothing registered as she picked up her keys and wallet and made her way to her pickup.

She got inside. Locked the doors. Pulled down the visor, though it gave her little privacy. She pressed a hand to her gut, sore from holding in her heartbreak. “How dare he?” she whispered as her jaw trembled. She slammed her fists against the steering wheel, wanting to call him names to match the sign he’d flashed at her.

But those words refused to exit her mouth. She hiccupped one sob. Heaved for breaths, then another sob broke loose. Followed by another and then a torrent of them.

How dare he curse at her when she’d worked her tail off to get where she was in life? He’d put her in this position. Him and that lousy recklessness of his. Maybe he was innocent of murder, but if not for his impulsive, rash behaviors, the jury might have found him innocent.

She wiped a sleeve across her eyes. Found a napkin and blew her nose. For all she cared right now, he could stay in there and rot.

Still sniffling, she started her pickup and made the hour-long drive back to the shop. It was closed now, thank goodness. She wouldn’t have to put on a happy face for customers.

Today, anyway.

Tomorrow would arrive, and she'd have to pretend to be happy.

She entered through the back door and went up to her apartment. It was early yet, but she climbed into bed without changing. She closed her eyes and prayed for sleep, yet dreaded waking in the morning. Real life had become worse than a nightmare.

When sleep came on, she dreamed that Chad had broken out of prison and became a tornado that terrorized the little town of Donaldson. She tried telling the residents that wasn't really him, that he was innocent, he wouldn't hurt anyone, but they didn't listen. Like during the trial, the judge and jury hadn't listened. They hadn't wanted to believe Chad wasn't the monster the prosecutor made him out to be.

But now, prison had turned him into a monster.

In the dream town, emergency sirens went off, warning the residents of impending doom.

The sirens wouldn't stop. They grew louder and louder as Tornado Chad wiped out nearly the entire little town.

At last, sunlight poked through the storm clouds, and the tornado faded away.

Jenn blinked in the blinding sun.

That wasn't right. She shook her head, chasing away the nightmare, and found herself tangled in the covers.

Oh no. Sunlight meant she'd slept in late.

She glanced at her clock and groaned.

Two hours late.

"Sally be there, please Sally be there," she mumbled as she ran a brush through her hair. She brushed her teeth then slipped on jeans and a Chad's T-shirt.

She hurried down the steps and saw a crowd of people in the shop. That meant someone had let them in, but it also meant that the barista was swamped. Jenn washed her hands, grabbed her apron, and pasted on her smile as she walked out front.

No surprise, Sally worked the counter alone, taking orders and making drinks.

"I'm sorry." Jenn swept behind her and started filling the orders.

"I knew you visited your husband yesterday." Sally frothed a hot cocoa. "Figured you needed the rest."

"You're a godsend." Jenn added caramel to a coffee drink.

"What are friends for?"

She almost scoffed at that. All she knew about friends was that they had left her in the lurch when Chad was convicted.

Sally knew about Chad, and she was still a friend.

"Thank you," Jenn said as she passed her friend. Oh, that sounded nice. She had a true friend.

Nine hours later, she closed the door behind the final customer and smiled.

Huh, who would have believed she could smile after yesterday's debacle?

Both she and Chad had overreacted. Not hard to do in their situation, but she needed to return as soon as possible and apologize. Tell him that he was welcome home anytime. They'd make do. They always did.

A minty hot cocoa in hand, she sat at a table and logged in to the prison visitor system on her phone. The earliest she'd be able to visit would be next Thursday, but she wanted it scheduled now.

She filled in all the info, but it didn't bring up her name as an approved visitor. That couldn't be right. She logged out and signed in, went through a few pages of forms, and was again denied.

What was going on? She could call the prison and ask, but she'd just reach a computer answering machine. Thomas had quicker access, didn't he? She called her friend and left a message, explaining the situation. Now all she could do was wait.

She may as well do that in her apartment while watching a rom-com. Those weren't usually her favorites, but after yesterday, she couldn't take anything serious.

Thomas didn't call that night. Or Saturday. Or even Sunday. Each day she attempted to sign in and was refused.

There was only one reason she could think of for the problem, but the answer made her sick to her stomach.

Monday morning as she dressed for work, acid reflux burned from her abdomen up to her throat. She should see a doctor, but she couldn't not work, especially since Sally was taking the day off, so Jenn was alone this morning.

She hurried to the shop, took care of the final steps for opening, and unlocked the door. No customers awaited, which was fine with her. That gave her time to wipe off the tables outside again. Brown leaves crunched beneath her feet, so she retrieved her broom to sweep them away. For now.

Seconds later, coffee addicts seemed to materialize out of nowhere.

By noon, she'd been popping antacids all morning and her feet throbbed and the shop had four more hours to go. Yippee . . . What she'd give to be back in the classroom. She'd thought that was tiring. Ha!

Thank goodness Elaine was here. Next to Sally, she was the best worker, though nothing was wrong with Kayla either.

With a lull in business, she sat at a table and elevated her feet. She reclined and closed her eyes as the bell jingled, signaling that a customer had either entered or departed. Whatever it was, Elaine could deal with it.

"Jenn?"

Thomas. Her eyes flew open, and she spun toward his voice. Why was he here? Wouldn't a phone call have sufficed? He pulled out a chair and sat beside her. "Tough day?"

"Busy day." She tugged her feet off the chair, removed a shoe, and massaged her foot. "Which is good for the bank account. Not so good for my health."

"Sorry to hear that." He set his briefcase on the table. "I hate to compound it, but I have news."

She pinched the bridge of her nose and sat up, prompting heartburn to streak up her throat. She ate another Tums. "Lay it on me."

"Are you all right?"

"Me? Other than the fight Chad and I had last week. Other than me not being able to make a visiting appointment, I'm peachy-keen."

He shook his head. "No, I mean with the antacids. Are you okay health wise?"

"Just heartburn."

"Or an ulcer."

"I didn't realize you were a doctor."

He half grinned. "Or someone who's had my share of ulcers."

That made sense.

"You're probably right."

"You should get it checked out, in case my diagnosis is wrong." He smirked again.

"In my spare time, I will."

"Jenn." He sighed. Removed his glasses and wiped them, then put them on. "You need to take care of yourself."

"I'm doing the best I can, all right?"

He hmphed.

I wonder what that's lawyer speak for.

"Tell me." She folded her hands on the table. "What's going on that I get a personal visit from our attorney that'll make my ulcer worse?"

Thomas stared at his briefcase then up at her. "Chad got himself in a little bit of trouble."

"Why am I not surprised?" Still, she'd hoped he wouldn't do something stupid after their fight. She could blame no one but herself for making him believe she didn't want him home. If only she'd worded her responses differently. Holding her breath, she asked, "What did he do?"

Thomas looked out the window and around the shop. Checking to see if other ears were listening? "He got caught with prison wine, and he'd obviously had more than one mug."

"Prison wine? I don't understand. He swore off drinking long ago."

"Oftentimes inmates find that's the only way to cope."

She covered her mouth with her hand. "And I caused this."

"No. Don't ever take the blame for his actions."

"But if I hadn't—"

"Jennifer, it was not your fault."

She looked upward at the tin ceiling. Sniffled. Blinked. "Is he all right?"

"He's in the hole for drinking and unruly behavior."

She wiped her nose. "That's like solitary confinement, right?"

He nodded.

Oh, he'd hate being alone. And all the research she'd done showed that isolation led to more mental health issues.

Why would he behave so foolishly? He had to know the consequences.

Maybe that was the reason. "Do you think he's intentionally sabotaging hope of early release?"

He shrugged. "That's a possibility."

"The jerk." She sniffled. "That's why I need to see him. To set things straight. Let him know we want him to come home."

"You see, that's the other problem."

"There's more?" What else had he done?

"There's no easy way to tell you this, but he's removed you from his accepted visitors list. You and the kids."

She sat silent. Stunned. Stared out the window at people pulling into the bar across the street, and managed to say, "You mean none of us can go see him?"

"That's true. I'm very sorry."

She laid her head on the table. No more tears were shed. Honestly, she didn't have any left. How could Chad do that to them? What about forgiveness? What about him being the one that others in prison went to for spiritual advice? Any headway he'd made there, he'd likely flushed down the toilet.

She felt a hand on her shoulder.

"Need a hug?"

She looked up into the eyes of someone who cared, someone who wouldn't overreact, someone who'd always been there for her. Someone who never did anything stupid. "Nothing would feel better."

Chapter Eleven

Chad trudged behind the CO toward the visiting room door. The only thing worse than being in prison was being here for the holidays. And since he'd removed Jenn and the kids from the visiting list, the holidays had become unbearable.

Yesterday, for Thanksgiving, the prison had served what they claimed was a turkey dinner, but working in the kitchen, he knew it wasn't real turkey. Every inmate grumbled about it, but what could he do? That was what prison officials gave them to serve.

Grumbling did no good at all.

Hope didn't either.

The door to the visiting room opened, and he spotted his dad where Jenn usually sat. The smartest thing he could do while in prison was to feel nothing, so why did he feel anxious about his dad visiting? Why was he in Minnesota during the wintertime, when he lived as a snowbird in Florida? Chad hadn't given a thought to removing Dad from his visitors list, yet he couldn't not show up for Dad's visit.

So here he was.

He sat at the table, foregoing the ritualistic handshake and hug for the man he'd once disdained. Then grew to love and even respect.

And now? Chad couldn't force out any words because they'd divulge his shame. He couldn't look his dad in the eye, so he focused on his own hands folded on the table, squeezing together from anxiety, knowing his dad could see right through him.

"What's the matter with you?" No love came through Dad's first words, not that Chad deserved any.

"What do you mean?" he mumbled, focusing on his hands.

"Look at me."

Chad sighed and forced himself to look his dad in the eye. Maybe Dad's tone didn't sound like love, but his eyes did. Undeserved love. God would call that grace.

Still, he said nothing, afraid he'd crumble right there in the visiting room. The gossip would make its way around the entire prison before he returned to his cell, and then he'd be labeled wimpy, which would make him an easy mark for gangbangers looking to beat someone up. 'Tomic wouldn't always be there to rescue him.

"Okay, I get it. You don't want to talk." Dad splayed his hands open. Had he learned Chad and Jenn's sign language? "Which is fine, 'cause I have a lot to say."

Yippee . . .

"You're being an idiot."

Okay, now that torqued him off, and he glared at his dad to prove it. "Watch it."

"Or what? You gonna take a swing at me like you did your fellow inmate 'cause he didn't appreciate you knocking his food on the floor?"

His breaths started coming in short waves. "Maybe he deserved it."

"And maybe you deserved three weeks in the hole."

"Maybe I did," he pushed out through gritted teeth.

"And so you're taking your childish behavior out on your wife and kids, who happen to be the best thing that ever happened to you."

Chad clamped his mouth shut, grinding his teeth. Sure, Dad was right about that, but Chad wasn't going to admit it out loud.

"Do you want to stay in here, is that it?"

Chad's jaw grew tighter.

And Dad responded with silence as the room around them was anything but quiet. Some couples arguing. Some kids telling their dad about school. Other couples doing all they could to edge across the line of what was allowed.

"I see." Dad finally broke his silence. "I'll let Jenn know she's free to move on. You don't deserve her."

"Don't you dare." He couldn't not respond, though that was what he'd wanted that horrible last day she'd visited.

"Oh, you do talk."

Chad sat as far back as he could, keeping his hands on the table where CO Vilas could see them. "What are you doing here?"

"Had to see for myself what a jack—" Dad cut himself off. "What a jerk you've become. Didn't believe it, but now I see it's true."

"What do you expect when your own wife and kids tell you not to come home?" There, he'd said it out loud. "I've set them free, so now what have I got to live for?" His breaths quickened, and unbidden tears glossed his eyes, but he forbade them to fall.

"You've got it all wrong."

"How? That's what Jenn said when she was here."

"Did you even listen to her? Or did you just go off on her?"

Chad looked at his hands and clamped his mouth shut. He'd done more than go off on her. "After what I did, I don't think she'll ever want to see me again."

"Ah, now we're getting somewhere."

"What are you, a counselor?"

"I've seen my share. Picked up on a few things here and there." Dad bent toward him. "And I know one thing. Your Jenn loves you more than you deserve. Your kids too. And you shutting them out has really hurt them."

"And she didn't hurt me?" *Good one, Chadster. Make it all about you, you selfish jerk.*

"How? Because she's afraid that you getting out of prison with your record intact will hurt you? And she doesn't want to see you hurt more than you've already been?"

"But . . ." But what? "I don't think she'll ever forgive me. I was . . . nasty to her."

"I know. But I also know that she'd forgive you in a heartbeat if you asked for it."

"Maybe I don't deserve it."

"Of course, you don't. That's what's called grace. At least that's what you've taught me. When you forgave me for my years of neglect, for loving the bottle more than you."

He finally met his father's eyes. "But you've changed."

"*God* changed me."

"And this place is changing me." He sniffled and wiped the back of his hand across his nose. "I see things. Hear things. Awful things. And they become normal in my life. In my thoughts. My dreams. Inmates call me Angel, but all I've been preaching lately is how to mess up. I thought for a long time God's plan was to put me here to lead others to Him, and in a few short weeks, I've undone all that work." He sniffled again. "I'm just a screwup."

Dad's eyes grew soft. "Exactly the kind of man God uses for His good."

Chad ran a hand over his face. "How can I fix it?"

"I ain't the one to ask."

Duh. Not like Chad had done a lot of praying over the past several weeks. Mostly he'd been running away from God, afraid of God's wrath. No, that wasn't true. He was too ashamed to face God's mercy.

"But I do have some suggestions."

Now that was more Dad-like. "What have you got?"

"First of all, you need to have a heart-to-heart with the Almighty. I know you're scared. Your earthly dad wasn't anything to brag about, but God? He listens. Trust me."

"I know." And he did.

"Then you need to add Jenn and the kids back on your visiting list. Give your wife a call. She's hurting and needs you."

Chad nodded vigorously.

"And then you need to see a counselor. You have those in prison, right?"

"We do." And he'd seen one years ago when he first arrived but had let the counseling sessions lapse because he thought he had it all under control. What an idiot.

"And lastly."

"Isn't that enough?"

"Nope. Not if you want to get out without adding to your sentence."

If that hadn't already happened.

Dad leaned forward, which meant this was serious. "You need to go to AA."

"What?" Chad jerked back. "I'm not an alcoholic."

Dad raised his brows. "No. That's why you spent three weeks in the hole for drinking."

"So, I had a bad few days."

"What happens the next time you hear bad news, have some bad days? That's how it started when your mom died, and I don't want that to happen to you."

"But . . ." Again, his excuse caught in his throat, and his gaze roamed the room, anywhere but toward his father. This latest foray into drinking wasn't his first run-in with abusing alcohol. The last time he'd struggled was the first time he'd shocked Jenn with an obscene gesture. Years ago, before he and Jenn started dating, he'd flipped her off, blaming her for his girlfriend breaking up with him.

And then he'd started drinking. At that time, Garrett had stepped in to wise him up before it went too far.

Garrett. His mentor. Father figure.

The man he'd been accused of murdering . . .

What Chad would give to talk to him now. He wasn't here, but Dad . . .

Chad finally looked his father in the eye. "You really think I need it?"

"Maybe the better question is, would it hurt you to go?"

No, no it wouldn't. The warden and COs would even look at it as a positive, as him trying to better himself.

"Now, understand, son, there's no guarantee that this will fix what you've broken."

Chad knew that too well. "But I can't keep going on like this." He wiped his nose again.

"Can I tell your family they're back on your visitor list?"

He nodded. "I'll take care of that today."

"Good." Dad winked.

"Can you tell me how they're all doing?" His heart ached with not knowing.

"As a matter of fact." Dad grinned. "I can."

For the remainder of the hour, Dad filled him in on what he'd missed over the past six weeks. The store's continued growth. The twins' schooling. His disappointment in Chloe's choice of boyfriends. Jason coming out of his shell a bit was the best news.

It all meant that Chad needed to straighten up. Talk to God. See a counselor. And yeah, go to AA if that was what it took to get home to his family. They needed him, criminal record or not, they needed him home as soon as he could get there.

"And then suddenly peas and turkey and mashed potatoes and gravy were flying through the air, and the dogs were barking their thanks for their best Thanksgiving ever."

Jenn fell back on the couch at Barbara's and howled with laughter. Just the image of this composed mayor slapping the table to make a point, accidentally hitting her dinner plate and sending that filled plate flying off the table, had Jenn gasping for breath.

"That's a typical Thanksgiving at the Webster household." Barbara plopped beside her. "I can run a city, but a meal? *Uff da*! Have mercy on all those I'm trying to feed."

"It sounds heavenly." Especially considering the day Jenn had spent with her parents. Flying food would have horrified Mom. The tension hovering over the Thanksgiving meal had been difficult enough to cut through.

So when Barbara invited Jenn to a post-Thanksgiving evening of pampering, she'd accepted the offer before Barbara had finished asking.

Feet and face masks followed by a Hallmark Christmas movie, and now, time for just being . . .

When was the last time she'd belly laughed?

Jenn crossed her legs and sighed. Not the sigh of anxiety or of one-more-thing, but of peace. When was the last time someone had waited on her? Listened to her? Been a friend to her? Even with Chad's cutting them off, she'd been able to relegate him to a do-not-open-tonight file drawer in her mind and enjoy a meal with a friend.

Yep, this was a little slice of Heaven.

"So." Barbara turned to her. "Tell me about your Thanksgiving."

Just like that, her view of Heaven took a dive. "Mom made the perfect meal. Was only Mom, Dad, Chad's dad, me, and the kids."

"Nice and intimate."

Jenn shrugged. "You could say that."

"Ah, obviously not a comfortable intimacy."

"Mom, in the middle of serving mashed potatoes, with Chad's father sitting right there, asked when I was going to wise up and dump Chad. Said she knew a great divorce lawyer. I couldn't have been more embarrassed."

"Oh no."

"Oh yes. Apparently, Chloe had let it slip that Chad had cut us off, and that was all the ammunition Mom needed."

"Did his dad say anything?"

"No, but I could tell he wasn't happy. He left as soon as his plate was empty. I apologized profusely, but still felt lousy."

"I'm sorry. Does your mom mean well?"

Jenn laughed. "Really, she wants the best for her only child, but her idea of the best has never been Chad."

"And your father?"

"Dad may be the breadwinner in the family, but Mom is definitely in charge. He just said, 'Whatever makes you happy, sweetheart.' Makes me want to scream. The kids couldn't take it either. Chloe took off to spend the evening with the professor—"

"Oh, speaking of Chloe, I need to tell you that I appreciate her stepping in to help with the soup kitchen."

"When she gets an idea, she's hard to stop. You don't know how much I appreciate you working with her and what a boost it's given to her ego."

"There's little I like more than working with determined young people."

"I always thought that would be Jason." She stared at the window and blew out a breath. "Now he's giving me reason to worry."

"Oh no."

"The fun of having twins." Jenn shook her head. "He left yesterday. Said he had a date."

"And that concerns you?"

"He never talks about her. I don't know her name." She turned to her friend. "Makes me wonder what he's hiding or why he's hiding and what I did to make him behave that way."

"Aww." Barbara laid a hand on Jenn's arm. "That does complicate things."

Jenn sighed, this time out of fatigue. "Is wanting a *Leave it to Beaver* family that much to ask?"

Barbara laughed. "Oh, honey, you wouldn't want that either. Making meals in a dress and heels?"

Picturing herself in that skirt and stilettos made her chuckle. "Not to mention perfectly coiffed hair and precision makeup? Yeah, you're right. That's not me, either. But can't I have a day or two with a little less drama in my life?"

"One thing I've learned is that as long as you have a husband and children, you will have drama. There's no escaping it. It's how you deal with that drama that matters."

"I'm working on figuring—" Jenn's cell phone played a generic ringtone.

"Go ahead and grab it. I'll find us something to drink."

"Thanks." If the kids were calling, they could wait. Mom and Dad would definitely wait. She looked at the phone. Thomas? This one she had to take. But first she said a quick prayer that he wasn't going to complicate her life further.

"Hey, Thomas."

"Is this a good time to talk?"

Barbara carried in a tray with two half-filled wine glasses and gave

Jenn a thumbs-up.

"Go ahead." Jenn sipped at the wine. Exactly what she needed for a lawyer call.

"You've been re-added to Chad's visitor list."

She gasped and tipped her wine, spilling drops on the couch. "Oh no."

"What?" Thomas asked.

"Sorry, talking to someone else, Thomas. One second." She set down the phone and her glass then leaped up, grabbed a napkin off the coffee table, and dabbed at the spill.

"Oh, don't fuss with that." Barbara brought in a damp cloth and pressed it on the mess. "This old couch has seen a bit of everything. Someday I'll get a new one."

"Are you sure?"

"Goodness, yes." She waved her hand. "I've got this. You take your phone call."

"Thank you." Jenn stood, retrieved her phone, and walked to the window. "Sorry about that. I got so excited with your news, I spilled wine on Barbara's couch." She inhaled a breath, calming herself and regaining composure. "How did you manage it?"

"You can thank your father-in-law. He visited Chad today and talked sense into him."

Jenn closed her eyes and lifted a *thank you* to God and to Hal. "I'll give him a call. My mom wasn't very kind yesterday. I'm surprised he didn't leave town." Another sigh. This one of relief and happiness. "Thank you for the news. That's exactly what I needed this Thanksgiving."

"Figured you'd appreciate it."

Jenn watched snow flurrying beneath the streetlamp. "How was your Thanksgiving?"

"It was good. My folks. Noelle. Some aunts and uncles and cousins. About twenty people in all."

"That's a houseful."

"They all wanted to see their Boston relative, I guess."

"How nice to be welcomed home."

"I admit, I did enjoy it."

"How can they not enjoy you?"

He laughed at that. "Family is still hanging around today, so I need to return and be social."

Oh, his not-so-favorite thing, but he did it anyway because it was the right thing to do. "Tell your folks I said *hi*."

"I'll do that."

"And thanks again for really making this a happy Thanksgiving."

"Not a problem."

"You're a good man, Thomas Nordberg."

They finally said their goodbyes, and Jenn turned to her friend. Barbara sat, her legs curled beneath her, in an accent chair across from the couch Jenn had spilled on.

She raised her glass. "Sounds like Chad's lawyer is also a friend."

"To be completely honest . . ." Jenn returned to her spot on the couch and picked up her wine glass. "We were once engaged."

"Interesting."

Jenn laughed. "Not so interesting. We were never in love. He was . . . safe."

"Hmm." Barbara stared at her glass, rotating it.

"What does 'hmm' mean?"

Barbara set her glass on the coffee table. "Mind a word of advice?"

"Not at all." But Jenn sipped at her wine to make the advice easier to swallow.

Barbara folded her hands and rested her elbows on her knees. "*Safe* can be very attractive."

"I'm not . . ." Jenn blinked, trying to figure out what Barbara was telling her. "I don't understand."

"How do I say this without offending you?" Barbara steepled her hands at her mouth, then lowered her hands, a move Jenn had seen before and come to interpret as her deep-in-thought move. "When life is chaotic, we often gravitate toward safe. A little something for you to be aware of."

Jenn looked at her wine, then at her friend. "I've fought for over seven-and-a-half years for my husband. From him being arrested, to the trial, to both of us losing friends. I was ostracized by our church. We lost our home, nearly all our belongings. I had to move in with my mom, who wanted to control my life. Worst of all, the kids lost their father. Through all of this, Chad and I are still in love, and we've worked hard to keep that love. If we've made it this far, through all of this, I think I can handle a friendship with Thomas."

Barbara smiled. "I'm sure you can. But know you and Chad and the kids are in my prayers."

"For which I'm very grateful."

They continued talking about family and being mayor and Chloe volunteering in the soup kitchen, but through it all, Jenn could not chase Barbara's words about Thomas from her mind. Yes, he was a dear friend, and she had no romantic feelings toward him. Yet . . .

Barbara was right. After years of being a prison wife, the idea of being with someone safe was very attractive. Too attractive, actually, which meant that until Chad was freed, her interactions with Thomas needed to be relegated to business only. She wasn't naïve enough to believe that she was perfect. Far, far from it.

Chapter Twelve

She was supposed to see Chad today.

Washrag in hand, Jenn glanced from the table she was cleaning toward the shop's picture window. Wind-hurled snow pelted the glass, making visibility outside nearly zero. The forecast had warned a winter storm was likely. For once, the forecasters were right.

Relief at not having to visit Chad flooded through her as if a dam had burst. Followed by anger at herself for having that feeling. Since Chad's meltdown, something inside her—what, she couldn't pinpoint—had broken.

On top of that, she hated missing time at the shop, especially during the Christmas season. They needed her here.

Didn't he need her more?

Besides, with the storm, few people were venturing out today. She surveyed the shop. A Christmas tree, bare of the Blessing Tree tags, stood proudly in the corner of the shop. When Jason had suggested they support prisoners' children through the program he and Chloe had benefited from, she'd been ecstatic. The last few years, he'd grumbled about the program and had said he couldn't wait until he was eighteen, so he'd age out. Who knew he'd be the one to sign up the shop and lead the charity's promotion?

The town of Donaldson had stepped up quickly, as well. Within one week of the tree going up, all the tags had been claimed. This town knew how to love.

But would they be as accepting when her husband returned home, especially if he still wore the convicted-felon label?

She was borrowing trouble again.

True trouble was that white stuff blowing outside the window, keeping customers at home.

Sally, the only employee working today, sat by the book nook reading. Otherwise, the shop was empty. Since the early morning rush, they'd had a total of five customers. Sally could easily handle the rest of the day on her own, and had offered to close. She lived close enough to get home safely.

If the shop didn't have a weekend Christmas special starting tomorrow, Jenn would reschedule her visit with Chad for tomorrow or Saturday, but she needed to be here.

Which meant, she had to visit today or miss this week altogether. Since opening Chad's, she'd missed too many visits already. If she left here three hours ahead of schedule, certainly she'd arrive in plenty of time to make her visit.

She sat at a table and checked the Minnesota 511 app on her phone to see the conditions of the roads. The map was filled with purple crash signs and red-highlighted roads. Travel wasn't advised, but it also wasn't prohibited.

She typed in the prison's address and tapped Directions. Three hours? On a normal day, the drive would take slightly under an hour. If she left now, she *might* arrive in time for her scheduled visit. Afterward, she could stay at her parents' home and hope the roads would be better in the morning, so she could open shop.

That involved a whole bunch of "ifs."

Going would be foolish.

Staying would disappoint Chad. Though he would certainly understand.

Still . . .

She verified the current time. If she wanted to make the appointment, she had to leave now.

She stood, removed her apron, and grabbed the washrag as she hurried to the dirty towel bin.

"You're still going?" Sally sounded incredulous.

Jenn tossed the linens. “I don’t have a choice.”

“He’ll understand, I’m sure.”

“He would.” Jenn turned to her friend. “But I need to do this for us.” Additional missed visits would only widen the fracture between them, and that she couldn’t bear. “Thank you for staying and closing.”

Without waiting for a response, Jenn rushed to her apartment. She changed into warm clothes and filled an overnight bag. Her pickup was already stocked with a winter emergency kit. Living in Minnesota, driving without one was foolish. One little ice patch could send the toughest of vehicles careening into a ditch, and tow truck drivers would be overworked today, so a pull-out could take hours.

She hurried from her apartment, an extra snow brush in hand, to her four-wheel-drive pickup hidden beneath about four inches of snow. One more delay, but that wouldn’t stop her. She turned on the truck’s ignition and window defrosters, then banished the snow from her windows and hood. That left her with two and three-quarter hours to get to the prison.

More than once, she’d been grateful that she’d spent the extra money to get a four-by-four pickup. Not only did it grip the road better than the average car, it also came in handy for transporting equipment. Plus, she sat up higher, giving her a greater view of the road ahead, all of which should help her arrive sooner than her phone’s GPS claimed.

She secured her phone on the dash mount so she could visually see the route and the time. If the weather worsened, she could always turn around. Then, inhaling a deep breath, she stepped on the brake and clutch, slipped the truck into first gear, and headed onto the mostly deserted main street. She took it slowly at first, periodically tapping the brakes to test the road for slickness. So far, her tires had a firm grip on the pavement. She sped up slightly, then a little more once she exited the town, but not too much. The road often hugged the river, and she had no desire to take a chilly swim.

The snow seemed to increase with her speed. Like fencers, her wipers whooshed back and forth, fighting off snowflakes. Snow was the victor, so she let up on the gas slightly. Any slower, and she may as well turn around and go home.

Taillights shone like a halo rainbow up ahead. She wasn't the only idiot out on the road this afternoon. Unfortunately, she had to slow to match their speed. The trick was keeping several car lengths between her and the vehicle in front as they continued to decrease their speed.

After about ten minutes of white-knuckled driving, she turned off the river road onto a highway that resembled a parking lot.

Home was fifteen, maybe twenty minutes away, and Chad a white-knuckling two-and-a-half hours. Growing up, she'd always done the wise thing, the safe thing.

Then she'd met Chad.

He'd quickly nudged her beyond her safe boundaries where she'd learned to take risks. Calculated risks, mind you, but they weren't exactly safe.

She checked her GPS, or as Chloe called it, Ginger. Right now, Ginger's calculations informed her that she'd still arrive early, so this was a risk worth taking.

Vehicles on the highway inched along, and snow began accumulating on her overworked wipers. She turned up the defroster and it helped enough to keep her windows clear.

Several agonizing minutes later, she turned onto the freeway that saw more movement. Again she touched the brakes to get a sense of iciness. So far, not a problem, but that could change in a foot or a second. A single patch of ice could send her pickup skidding into a ditch, already occupied with stuck travelers.

That alone made her slow down. Taking risks was fine, but only if she showed wisdom in the taking.

An hour passed, followed by another. Ginger said she had another ten miles to go and guessed at it taking thirty minutes. That would leave Jenn plenty of time to park, sign in, and make her way to the visiting room.

The snow let up and visibility increased. Even fewer cars traveled the road now, but these last, less traveled roads hadn't been plowed recently. A vehicle cruised up too quickly behind her, almost hugging her bumper. The last thing she needed was to be shoved into the ditch by a bully, so she watched for a side road or a driveway to pull into, to allow the driver to pass.

There. Just ahead. She flicked on her blinker, and slowed her truck. The tailgater drew closer. To not overshoot the driveway, she'd almost have to come to a stop to make the turn. With the truck only feet behind her, that would be nearly impossible.

Still, she'd take the chance to get him off her bumper.

The driveway neared. She raised her foot off the accelerator.

Wait. Wasn't that the prison tower beyond the hill?

Yes!

With the truck nearly hugging her tailgate, she gave her pickup a little more gas. The wheels skidded, tugging her sideways, toward the ditch. She turned into the skid, but snow on the shoulder had her tires in a vise grip. It pulled her off the pavement and plowed her into a ditch with a chin-high drift.

The bully truck zoomed past, and she got a glimpse of the large man filling the cab, laughing at her.

Laughing, but not stopping, the jerk. Oh, it made her want to say words she'd forbidden her kids to say. But she behaved and focused on the problem at hand.

If she could get out, she'd walk the last mile to the prison and call a tow truck on the way. As busy as towing companies likely were, no way would they arrive before her visiting hour was up.

The challenge was getting out of the pickup with snow up to her windows on both sides of the cab. She tried both the driver and passenger doors. They wouldn't budge. The rear window opened enough to pass a child through, but not an adult.

So, she was in a ditch, within sight of the prison, and she was trapped inside the pickup. That word she'd held in earlier slipped past her lips. Not only would she miss out on her visit with Chad, but she could be stuck here for hours.

Chad paced the concrete hallway outside his cell, praying for Jenn, for her safety, periodically checking his window that was plastered with snow. Jenn would be nuts to drive in this, but he hadn't heard that she'd postponed the visit. If she didn't make the trip, though, he'd be disappointed.

Why were feelings so stupid?

Still, he made his way toward the visitors center, dread and hope taking up equal shares in his gut. He needed to see her. While Jesus was his hope, Jenn's presence offered reassurance, and he anticipated even the slight physical contact they had to help him make it through the week until her next visit.

But more so, since the time he'd shut her out, she hadn't been the same. Not that he blamed her, of course. What he'd done to her had been despicable. God had forgiven him, and Jenn had said the words, but he'd felt a distance between them that could only be repaired with time spent together, so she could see for herself that he was changed. But how do you get time together when prison, miles, and winter all stood between you?

Thankfully, he knew that God was bigger than all those obstacles. If God could change his father's life, God could fix anything.

CO Wilson nodded at Chad as he neared the cage that separated the prisoners from the visitor center. "Come to see your wife?"

"I hope so, but with the weather . . ."

"Doesn't she live around here?"

"She used to."

CO Wilson nodded again and said nothing more. The man was good at keeping a line between himself and the prisoners, but he also didn't rebuke them like CO Bulldog would for even the tiniest infraction. Or a crosswise look. Wilson was at least human.

Chad took a seat on an unforgiving concrete bench outside the cage. His leg bounced to a rhythm of a song that had become an earworm, one he'd never allow his kids to hear but was popular on the inside.

Seconds ticked by with the beat of the music, then bled into minutes. He looked up at CO Wilson, who shook his head.

"What time is it?" Chad stood and tried to read the officer's watch upside down.

"Four fifteen."

Fifteen minutes eaten away already. Still, he paced the hallway, hoping, praying that Jenn was safe, wherever she might be.

Another five minutes slid by. Ten. Fifteen. *Face it, Doofus, she's not coming*. He balled his fist and resisted the urge to pound it into the wall.

"Have you tried calling her?"

He'd thought of it, but his account was low, having spent the majority on presents for his family, and the rest on booze. Idiot. He'd never been good at budgeting money. Which was one of the factors leading to his appearance of guilt. You'd think he'd learn.

"I s'pose . . ." He kicked at the floor. "I'll check my O-mail, see if something came through." He aimed for a cage that would allow him into the common area.

"Sorry about that, Angel. I know how important this was for you."

The CO called him Angel . . . Affirmation of Chad's humanity, of him standing out among the prisoners in this snake pit.

He spun and nodded his appreciation then headed again for the cage. He'd see her next week, assuming another winter storm didn't hit the state, which was never a certainty.

"Hold up, Angel."

He stopped and turned, trying not to get his hopes up, yet the excitement buzzing in his stomach told him he'd failed.

CO Wilson removed a hand from his ear, then gestured toward the cage. "Guess who just arrived."

Jenn sat at the table, trying to still her breathing. One thing she'd learned since moving from the cities was that farmers were unsung heroes. The young farmer had stopped, dug out her driver door, and then delivered her to the prison with a promise to free her truck. Then he'd told her to call when her visit was over, and he'd give her a ride back. All without accepting payment. She'd make sure to send him a care package from Chad's.

Speaking of which . . .

The door to the prison opened and Chad stepped through. An array of emotions passed over his too-readable face. Relief. Joy.

Anger.

Oh boy. Unbidden tension stiffened her arms at her side, making her smile a forced one as she stood to receive the too-quick hug and kiss.

They sat across from each other, and the anger seeped from his features. "You had me worried," he said through his teeth. He drew a hand over his face and took a breath. "I've been praying for you all afternoon."

"Thank you." She looked down, ashamed to admit that prayer hadn't crossed her mind.

"But you should have stayed home."

"I know, but I needed to see you. I took a calculated risk." He didn't need to know about the ditch dive.

His frown curved up into a smirk. "I'm worth the risk, huh?"

"Of course, you—" A new guard shuffled to the door of the prison, and she gasped.

"What's wrong?" He started to turn his head, but apparently thought better of it. Good thing, too.

"That guard, the new CO." Whispering, she nodded toward the door. "He practically drove me off the road earlier."

His hands tightened into balls. "That's CO Bulldog. He's always got bees up his . . . butt."

Jenn covered her mouth and chuckled. "His butt, huh?"

He shrugged with a smirk. "That's prison life for you. It's reforming all of us into saints."

She laughed, then sighed. "Oh, I miss you."

"Soon, Cocoa, soon I'll be home. I know it."

That was what she hoped for. And feared. "Hear anything from Thomas?"

He shook his head. "No hearing date set yet."

"So we wait."

"Like everything having to do with the law. Nothing's fast. But while we wait, I have some questions." He reached into his pocket and pulled out a piece of paper. "Chloe wrote me."

"She did?" Jenn clasped her hands together as if in prayer. Both kids had become terrible at writing letters. To be honest, she wasn't much better, and had gotten even worse upon the store's opening.

"Yep, and I've got a bunch of questions."

"Okay . . ." Hopefully not about the professor boyfriend Jenn still had never met.

"Uh, yeah. She's using all this terminology for the coffee shop that I've never heard before." His eyes scanned the letter, then he looked up. "What's a flight?"

Oh . . . More changes for Chad she hadn't even considered. Whenever he did get out, even the coffee shop was going to be a culture shock for him.

"We use it in a few different ways. If someone orders a flight of coffee, we give them three small cups with different flavors of coffee. We also have an all-cocoa flight and a mixed flight that has one coffee, one hot cocoa, and one mix. And our pastry maker offers a brownie flight, with three flavors of brownies."

"Wow. That's something." His forehead wrinkled as he absorbed the concept then glanced at Chloe's letter. "She said chocola . . . choco-ter . . ." He shook his head.

"A choco-terie board, a play on charcuterie board from French tradition. Ours is a platter decorated with different kinds of chocolate and fruits and cookies, all artfully organized so it looks pretty. Chloe came up with the idea, and arranges them, so we call it Chloe's Choco-Terie Creations. They're very popular right now with the holiday season."

"Makes sense, I guess." He perused Chloe's letter, his brows sliding together. "And what's a NowPic? Is that the new name for those Polaroid instant cameras?"

Jenn laughed, then, seeing Chad's frown, she cut herself off and cleared her throat. “That’s a popular new picture-sharing app that allows friends and followers to see images she posts from her phone.”

“Oh . . .” He scratched his head.

It was so easy to forget that he was out of the loop on all the latest trends. Technology had changed so much during these past years.

He shook his head and slumped. “I feel like you’re talking a whole different language.”

“It really is a different language, but you’ll catch up quickly when you get out.”

“I hope so. I’ve only been in for seven-and-a-half years, but it feels as if I won’t recognize the world when I get out.”

She had nothing to say to that, other than to agree. “I’m sorry.”

“No.” He shook his head and sat up straight. “I’m the one who’s sorry. I’m turning everything into a downer, when I have this good news.” He held up the letter. “Tell me how Chloe uses this NowPic for the coffee shop.”

Chad’s ability to switch emotional gears sometimes made Jenn dizzy, but in this case, she was happy for the turnaround. Besides, bragging on her kids was a mother’s right. “She shares images of the chalkboard menu and Paula’s Pastries, seasonal beverages, store décor, schedule changes. It’s a free and easy way to advertise.”

“Sounds like smart marketing.”

“That’s Chloe’s gift.”

“But she’s going to school for teaching?”

“Because tuition assistance from my parents came with a hook. Mom insisted Chloe get a teaching degree.” Jenn shrugged.

Darkness shadowed Chad’s face again and he flexed and unflexed his fists. “If I were home . . .”

“Sweetheart.” Oh, she wished she could reach across the table and take his hand. “Soon.”

“I hope so. I’d do anything to be free.”

Even accept a deal that would still label him guilty, and that broke her heart for him.

A buzzer went off, warning them they had only five minutes left, which meant she had to get in as much conversation as she could.

"I do have some other news." She laid her hands palms up on the table. "Did Jason tell you he got Chad's to sponsor a Blessing Tree?"

"He did?" Light returned to Chad's eyes. "Good for him, but I thought he hated getting gifts through that."

"He didn't dislike the gifts. He disliked that people saw him as a prisoner's kid. He didn't like the label or the pity. I'm afraid that attitude trickled down from his mother."

"Not like you had much choice."

"We could have said no, but I didn't want the kids to feel cheated."

He sighed.

All she'd done was take good news and make her husband sad.

"It's not your fault, Chad. Or mine or the kids. It just . . . is, and we're all dealing with this the best way we know how. That means loving you and the kids the best I can."

He reached as far across the table as the rules allowed. "You still love me?" His eyes searched hers, as if doubting.

Problem was, all too often, she did doubt, but she wasn't going to burden Chad with that. Instead, she spread her palms on the table as if grasping his hands. "I love you more than cocoa."

That made him smile. "And I love you more than coffee."

"That's saying something."

"Tell me about it." His smile grew into a grin. "And I love how you've done an amazing job with the kids, that they're both thinking about others."

"*We've* done a good job. And I mean that." She laid a hand on the side of her face, communicating that was how she yearned to touch him.

He copied her gesture, and she swore she felt the warmth of his hand covering hers. "Tell me how you're celebrating Christmas."

Another tough topic. She'd never learned to enjoy Christmas. How could she when the holidays meant no visitors for Chad because prison staff got time off to spend with their families? So, no special meals. No real celebrations for him. She'd done her best to normalize the day for their kids, but nothing was normal when your father was in prison.

She'd also learned that telling her plans brought Chad joy, as if he could celebrate vicariously through her.

"I'm closing the shop at one on Christmas Eve, so I should be out of there by two. We're going to Mom and Dad's, and she's making her usual roast beef meal."

"Oh, my favorite." He licked his lips then wiped a hand across his mouth.

"Everyone's favorite." Though Chloe had been talking lately about possibly going vegan like the professor. "And then I'm going with the kids to see the Christmas lights at the Arboretum, assuming we don't have another blizzard. I told Chloe to invite Nicholas so I can finally meet him."

Chad scanned his letter from Chloe. "She said nothing about him."

"She never does."

"I guess I can only hope that they both find someone to love like I love you." He pressed his fingers to his lips.

She did the same while closing her eyes, trying to remember the feel of his lips on hers, his arms wound around her, his fingers combing through her hair.

Bzzz.

The times-up buzzer sounded, jarring her from her daydream.

Like robots, they stood and met at the side of the table for their handshake and hug. The peck on her cheek. Then he backed away and blew her a kiss. "I really do love you more than coffee."

She captured the kiss with her hand and pressed it to her heart. "And I love you enough to try coffee."

He laughed at that.

"Come on, Taylor, hustle." CO Bulldog's voice echoed through the room.

Her fists clenched. What she'd give to tell him off, but she knew that would only make things worse for her husband.

Chad spun away. Seconds later, he disappeared inside a cage that led him to who knew where. What was it like on the other side? How could he even smile?

She turned to leave and touched a hand to her lips, hoping to feel his warmth again, but the moment had passed. What would it be like to touch him again?

And why did the idea of intimacy frighten her?

Why did the whole idea of him returning home scare her to death, when that was what she'd spent the last seven years fighting for?

Chapter Thirteen

Joy.

Was that the sensation Jenn was experiencing right now?

She walked behind the twins as they all took in the Christmas lights at the Landscape Arboretum. The kids weren't fighting. The professor had made some excuse not to show up, which was fine with her. The temperature held at a balmy twenty, which was perfect for Christmas Eve. Business this past month had been far better than she'd anticipated, much of that due to Chloe's creations, including the widely popular Choco-Terie board.

The pastor's Christmas Eve sermon this afternoon, at her parents' church, had been uplifting as he explored what was going on in the world at the time of Jesus' birth. To think, Mary could have been stoned for being an unwed mother. On top of that, she was completely innocent of any wrongdoing.

Now that was injustice.

Another Easter connection.

Jesus and Mary were innocent. Chad was in very good company, in that regard.

The kids oohed over a tall pine up ahead with multi-colored lights covering nearly every inch of the tree, hiding any defects it might have.

Because of Jesus' sacrifice, her defects weren't just hidden, she was truly clean.

Yeah, that was definitely a cause for joy.

But . . .

Perhaps it was the compliment from her mother at suppertime, when she'd echoed Dad's pride in her and the kids for turning Chad's Choco-Latte Corner into a success. Compliments from Mom were rare, so when Jenn did receive one, it buoyed her.

Maybe it was the entire day's events that allowed her to experience joy. When was the last time she'd felt stress-free?

Probably eight years ago.

The last Christmas they'd spent together as a family. A year later, Chad had not only been arrested, but by Christmas, he'd been found guilty and sentenced to a hundred fifty months in prison, sending the entire family on a downward spiral.

After landing at the bottom, she'd clawed her way to the top, all with a heavy weight on her shoulders.

Well, they were almost to the top.

That would happen when Chad stepped onto free soil again.

Maybe soon?

Add that to her list of reasons to be joyful.

Fight until he's free!

"Mom, hurry up." Chloe ran back and grabbed Jenn's arm. "The best part is up ahead."

Chloe practically dragged Jenn around the tall pine then spread her arms. "Ta-da!"

Jenn gasped. White twinkle lights hung from branches for as far as she could see. She could barely tell where treetops peaked and starlit sky began, returning her to a much happier time. She blinked away tears.

"It's like your wedding pictures, isn't it?" The frozen air cloud created from speaking added to the ambiance.

Jenn nodded and wiped at her nose. "It's breathtaking."

"I know, right?" Chloe gestured toward a bench. "I know you want to sit and take it all in."

That she did. She sat and the kids joined her, one on each side. Other visitors oohed and awed at the sight as they walked through the forest of lights.

Jenn closed her eyes and pictured Chad handsomely decked out in black for their evening wedding. White twinkle lights, matching the twinkle in Chad's eyes, had hung from trees on both sides of the Mississippi River near the headwaters. Her bouquet was purple hyacinths and baby's breath, with more lights glimmering from the flowers. The bridesmaids carried candles.

The groomsmen . . .

She squeezed her eyes, willing away that memory. Chad's arrest had not only sent their family reeling, but it had stolen what had once been happy memories and the joy she'd felt moments ago. She'd loved everything about their wedding, but now she couldn't think of it without becoming sick to her stomach.

"Jenn?"

What? Thomas? She shook her head and looked upward. It was Thomas. And his daughter. Why were they here?

"Fancy meeting you here." He gave a half smile. "Remember my daughter, Noelle?"

Jenn nodded. "Of course. Nice to see you again, Noelle. It's your birthday, tomorrow, right?" Jenn only remembered that because Noelle had been born on Christmas day.

"I'll be seventeen." Her face beamed like the lights surrounding her.

"Almost an adult." Jenn glanced at Thomas who shook his head, then back to Noelle. "How's college going?"

She shrugged. "I'm sure it'll be more challenging my senior year."

More challenging than a nearly-seventeen-year-old taking junior-level classes at one of Minnesota's top-ranked schools?

Thomas smirked. "She got her smarts from her mother."

"Or she added both yours and your wife's together."

"Probably."

Noelle rolled her eyes. So, she was a normal teenager after all.

"Mom, Uncle Thomas?" Jason broke his silence. "You mind if the three of us go ahead?" He gestured to Noelle to join them. "The two of you can catch up."

Hmm. *Methinks this wasn't a chance meeting after all.*

Thomas waved the kids away. "We'll catch up soon."

She scooted over on the bench, leaving plenty of room for Thomas to sit. "Why do I have a feeling that this meeting wasn't serendipitous?"

"Aw, good word."

"Thomas."

"Okay, I plead guilty."

"Good, because the evidence was stacked against you." She steepled her gloved hands together and tucked them between her legs to warm up. "Do you mind if I ask you a legal question?"

"Of course not."

She looked around at the lights that had enchanted her moments ago. "There's a thief I want arrested."

"You haven't contacted the police?" He cocked his head to the side.

"Nah. I think they'd be upset if I called 9-1-1 with this problem." Her throat grew raspy, and she cleared it, wishing she had some water. "You see, I'm talking about a joy thief."

"Aww, yes. One of the most insidious criminals out there. I know."

Yes, he would. His marriage had been far too short.

She nodded toward the lights. "This reminded me of our wedding." As her ex-fiancé, Thomas hadn't been invited, but he'd probably seen the pictures. "It was the perfect wedding. Perfect temps. No clouds. Just a handful of friends and family. And then the wedding night . . ." Camping under the stars—making love beneath those stars—on private property owned by Garrett.

Chad's mentor.

And best man.

Chad would have given his life for the man, not murdered him.

If only the jury had understood their connection, they'd have known Chad wasn't capable of doing what he'd been found guilty of.

Sometime in the middle of her musing, Thomas had taken her hand.

She gripped his tighter. "I can't think about our wedding anymore without becoming depressed. I see Garrett and then I see Dajon." The other groomsman, Chad's best friend. The one who'd made the accusation of murder and the key witness in the trial.

"My maid-of-honor and bridesmaid vanished after the trial, not wanting anything to do with a prison wife."

"I'm sorry you're going through this, Jenn." His thumb caressed the back of her hand. If he were someone else, the gesture would have been too intimate, but this was her good friend, Thomas.

"I realized something earlier tonight." She closed her eyes, trying to recall all the reasons she'd felt joyful earlier, but all those reasons had vanished. "It's been nearly eight years since we've shared a Christmas together. I felt joy earlier tonight, but now, now I feel rotten for having that feeling. Chad being convicted right before Christmas has ruined every Christmas since then."

The twins had only been ten at the time, and she'd done her best to give them a happy Christmas, but how do you convince a child God is good when their father is sent to prison for a crime he didn't commit? She'd had enough difficulty convincing herself.

"It's okay to feel joy." He released her hand and folded his together. "Lacy has been gone for eight years, and I still miss her like crazy. Especially around the holidays. They were special to her, and I've never been able to replicate what she did to make them special. It's very lonely."

Yes, it was. Even with children. "The loss of a spouse leaves a different-shaped hole in your heart, one no one else can fill."

He nodded. "So true. But." He sat up straight. "Some memories with her no longer bring sadness. I'll find myself smiling at them, then berate myself for feeling happy."

"I'm not alone, then."

"Not at all. And your situation is unique. I know Lacy is with Jesus. She's free and healthy and happy. How can I be sad about that?"

Compared to Chad . . .

Enough of that talk, and those feelings. Mimicking Thomas, she sat up tall. "I'm sure you didn't come all the way over to the Arboretum to be a counselor."

"That depends upon if you're talking about the therapist type of counselor or legal counselor."

"You've developed a sense of humor."

Thomas shrugged. "I try." Then he removed his gloves, blew hot air into his cupped hands, and put his gloves on. "I have news."

News. That word could be good or bad, and Thomas was never good at tipping his hand.

So, she waited for him to continue, while watching the lights and the people walking past, wonder evident on their faces. Oh, to feel that again.

"Chad has a court date."

Jenn bit her lip, trying to tamp down her hope. A court date meant nothing other than they were closer to another waiting period.

"January twenty-fourth."

A month from today.

"Does that mean Dad can get out of prison then?"

Jason? Jenn glanced to her right, where the three kids were huddled together. Had they been listening the entire time?

"Come here." Thomas waved them over, and the kids stopped in front of them. Hope was written in Chloe's large, glistening eyes, but Jason gave nothing away emotionally, as usual. Regardless, they were about to be disappointed.

"The post-conviction hearing will be to determine which direction your father's case goes. We present the new case, the prosecuting attorney will present their side, then it's up to the judge to make a decision."

Jason crossed his arms. "If the judge decides that Dad's not guilty or that he could get off with time served, would he come home that day?"

"No." Thomas sighed, shaking his head.

"That's bogus." Jason stomped a foot. "When can he come home?"

"That's determined by how long the judge takes to make their decision. Could be anywhere from a few days to ninety days."

"So, the judge gets to go home to their family while Dad rots in jail for something he didn't do."

"I understand it looks like that."

Jason snorted. Kicked at the hard-packed snow path. "Does Dad go to jail or prison while waiting for the judge to make up his mind?"

Thomas stood up and laid a hand on Jason's shoulder. Jenn could tell Jason wanted to shake it off, but he behaved himself. For now, anyway.

"You have a lot of good questions, Jason. I appreciate your maturity."

Jason snorted again. "Well? What's the answer?"

Yep. really mature.

"The answer again is determined by the judge. If he or she believes they'll make a decision quickly, they could have your father moved to the local jail."

"Up in Bag . . ." Jason squished his eyes closed, thinking.

"Bagley." Jenn offered the name of the county seat where the hearing would be held.

"Yeah, that's it. So, he'd be farther away from us again?"

As if Jason had spent a lot of time visiting his father this past year.

"If he's sent to jail, that's where he'll be." Thomas answered so calmly, very unlike Chad. "It's likely that he'll be transported to prison. Inmates would prefer that, as there's more to do."

"We wait until January twenty-fourth, then." Chloe joined the conversation, copying her brother's crossed-arm stance. "Then we wait another maybe ninety days to find out that Dad *might* be released, or he *might* get another trial, which could last years, or he *might* have to serve the rest of his sentence, which would be another five years from now."

Thomas dipped his head to the side. "Close enough."

"Like Jase said, that's bogus." Chloe added a stomped foot to the word.

Oh, Jenn would dearly love to stomp her foot and shout, "Bogus." She'd like to teach the legal system something about the Sixth Amendment, which promised a speedy trial. Thomas had explained all this years ago, and still today, she was dumbfounded by the sloth-like speed of the legal system. Thomas had explained why, but it was a bunch of legal mumbo jumbo that made no sense to her.

"To sum it up." Like her kids, Jenn crossed her arms. "Chad could be home anytime between the end of this coming January and four years from this coming October. There's zero guarantee of him being acquitted."

Thomas sighed, his first sign of emotion. "I'm afraid so."

"To echo the kids, that's bogus." And she did an exaggerated foot stomp.

The trio of kids stared at her as if she'd grown horns.

Then she grinned. Smiles slowly inched their way to the kids' faces, then they laughed.

"Mom." Jason pointed to her leg. "Don't ever do that again, okay?"

"No promises." She grinned, hoping to remove the darkness that had overshadowed the evening. "I think we should celebrate knowing the hearing date with dessert from Baker's Pantry. What do you all say?"

They all cheered for that. Even Thomas.

She pretended to cheer. She was the mom. She needed to show happiness for their sake, even if she preferred to spend the evening by herself, crying.

Because that was what single moms did.

Chapter Fourteen

CO Bulldog stood too close behind Chad as he awaited entrance into the courtroom. Of all the guards to be assigned to him for his hearing, why did it have to be Bulldog? The jerk had spent the entire road trip attempting to provoke Chad, but so far, he'd resisted taking the bait. Unfortunately, the day was far from over, and where Chad would wind up at the end of the day was a mystery.

The only thing he knew was that going home today wasn't one of the options.

He'd either be spending a few days at the county jail, which he despised, or he'd be transported back to prison, which was only slightly more palatable. At least in prison, he could work, go outside, hang out in the common areas. In the county jail, you were stuck in a cell with a bunch of crazies whose behavior was unpredictable.

In order to survive, you kept your head down, didn't make eye contact, didn't react to goading. He'd mastered all of that. Well, maybe not mastered, but he knew what he had to do to stay out of most trouble. Some trouble found you whether you looked for it or not.

The door in front of him opened.

"Get goin'," CO Bulldog growled.

I'm going as fast as I can with these shackles on my ankles. Chad shuffled through the doors and glanced to his right. Caught his breath. They were all here. Jenn, Jason, Chloe. Dad.

But so was his former best friend, Dajon, along with half of Clearwater County. People he'd served coffee to for years. People who used to come into Cuppa Truth to see him, to have him listen to their woes. Now they all wagged accusing fingers. After all, he was the son of the town drunk. No one was surprised when he went rogue.

Though it hadn't been him. Hopefully, today, the judge would not just listen to the evidence, but he—Chad glanced at the raised bench in front of the courtroom—*she* would hear the truth. Maybe having a female judge would play in his favor. Or maybe it would be worse.

Lord, help me give it up to You, he silently prayed for the hundredth or so time since he was escorted from prison earlier today.

CO Bulldog gripped his arm and led him to the table where Thomas sat. He unlocked the arm shackles, and Chad audibly sighed with the relief. Not only were they painful, but being chained made him feel less human, though his pride couldn't really dip much lower than it already had.

Still, he glanced at Jenn, who blew him a kiss. Jason gave him two thumbs up, and Chloe showed the I Love You sign. Dad mouthed, "You've got this."

Oh, he hoped so. He couldn't have a better representative than Thomas, who'd managed to help free several wrongly incarcerated prisoners. Why shouldn't the same happen for Chad?

Still, perspiration filtered through his orange prison uniform. This hearing held his life in its hands. Would he be going home in ninety days? Or would it be another fifty-seven months?

Jenn did her best not to tear up when Chad was led into the courtroom, shackled like some monster, followed by that Officer Bully or Bulldog, whatever Chad had called him. She could practically see steam billowing from Chad's head, but he kept his cool and didn't react, like she really wanted to. Jesus said they were to love their enemies and pray for those who persecuted them, but oh that was difficult.

The only thing she could do right now was pray, so that was what she did as Thomas addressed the judge, sharing the found evidence. Then the other attorney whined that the evidence wasn't solid enough. To Jenn, it was more solid than granite, but when it came to the legal process, what did she know?

She prayed for the prosecuting attorney as well.

"Mom." Someone—Jason—shook her. "Dad's talking."

What?

She opened her eyes and looked forward. Listened to her husband make his plea.

"I know everyone says they're not guilty, but I believe this evidence proves my innocence. Garrett Wright was my mentor, a friend, a father figure even, though he was only twelve years older than me. Yes, I had a tough childhood, but Garrett saw something in me and rescued me from what could have been. He allowed me to dream. If I'm guilty of anything, it's of dreaming too much. Of wanting to be too much like Garrett and not enough of who God made me to be."

Jenn closed her eyes and nodded. They were both guilty of that.

"Your Honor, my only dream now is to be reunited with my wife, Jenn, who's stood by my side during this entire ordeal. And my kids, who were only ten when I was arrested. I've missed almost their entire teen years. I missed teaching them to drive, their first dates, their high school graduations. They just turned nineteen but still need a dad. And I need them."

Jenn glanced at the judge to see if she could read her expression, but she had a poker face. Was anything Chad said sinking in?

"I know that before Christmas I got into some trouble. I have a ton of excuses, but none that matter. What matters is that I'm now taking steps to insure that will never happen again. I see a counselor weekly and I'm attending AA meetings. I plan to continue with both when I'm released."

Jenn steepled her hands and whispered, "Thank You, Jesus."

"Your Honor, I ask that when you make a ruling, you'll take not only the evidence into consideration, but that you'll also consider my family." He turned and gestured toward Jenn and the kids. "They deserve to be free, too."

Both attorneys spouted a lot more of the legal mumbo jumbo, then the judge banged her gavel. "You'll have my decision within ninety days."

Ninety days . . .

Chad stood and was handcuffed. He mouthed the words, "I love you," but she couldn't hear them above the din in the courtroom, as Chad was led away once again. All she made out were complaints from the gallery that he better not get off. What she'd give to go over to those people she used to call friends and serve them a not-so-nice piece of her mind.

For half a second, she connected gazes with Dajon, but he looked away too quickly, as if he was guilty. Maybe not of killing Garrett, but of attempted murder for breaking up her family. She'd show him. Chad would be released, and their family would be stronger than ever.

"Come on, kids." She put on her coat and gloves and snatched up her purse. "The air is stuffy in here." She steered them out of their row.

"Jenn, wait."

She turned to see Thomas hurrying toward them while putting on his jacket. "Can I treat you all to dessert?" His eyes searched hers, meaning *dessert* was code for, "We need to talk."

The kids and Hal missed the hidden message and accepted before she agreed to the talk.

"I guess you have the answer, counselor. But not in this town. I'd prefer not to have a pie shoved in my face."

"Understood." Thomas held her arm lightly, escorting her out of the courtroom then out of the county courthouse into air colder than a freezer. The entire family did a masterful job of ignoring the jeers from the townsfolk. Yes, they'd all loved Garrett, but they'd loved Chad and her, too.

Guess she needed to add them to her burgeoning prayer list. Good thing their little house church was meeting this Sunday night at Chad's. She needed to share some of this burden. They'd all been far more supportive than she'd believed people could be. Her church was reminding her what being a Christian was all about.

Once in the parking lot, the group decided on an eatery in another county, a little mom-and-pop café she and Chad used to frequent on trips to the cities.

"Jason, Chloe, ride with me." Apparently, Hal had deciphered Thomas's *dessert* code. "I need some grandpa time with my kids."

"That helps." Thomas whispered to Jenn and gestured across the lot. She followed him, keeping her head down to block the wind and to avoid eye contact with townsfolk. She was a pariah-by-association in this area she'd loved, where she and Chad had talked about raising their kids. Retiring. Now, if she never set foot in this county again, it would be too soon.

Guess that meant she was rooting against another trial for Chad, though that would likely be the only way he'd avoid the "ex-con" label. Was it worth the years and the heartache if there was no promise of winning?

There was no good answer.

Thomas's Infiniti SUV was already running, already heated, when he opened the door for her, but she still shivered when thinking of this mess her life had become. How different things would have been if she'd ignored her heart and gotten married to Thomas. He was a good man, and she would have been happy. Wouldn't have had to worry about people shunning her—especially her own mother. She wouldn't have to worry about the kids' college, about medical expenses, finances in general.

Thomas said nothing as he drove from the parking lot, and she relished the silence for several more minutes, but knew they'd have to discuss what had transpired. She should have been paying attention, but prayer seemed more important. Besides, would she have understood what was happening? Not that she was a dummy, but legal-speak always made her brain swim.

Although Thomas was good at turning that jargon into ordinary speech.

She was getting warm, so she removed her gloves and watched miles of snow-covered ditches fly past. Going straight home would take about three and a half hours. The detour and stop would add another couple hours, so the shop would be closed long before she arrived. Which was fine. All she wanted to do once they got there was sleep until morning woke her.

But the shop needed her.

She loved the place, but sometimes it seemed as if she'd traded one prison for another. Taking days off meant that she'd be paying someone else for those hours worked, and that ate into the profits, which determined what type of groceries she'd be shopping for the next week. Times like this, she really missed teaching.

A life with Thomas, even a life without romantic love, would have been much easier.

"What are you thinking about?" His question, which she would not answer, cut through the silence.

"Life." Which was true.

"I'm sorry it's been so difficult for you."

Translation: if you'd chosen me, it would have been easier.

"Guess God wants to build up my faith muscles." They should be super strong, considering how hard she had to work at her faith.

"I object."

"Object? What's the lawyer-speak for?"

"You have faith, Jennifer." He quickly glanced her way then at the road. "I'd say trust is the word you're looking for."

"Aren't they the same thing?"

"Are they?"

Oh, she hated it when Thomas went therapist on her. Still, she mulled over his question. She believed in God, believed Jesus received the death sentence all people deserved. That was faith. But did she really trust that God would spend time concerned with their little lives, though the Bible said He did?

"Hmmm," was all she could say.

"What's that Jennifer-speak for?"

She laughed at that. "I guess it's an admission that you're probably right, that I've developed major trust issues. I pray, but do I expect God to answer with a 'Yes'?" She grunted. "I used to." She stared out the window at pines God had taken special care to flock with snow. She believed that, so why was it so difficult to believe He'd want her to have good in her life?

Dang, Thomas could be a therapist with what he'd gotten her to admit to herself. "I'm assuming this counseling session isn't what you wanted to talk about."

He grinned, which was nice to see, but then his lips immediately flattened. "What's your perception of how the hearing went?"

She looked at her fingernails, which Chloe had polished just for today, so she'd look her best for Chad, even though he never got close enough to see her hands. "Can I plead the fifth?"

"Interesting."

"What?" She sat up straight. "Why is that interesting?"

"I thought it went well. Judge Bonner is fair. I felt the prosecution tried too hard to convince the judge not to retry. In my opinion, their case wasn't compelling. And Chad's talk was exactly the type of speech that might sway Judge Bonner."

"You really think so?" Was that hope seeping in? Maybe some joy again?

"That was my impression. I'm rarely wrong, but not never."

"So it's okay to hope."

"It's always okay to hope, Jenn. But place that hope in God doing what's best for you, for Chad, the kids. Trust Him."

She sat back again. Quiet. Processing. "I didn't hear what was going on because I was praying. For CO Bulldog—"

"Bulldog?"

She rolled her head from shoulder to shoulder. "Technically it's Bullock, but according to Chad, Bulldog fits."

"Don't let him hear you say that." He grinned again. "But you are not the first to label him with that . . ." He cleared his throat. "Endearment."

"And I won't be the last." She folded her hands as if in prayer again. "I also prayed for the other attorney and Dajon, the people in the county, the judge. Chad . . . You."

His eyes crinkled with that. "I felt it."

"But now we wait again."

He drummed his fingers on his steering wheel, a frown taking over his smile. "I wish I could tell you something different."

"It is what it is. Doesn't the Bible tell us to rejoice in today?"

"It does."

"Good." She reclined her seat, closed her eyes, and felt the muscles in her shoulders relax. Thomas had a way of calming her. "Then that's what I plan to do. We did everything we could do, and now it's in His hands. Pray that I leave it there."

"I always do."

She peeked at him through barely raised eyelids. Yeah, she had no doubt those were his prayers. Thomas was a good man.

Chapter Fifteen

"I'm so glad you joined us tonight." Jenn opened the coffee shop door, letting in fresh April air. Those two home church newcomers were the last of a full house to leave tonight. "You're welcome back any time."

The twenty-something couple smiled at her, and the husband said, "Thanks. We were nervous. I mean, it's a different type of church model than we're used to, but it felt good to be seen and heard."

"I understand." More than he knew. "We're grateful that was your experience."

They walked out and she locked the door behind them, leaving her and Barbara, who always stayed to help straighten things for the morning.

After cleaning up, Jenn poured two cups of hot cocoa, and she added a dollop of whipped cream to each, plus candy canes to stir the drinks. That always upped the hot cocoa a notch. Her personal favorite was adding a scoop of mint chocolate chip ice cream. Simple but delectable.

"Yum." Barbara sipped at her drink as she sat in one of the two padded chairs by the window, a new addition to the shop. Customers found they liked them for reading. They'd choose a book from the little library, read, and sip away their afternoon. Others, like her and Barbara, found it to be a cozy conversation nook.

Jenn sat opposite Barbara and put her feet up on another chair. Sundays always seemed long. Often, she was here by herself since the shop closed at two in the afternoon. The intent was to give herself a break, but she found that she used that time to spiffy up the shop. Put up new artwork to replace the pieces that had sold. Try a different seating arrangement.

Recently, she'd been working on the attic. Under the tutelage of Caleb—the carpenter who'd worked on the shop—she was learning some useful and money-saving skills. Besides, if—when—Chad came home, he'd need a place of his own to unwind. Something she'd read in a lot of different husband-getting-out-of-prison groups and blogs.

She'd read far too many. The latest thread on an online board had her nerves zinging.

"What's on your mind?" As usual, Barbara initiated the conversation. The talk wasn't always about Jenn. Barbara's first husband—a control freak—was also a frequent topic of conversation. But tonight, Jenn didn't mind leading off.

"Ninety days of waiting is almost up."

"Does your attorney"—Barbara had stopped saying Thomas's name long before Christmas—"have any idea what the judge is going to rule?"

"No clue." Jenn shook her head. "But I'm preparing for Chad's homecoming in a week or two, even though there's a good chance he won't be home for four-and-a-half years."

"That's very wise."

"I've been doing some reading . . ." She sipped her cocoa.

Barbara smirked. "Why do I get the impression that's not a good thing?"

Jenn put down her drink and narrowed the gap between her and her friend. No one else was around, but the topic was so delicate, she felt the need to whisper, or at least speak in hushed tones.

"I've been reading boards run by prison wives and about what their husbands expect when they come home and . . ." She shivered.

"That bad?"

Jenn puffed out a breath, hating to talk about this, but she needed another perspective. One from an adult. It definitely wasn't something she'd share with Chloe. "It was all about sex."

Barbara's brows shot up, but she remained silent.

Here goes nothing. "All these boards I looked at, that's what the women talked about. When their husbands came home, that's the first thing they wanted to do."

"Not a surprise."

"No, but . . ." Jenn rubbed her goose-bumped arms. "Is it getting chilly in here?"

"Jenn." Barbara set down her mug. "If you don't want to talk about it, that's okay."

She didn't want to, but she needed to. She wrapped both hands around her mug and stared into the cocoa. "These women say it's not about love, it's just a release, and that scares me to death. Chad was always . . ." She felt her cheeks blush. "Gentle. Loving. But this . . . ?"

Barbara leaned forward, enough so Jenn couldn't ignore her.

"You are his wife, not a slave," she said with a forcefulness Jenn hadn't heard before.

"But it's almost been eight years."

"Which means he can wait a bit longer. Sex should be a loving, mutual act, especially between a husband and wife."

"But—"

"Period."

"I do love him."

"Good."

"And he loves me."

"Also good, but that doesn't mean he'll be ready."

"Oh, he'll be ready." If the boards she'd read were any indication.

"I mean, ready to *love* you, not use you." Barbara reclined in her chair. "I speak from experience, remember?"

"Oh." Jenn took a long sip of her cocoa, then locked eyes with her friend. "It feels like one more thing to feel guilty about. *Hi, Chad. Glad you're home. Your bed's in the attic.* After all he's gone through, it doesn't seem fair."

"After all you've both been through. Whenever he gets home, life won't be easy. But you know that already."

Jenn sighed. "I do. And it all scares me."

"Don't forget, he's going to be frightened too. He'll be coming home to a brand-new world. Really, brand-new kids. A different wife. Be kind.

Understanding. But don't give in. That only hurts both of you."

"I know," she whispered. And she did know all that, but it still felt unfair.

"Yes, you do." Barbara got up and carried her mug to the sink. "Sometimes the truth needs to be repeated or stated aloud. I don't know how many times I had to hear that the only control my ex had over me was the control I gave him. Eventually, it sank in."

Jenn got up and met Barbara at the door. "I appreciate the counseling session."

"I'm always here for you."

"Same here." The friends hugged and Barbara left.

Her friend was right. Jenn was borrowing trouble again, worrying about something that hadn't happened, or may not happen. Chances were, Chad was going to serve out the remainder of his term, even if he got a new trial. Then all this worrying would be for naught.

Thomas would remind her to trust God, which meant tonight, before she got in bed, she'd kneel and, once again, give her husband and the judge and the attorneys and all the problems that came with them, over to God and pray that tomorrow she wouldn't pick those problems off the ground.

Chad made another hashmark in his notebook as daylight dawned outside his slit of a window. Good Friday. He'd never understood what was good about it. One of Jesus' best friends had turned him over to the Sanhedrin, a council of elder rabbis, which led to Jesus' crucifixion.

Yes, but it also led to Jesus' resurrection, Chad reminded himself. Did that mean that Dajon was the equivalent of Judas? Nah, not really. Dajon saw what he saw, and Chad couldn't blame him for his testimony. Still, it felt like a betrayal.

But with Judas, Jesus knew that betrayal was coming, and yet He washed His friend's feet, served him communion.

Hmm.

Chad clutched his pen.

Was that what God required of him? Forgive his friends by washing their feet? He laughed at that image. Dajon wouldn't let him be in the same city, much less wash his feet.

Still, the image remained.

He'd read about the Last Supper the previous night. Maundy Thursday was what they called it at his home church. He sighed. Looked out the window, imagining a steeple reaching up beyond the walls of this prison. Someday he'd get to go to a real service again. Worship alongside others as a free man. Being able to spend holidays together with family would be a blessing.

In here, he hated holidays. Easter and Christmas were the worst, because those were the most fun on the outside.

"What are you up to?"

Chad froze at that voice. Warned himself to not respond in any way other than neutral. Not to make eye contact. No way was he going to blow his chance of getting out of here early.

"Angel, I asked what are you up to."

Chad set his Bible on the bed and responded as monotone as he could. "Reading."

Iron laughed. "Sissy's gotta read his Bible."

Well, maybe you should read it sometime, then you wouldn't be such a jerk, Chad responded in his head to keep from blowing up.

"Guess I should give it a try." Iron picked up the Bible and paged through it. "Nothing in here but words. No pictures or nothing." Iron ripped out a page. "That's what I think of your Bible."

Chad clenched his fists but sat silently.

More pages tore, followed by one slow, agonizing rip. *Don't show your vulnerability. Don't show he's getting to you.* But those tears certainly wanted to fall. That Bible was his first, the one Garrett gave him years ago.

"Gonna cry over a broken book?" Iron threw the remains of the Bible at Chad, who closed his tear-filled eyes and counted down from ten.

"Waaaa."

Lord, please, stay my hands and voice.

"What do you have here?" Iron moved to the spot on the wall where Chad kept pictures of Jenn and the kids. "Oooh, you got this waiting for you back home?"

Chad deepened his prayer, begging for restraint.

"I only got three more years. How about I make a visit to your lady? She needs a real man to keep her warm at night."

Chad jumped up from the bed, his fists clenched, and his heart palpitating hard enough to break down Jericho's walls. "If you so much as—"

"Problem here?"

Chad spun toward CO Wilson. Looked at Iron, then at Wilson. Snitching was about the worst thing one inmate could do to another, so he lied.

"No problem but my hand." Chad showed his fist, thinking of some way to remove himself from this situation. "It hurts. Iron here said maybe I have arthritis. Could I have it checked out?"

The CO grinned. "You might want to wait until you get home for that."

"But it . . ." Chad unfurled his fist. "Say what?"

"Iron." Another CO appeared behind Wilson. "Go to your playpen before I write you up."

"We ain't done." Iron picked up what remained of Chad's Bible and sauntered out of his cell.

Wilson eyed Iron and nodded toward Chad. "You don't want your Bible?"

"If anyone could use it, that would be Iron." Though Chad still wanted to pummel the guy for ruining it, and even more for what he'd said about Jenn.

"Are you ready to go home?" CO Wilson remained in the doorway.

Chad blinked. "Now?"

"You're welcome to stay another night, but there's no promise Iron won't come visiting again."

"You mean, I'm free?" Chad looked beyond the door, then at the CO. "You're not—" He stopped himself from using a curse word, something he'd have to be even more careful of on the outside. "You're not kidding me?"

"I don't kid about something like that. Grab your things, and let's go."

Chad fell to his knees and covered his eyes with the palms of his hands and thanked God.

He was finally going to be a free man!

FREEDOM!

"So they are no longer two but one flesh. What therefore God has joined together, let not man separate."

Matthew 19:6

Chapter Sixteen

Freedom began on Good Friday.

That had never occurred to Chad before, but it was right. Without Jesus' sacrifice on Good Friday, His resurrection wouldn't have happened two days later. Redemption wouldn't exist.

"Thank You, Jesus," Chad said as he walked toward the door leading outside. Not to the prison yard, but to freedom. He was still trying to wrap his mind around that. Nearly eight years to the day he was arrested, he was a free man!

Plastic bag in hand, filled with all his possessions from the last eight years, he turned the knob on the solid door and pushed it open. Sunlight poured through the opening and cool air rushed in. Fresh air. He breathed in, letting it fill his lungs. Somehow, the air seemed cleaner out here than on the inside.

Then he looked ahead.

People crowded on both sides of the sidewalk. To the right, they were cheering, but those on the left were jeering while holding signs protesting his release, not unlike those calling for Barabbas to be released instead of Jesus. Dajon, his former best friend, led those jeers. Any other day, that might have bothered him, but nothing was going to mar his freedom day.

But where was . . . ?

Jenn!

She walked toward him, flanked by Jason and Chloe.

His brain said to run to her, but his legs turned to jelly, and he fell to his knees. Tears he'd held in for years flooded from his eyes.

Jenn knelt in front of him and embraced his cheeks. He startled and gasped at the touch—it had been so long since he'd experienced human touch—then he leaned into it as more tears fell. They might never stop.

He lifted his gaze to hers. How was it that her cocoa-colored eyes seemed richer? Brighter than they had in the visiting room? He brought a hand to her cheek, caressed a corner of her lips. He wanted to kiss her so badly, he could taste it. His voice hoarse, he managed to squeak out, "Can I kiss you?"

She nodded and sniffled.

That was all the encouragement he needed.

He feathered his lips over hers, afraid to take the kiss deeper, afraid he wouldn't be able to stop. That, he'd save for tonight. Who needed sleep, anyway?

For now, he curved a hand around the back of her neck and gazed into her cocoa eyes again. She was the most beautiful sight he'd seen in years, and he never wanted to stop looking at her, studying her every feature. Touching her. He'd never take her for granted, ever again.

He felt a hand on his shoulder and looked up. Jason. Wow, it was as if he were gazing in a mirror that subtracted twenty years. Beside him, Chloe looked like an angel. She'd accented her blonde hair with green streaks that fit her creative personality. Standing, he took Jenn's hand, gripping it as if this was all a dream. If he let go, she'd be gone, and he'd be on the inside again.

He risked releasing her hand to hug the kids. He wrapped his arms around Chloe, tucking her head beneath his chin. When he'd gone to prison, her head barely reached his chest. "I love you, Chloe," he whispered into her strawberry-scented hair.

"Love you, too, Daddy." The dampness he felt on his neck told him he and Jenn weren't the only ones crying.

Then he looked Jason in the eye. Actually, looked up to him a little bit. Jason offered his hand, but Chad fully embraced his son. At first, Jason stiffened, but then he relaxed into the hug.

"I've missed you," Jason whispered so softly Jenn and Chloe probably hadn't heard. All that mattered was that Chad heard the heartfelt words. His kids had missed him. Man, he was blessed.

He looked upward and shouted, "Thank You, Jesus!" He didn't care what others thought. He needed to properly thank the One who saved him, who freed him, and he wanted everyone to know the Truth. Especially on this Good Friday.

"We brought you something, Daddy." Chloe held out a covered mug that had the words World's Best Daddy printed on the side. "Freshly poured from a Thermos, so it's hot. It's a new drink we made up special for the store, to honor you. And it's been a favorite. We call it Chad's Choco-Latte."

He accepted the mug and wanted to cry over the words imprinted on it, but he held them in as he sipped. Heaven on earth. He felt his eyes roll back with the deliciousness. So, this was what real coffee tasted like.

"You like it?" Chloe had her hands folded in front of her chest.

"Baby girl." He kissed her forehead. "It's the best thing I've tasted in eight years."

She beamed at the praise.

"I'd like to introduce you to the team."

Who said that?

Chad looked around, then up at Thomas. Where had he come from? Chad's gaze traveled from Thomas to the crowds on both sides of the sidewalk. He'd been so focused on his family, he'd forgotten about all the others. Yes, they were making noise, but prison was never quiet. Prisoners learned to ignore all but what they were focused on, or they'd go crazy.

"Uh, sure," Chad finally responded. He handed the mug to Jason, then gripped Jenn's and Chloe's hands and followed Thomas to those cheering for him. Strangers at that. The only one he knew was Thomas. Ironically, on the jeering side, he recognized almost everyone. He'd thought life inside was lonely, it hadn't occurred to him before how alone Jenn must have felt, being rejected by everyone she'd known.

Thomas introduced them to the head of Minnesota's Guilt-Free Project, then to the attorney he'd been working under on this case. And finally, to the rest of the team. Jenn introduced him to her new friend, Barbara, Donaldson's mayor. Good for Jenn to be making new, better friends. Then to Caleb and Lissa Johnson. Apparently, Caleb had done a lot of work on the coffee shop, and Jenn had become friends with the couple.

Those he didn't previously know had driven across the metro to celebrate his release, while his former friends had driven three-and-a-half hours to accuse him. He claimed the cheering section as his new best friends. He should want to chat with them all, get to know them, but a queasiness in his stomach told him it was time to leave. Could it be those few sips of coffee he'd had?

Regardless, he had a strong desire to get away from the crowd, almost a panicky feeling. Made no sense, because he'd always loved being around people, loved being the center of attention.

Had prison changed that about him too?

Make a short speech, then get out of here. His mouth suddenly dry, he clung tighter to Jenn's hand. Feeling his heartbeat ramp up, he wiped a trembling hand across his lips.

"Thank you," came out hoarse, so he cleared his throat. Someone, a news station reporter, it looked like, stuck a microphone in his face. Took all the strength he could muster not to swat it away. That would look amazing on TV.

"You're doing fine, hon." Jenn whispered in his ear. "Say 'thank you,' and we'll get you home."

Home. What a beautiful word. He cleared his throat again, and tried to ignore the microphone. "Thank you all for coming today, for supporting Jenn and Jason and Chloe. I can't begin to tell you what that means to me. A huge thanks to Thomas and the team at Guilt-Free Project. You believed in me when others didn't." Namely those making noise behind him. "I'm indebted to you all, but right now, I admit, all I want to do is go home."

Home . . .

He was going home!

His new friends cheered as Jenn led him away and into the parking lot to a shiny, expensive-looking SUV. The store had been doing that well?

"Jase, can you sit up front with Thomas?" Jenn tugged open the back door while Thomas opened the driver's door. Duh. Thomas's car, not Jenn's. "I need to sit with your father."

"Can I drive?" Jason looked over the top of the car at Thomas, who laughed.

His kids drove . . .

Yes, he knew that, but still, the last time he'd seen them, spent time with them, they were speeding radio-controlled cars up and down the driveway. He used to look forward to the day he'd get to take them out driving for the first time, but he hadn't been around.

He'd missed nearly half their lifetime. What else was going to take him by surprise?

Chloe climbed into the third-row seat, leaving him and Jenn in the middle. He sat near her, his left hand forever melded with hers, his right hand holding his new favorite mug filled with his new favorite beverage.

He sipped again and sighed as Thomas parted the picketers with his car and drove from the parking lot.

Like Lot's wife, Chad was tempted to glance back, but he overcame it and looked straight ahead. No more reminiscing about what he'd missed. From now on, he was only looking forward.

After he had some answers. "Thomas?"

The attorney gazed in the rearview mirror. Nodded.

"Was I acquitted, or am I considered an ex-con?"

Beside him, Jenn sighed. That was all he needed to know as he blocked out Thomas's explanation of his release. Released for time served. Blah, blah, blah. It was what he'd expected, but he'd be lying to himself if he said it didn't hurt.

For the rest of his life, the world around him would see a lie. They would see him as a murderer. The chaplain had encouraged him to see himself through God's eyes. He was still working on that.

Instead, he clung to Jenn's hand as quiet overtook the vehicle. She believed in him. The kids did too. That was what mattered.

An hour later, the car slowed to enter a sleepy town bordering the Mississippi. He'd caught glimpses of his favorite river through the trees that were just beginning to bud again.

For him, life began today. Ironically, on the day they commemorated Jesus losing his life.

The road made a big S-curve through a residential area, and then he saw it. There was no mistaking the azure door on the brick building and the Chad's Choco-Latte Corner sign out front. The building was exactly how he'd pictured it. Hadn't Jenn told him it was the only business on the block, besides the bar across the street? But there was a pizza pub two doors down and a flower shop a couple next to that.

"There are more businesses," he said as Thomas pulled curbside.

"Brand-new businesses." Jenn pointed to the flower shop. "That opened in time for the Valentine rush, and the pizza place opened last week."

"I haven't had good pizza in years," he said, not to complain or gain pity, but more as a statement of fact as he got out of the car, momentarily releasing Jenn's hand.

"We can have pizza tonight." Jenn accepted his extended hand. "I guess that's a yes."

"What?" He looked down at her pretty face. "I didn't say anything."

"You didn't have to." Jason laughed. "The drool on the side of your mouth said it for you."

Chad raised a hand to his lips. He wasn't drooling.

"It's a joke, Dad."

"Oh, yeah, of course. Funny. Ha ha." Why hadn't he caught the obvious humor? What was wrong with him?

He shook that off. *Stop doubting, Chad.*

"Hey, I'm taking off."

Chad looked at the SUV. Thomas stood on the other side of the vehicle, the door open. Should he go thank him with a handshake, or say *thanks* here?

Jenn hurried to Thomas and gave him a hug, prompting a visit from that green-eyed monster known as jealousy. Chad banished the monster but chose to wave from the opposite side of the car as Jenn returned to his side. Once again, he took her hand and didn't look back as Thomas sped off.

"Come on." She nodded and led him to the front door of Chad's Choco-Latte Corner. Oh, he loved that name.

"Normally we go in the back door." Jenn handed him a key. "But we figured you'd like to enter through the café side."

He stared at the key. The key to *his* coffee shop. It still felt like a dream. He released Jenn's hand again to jimmy the key into the lock. Turned it. Then opened the door. The scent of coffee rushed toward him, and he breathed it in as if it were fresh air. Perhaps to him, it was equally as good.

Jenn reached around him and flipped on a switch.

He gasped. Stood frozen in the doorway. This had to be a dream. He floated to the bar, lacquered to a brilliant shine, and ran his hand over the top. Water rings and other dings beneath the lacquer made it more beautiful. He closed his eyes, envisioning himself on the other side, hamming it up with customers, listening to their problems, sending them home with a better attitude than the one they'd had when they arrived. Jenn would be working the register, and he'd be drinking in her every move.

"Like it?" Jenn's hand covered his.

A nod was the only answer he could give without breaking out in tears again.

"We knew you would." She touched his arm and pointed upward. "Tin ceilings." She gestured downward. "Hardwood floors."

It was like someone had reached into his daydream and recreated it. "I have no words."

Jenn's face beamed right before she kissed him on the cheek.

He returned her kiss and whispered so the kids wouldn't hear, "Just wait until tonight . . ."

Was he mistaken, or did she stiffen at that? Nah. He'd probably forgotten how to read body language by now, too.

But something else was off. He glanced around the room. Tables, chairs, barstools. A nook with books. A little food pantry? Huh. What a great idea. Artwork hung on the walls with prices attached.

"You're selling artwork?"

Jenn gestured to their daughter. "Chloe's idea. We make a small commission off of it—Jason's idea—but the main goal is to provide a venue for local artists to display their works."

"Brilliant idea, Chlo." He ruffled her hair like he used to do eight years ago, then froze. "I'm sorry. You're probably too grown up for that."

"It's okay, Daddy." She leaned into him. "I've missed it."

He kissed the top of her head and curved an arm around her shoulders. "And I've missed this."

The lack of loving human touch had to be one of the cruelest realities of prison.

Aside from that, something niggled at him. He studied the room once again, and then it hit him.

"Where are the customers? Aren't we open in the afternoon? Or did you close for Good Friday?"

"We closed for you." Jenn squeezed his hand. "We figured coming home to a crowd would be a bit much. Besides, then we wouldn't be able to spend today with you. We'd be working."

They'd taken the day off for him. Not that it should surprise him, but it had been eight years since he'd been treated special. Right now, that was difficult to wrap his heart around.

"You're open tomorrow, right?" The mere thought of making drinks and shooting the breeze with customers energized him. Once again, his life would have purpose.

"Only if you're okay with it." Jenn climbed onto a barstool. "Sorry, I stand all day, so my feet need a break."

"Of course. To both. You should definitely open tomorrow. I can't wait." He rubbed his hands together and sat beside her. Took her hand again. Was he imagining things, or was she holding his hand looser now? Nope. No doubting or questioning. That insecurity was the prison talking. Take everything in without seeing ulterior motives in every action and word.

"Can't we show Dad the rest?" Jason shifted from resting on his right foot to his left.

"Patience, dear."

Ah, there was a familiar phrase. So, Jason was still impatient, needing things to be done now. Like his mother. Where Chloe took after her father, tending to be more laid-back. It was good to see that not all things had changed.

But this time, Jason was right. Chad was more than eager to see the rest of the home. He leaped from his stool and helped Jenn off hers.

"Go ahead, Jason, lead the way. Dad and I'll follow."

The twins aimed toward a hallway. Jason flung open a door to the right. "Bathroom."

A stool and a sink. Both were throne-like compared to what he'd had for the last eight years.

To their left in the hallway was the employee breakroom and storage room. Straight ahead was another door. Outside perhaps?

Jenn pointed to a door on the right. "Our office."

Then Jason used a key to open a door perpendicular to the outside door. "This is your home." He held the door, and Chloe remained beside him.

"Go on up." Jenn prodded him in his back. "It hasn't been fully renovated, but that'll come someday."

He walked upstairs into an apartment that was clearly Jenn's. Light purple walls. Orderly with few items cluttering the small space. But still, it looked cozy, even with the green appliances.

"This is my bed when I visit." Chloe bounced on a couch.

Jason pointed to the floor space between the sofa and accent chairs and smirked. "That's my bed."

"Not anymore." Chloe socked Jason in the arm. "What're you complaining about?"

Chad grinned and then laughed. Oh, how he'd missed the twins' banter. To think, he used to get so upset with them. Never again.

"And Dad, check this out." Chloe jumped up, grabbed his hand, and dragged him toward the window in the living room.

He gasped at the view of the river. Tears again? Man, he was lame. In prison, all these tears would have been a death sentence, or at least an invite to a beating. His. Inmates didn't like sissies, and only sissies cried.

"It's okay." Jenn leaned into him as he stared at trees budding. At a river flowing freely. A lonely swing set overlooked the river. It needed company. "What do you think?"

A sad memory thrust forward, so he kissed her temple. "I need to make a confession."

"Nope." She touched his lips. "This is enjoy-the-family night."

"But I need to say this." He pointed at the window, the living area, toward the steps. "I've been jealous and scared that you were moving on without me, but now, now I see why you started the shop. You didn't open it to move on without me. You bought it for me. I see that in everything. I'm so sorry I doubted."

"And I'm sorry it took so long to tell you." Her hand caressed his back.

And he shivered. Why did every touch unnerve him when his body was begging for human contact?

"Let me show you the rest." She pointed out a bathroom he couldn't wait to use.

Literally.

"Uh, I gotta go." He started unzipping his jeans, the ones he'd worn to jail that now were a size or two too large.

"Wait a second." Jenn grabbed the doorknob and closed the door.

Oh. He shook his head. Stupid idiot. Made him want to bonk his head on the wall. In prison, there was no privacy, so you just went. Guess he'd gotten used to that. How many other things had he become used to and wouldn't think twice about, that would embarrass his family?

He finished and washed his hands, with fruity-smelling soap that softened his skin. Now to face his family and apologize again. He inhaled deeply then stepped out of the bathroom. Jenn was in the kitchen, pouring water into glasses, and the kids were on the couch looking at . . . what were they so focused on?

"What is that?" He stood over them as they tapped the screen. "A game?"

"It's a photo app." Jason took the item and pocketed it.

"Huh?" He tossed the somewhat familiar phrase around in his head. "Oh, your mom mentioned Chloe uses a photo app for marketing."

"Yep." Jason shrugged. "I've got like a zillion apps on my phone."

"Your phone? Apps?" Chad rubbed his temples. The last phone he remembered having was an old *Star Trek*-like version that flipped open like a communicator and made phone calls. The computer phones were popular at that time, but they'd also been out of his family's budget. "All I need is a regular phone." He looked around the room. "Where is it, by the way?"

"A phone?" Jenn came around a rolling island and handed him a glass of iced water. "I don't have a landline anymore."

"You don't?"

"Didn't make sense." She shrugged. "Not when my cell phone does so much more."

"You have one of those, too?" He pointed at Jason. "Aren't they expensive? They used to be."

"They're still pricy, but when it functions as a computer, it's worth the expense."

He shook his head. "Nope. Give me a regular *Star Trek* phone."

Jason laughed. "You mean a flip phone? That's so uncool."

Uncool. Once upon a time, that phrase would have stung. Okay, guess it stung a little bit now, too. Truthfully, he didn't need a phone. Who would he call?

"I'll show you cool." He hiked up his pants like that nerdy kid on *Family Matters*, a show his dad used to love. It had been popular at the same time Chad's favorite show, *Friends*, was on. He pushed up pretend glasses. "Show me the rest of the place."

"You are so dorky, Daddy." Chloe laughed and led him to the back of the apartment. The bedroom. It also looked very much like Jenn with deep purple walls and simple décor. It wasn't girly, but it sure wasn't manly either. The king bed seemed massive, but it didn't take up the entire room. He caught Jenn's eye and waggled his brows. She blushed and glanced away. Exactly the reaction he was shooting for.

But they did have one problem. The kids. How could he have privacy with Jenn while the kids were only feet away. No doubt, these walls weren't thick. He'd have to think on that.

"That's it?" He walked from the bedroom because his mind was going places it wasn't time for yet, and he needed to distance himself.

"Not quite." Jenn opened another door he'd assumed was for a closet, but it led to more steps.

He'd forgotten about the attic she was finishing.

"Be my guest." She gestured upwards. "It's far from done, but it's insulated now, and the drywall's up. With the window AC, it's not too bad."

He climbed the steps and looked around a wide-open space. At one end, there was a bed, and on the other side, an old couch faced a really skinny TV.

"What do you think?" Jenn whirled around, with her arms out. "Caleb showed me how to put up drywall, and the kids and I did it together. Jason sleeps here when he visits, and it's been the kids' space, but now it's your man cave. For those times when you need to get away. Destress."

No surprise, she'd thought of his unique needs. She'd always put others before herself.

He studied his wife, beaming at her accomplishment. "You're amazing, Jenn."

She shrugged and headed down the stairway with him close behind.

"Just resourceful. When you're a single mom, you learn to take care of things by—" She slapped a hand over her mouth. "I'm sorry."

"Hey, it's okay." That was not something that bothered him. Yeah, she'd basically been a single mom, but it wasn't his fault. About that he had no guilt.

His stomach rumbled loudly as he entered the living room.

Jason and Chloe snickered. Jenn laughed.

He did too. "Uh, did someone say something about pizza?"

"We did." Chloe grabbed her brother's arm. "We'll go order. You still like meat-lovers?"

Did he? How would he know? It was food. Any food on the outside would be better than what was served in prison. "Yeah, sure. Whatever you guys get is good."

"Gotcha." Chloe hustled toward the steps. "See you in half an hour or so."

The kids pounded down the steps. That hadn't changed either.

Like his feelings for Jenn hadn't changed. He glanced at her, then at the bedroom. Half an hour? No problem. He approached her. Kissed her forehead. Her nose. Her lips. "How about you and I—"

She pushed away as if in a panic. "I have one more space to show you."

Okay . . . What was that about? Or had he misread her?

He stuffed his frustration as she aimed for the stairs. He followed her down, then out the back door. They crossed a gravel parking lot with a pickup and a small sedan. Jenn's and the kids' vehicles? She took his hand again—okay, now he felt better—and led him toward the river, stopping at the swing.

"Remember when you used to push me on the park swing?"

He grinned at the fond memory of their early years together. He'd push her for a bit, then they'd switch places and she'd push him until it was high enough for him to make a grand leap from the swing. She'd laugh. They'd kiss . . . Ah, he liked where she was going with this.

She sat and he grabbed the chains to pull her back.

"Not yet." She gestured to the other swing. "Let's just sit and be together."

Okay. He could do that too.

He sat and reached across to her, and she held on. They both rocked while watching the Mississippi roar past not too far from them. With the spring waters, the river was full, beautiful, and dangerous.

"I would come here when I really missed you, which was often." Her thumb played across the back of his hand. "I can't tell you how many nights I cried, but out here, only God and I knew."

"I'm sorry."

"No." She shook her head. "I'm not trying to make you feel bad. What I'm trying to say is that I'm overwhelmed knowing that you're finally home. That I don't have to come here alone anymore. That I don't have to parent alone anymore."

She sniffled and turned to him, waited until he looked her way. "I was wrong when I told you I didn't want you home early. You here, now, is the best day of my life. Period."

"You really mean that?" He blinked and wiped a hand across his nose.

"More than anything. I've been so lonely and now, now you're here, and I'm pinching myself, thinking that maybe you're going to disappear, that you getting out is only a dream."

"I've been doing the same thing." He toed the ground and made his swing go higher, then remained silent until it slowed to a near stop. "When I woke up this morning, I was in prison, and now?" He watched the river that wouldn't let anything stop its flow. "Now I'm free. And I'm with you. And the kids. And you have this amazing shop. And I can't believe it's real. I keep seeing boogeymen out of the corners of my eyes, thinking they're going to snatch me up and take me back."

"Nope. You're home for good. I won't let the boogeymen take you."

"I can't think of a better guard than you."

She smiled that cute, shy smile he used to see years ago before familiarity had worn off the shyness. But it slipped away too quickly.

"It's not going to be easy, you know."

He knew that, too. He'd heard that from Thomas and his counselor and from all the books he'd checked out. Too many ex-con marriages ended up in divorce. So, he was fortunate that Jenn hadn't divorced him already.

"But we have something that others don't." Also affirmed by his counselor. "We have that third strand of the cord bonding us."

"As long as we keep God involved in our marriage."

"He's the only way I survived prison."

"He's the only way I survived without you."

They continued to swing, letting nature do the talking for them. How he'd missed this, having spent years on the inside where little was green or soft.

"Um." She rubbed her hands up and down her legs, a nervous trait he remembered. She was going to tell him something difficult.

Which meant, whatever it was, he needed to school his reaction. The counselor said his reactions to things would likely be over the top, because where he was coming from, nothing was normal.

"Whatever you want to tell me, I'm good with it." Which was probably a lie, because if she told him she'd been seeing someone else, he'd have a right to explode.

She stood, barricaded her chest with her arms and walked toward the river.

He followed. Stood alongside her. Waited. Imagining the worst. She had cancer. Jason was dropping out of school. Chloe was pregnant. *Jenn* was pregnant. Oh, God help him.

"It's about our sleeping arrangements."

That he hadn't anticipated. "What about them?" he asked, much harsher than he intended, and she winced. "Sorry. It's going to take me a while to adjust from prison voice to home voice. My counselor warned me about overreacting."

Her gaze fixed on the weedy grass beneath her feet. "I don't know if we should sleep together."

What? She couldn't mean that.

"I mean." She puffed out a breath. "Sleep together, but not, you know, make love."

He squeezed his fingernails into his balled fists as those same insecure questions charged through his thoughts. "Do you still love me?" He had to ask. Had to know the truth. He certainly wouldn't be the first inmate to come home and find that their spouse had moved on. Who could blame them? She'd started the business without him, had kept that a secret. What other secrets did she have?

"Oh, Chad." She turned to him, gripped his arms, looked up at him with eyes that had seen too much sorrow. She pressed a hand to his cheek, and he groaned with the touch he'd missed for too long. "I don't just love you, I'm in love with you."

Thank You, Jesus. But then her not wanting to make love made no sense. His counselor would advise him to be honest, to express his feelings. Not easy to do after you'd stuffed them inside for eight years, but he could do it. He swallowed then forced out, "I don't understand."

She hugged herself. "It's that . . . I'm scared." She stared out over the water. "I've read all these, these stories from women when their husbands come home, and it's not pretty. I don't want that to be us. Sex is more than that to me."

"I still don't under . . ." Or maybe he did understand. She'd listened to the wives' side, but he'd heard the husbands'. Those who were frequent flyers in prison. Their first night home wasn't about making love to their wife, it was about a conquest. Or a release from being apart. That was why even non-homosexual prisoners used other prisoners. It was only by the grace of God that he'd avoided that fate. He still shivered, thinking of that time a half dozen inmates had him cornered, and a true miracle had happened.

But he wasn't those guys. He wasn't those husbands who didn't respect their wives. He touched her cheek as gently as he could, and said softly, "How can I make you less afraid?"

"I don't know." Her quiet words were carried away on the wind. "I caught all your remarks inside, and I get it. I do, but . . ." She clenched her fists. "It makes me feel like a trophy."

Now that made him angry. He rubbed a hand over his mouth to avoid saying something he'd regret. "Wanting to love my wife is not a sport."

"Then show me that." She turned to him. Gripped his arms. Her eyes hooded. "I know it's not sport. I know that's not how you think of me, Chad. This one's on me. I love you. I want to love you, it . . . it frightens me because I'm not the woman you married, and you're not the man I married. We've both changed, and I need time to adjust."

He tempered his tone, so he didn't growl like he wanted to. "How much time?" As if she could put a date on it, but he needed something to hope for.

She shook her head. "I don't know. A day. Two days. A week?" She shrugged.

What was stopping her from waiting a month? A year? Or was he worrying about nothing again?

She took his hand. Held it, maybe hoping to soften him to the idea. "Does that make sense?"

His jaw tightened. Nope. Not at all. They were husband and wife, and he wanted to . . .

A word he'd heard too often—said more than once—in prison flitted through his mind, one that would shock Jenn.

His counselor had warned him about this. Adjusting to each other wasn't going to be easy. Chad had mistakenly assumed he'd meant emotional adjustments, not physical. He looked at the grass beginning to green up, at a dandelion sprouting among the grass. He kicked at it, knowing weeds left alone to grow could easily take over. "I don't like it," he mumbled. "But it makes sense. Just so you know, I'm gonna be frustrated."

"And probably growly like a black bear." She looked up at him with a forced smile, poised her hands like bear claws, and raised them above her head, her attempt to get him to loosen up.

He laughed to go along with her, but he wasn't laughing on the inside. "Much worse than that. Maybe more grizzly bearish. Unless . . ."

"Unless what?" She propped her hands on her hips.

"You won't mind a kiss now and then?"

She blushed, which was reassuring. "Maybe." She tapped a finger to her lips.

That alone made him want to envelop her in his arms and . . . his insides twisted like a pretzel.

Dang, she was right, so right. He looked upward to send God a silent apology. He didn't want to make love to her. Well, he did, but right now his feelings were a lot more about lust than love. He may not like it, but waiting was the right thing.

But flirting wouldn't hurt. He grinned and closed the gap between them without touching her. "Just now and then?"

Her blush deepened. "I think I'd like it."

He drew closer and smirked. "I know you'd like it."

Her cheeks were nearly flaming red.

"You're okay with cuddling tonight?" She nibbled at her lower lip, making her look way too adorable.

"For now."

"We've got a deal then?" She squeezed her hand between them, offering to shake, the tease.

"Nuh-uh." He edged closer. "You said kissing's okay. This deal is only sealed with a kiss."

"If you must." She looked at her foot doing a slow dance over the dandelion. It reminded him of the young woman who'd come into the coffee shop asking for hot cocoa. Shy, yet not afraid to stand up for herself. That was when he'd fallen in love with her.

He rested his fingers on the bottom of her chin. Before lifting, he'd ask again, to make sure. "Jenn—Cocoa—may I kiss you now?"

She nodded, and he lifted her chin. He could feel her heart galloping as he wrapped his arms around her and gently pulled her close. He bent over and held his lips a paper-thin width from hers, long enough for a bird to call out to its mate. Then he brushed his lips across hers, lightly, enough for her to moan and pull him closer. He took the kiss deeper, tasting Andes mint. And love. About that he had no doubt anymore.

"Ewww. PDA." Jason, the little brat. The kid always did have rotten timing.

"Get a room, guys." Chloe was no better.

Chad didn't let Jenn pull away, but they both scowled at the kids carrying boxes of pizza and a blanket toward them. Clearly, Jenn wasn't any happier about their intrusion than he was. Point for him.

The scent of the pizza wafted toward him and made his mouth water. He couldn't remember anything smelling so good.

He released Jenn and hurried to the kids and raised the pizza box cover. He breathed in the mouth-watering scent. Pepperoni and pineapple. His favorite. He grabbed a triangle and brought it to his mouth, then stopped, remembering what day it was.

"Something wrong?" Jenn sat on a corner of the blanket Chloe spread out on a yard just beginning to green up.

Chad looked from Jenn to the kids, to the sky, and back at Jenn. "It's

Good Friday. Do you think it's a good idea to eat pizza?"

"I'd forgotten." Jenn puffed out a breath, then gestured for everyone to sit. "But I have a feeling that Jesus would celebrate with us. He wouldn't want us to be sad."

Chad joined the family on the blanket. On free ground. With no bars or prison walls or barbed wire containing him.

Yeah, he could see Jesus enjoying pizza right with them, so he grasped the twins' hands, and Jenn closed their intimate circle. They bowed their heads and Chad invited Jesus to dine with them.

"Lord, I can't believe this day is here. I'm free." He sniffled but didn't bother to wipe his eyes. "I can't begin to tell You how thankful I am to be here with Jenn and Chloe and Jason. It's an amazing gift that I get to celebrate Your resurrection with my family. Thank You, Jesus."

Jenn echoed her gratitude.

"And thank You for this pizza. It's the best-smelling food ever, and I can't wait to taste it. I'm grateful You're sharing it with us. In Your holy name, amen."

His family echoed the amen as he took a bite. And moaned.

"Good?" Jenn asked.

"The best ever."

His family agreed by scarfing up their slices.

His family. So grown up. So very different from when he'd gone to prison, and prison had changed him in ways he couldn't name.

Yes, Jenn was right. They needed to get to know each other again, and it wasn't going to be easy. What if she learned that she didn't like the man he'd become? Would she still be "in love" with him then?

Chapter Seventeen

Jenn watched in the mirror as Chad stared into the dresser drawer she'd filled for him with new clothes. When Thomas had told her yesterday about the judge's ruling, she'd hurried out to get a few items that she hoped would fit Chad. It was clear he'd lost a lot of weight in prison. Not that he had been overweight when he went in.

Unlike her. She wiped mascara from her tired eyes. Eight stress-filled years apart doesn't do kind things to a woman's body.

He pulled out a T-shirt, unfolded it, and turned to her with a grin. Aw, he'd found the oversized T with the Chad's Choco-Latte Corner logo on it.

"Like it?" She spoke toward the mirror, her eyes connecting with his.

"Love it!" He removed the loose-fitting polo he'd worn home from prison, and she gasped. He may have lost weight, but what was left was solid muscle. So, that was what a six-pack looked like.

"What?" He followed her gaze, and looked down. Smirked. "Oh. Guess I look a bit different, don't I? There's not much to do in prison, so you work out a lot." He shrugged then grinned at her. "Like it?"

She nibbled on her lower lip. "Not bad for a forty-something man."

"Not bad." He flexed his arm muscles. "I look pretty darn good." Only, he didn't say "darn."

"Yeah, you do." A whole lot better than she did, that was for sure. For now, she'd be undressing with the lights off.

He pulled the T-shirt over his head, then climbed into bed.

"Oh, man." He moaned and stretched out on the king mattress. "It's like sleeping on a marshmallow."

Really? And she'd thought it was hard. She mentally added that to her list of don't-take-for-granted items.

"And I can stretch out, and the blankets aren't itchy. And"—he sniffed the bedding—"it even smells nice, like lilacs." He looked toward her as she finished cleaning her face. "Smells like you."

Hmm. Had to be the laundry detergent she'd gone nose-blind to. Jotting *space*, *soft blankets*, and *fresh linens* on her don't-take-for-granted list, too.

She flicked off the overhead light and dug the ancient, oversized T-shirt, that she'd worn when pregnant with the twins, from under her pillow. It was broken in perfectly for sleeping. She turned away and slipped her sweater over her head.

"Cocoa, we are married."

"I know," she said without conviction. "I'm . . ."

"Shy. Like on our wedding night."

True, but now she had a lot more insecurity. She undid her bra and quickly slid on the old T before undressing the rest of the way and climbing into bed.

Beside her husband.

And it wasn't a dream. She sniffled. Now tears wanted to come? She wiped an arm across her eyes.

"Hey, babe, what's wrong?" He sat up, leaned over her.

"Nothing." She sat up, hugged her blanket-covered knees against her chest. She breathed through the emotions that wanted to waterfall out. "Nothing's wrong. It's just that I've waited for this for years, and it's finally real. You're actually here, beside me." She touched his whiskered cheek. "You're not an illusion."

He kissed her nose. "I've had the same thoughts all day. Keep waiting for someone to wake me up." He took one of her hands and kissed the backside. "As long as I can keep touching you, I'll know it's real."

"You're not upset with me?"

"Upset?" He kissed her forehead where wrinkles sprouted.

"You know, for what I said earlier? You believe I love you?"

"I do believe." He kissed her lips, but didn't linger.

"I didn't hurt you?"

Silence this time, with no kiss. Over pizza—which he'd said was the best ever—she'd worried that he was feeling hurt. She'd fretted as they watched a movie and had popcorn—also the best ever—in the man cave. She'd pondered his pain while getting ready for bed. He'd shown no signs of hurt feelings. Before prison, he hadn't been able to hide his feelings, but after prison? During prison, he'd probably learned to stuff his feelings.

Before Prison, During Prison, and After Prison. The divisions of her life with Chad. Would those terms forever be the lenses through which they viewed their life together?

It was dark, so she couldn't see his face, couldn't read if he was pondering her question or angry or sad.

Finally, he took her hand, rubbed his thumb over the back of it. "Yeah, it hurt, but I get it."

Did he really, or was he trying to make her feel good?

Wasn't this where the Bible said, don't worry about tomorrow? *I'm trying, God, really I am, but my life has flipped on its head again, and I'm struggling to regain my footing.*

"Lie on your stomach, babe. You wouldn't object to a back rub, would you?"

Never.

She rolled onto her stomach. His fingers, stronger than she remembered, kneaded the sore muscles in her shoulders, down her back, along her arms. Her head. Muscles that had been coiled tight like springs moaned *thank you*, and her eyelids grew heavy.

Her phone alarm played, "Wake Up, Sleeper" by Austin French, and she forced her eyelids open. Sunlight poked through holes in the shade. It was morning? She sat up. Stretched. Smiled. That had to be the best night's sleep she'd had since . . .

Chad!

Chad was home. She spun to her right, hoping to greet the day with a kiss.

His side of the bed was rumpled, but he wasn't there.

Wait . . . had yesterday been a dream? Was she waking only to find that Chad was still in prison, that she was still a single mom?

No. She could still taste the pizza and popcorn. And his kiss. Feel his newly strong hands unknot muscles that had been bound for eight years. She climbed out of bed and started for the bathroom.

Heard a snore coming from the other side of the room.

She followed the noise around the end of the bed.

There he was, scrunched in the small space between the wall and the bed, stomach down, an old towel his only blanket, his arms his pillows. He lightly snored, showing he was asleep, but he had to be uncomfortable.

Was this her fault somehow?

She bent to wake him, then stepped away. He appeared to be sleeping soundly, so she hated waking him.

Instead, she dressed and hurried downstairs. Paula would be arriving any moment with Easter-themed pastries. Jenn could practically taste them already. In the meantime, she did a quick check to make sure they were ready to go for the day. Jenn started brewing the day's first batches of coffee, woke up the sleeping espresso machines, double checked their house-made syrups and sauces, and jotted a mental note to make more vanilla flavoring, as they were running low.

She checked the time. Hmm. Paula was late. That was different. The woman was as punctual as winter's arrival.

Speaking of punctual, where was Sally?

She checked the time again, then the employee schedule. Yes, Sally was due to work today, and had even told Jenn she'd be glad to get out of the house with the kids all home from school for Easter break. Had something come up?

She checked her phone for messages. Nothing.

How strange. She texted both with a polite reminder.

Life happens. Paula and Sally would have good excuses, so Jenn refused to be angry with them or frustrated. This was all part of being a business owner, and Jenn had planned for such eventualities.

Besides, her two best (and cheapest) helpers were upstairs.

She sent a brief message to both Jason and Chloe.

| No pastries. No Sally. Need you both ASAP. |

She didn't have to hear them to know they were grumbling about having to get up so early, when she'd told them last night that this morning was covered. Seconds later, feet thundered down the steps from the apartment. That would be Jason, because Chloe wouldn't be seen outside the apartment without being perfect.

"Got your message." Jason skidded to a stop by the bar and stared into the empty showcase. "No pastries?"

Naturally, he'd be worried about food.

She shrugged. "No Paula. No message from her. And silence from Sally's end, too."

"That's strange." Jason headed straight for the cash register. "Done the till yet?"

"Nope. Saved it for you."

Her phone pinged, and she grabbed it out of her pocket. "It's Paula." She opened the message and read it twice to herself before reading it out loud. Even then, she could hardly believe what it said.

"Fiona at the flower shop offered me a better deal. Will be selling over there starting today."

"You gotta be kidding me." Jason slammed his fist on the counter by the register. "Whatever happened to following through on commitment?" He banged the cash drawer shut. "Did you have a contract with her?"

She continued to stare at the message. This was so unlike Paula. She'd always been reliable. Finally, she looked to Jason. "Yeah, we had a contract, but I'm not going to hold her to something she doesn't want."

"Even if it hurts the store? What are we gonna serve today? People are going to want pastries."

Translation: Jason was going to want pastries. "I guess they'll go to Fiona's Flower Fiesta then." Though Jenn would love to go over there and give the woman an unsavory piece of her mind. Nope. She wasn't going to let Paula ruin Easter weekend.

She started to delete the message, then thought better of it in case she did change her mind about suing for breach of contract. Thomas could let her know if it was worth the trouble or not. Probably wasn't, but it gave her some satisfaction thinking about it.

She began wiping off the tables and chairs, though they'd been thoroughly cleaned two nights ago after she had heard that Chad was going to be released. They'd even had a little party. Sally, Elaine, the kids. Jason's friend, Carlos, had hung around too.

"There's Sally." Jason's words transported Jenn to the present.

She hurried to the front door to open it. "I was worried you weren't going to make it."

Sally didn't come in, her eyes focusing everywhere but on Jenn. She handed Jenn a key. The key to the shop?

"What's this for?" Jenn held it loosely.

Sally heaved a sigh. "My husband doesn't want me working here anymore."

Her husband? The few times Jenn had met him, he seemed reasonable. "Why? Is it something I did? Please be honest with me. I can take it."

Finally, Sally looked up, but her gaze still didn't reach Jenn's. "He doesn't want me working here with your husband around."

"I still don't—"

"I do." Chad growled behind her, and both she and Sally jumped. "I wouldn't want my wife working with a convicted killer either."

"That's not . . ." Jenn looked from Sally to Chad and back again.

"I'm sorry." Sally retreated. "I told him it wasn't a problem, but . . ." She shrugged. "I'm really sorry, Jenn. I've loved working here. You were the best boss."

Jenn had no words as Sally hurried down the sidewalk.

Behind her, Chad used words she wouldn't allow in the shop, but right now, she didn't care. She felt the exact same way.

"Well, screw her." Jason slapped the bar.

"Jason!"

"Dad said worse words."

"You're right." She locked the door and looked at Chad. Anger turned his face red as a Hot Tamale candy. "I'm sorry you had to hear that." She walked toward him, and he held up his hands, giving the stop signal.

"I need a moment to clear my head, so I don't say something else I'll regret." He stalked through the hallway then outside.

Her heart thumped inside her chest and stress tightened every muscle in her body. She'd join Chad if she didn't have to get the shop opened. At least he recognized the need to step away. According to her research, over-the-top reactions were to be expected. Although anger, at this moment, wasn't an extreme reaction.

"Do you suppose Dad's the reason Paula went to the flower shop?" Jason came around the bar and hopped up on one of the stools.

She glanced at the empty pastry bin, then out the window. A few stores away, Paula was essentially cheating on her. She was breaking their contract. Why would she risk Jenn filing a lawsuit? Jason was probably right. Paula didn't want to support a business co-run by an ex-con. Didn't matter that he was innocent, because in the eyes of the law, he was guilty, and he'd have to wear that damning label for the rest of his life.

Made her want to curse like an ex-con too. It wasn't fair that he'd have to prove himself innocent to everyone.

Like it hadn't been fair of her to make him prove himself yesterday. Oh, she'd made a huge mistake. But not one she could rectify right now. She had a business to run, one that was going to open in thirty short minutes, and she had no food to offer the guests. If she were feeling charitable, she'd send them to Fiona's, but fat chance of that happening today.

So that meant she and Jason would have to brainstorm, come up with something else that customers would want to serve for Easter.

She nodded to the clock and sat on a barstool beside Jason. "We have thirty minutes to come up with Easter treat ideas. No idea is stu—"

"How about this?" Chloe entered the room carrying one of her Choco-Terie boards and a basket of bite-sized muffins.

"Is that what you were going to bring to your grandparents' place?"

"Yep. Jase messaged me the problem. What's wrong with people?" Chloe rolled her eyes. "Since we're not going to Gran's tomorrow, we have a good start for today." Chloe tucked the board into the fridge and stocked the muffins in the pastry showcase. They wouldn't last long, but it was something.

"Thank you, Chloe." Jenn got off the stool. "What other ideas do you have?"

"If you two can handle the store, I can do some baking. It won't be Paula's, but it'll be good and fresh."

Jason snorted. "It'll be better than Paula's. I didn't care for her stuff anyway."

Liar. But Jenn let that one go. "Perfect. Thank you." She briefly considered calling in Kayla, who'd quit a few weeks ago to be a plumbing apprentice, but decided against it.

"I'll call Elaine." Jason jumped off his stool. "See if she can come in early, work the entire day."

"Have I ever told you kids how amazing you are?" Jenn resisted wiping stress perspiration from her forehead. As it was, she needed to run upstairs and refresh her deodorant.

"Not since yesterday," Chloe yelled as she jogged down the hallway.

"Then we can do this," Jenn said partly as prayer and partly to herself. This was their first day-before-Easter, so she had no clue how busy it was going to be. Regardless, she and Jason would have to handle it. She hurried upstairs, refreshed her deodorant, then calmly made her way to the store.

Jason was still in the breakroom, talking to someone. He startled when he saw Jenn watching him. Why? "Yeah, see ya soon." He jabbed at his phone, as if embarrassed to have been caught talking, then pocketed it.

"Uh, that was Carlos. Chloe said she needed more ingredients, asked if Carlos could get them for us. He said he would."

"Hmm." Then why the drama with the phone? And why couldn't Chloe call Carlos herself? Did that really matter at this moment? Instead,

Jenn smiled, said something about Carlos being a good kid, then asked Jason if he'd called Elaine.

"Yep." He wrote in her name on the schedule. "She'll be here after ten. They're doing an Easter thing with her dad this morning, but she can stay 'til closing."

"That's wonderful." They'd survive the first three-and-a-half hours without her. Now, it was time to get those doors open and welcome the Easter crowd. Part of her hoped for a busy day, but another part wanted to sit and feel sorry for herself. And Chad.

He'd need to be retrained before handling drinks or money—and that needed to be done on a slow day—but nothing said he couldn't do dishes or clean tables. That would certainly help.

She hurried to the back door to call Chad inside. She opened it, looked ahead. Saw no one.

"Need something?"

She startled and glanced to her right.

Chad sat on the ground, his hands extended.

She knelt in front of him. "Are you okay?"

"Yeah. I'm good." He looked to the sky and mouthed something. "God and I were having a conversation."

Oh.

Had that even been a thought with her? On Easter weekend, of all times.

She grabbed his extended hands. "Can I pray with you?"

He nodded. Smiled. Then closed his eyes. "Lord, You know what's going on with Jenn, the kids, and the store, the problems with me coming home. I'd be lying if I said I wasn't upset. But I do know You'll use this for Your good, somehow. Give Jenn guidance today, and for all those who enter the shop, I pray that they will be blessed. Amen."

"Amen," she said so quietly, Chad probably didn't hear, but God did. He always did. So, why hadn't she gone to Him first with the problem?

"Thank you." She kissed Chad, and he beamed. Oh, she did love seeing his smile again. "Now it's time to get to work."

He leaped up and offered his hand to help her. It was a small gesture, a very Chad-like gesture, but she'd become so used to doing everything on her own, that it took her a second to respond.

"How can I help?" He followed her inside.

"First." She pointed to the door. "It needs to be locked on the outside at all times."

"Yeah. Of course." He responded too softly, and she realized she'd made another mistake. His fingerprints on an unlocked coffee shop back door had been part of the evidence against him.

"I'm sorry."

"Cocoa, it's okay." He closed the outside door and made sure the door to the apartment was locked. "I'm hyper-sensitive to everything right now. Put me to work, and I won't have time to feel sorry for myself."

"Gladly." She nodded toward the shop. "It's time to open."

He should be thrilled for this opportunity, but Chad's heart beat erratically as he followed Jenn into the shop. Chad's Choco-Latte Corner. Even though he'd known of the store for months, he still found it hard to believe that their dream had come true. No surprise, his Jenn had made it happen.

He followed her behind the bar. Studied the coffee-making equipment, the cash register. Nothing was familiar. How would he be any help?

"Do you mind doing cleanup today?"

He could have kissed her right there. "I'd love it."

"Thanks." She blew out a breath as if relieved. No doubt, she'd anticipated him wanting to make coffee, which he did, but the new machines intimidated him. They shouldn't. He used to love working on new machines, but that was before prison.

She gestured to the sink and opened the doors beneath it. "Everything you need for dishes and cleaning tables is here." She hurried to the breakroom and unlocked the door, then handed him a key.

He followed like a child tethered to their mother.

"Broom, mop, and cleaner are in that closet." She pointed off to the right. "I'm sure there's something I'm missing, so feel free to ask."

He nodded, feeling a lot like a toddler.

"It's go time." Jenn strode to the front door, stopped with her hand on the knob. She snapped her fingers and looked back. "I almost forgot." She walked back to him and extended her hand. "I like to begin each day with prayer. I can't believe I almost forgot." She winced.

Not a surprise with the mayhem they'd begun the day with. "May I?" He nodded at Jason, summoning their son over.

"Please do."

He gripped Jenn's and Jason's hands. "Lord, what a privilege it is to begin the day workday with You and with my family. I still can barely wrap my mind around the fact that I'm free and I'm standing inside a coffee shop."

"Cocoa, too." There was a grin in Jenn's voice.

"Yeah, cocoa too." He squeezed her hands. "Bless our day and our customers. Help me adjust and learn. In Your Name, amen."

"Amen." Jenn squeezed his hands and returned to the door.

Jason took his place by the cash register, if that was what you called it. Didn't look like any register Chad had ever seen before.

A bell jingled from the front of the store, and he froze in the hallway entry. His palms began to sweat. His heart palpitated as if he were hanging off the side of a bridge. People—not prisoners or COs—were about to enter. He'd always been a people person, so what was the problem?

Customers hurried in. He recognized that urgent walk of someone needing their coffee fix to begin the day.

Speaking of which, he hadn't made himself a coffee. Well, it was too late now as a line six people deep had already formed in front of Jason.

He handled that register thingy like a pro. Smiling at the customers, listening to them, treating each as if they were special. Not bad for an introvert.

Minutes later, the pastry bin was empty, and the tables were full, and more people crowded into the store. He hadn't moved from the hallway. It was as if he were paralyzed.

No, that wasn't it. He couldn't force himself to move forward, but if given permission, he would run to his safe space, wherever that was. Maybe where he slept last night when he couldn't adjust to the oversoft mattress, blankets, and pillows. He wiped an arm over his forehead and squared his breathing—as his counselor had taught—to curb the panic. This would pass.

Crash! Bang!

He fell to the floor, covered his head, protecting it from flying food trays and pummeling fists. Silence smothered him, and reality hit. He wasn't in the prison cafeteria. He was home, at the coffee shop. Slowly, he brought his hands to his sides and looked outward. No one was drinking or eating, but they were staring at him lying stomach-first on the floor.

Then Jenn was at his side, kneeling beside him. "It's okay," she whispered. "Just some broken dishes. Happens all the time."

Right. He swallowed. Nodded. Stood. But couldn't make eye contact with the customers.

"Can you get the mop and broom?" Jenn pointed toward the breakroom. "I need to make drinks."

"Oh. Yeah." He retreated to the breakroom. Finding the mop, broom, and rags was easy. Forcing his feet to go forward into the shop, though, every step was filled with lead. He made it to the spill. Bent over to pick up the large pieces.

"I'm sorry," a voice above him said.

"It's okay." He wiped up the coffee with a rag, all while his body was urging him to flee. Each customer appeared to be a multi-fingered monster, condemning him for what he'd been convicted of, or wanting to pitch a fight.

He finished cleaning and hurried to the breakroom where his breathing normalized. He cleaned the mop and hung the rag over the sink. But now he had to go back out there.

The door opened, and he stood tall, squared his shoulders, making himself look as large as he could. His fists ready to defend.

"Are you okay?" Just Jenn.

He relaxed, squared his breathing again. His prison counselor would remind him to tell the truth, but how could he admit to the woman he loved that he was terrified? And so very broken. He hadn't realized how much until this morning. Yet, she'd see right through him if he tried to hide it.

Finally, he shook his head. "No." He swallowed. "But I promise to work on it."

"If you need to—"

"I said I'm working on it," he barked.

Jenn's eyes grew round as a coffee mug as she backed from the room.

"I'm sorry."

The door closed before his apology could reach her, and he cursed.

"I'm sorry." He looked to the floor, hoping God would still be listening to him after such a horrible display. His fists balled, needing something to punch. In prison, he used the weight room. Or his pillow. Neither of which he had right now, which meant he needed to come up with some other way to redirect his pent-up feelings, whatever they were.

Right now, the answer was to man up and head out to the front of the shop and do his job. He forced his feet to move from the breakroom, closed and locked the door behind himself, then shuffled forward through the hall, his breaths coming faster than the Easter Bunny delivered baskets.

More people filled the shop now. Great for the business. Heads pivoted toward him then jerked away. So, he'd become the elephant in the coffee shop. Nice. Some customers didn't even try to whisper their comments about the ex-con working there now. His fists balled. What he'd give to pop them—

Ignore them. And ignore those abusive voices in his head calling him no good. He'd show them. He went behind the bar, observed Jason at the till, Jenn concocting beverages she didn't like.

Her gaze caught his as she frothed a drink. She nodded toward the seating area and mouthed, "Clean the tables."

Okay. He could do that. He found spray cleaner and a clean rag beneath the sink and forced himself to head into the seating area. He didn't have to listen to the customers. Didn't have to talk. He only had to clean.

He wiped down a couple tables then headed behind the bar for a clean rag. A guest pushed away from the table as he was walking past. They bumped.

"Watch it, klutz." The teenaged boy sneered at Chad. "Or I'll call the police on you."

"You—" Chad cut off his sentence and secured his balled fist to his side. "Sorry." Clenching his jaw, he made his way to the sink.

"Are you all right?" Jenn handed him a large paper cup with the shop logo on it.

He took a long swig of regular coffee before daring to answer. "I am now. Thanks."

"Don't let that kid rile you up. He loves to give everyone a hard time."

"So I'm not alone."

"Not at all." She nodded to the sink. "Doing dishes might help."

Throwing dishes would help even more.

But he filled the sink with warm, suds-filled water and washed plates, coffee cups, dainty tea mugs, silverware, none of it matching. In too short a time, the dishes were done.

Now what? He looked to Jenn, and she nodded toward the dining area. More tables to bus. He showed her a thumbs-up, grabbed a gray tub, and headed to the dining area. New customers filled the place, ones who hadn't witnessed his panic attack, who wouldn't label him a head case, so this round would be easier.

More plates filled the tables than the first time. He glanced toward the bar and the pastry display. It was full? When had that happened? Chloe probably came down when he was pouting in the breakroom.

His stomach growled as he wiped off a table and chairs. Guess since he didn't have a bell telling him it was breakfast time, he'd forgotten to eat. His stomach talked louder so that young girls at a nearby table giggled. How dare they laugh at him? In prison, that would get you a punch in the face, for sure.

He carried the bin behind the bar and restrained himself from slamming it down. He looked to Jenn, but she was talking with a customer, so he caught Jason's eye and asked his son what he should do next.

Did he roll his eyes? Nah, he was seeing things.

Jason waved Chad over then pointed out in the dining area. "It needs to be swept."

"I'm on it." Chad found the broom and dustpan and banished every crumb off the hardwood floors. That took all of fifteen minutes, with no customer interactions. The morning was getting better.

After putting away the broom, he approached Jenn again and asked her, "Now what?"

She closed her eyes, shook her head, as she finished filling a cup. "There are more dishes to do."

"Sure." He went to the sink and looked at his wife, whispering with his son. About him, no doubt, but he had no clue why.

"Hey, this plate is chipped." Someone complained behind him. Chad turned toward the man, then looked to Jenn and Jason. Both were busy with customers.

"Gonna do somethin' 'bout it or not?" A bushy-mustached man waved the plate in Chad's direction, spilling crumbs all over the newly cleaned floor and counter.

What was he supposed to do? He stood there, frozen. Glanced again at his family for direction. They were still busy.

"Hey dummy, I'm talkin' to you."

Okay, that was it. Chad threw the dishrag into the sink and rolled up his sleeves. "Who you calling dummy?"

"Oh, tough guy. Heard you just got out of prison." Bushy-stache smirked. "How long ya gonna last on the outside?"

Chad bellied up to the backside of the bar. Good thing it was between them, or he'd have shoved his fist right up Bushy-stache's nose.

"Chad." Jenn's voice seemed distant as she grasped his arm, tugged it away. "Stand down, Chad."

He blinked several times, barely registering Jenn telling Bushy-stache to leave and return only when he'd learned some manners.

Then it sunk in. What had he almost done?

He looked at Jenn. She wasn't angry, but sad. Probably disappointed. Heck, he was disappointed in himself.

"I'm sorry."

She glanced down then up, meeting his eyes. "Chloe said she'd like some help baking. Would you mind?"

In other words, "Chad, you're a screw-up. Get outta here."

"Yeah. No problem."

He strode from the dining room, though he wanted to stomp like a child. His first day working was a massive mess. Just like his life had been for the past eight years.

Chapter Eighteen

Jenn sagged onto a newly cleaned chair and sighed. Business had remained steady long past their planned closing time of two p.m. They'd finally locked the doors at three. And thanks to Chloe's muffins and molded chocolates, they'd survived the day. Not to mention Elaine coming in early and Carlos running for groceries. Maybe Sally and Paula had let them down, but others had quickly lifted them up.

No doubt it was all aided by Chad's prayers. The fact that Jenn hadn't thought of bringing the problem to God first still nagged at her. Perhaps that was a wake-up call. Which meant, now was a good time to give thanks.

She splayed her hands, copying Chad's open praying style. She thanked God for providing today, for her workers who did show, for the customers supporting them, for Chloe. Jason. Chad.

Oh Chad.

She doubled her prayers for her husband. The last she'd seen of him was after she'd recommended he help Chloe. He'd disappeared down the hallway toward the apartment, his shoulders hunched and head hanging low. Likely, he was angry with her now, but what options had she had? She'd read that ex-prisoners needed a lot of instruction but hadn't comprehended the difficulty in dealing with it in real life. That was compounded by his panic attack—PTSD from prison?—and his near-fight with Mr. Carter, a customer she wouldn't mind never seeing again. She added a prayer for Mr. Carter, also a child of God.

She said, "Amen," but her eyes remained closed as she pictured a long soak in her tub, lit candles, music. Then she'd be able to get a good night's sleep and be in the right mindset to celebrate Easter tomorrow, the first in their new home. With Hal and Mom and Dad joining them, it would be an intimate celebration, not so large that it would overwhelm Chad.

"Jenn?"

Chad. Why did her shoulders tighten at him saying her name? She should be thrilled that she could hear his voice in person, not over the phone, not across a table in a noisy visitors room.

She opened her eyes and turned toward his voice. He hovered in the hallway, a step away from entering the customer area. Had he felt her tension? She lifted a quick prayer that God would remove whatever stress she felt and replace it with gratitude. No doubt, that would be a prayer answered over time, not in the second she wished it would be.

So for the moment, she smiled, and, with her foot, she pushed out the chair across from her, an invite for him to sit.

Relief unhunched his shoulders as he strode to the table and sat.

"Hey," she said and reached across the table. His hand eagerly gripped hers. No more sign language was needed to substitute for touch. "How'd it go with Chloe?"

"She's quite the baker."

A deflection, not an answer to her question, which communicated what she needed to know.

"She's good at anything creative, it seems. All right brain. And Jason's the opposite. Put the two together, and they're a dynamo."

"Like us?"

She nodded. Smiled. *Like we will be again.*

"Would you be up for a walk?" He looked toward the front of the building then back at her. Uncertainty written in his raised brows. "I'd like to see the town."

And there went her tub time. Could she be any more selfish?

"I'd love to go for a walk. With you."

His face lit up. Yep, her thoughts had been very selfish. She accepted his offered hand to help her up, and he didn't let go as she led him out the front door of the shop. The usually busy street had quieted to only the occasional passing car, though business was ramping up in the bar across the street. They headed right on a now-empty sidewalk which took them past the neighboring building, the only vacant storefront. To think, their little coffee shop had spurred a downtown revitalization, as their realtor had suggested it might. That was certainly something to be proud of.

Next door to the vacant spot was the pizza place called Slice of Heaven. A peek through the window said that their business was booming.

"Is this where the kids got the pizza from last night?"

"It is."

"Best pizza ever." He licked his lips as if tasting it all over again.

"Can't argue with that." Which was mostly true, especially for their choose-your-favorite-toppings personal-sized pizzas. She could create something healthy, but after a hard day's work, healthy was rarely on her menu.

Chad squeezed her hand as they walked in front of Fiona's Flower Fiesta. "Is this where your pastry chef went?"

"Yep." Jenn grimaced. "If I wanted to be mean, I wouldn't set foot in Fiona's again, but it's not her fault that Paula decided to leave with no notice. Besides, I really like Fiona, and she always gives us discounts on arrangements."

"I've learned it's best not to harbor anger," Chad said with no malice whatsoever. If anyone had a reason to be angry, it would be him. Especially toward his former best friend.

"Not even toward Dajon?"

"To serve what purpose?" Chad shrugged. "The only one I'd be hurting would be myself. Not long ago, I learned to give him to God. Over and over, the Bible tells us to love and pray for our enemies. Knowing that helped me survive without becoming bitter. Someday, I'd like the opportunity to tell Dajon I forgive him."

Jenn studied the man walking beside her. He was telling the truth. Neither malice nor deceit showed in his eyes. How did a good man go into prison and come out better?

Clearly, there were lessons she needed to learn yet. She added Paula, Sally, and Sally's husband to her prayer list. If Chad could forgive the man who'd given the most incriminatory testimony against him, she could forgive others for walking out on her today.

Besides, this was Easter weekend, the time when people celebrated what forgiveness truly meant.

They walked in silence to the end of the sidewalk, then crossed the street to return. Mostly residential homes lined the road, with a park in between. Then the dive bar. Right across from the coffee shop.

Would that be a problem? He had been going to AA meetings, but was temptation too close?

"Don't worry about it." It was as if he'd read her mind, like he used to do. "I'm sober since before Christmas. Nothing can be as dark as prison."

"I'm not worried." She gave his hand a reassuring squeeze. Well, maybe her worry was about the size of a mustard seed. She didn't plan to water that seed and let it grow.

From there, they walked across the street and down by the river, where they each took a swing, letting silence take over as the sun began its too-quick descent. That meant it was nearing suppertime. She'd still have an hour to soak in the tub before bed.

As for bedtime, they had issues to work out. Her last image of Chad in the bedroom was of him squished between the bed and the wall, no pillow, no blanket, and that broke her heart.

Jenn pushed up on her tippy toes and held the swing there. "Can I ask you a question?"

"You just did." He grinned.

"Ha ha."

"Ask away." He also pushed back on the swing and held it in place.

"It's about bedtime."

"Oh." He swung forward a couple times, then dragged his feet to stop it. "What do you need to know?" His expression-free gaze was fixed straight ahead.

"You slept on the floor last night. Was that because of me? Because I didn't want to, you know . . ."

"Have sex?" He looked toward her, wearing that teasing smile she'd once found so adorable.

Why did that phrase bother her so much? They were husband and wife, for goodness' sake. She finally nodded in response.

"Cocoa, it had nothing to do with you." He reached over and caressed her cheek, but then turned quickly toward the river, his eyes downcast. "The bed was too soft. So was the pillow. The blankets. The space was too big. It was all too quiet."

"I'm sorry." And she was, more than for the years of hard beds and itchy blankets and skimpy mattresses. "It's not fair."

"Maybe not, but I'm trusting God for a purpose."

Which meant, Chad still hadn't seen a heavenly reason behind his incarceration. Maybe he never would.

"Can I ask you a question now?"

"Sure." She gripped the chains tight, preparing for anything.

"Why didn't you have Chloe invite Nicholas to Easter dinner tomorrow?"

Nicholas? Oh, Nicholas Christopher the third. Chloe's professor. The answer to that was easy. "Chloe didn't ask if he could come."

"Because she was afraid to ask you."

"Afraid?" She looked at the house then at Chad. "What do you mean?"

"She knows you don't like him, though you've never met him."

"That's because he's a nearly thirty-year-old man dating a nineteen-year-old. So, yeah, I don't need to meet him to know I don't like him. Jason doesn't like him either."

"Makes sense." Chad backed up then swung forward. He pumped slightly to make the swing bob back and forth.

No doubt he disagreed with her. "What would you do?"

"Probably the same thing." He dragged his feet and came to a stop. "Personally, I'd like to punch the guy."

So, Chad was on her side.

"But we're alienating Chloe in the process."

Or maybe not. "That brings me to my question, 'What would you do?'"

He breathed in and slowly blew it out. "Personally, I want to meet him. I want to show Chloe that I trust her decisions."

"Even if you don't?"

"Maybe I should. I mean, look at how she jumped in and offered ideas for today. That's not the actions of an adolescent."

Huh.

Jenn pushed back, released, and let the swing's momentum take over. How was it that Chad had spent eight years in prison, and yet he was a wiser parent than her?

She slowed to a stop and spoke to the river. "You're right."

"I am?"

"I've messed up." A frog leaped in front of her, and Jenn startled, then refocused. "If I trust her with all the store responsibilities, shouldn't I trust her with her personal life, too?"

She owed her daughter a big apology. She whipped out her phone, typed a text to Chloe, and pressed Send. "There. I told Chloe that I'm sorry and that she should invite Nicholas."

"Our daughter will be very happy. And we'll have to behave ourselves tomorrow."

"I'll be on my best behavior." She drew an X over her heart. On top of that, she still owed Chad an apology. "Leapfrogging back to an earlier topic."

He chuckled.

"Glad you still appreciate my humor."

"I've missed it, Cocoa."

"And I've missed you." She got up from the swing and knelt in front of him. Held out both hands, which he immediately took. "Last night, I was wrong. I was frightened. And it wasn't fair to you."

"Jenn—"

She pressed a finger to his dry, cracked lips. "I know I hurt you, and I want to make it right. I want to be your wife, in every sense of the word."

A smile grew on his face, slow as a turtle, making it all the more beguiling. "Are you sure?" He touched a hand to her cheek, and his thumb caressed her lips.

She kissed his thumb, the palm of his hand. "I am." And she really was. And now that she'd allowed the words their freedom, she anticipated their time alone tonight.

"Then . . ." He leaned toward her.

"Mom. Dad."

Uh-oh. Jenn pulled away and fell on her backside. She knew that tone from Chloe, and it wasn't a happy one.

"What's wrong, hon?" She stood and wiped the grassy dirt from her behind. Chad stood beside her, parenting side by side like they should have been all along.

Chloe held out her phone. "Got your message right after I got one from Jerkface."

Jenn assumed Jerkface meant Nicholas, but she held her tongue. Thankfully, so did Chad.

"What kind of low-life . . . ?" Chloe sniffled and wiped her eyes. ". . . breaks up in a text?"

Oh, now she really wanted to introduce Nicholas to her fist.

Instead, she rounded the swing and drew her daughter into her arms. "I'm so sorry, Chloe." Jenn knew all about broken hearts from breaking it off with Thomas years ago. Didn't matter who broke the heart or the reason for breaking. It hurt all the same.

Chloe jerked away and tased Jenn with a look that sizzled. "If you'd been more supportive, maybe he wouldn't have broken up."

"I know, your father—"

"Was the first one who listened."

Jenn closed her eyes and reined in her own tears. She thought she'd been supportive, thought she'd listened, but apparently, Chloe felt differently. "I'm sorry. I messed up."

"You better give thanks that Dad listened, because if it weren't for him, I'd be done with the coffee shop, and you'd be stuck without a barista and a pastry baker. When it comes to being a mother, you're just like Gran."

Jenn gasped as the verbal shot smacked her right in the heart. No, she wasn't like her mom. Not one bit.

Problem was, Chad didn't defend her, which meant he believed the same as Chloe.

Chapter Nineteen

Jenn raised the lid on the slow cooker, and the aroma of a well-cooked ham wafted through her apartment. If Easter had a scent, it would be slow-cooked ham.

"Oh, man, you're making my stomach rumble." Chad wrapped his arms around her from behind and rested his chin on her shoulders.

"Soon." She put the lid in place and turned into his embrace. "But we'll eat much sooner if you let me work."

"Ah, do I have to? You look awfully sexy in this apron." He kissed her good and long, taking her back to their previous night. All her worries about their lovemaking had been for naught. Maybe that boded well for the rest of the things concerning her about Chad's adjustment to life on the outside.

"Yes, you do." As much as she could remain in his arms, making up for lost years, she struggled from them and gestured to the plates she'd set out on the island. "Mom and Dad'll be here any minute, and I'd love for everything to be ready." If not, Jenn would certainly hear about how Mom's meals were always perfect and on time. It would have helped if Chloe weren't hiding, but Jenn wasn't about to nag her daughter today. Not after last night's drama.

"Aye, aye, captain." Chad lifted the stack of plates. Glanced at the long folding table loaned to them by city hall. "Where do you want them?"

"Let's see, there are seven of us." She did the math in her head to recheck. Her, Chad, the kids. Mom, Dad. Hal. "Yep. Seven, so put one plate on each end. Three on one side and two on the other."

"Got it."

While he set out the plates, she pulled glasses and cups from an upper cupboard and silverware from a drawer. "When you're done, set these out too, please."

"Sure thing." Chad picked up the knives, glanced at the table, then at her. "Where do you want these?"

Chad knew this. Was he that afraid of doing anything without instruction? She held in a sigh. This was all part of their adjustment. "Knives and spoons to the right of the plate. Forks on the left." She gestured to the napkins on the island. "And put the napkins beneath the forks." In some ways, it felt like she was teaching elementary school again, but she could never let that show.

The doorbell from the driveway side of the building ding-donged.

"Company's here." She glanced out the living room window. "My parents and Hal. Looks like they drove in at the same time. Mind getting the door?"

"Sure," he replied without enthusiasm, probably not wanting to face her mom, not that she blamed him. This way, though, they'd get that first meeting over with. And she could get food on the table.

Thundering footsteps came down from the attic, and Jason appeared in torn jeans and a T-shirt with some rock band label. Should she make a big stink about dressing up for Easter?

Nah. Not this year. They had bigger problems than Jason's wardrobe. Besides, now he could lend a hand.

"Morning, hon." She pointed to the rolls in the basket on the table. "Would you mind nuking them for a few seconds?"

"Sure." He sniffed and sighed as he grabbed the rolls. "Oh, man, this place smells like Heaven."

"Right?" She removed the cheesy potatoes from the oven, and more delicious scents were released into the air. Chad's favorites. She couldn't think of a more perfect welcome-home meal. If Chloe felt better, the meal would taste better too, but that they could do nothing about.

The microwave dinged and Jason removed the rolls. "Put them on the table?"

"Yep." She nodded and grabbed a trivet for the potatoes. "Please let Chloe know that lunch is almost ready."

He groaned. "She's being a brat."

"Yeah, well, she's got her reasons."

He hmmphed and shuffled toward the attic door. He opened it and yelled, "Chloe. Lunchtime."

"That's a nice Easter greeting." No surprise, Mom's entrance had no saccharin at all. At least she could pretend to be sweet. Well, she was carrying the sweet. Literally. No one could beat Mom's lemon meringue pie or carrot cake.

Jenn faked a smile and greeted her parents with kisses on their cheeks. "Happy Easter." She greeted Hal the same way. "I'm so glad you could make it."

"Wouldn't miss it for the world." He wrapped an arm around Chad's shoulders. There were even tears in his eyes. "To see my son come home is the best Easter a man could ask for."

"I couldn't agree more." Jenn removed a pitcher of punch from the fridge, plus a bottle of sparkling grape juice. "Everyone sit wherever you want. Chloe should be down in a minute. In the meantime, Chad, would you mind plating the ham?" That had been his job before prison, so hopefully it was something he could do post-prison.

"Sure." He joined her in the kitchen.

Jenn handed him a platter and a couple of meat forks. It was a pre-sliced ham, so it should be pretty easy to work with.

"Coffee anyone?" She held up the carafe of coffee Chad had brewed that morning.

"Yes, please." Chloe slumped toward the table wearing a robe. Her hair was unruly and her face blotchy as if she'd spent the entire night crying. Maybe she had. Which added a dagger to Jenn's heart. If she had been more accepting of the professor, maybe Chloe wouldn't be going through heartbreak right now.

"My goodness, Chloe, is that how—"

"Mom." Jenn lasered a look toward her mother. "Not today."

"Whatever. It's your house. Your rules." But Mom's pursed lips showed she wasn't happy about being silenced. Tough.

Jenn poured coffee for everyone but herself. For herself, she poured a glass of sparkling grape juice, though something stronger would taste very good with Mother around.

"How's this?" Chad carried the platter of ham over to the table. It looked delectable, but his downcast eyes showed insecurity that needed to be flipped upside right.

"That's perfect." She gestured to an open spot on the table, and he blew out a relieved sigh. "Go ahead and sit. I'll get out the veggies."

No, it wasn't the cooked carrots, asparagus, and string beans Mom always made. They were sacrificed to give Jenn more time to focus on the necessary entrees. Instead, she set out a pre-cut veggie tray Jason had picked up from the grocery store yesterday.

At last, Jenn sat at the only open spot, at one end of the table. Mom, who'd sat first, had taken the other end. Jenn offered her hands to Chad on her right and Jason on her left, and they all bowed their heads.

"Dear Lord," Jenn began. "Wow, I can't think of a better way to celebrate Your resurrection. Having Chad home for Easter is a miracle we thought we'd never see. Thank You for opening doors for him. I pray they will continue to open and that You will bless his freedom. Thank You for those around this table today celebrating both You and Chad. Thank You for the feast as well. We are blessed. Amen."

"Amens" echoed around the table, followed by Jason asking for the ham.

"One moment." Mom quieted the hungry group. "I have some news of my own first." She looked across the table at Jenn. "I received a call from Warren Liekhus at Apple Lake School, and he practically begged you to return."

Jenn blinked. Shook her head. As appealing as returning to the classroom sounded, that was the last thing on her mind today. She smiled, as best she could. "You may pass along that I'm not interested."

"But—"

Jenn held up her hand. "Please, Mom. My life is here. At the store, with the family."

"A woman could hope." Mom scooped herself some potatoes. "Anyone else?"

"I'd like to say something, too." Chloe focused on her lap while others passed food around the table. "Um, I was wondering, since Paula pulled out . . ." Chloe peered at Jenn, then down. Her poor daughter looked ready to cry again. Oh, if only Jenn didn't have a table surrounded with guests, she'd sit and hold her daughter.

"I was wondering if I could make chocolates instead." Chloe peered up. "It would be different from pastries and would fit the shop's theme, with chocolate."

"I think that's a brilliant idea." Jenn accepted the meat platter and forked a couple slices of ham.

"Really?" Sun broke through the clouds on Chloe's face. Seemed dramatic, even for her daughter.

"I'm with your mother." Chad took a bite of ham and moaned. "Best ham ever."

"Dad, to you, everything's the best ever," Jason said while devouring a slice.

"True." Chad grinned, then focused on Chloe. "I love the idea of you making chocolates. People could add them to their coffee."

"Or hot cocoa."

Chad shrugged. "If they for some reason don't want coffee."

Mom sighed loudly, ruining the light moment. "I too think it's a good idea, as long as you don't let your studies lapse."

"About that." Chloe pushed food around on her near-empty plate. "After this semester, I'm not returning to college. I don't want to be a teacher. Never did."

Silence saturated the air, everyone waiting for Mom to pitch a fit.

But then Chad cheered. "Good for you. I knew you didn't want to go into teaching."

"She should go into something that won't leave her destitute like . . ." Mom stopped, which Jenn was very thankful for, because she would have had unkind words for that woman.

"Chloe." Jenn set down her silverware to focus solely on her daughter. "I applaud your decision." Maybe *applaud* was a bit strong, but Chloe needed affirmation more than anything.

"That was a—"

"Mom." Jenn cut off whatever selfish thing her mother was about to say.

"Fine." Chloe slammed her knife on the table. "Gran, I know what you were going to say, that I wasted your money and time, but I don't care." She pushed away from the table. "I don't care about anything." She ran toward the attic.

Jenn rose.

"And I don't want you to follow." Chloe glared at Jenn then stepped through the door and slammed it behind herself.

Jenn slumped. *Happy Easter, everyone*, she wanted to say.

But Chad got up, leaving his plate full of his favorite foods. "I think she'll talk to me."

Thirty minutes later, he returned to the now-cleared table. Mom snored ungracefully in one of the chairs, and the guys had some adventure flick on Jason's laptop.

Jenn microwaved Chad's food, which she'd refrigerated, and joined him at the table. "How is she?"

He didn't look up, but concentrated on his plate. "Her heart's broken." He took a bite of meat and said nothing else.

This was all her fault. If she'd been kinder about the professor, paid more attention to Chloe's feelings, listened instead of judged, she would have known Chloe was really in love, because only true love would cause this much heartbreak.

Jenn jerked up in bed, hip-hop music blasting in her ears and making her heart beat in an erratic rhythm. "What in the world?" She blinked. Looked around the room. Oh, the Zena smart speaker on her dresser. It had gone haywire. "Zena, shut off music."

Thankfully, the noise quieted, but didn't stop as it played on in the living room. Still, her heart and breaths slowed. The speaker had never turned on by itself before, but with Chad home, a whole bunch of things had never happened before.

Her phone started playing, "Wake Up, Sleeper," the signal that it was five a.m. and time for her to get out of bed. So, she'd been awakened seconds earlier, but with such a rude awakening, no doubt she'd be crabby all day. Not a good way to begin the work week.

"Sorry, did that wake you?" Chad strolled into the bedroom, his hair wet, and a towel wrapped around his midsection. His tight muscles still shocked her—it was almost too much.

"I was about to get up anyway," she said, rather than criticizing him for the annoying music.

"Still, I'm sorry it came on so loud. I'm not used to silence. Prison was always noisy."

Ah, now it made sense. She'd read that ex-prisoners couldn't take the quiet. Unfortunately, silence was necessary for her to begin the day. One more thing they'd have to work out together. For now, she'd compromise. "In the future, would you mind lowering it a few decibels, please?"

"Yeah. No problem. Chloe taught me about the magic Zena box on Saturday when we were baking, so I tried it out this morning." He grinned. "Didn't intend to wake the neighborhood."

Chloe.

How could a mother not worry about how her heartbroken daughter was doing? She only had a few more weeks of classes, but being on the same campus as the rotten professor would be difficult.

"Do you think she'll be okay?" Chloe had barely spoken two words to Jenn before she and Jason left last night.

He shrugged. Turned toward the mirror. "Broken hearts are painful, but people recover."

"I suppose. I wish she'd speak to me."

"She will. Give her time."

And a whole bunch of prayer.

He ran a comb through hair that was far too gray for a forty-three-year-old. Wait, what was that on his shoulder blade?

She looked closer. A tattoo? Appeared to be a very crude cross.

His gaze connected with hers, and his shoulders drooped. "You see it."

She rubbed her finger where she'd had a wedding band tattooed. Once upon a time, they'd scoffed at the idea of tattoos. Now they both had one.

"Tell me about it." She sat on the edge of the bed and patted the space beside her. When he sat, she traced the image with her finger, and he shivered.

He shook his head. "It was protection. Identified which gang . . ." He made finger quotes and sighed. ". . . I belonged to."

"Gang?" She couldn't wrap her brain around that thought.

"Not like what you're thinking. It really saved me from being recruited or attacked." His head remained down, which told her there was more to the story than he was telling. No doubt he had many stories she'd never hear to completion. She had to allow that. Likely, he had many stories she honestly didn't want to know about.

She kissed the tattooed area then rubbed her kiss in with the palm of her hand, feeling overtight muscles. "You are protected by Jesus' sacrifice on the cross."

With that, he looked up, and their gazes met in the mirror. "What did I do to deserve you?"

That was what she should be asking him. Prison may have broken him, but God had pieced him together in beautiful ways she was just beginning to see.

She gave his back a light tap and smirked, hoping to loosen him up a bit. "You won't be saying that after our training today." She got up and walked toward the door. Looked back. "You'll probably want to call me a lot of not-so-nice names."

"Oh yeah?" He grinned. "If you snap, you have to take a full sip of coffee."

"A full sip?" She wrinkled her nose, practically tasting the rancid drink already. Definitely an incentive for her to keep her cool. "And if I'm calm and nice all day?"

"Then I have to give you a foot rub." He grinned. "Of course, either way, I win. We both know what a foot rub led to the other night."

She blushed at the thought of their Saturday night together. It wasn't at all like the horror stories she'd heard from other prison wives. By his chuckle, she could tell he saw the red in her cheeks, so she turned her head toward the living area before saying, "It's a deal."

After grabbing a quick breakfast, she prepped for work and told Chad to meet her downstairs. She hurried to the shop with a box of chocolates Chloe had made last night after her parents and Hal had left. Since Chloe had no classes today, she planned to make more during the day, enough to last the week. Jason would deliver them tonight once classes were over.

Hopefully, the customers would like the new addition. And Jenn would graciously—or through gritted teeth—tell those who wanted pastries to stop by Fiona's.

Glorious silence met her in the shop. She stood by the counter and took a moment to breathe, to bask in the quiet before Chad joined her. Before customers' voices and background music filled the next ten-plus hours. She used to relish the peace when she'd get off work. Now, would she ever have any? That was an adjustment *she'd* have to make. Chad had already endured his share.

Whistling came from the hallway. Oh, to feel that happy when morning dawned.

"Ready for my first day of barista training, boss." He grinned and rubbed his hands together.

"Come here." She swept past him to the breakroom, where she handed him an apron with their logo on it, then pointed out the Opening Duties chart. "Usually, I'll assign my morning person half the duties, but since she quit, you and I get to do them all. The plan is for you to take over for Sally."

"Got it." He gave two thumbs up.

If only all workers were that eager.

"This way." She felt a lift in her own step as she led the way to the espresso machines. She loved the training part of the job—reminded her of being in the classroom. Oh, she missed it, but not enough to apply for the job Mom had mentioned. Not when the coffee and cocoa shop had become a reality. Watching Chad's face light up as he walked behind the bar made the sacrifice worth it.

She had him put the espresso machines together and turn them on, then empty and rinse the coffee canisters. While the coffee brewed, they organized Chloe's chocolates in the display case. Milk, dark, and white chocolates. Some with peanut butter, others with coconut, and, naturally, one flavored with coffee.

Together, they added clean pumps in the syrup and scoops in the toppings. Made sure the espresso shots were timed correctly, then emptied fresh cold brew into clean jugs.

"That was easy." Chad swiped his hands together.

"But we're not done yet." She gestured to the register that was very different from the old-fashioned register he'd used at Cuppa Truth. "It's all Wi-Fi run, and really, it's almost self-explanatory."

"Like Zena?"

"Remind me to have a talk with your daughter about teaching you about her." If Chloe was still talking to her.

Jenn showed Chad the very basic steps. Coffee, cocoa, and type of chocolate. Small, medium, or large. Jason had programmed it so she could easily add smoothies or juice or other items to the register. But for now, she wanted to keep it simple for Chad.

She had him count out the petty cash in the drawer, then showed him how to process credit cards, which was what most customers used. No surprise, he was a fast learner, but then he had worked as a barista for roughly sixteen years before his arrest. Even with the upgrades, he could do this in his sleep.

"To encourage others to follow suit . . ." He dug into his pocket, pulled out a couple dollar bills, and squeezed them into the tip jar next to the register—a mason jar with the logo, along with the word TIPS printed on it, which they'd Velcroed to the counter so it wouldn't easily walk away. Chloe had tied an azure ribbon, matching the front door, around the neck, and Hal had cut out a slot for bills and coins, again, making it difficult for money to magically disappear. Lessons learned early on in the business's opening.

But she hadn't ever considered beginning the day with money in the jar. Chances were, this was the first of many lessons he'd teach her.

"How am I doing, Mrs. Taylor?"

"Hmm." She tapped a finger to her chin. "We're opening in a few minutes, but think you can handle a quick lesson on the espresso machine?"

"Thought you'd never ask." He rubbed his hands together. "Teach me how to make a Chad's Choco-Latte. Would be the perfect wake-up."

"Gladly." Then she wouldn't have to make drinks that she didn't want to sample.

Again, he caught on quickly, blending the espresso, steamed milk, chocolate, and a dash of English toffee sauce, the unique ingredient added by Chloe, of course. He took a sip and moaned his delight. "You know." He licked his lips and held up a finger. "All it needs is a little Irish cream."

She froze. Stared at him. Held her breath.

"Kidding." He held his free hand. "No Irish cream for me. Ever. Okay?"

"Don't you dare joke about that."

He drew an X over his heart. "Promise. Never again. Sorry."

She released her breath. "You're forgiven." She'd shocked herself with how much she'd reacted to his joke. But that was all it was. That was who he was. She'd fallen in love with a man who loved to tease and joke around. Guess that was something else she'd have to get re-used to.

In the meantime, coffee-craving customers awaited outside the door.

"I'll teach you more during lulls, but it's time to open up. Can you man the till, and I'll play barista?"

"Got it, boss."

Despite his bad joke, she did love seeing that broad smile on his face. This was his happy place. Soon she'd be able to snatch a break here and there and not have to hire anyone to replace Sally. What a deal that would be. Still, money was going to be tight. The store was barely making enough to support her on a very tight budget, much less two adults. One more item to add to her prayer list. God had provided thus far, right?

Before opening, they prayed over the shop—together. Another prayer answered.

Then she unlocked the door and headed for the back of the bar, ready to begin the day. With Chad returning as barista, it was going to be the beginning of good things for Chad's Choco-Latte Corner.

Coffee-crazed people walked in through the door, and Chad froze. No welcome came from his lips. No "Good morning." No "Which coffee will begin your day?" He stood there, mute. Tried to lift his eyes to theirs, but couldn't force them. He'd spent so many years training himself to avoid looking others in the eye, that it was impossible now. He'd thought for sure it wouldn't be a problem working as a barista. Jenn was going to think he was a head case. If she did, she'd be right. Prison had royally messed with his head.

Still, when a well-dressed woman stepped up to the counter, he forced a smile and the words, "Welcome to Chad's Choco-Latte Corner. How can we begin your day?"

"I'll have a skim-milk cappuccino, milk steamed to exactly a hundred and fifty-seven degrees, two-and-a-half pumps of vanilla flavoring, extra foam."

Chad stared at the register as she rattled off her order. How did he ring up an order so precise?

Within seconds, Jenn appeared at his side, rescuing him. "May I help?" she whispered.

He nodded.

"I'm sorry." Jenn took his place at the register and smiled at the woman. "Would you mind giving me your order again, please?"

The woman gave an exaggerated sigh and repeated her order. Not once did Jenn lose her smile, whereas with each instruction, steam brewed hotter inside Chad. The next customer's order wasn't any easier. Why did this surprise him? It was no different than when he'd worked at Cuppa Truth. He'd handled it fine back then.

Jenn took both orders, then made both, as the line stretched to the door and some customers walked away. Not once did she complain, and if she had, she would have had every right. Instead, she directed him to clean the tables, the floors, and the dishes.

What was wrong with him? He should be able to do this in his sleep. He should be able to smile at the customers, joke with them, flirt . . . No, no flirting, but still, being a barista should come naturally.

Because of prison, he was now a failure at the one thing he did best, the only thing he'd ever wanted to do. If he couldn't do this job, what was he good for?

Jenn plopped down on a chair during a break in customer traffic. She should be training Chad during this time but had no energy to do so. To see him stand there, unable to look a customer in the eye, unable to speak, much less be the friendly, outgoing man she'd fallen in love with, had shattered her heart. Made her want to rescind the prayers she'd lifted for Dajon and for all those responsible for calling Chad guilty. They'd done this to him. To her and to the kids.

"I'm sorry," Chad said from his hiding place in the corner booth.

"Hey." She got up and joined him. Stretched her hands across the table to him. For a second, he hesitated, but then he grasped hers so hard, she almost yelped.

"It'll get better," she said, but couldn't add that all was okay, because clearly it wasn't. "Elaine is coming in at noon when she's done with classes. Jason said he can do classwork online, so he'll be out here all week. I can train you while he's manning things."

"Are you sure?" Just like with the customers, his eyes didn't lift to hers.

"We expected this, right? We knew things weren't going to go smoothly."

"Yeah, in life, but not as a barista. I froze, Jenn. I couldn't make eye contact. Her order flew over my head faster than a bullet." He glanced to his left, and she followed his gaze. The dive bar? No, that was simply coincidence, not a longing.

"Chad." She shook both of his hands. "We've only been at this for three hours. When I train someone, it takes a lot longer than that. Give yourself a break."

His lips raised in a half smile. "I suppose this means you get a foot rub tonight."

"Foot and back, mister."

"And back, huh?"

"Yep. No reneging."

"If you say so, boss."

"Uh-uh." She stood and wagged her finger as a customer approached the door. "Foot and back rubs are for your wife only, not for your boss, got it?"

"I love you, Cocoa."

"And I love you more than cocoa." Which she did, really, she did, but this scared her. Clearly, she'd been expecting too much for his first day. By the end of the week, he'd be a pro again. By the end of the month, he'd be pulling in double the customers with his quick wit and engaging grin. They'd all appreciate his willingness to not only listen when customers had a bad day, but to hear what they had to say.

They'd fall in love with him, like she had, like the old customers at Cuppa Truth had. She had to believe it, because if that didn't happen, Chad's Choco-Latte Corner was in deep trouble.

Chapter Twenty

Where was Chloe?

Jenn stared past the line of customers waiting to be served at the tables that needed to be wiped. Wednesday mornings weren't usually this busy. She should give thanks that so many people wanted to drink their coffee and cocoa, but she couldn't, not when working alone. You didn't rush making a quality drink.

As soon as she had a moment, she'd give Chloe a call. If that girl was still sleeping . . . Oh, how Chloe had tried Jenn's patience this past month since Chad was freed. Jenn hadn't expected her broken heart to last this long. In the past, her daughter had moved on quickly from broken relationships, of which there were many.

Even so, Jenn plastered on her work smile and greeted the next customer in line, a twenty-something woman she hadn't seen in the shop before, so Jenn needed to make a positive impression. "Welcome to Chad's. Thank you for waiting. What can I begin for you?"

The door chimed as she took the order, but it barely registered as she focused on making a positive impact on the customer. Either an impatient guest was leaving, or more were being added to the waiting line. Jenn began tamping the espresso grounds and heard water running in the sink behind her. Who was—?

She glanced over. Thomas? With a wet washrag and a spray bottle of cleaner in hand, he hustled out to the dining area and began wiping tables. It practically made her want to cry. When was the last time someone—namely, Chad—had taken the initiative to work without needing every single instruction?

He'd been out of prison an entire month, and still struggled with independence. Guess that is what happens when you have eight years to learn a habit. The least she could do was give him more than a month to unlearn it. She was certainly trying, which was why she'd gladly told him to take the morning off to see his counselor, gladly volunteered Jason to drive him. Chloe would be here. They could easily handle it.

Ha!

She began steaming the milk for the customer's thankfully simple latte.

Chloe was going to receive a piece of Jenn's mind once she showed up.

As Thomas cleaned, Jenn continued taking orders and making drinks, most of which would never pass her own lips. Every once in a while, a kindred hot cocoa or smoothie drinker would enter, but by far, coffee was the beverage of choice. Why, she'd never understand.

The door jingled, and Jenn looked beyond the now shorter line. Chloe? So, she hadn't been sleeping.

Her daughter swept around the counter. "Sorry, Mom. I'll explain later." She took over at the register.

She'd better explain, and it had better be a good explanation.

A half hour later, the line had dwindled to the occasional walk-in, Chloe had taken over all barista duties for the time being, and Thomas had thoroughly cleaned the place. As a neat freak, he'd done a better job than Jenn would do.

Which meant she could take a breath.

She created a hot cocoa with ice cream for herself, then an Americano for Thomas, and joined him at a table.

"Thank you." She sighed. "You were a lifesaver today. If someone had warned me that running your own business would be more tiring than teaching, I would have laughed."

"Your mom probably warned you."

"Her many warnings about my life choices usually fall on deaf ears." She sipped her cocoa. Now this was delicious. Chad would tease her about adding a hint of coffee to improve the flavor, which would stiffen her resolve not to drink coffee. Ever. Chad was one of those things Mom had warned her against.

Whereas she'd encouraged a relationship with Thomas. At least they were still friends.

"Can I join you?" Chloe stood by a chair, clearly nervous about speaking with Jenn.

"Of course." Jenn reminded herself to listen and not react, to not judge or jump to conclusions.

"Um, about this morning." Chloe wrapped her hands around her drink that was piled high with whipped cream. She spoke toward the beverage. "I'm sorry I wasn't here for you, but I got a call from Barbara—"

"Mayor Barbara?"

"Uh-huh. She said that a new resident at the homeless shelter didn't have any clothes that fit him and asked if I would get some. How could I say no? You were in the shower when I left, and I meant to call and let you know I'd run into town, but then I forgot until I was driving again and—"

"Chloe." Jenn raised a hand, then stood and gave her daughter a hug. "I'm proud of you. No further explanation needed."

"You are?"

Jenn moved her chair so that it faced her daughter. "For all you've done volunteering at a place where the homeless can live and eat . . ." Jenn shook her head, trying to wrap her brain around her daughter's selflessness. "What nineteen-year-old does that? So yes, I'm immensely proud of you."

Chloe slouched in her seat and blew out a breath. "I thought for sure you'd be seething mad, and I'd be on your naughty list again."

"I think this gives you a get-off-my-naughty-list-free card for the rest of the year."

"Sweet!" Chloe reclined, clasping her hands behind her head. "That means I can do whatever I want for seven whole months."

"Not so quick. Remember, you also have a father."

Chloe waved her hand. "Nah, he's never mad at me. He listens."

"That's your dad for you." But Jenn felt herself wilt. When had she stopped listening to her kids? Chloe's words hadn't been intended as a slam against her, but the truth hit hard. Since Chad's arrival home, he'd adopted the good-cop part of parenting, while Jenn always had the bad-cop role. That needed to change now.

She took Chloe's hand, looked in her eyes. "I'm sorry I've been so tough on you lately. Sorry I haven't listened. Sorry I've been so judgmental. I promise to do better."

Chloe blinked, likely holding in the tears that she shed so easily. "It's okay. I've been a jerk, and you were totally right about Nicholas. I didn't want to listen to you either."

"Are we good then?" Jenn examined her daughter's smile, looking for any pretense, but saw none.

"We are." Chloe hugged her mom and stood as a new customer entered. "I've got this. You take a rest."

Gladly. Jenn shifted her chair toward Thomas. "Sorry about the drama."

He smiled. "Nothing I'm not used to. See it in court all the time."

"With a seventeen-year-old, you'll be seeing it at home too."

"Already am." He shook his head. "The problem with a child attending college two years early is that the boys she meets are that much older. Thankfully, my folks back me up in the boyfriend department, because I'm returning to Boston soon. Decided to keep my practice there rather than move here. That's why I stopped in today. I had an appointment not too far from here, and I wished to speak with you in person."

Disappointment thudded through her. "I'm sorry to hear that. If not for your perseverance, Chad wouldn't be home."

"And now that he's home, I can go home. Lacy had begun projects around the place. It's time I honor her and finish them."

"You still miss her?"

He glanced toward the picture window. "Every day. I'd be lying if I said I wasn't lonely."

"You're a good man, Thomas." One she was really going to miss. Too much so. His going home was a good thing for both of them, because too often Thomas reminded her of the life she could have had if she'd made different choices. "Will you stay for pizza?"

He checked his watch and stood. "Sorry. I have to get going. Noelle's got an end-of-the-year choir concert tonight. I can't believe my baby girl is going to be a college senior in a few months."

"Definitely not a surprise to me." Jenn stood to walk him out the door into fresh, coffee-scent-free air. "Before you leave for Boston, please come say goodbye."

"I'll do that. And you take care of yourself, got it?"

She shrugged. "I do my best."

"Do better. And love Chad. Transitioning from prison to home life isn't easy. If you're going to be a statistic, make it a positive one."

"Yes, counselor." It was as if he had insight into her marriage. Yeah, life wasn't easy for the ex-con, but it wasn't easy for the wife either. "Now give me a hug before you go. Tell Noelle and your folks, *hi*."

"Will do." He wrapped her in a hug before striding to his Infiniti. She hugged herself, trying to convince herself his leaving was for the best, but her heart was having none of that.

"Was that Thomas?" Chad craned his neck to see who Jenn was hugging on the shop's front sidewalk before Jason turned the car aiming toward the rear of the shop.

"Looked like it." Jason drummed his fingers on the steering wheel to music Chad had chosen. At least Jason seemed to like his music preferences. Hip-hop was all he'd heard for years, and he appreciated how it didn't gloss over the messy parts of life. Jenn despised the language, and he didn't blame her, but when you were used to hearing certain words every day for years, they became part of your thought process and your daily lexicon. What had once been offensive to him, wasn't any longer, though he felt it should be. It seems he prayed *ad nauseum*, King David's words from Psalm 51. God was probably tired of hearing the words with as little effect as the prayer seemed to have on his life.

Especially when it came to jealousy.

What was Thomas doing here? Again? Chad's case was done. He was free, which meant Thomas was free to return to wherever he came from and leave Jenn alone.

No, his thoughts toward the man who'd helped free him from prison weren't very charitable, but his brain and heart were at odds.

Jason parked beside Jenn's pickup. Someday, soon, Chad would get to drive it. All he had to do was pass his written driving test next week to get his permit, then he'd have to pass the road test in ninety days, if he could get an appointment. That meant ninety more days of Jenn and the kids chauffeuring him to the counselor every week, plus other appointments. Thankfully, his AA group was within walking distance.

He was such a burden on them.

Words that Avery, his post-prison counselor, had forbidden him to say or think, but it wasn't easy to expel words that accurately described his situation. If Jenn left him for Thomas, he wouldn't blame her. Avery would tell him to be open with Jenn, to tell her his feelings and not stuff them away, to state what he observed. But did Jenn deserve to carry that additional burden?

"You coming, Dad?" Jason peeked inside his car.

"Yeah. Just thinking." Chad got out of the sedan that was older than his son, but which Jason was proud of. He'd bought it entirely on his own.

Chad slogged toward the shop and followed Jason inside. Jason hurried upstairs to the apartment, yelling something about his shift starting soon. Friday would be the last of his weekday shifts as he'd be starting an accounting internship on Monday.

Chad couldn't be prouder of his son. Both of his kids. Jenn had taken their lemon-filled situation and made cheesecake from it. But no matter what Avery said, Chad couldn't chase the belief that his arrival home had added a bunch more lemons to Jenn's burdens, and the pile was about to topple.

Thomas's presence solidified that feeling.

Shake it off, Taylor. Man up. He gave himself the pep talk as he made his way to the front of the shop. Chloe was working, as was Elaine, that young Asian girl who always put him on edge. Made no sense, but the sight of her and that friend of Jason's—Carlos—raised the hackles on his back, like in prison when he'd pass by anyone in the Asian or Hispanic gangs.

Another horrible lesson taught to him in prison that he had yet to unlearn. Would it take as long to forget those lessons as it had taken him to learn them?

He waved to Chloe, forced a smile for Elaine, and spotted Jenn in her quiet spot, the corner booth.

"Mind if I join you?" He'd learned to never assume.

But she smiled and pointed to the seat opposite her. "How'd it go this morning?"

"I should be asking you that."

"Sounds like you're deflecting." She crossed her arms.

"Pot calling the kettle."

She laughed. "But seriously, did it go well?"

"Did the doctor get a good peek inside my head? No clue. I want to be better. I want to put those years behind me, but they dog everything I do and think. They hurt you."

She peered down, affirming his words.

"Those years made me insecure, dependent, even jealous, when I know up here"—he tapped the side of his head—"I have no reason to be."

"Jealous?"

He watched her for signs of deception, but saw none, not that he was an expert on body language.

"Yeah. I saw Thomas out front, and . . ." Avery had instructed him to be open and honest, so here goes. "And I got jealous."

"Oh, Chad." She reached across the table. "Then you'll be very happy to know that Thomas stopped by to tell me he's returning to Boston, now that your case is done, and Noelle's school year is over."

Relief flooded through him like a cool river on a hot day. "That's all?"

"Chad Taylor." She came around the table and scooted in tight beside him. She cupped a hand on his chin and said, "Look at me."

How could he refuse to look into her chocolate brown eyes? At least that was becoming easier, but he still averted his eyes when it came to strangers. And customers.

Her face drew near enough to his, he could feel her breath.

"You, Chad Taylor, are the man I'm in love with. Thomas was, is, and always will be, just a friend." She closed the distance between them and gave him a kiss that promised more for this evening. Too soon, she drew away and rested her forehead on his. "You understand?"

He nodded.

"Good." She kissed him again. "Keep that in mind, mister, if you want dessert tonight."

"Dessert, huh?"

"Yep."

He grinned. "I guess I'll remember that."

"Good." She winked. "Come to the bar. Let's get some more training in while we have help and quiet."

"Yes, ma'am."

Well, maybe he wasn't such a loser after all. Maybe he and Jenn had a chance to beat the odds and stay together.

Chapter Twenty-One

With June's evening heat beating down on her, Jenn took her time walking the backstreets of Donaldson to Barbara's house, appreciating the quiet of nature. Their home was never quiet, one of the concessions she'd made to preserve Chad's sanity, but the music he listened to made her shiver.

How had it already been two months since he'd been released? Two excruciating, amazing, dreadful months? Jenn had hoped that, by now, things would be easier.

So nature walks helped preserve her sanity. That and venting to Barbara, who understood from experience the need to express feelings out loud. Talking to her was as valuable as seeing a counselor. Besides, paying for Chad's therapist already stretched their budget to the point of having no margin. Counselor Barbara was all they could afford for her.

She turned onto Barbara's street as her friend came out her front door. She waved and Jenn hurried to meet her at the end of the home's sidewalk. They hugged, exchanged good-to-see-yous, and continued up the street. They didn't have a walking plan other than follow where their feet led, always exchanging small talk before getting to the nitty gritty.

After walking several blocks, they passed city hall, which signaled an end to small talk.

"How'd the meeting go last night?" Jenn asked. Replacing the sidewalks was supposedly on the docket. Jenn had wanted to go, but once she got out of the shop, she had no energy for more work. They'd extended their summer hours until seven p.m. and offered a wider selection of lemonades, teas, and smoothies.

"You'll be happy to know that the council voted unanimously to not just fix but replace the sidewalks. The town should get money from the state to help fund it—that sold our toughest council members on the deal. Having the retail area filled also helped."

"Filled? You mean the store next to mine is sold?"

"For a hair salon."

"That's fantastic." One more place she could walk instead of drive to.

"Two other businesses vied for the spot, a vape shop and a bookstore. I was happy the vape idea was nixed but disappointed for the bookstore, although Fiona said she might be willing to share space in her flower shop. The town's in talks with a grocery chain, a gas station, and a brewery, and a few food truck ideas were bandied about. We'll probably look at those more seriously next month."

"Your little town is growing up. You must be proud."

"It really began with you taking the chance on the coffee shop. It showed others that this town could support small businesses again, and it also helps draw new residents to the area."

"Yeah, well our little coffee shop is struggling right now." Jenn huffed and sped up.

They turned a corner, heading down another residential street.

"I'm sorry to hear that." Barbara hurried to Jenn's side. "My short legs have difficulty keeping up."

"Oops. Sorry. I tend to go faster when I'm upset."

"And I tend to eat chocolate, which is why I need these walks with you." Barbara patted her hips. "Tell me about the store. It always appears busy."

"Maybe it isn't so much the shop's lack of success as our need for more income. Right now, it's supporting four adults. Elaine is our only non-family employee, which helps. But adding Chad to our household has pinched an already tight budget. We don't go out. The only thing extra we spend money on is Chad's therapy sessions, and those are necessary. He offered to get a job, but what can he do without a driver's license? His road test is two months away. Then there's his insurance. Auto. Health."

"It's been a lot for you to take on."

"I shouldn't complain." Jenn kicked at a stone in the road, but the summer's heat had sunk it into the asphalt, so it didn't move. She shook off the pain and kept moving. Story of her life. "I mean, Chad's home. Chloe's talking to me again. Jason's got a fabulous internship. What more could I ask for?"

Besides a husband who behaved more like a grown man than a young child? One who didn't depend on her for every little thing. A husband who didn't fly off the handle at any little incident or give sideways looks to Elaine and Carlos. One she didn't have to chauffeur or financially support. Along with running a start-up business, it was all too much.

"What else is going on?" Barbara slowed, prompting Jenn to slow. Her way of making Jenn face an issue rather than try to outrun it. "You seem more stressed than usual."

"Do I?" Jenn wiped perspiration from her forehead. "I'm exhausted. Sometimes I feel like I'm more Chad's mother than his wife. And then I feel like an ogre. Chad'll bring up ideas, most of them are outdated, and then he gets all depressed or he explodes. There's no in between. Yesterday, he brought up adding ice cream to the menu. Not a bad idea, especially since there isn't an ice cream shop in town, but that would also mean we'd have to purchase new equipment and supplies, plus the ice cream. The little bit of ice cream we use for our drinks barely fits in our freezer, so selling it isn't financially feasible. He told me the only reason I said *no* was because it was his idea, not mine. To keep the peace, I said we'd look into it."

They approached the park that was across the street from Chad's, adjacent to the bar. Barbara gestured toward a bench. "Care to sit?"

"Sure." They sat side by side. The coffee shop was in full view from here. "My heart breaks for him. Everything he tries is met with roadblocks. To help with finances, he applied at a couple machine shops nearby. Online applications don't have a place for him to explain why he hasn't held a job for eight years, or where his previous address was. Is he supposed to enter *Prison*? Both had that stupid box to check indicating he's an ex-con, so of course he wasn't even interviewed. It's so not fair.

Our legal system says he's guilty, therefore that's what the world believes. He's had customers spit at him. People cross the street to avoid him. But then I also notice that he's not as friendly, though not outwardly rude, toward Elaine and Carlos and people of color in general, which is weird because his former best friend, Dajon, is black."

"Do you suppose that's why? Some underlying anger toward Dajon?"

"Maybe." Jenn shrugged. "He's very closed about what went on in prison, but I do know that it was very divided racially. He probably has no clue he's behaving that way, and I refuse to point out one more behavior flaw. I've done it too often, and I get so impatient with him."

"Hmm."

Okay, that *hmm* always meant Barbara was going to say something profound, so Jenn steeled herself to listen, whether she agreed or not. Usually, Barbara's advice was to be nibbled on slowly, not swallowed immediately.

"When I was married to my first husband . . ."

Jenn shifted to view her friend, who had learned many lessons from her first marriage.

"As I've told you, he controlled most everything I did. He had me believing I was lazy and dumb and ugly."

All of which were far from true.

"And the only thing I could control was my food intake, so I ate. Made me feel better for that moment, made me forget my pain. A hundred and fifty extra pounds later, plus the loss of many friends and family, I finally fell to my knees and whispered, *Help*.

Help! was a daily prayer for Jenn, so that wasn't her issue, but she continued to listen for some important nugget to glean from Barbara's experience.

"I learned that those who don't take care of themselves continue to make unhealthy decisions until their core issue is faced. With me, I finally acknowledged that my ex was bad for me. I acknowledged that I wasn't taking care of myself, and my first step in getting out of that situation was praying. I still have extra weight—don't know if that will ever go away—but I don't beat myself up over it anymore."

Jenn chewed on Barbara's words. True, she spent most of her time taking care of others, and very little on herself. But when did she have the time? Nights off, like this one, were rare. Chad and the kids had gone to a movie, the first he'd gone to post-release. She hoped it went well. She never knew what would set him off. But tonight, that wasn't her problem.

Problem.

Chad.

Dear God, in her mind, the two were synonymous. She and Chad would never move forward as a couple as long as her subconscious—or truthfully, her conscious—thoughts defined him as a problem to be dealt with. And here she'd been upset with society labeling him. She wasn't any better. The difficulty was in turning around her thought process, but she could do it.

That was the core issue she needed to deal with. Chad wasn't a problem. He was her husband, the man she loved, and now that she recognized the enemy, she planned to fight for him and wouldn't give up, no matter what happened.

Even though he was no longer in jail, she was still fighting for his freedom.

Life at Chad's Choco-Latte Corner was good.

Chad hummed along with the music playing over the store's speakers. Christian pop wasn't his preference anymore, but he was becoming acclimated to it again. The lyrics were definitely more positive than the hip-hop he'd grown used to.

He glanced at the clock above the exit as he finished making a customer's drink. Only one hour to go before he, Jenn, and the kids could enjoy a family evening. The way life should be. He topped off the frozen hot cocoa with oodles of whipping cream and slivers of mint chocolate, and handed it to a young teen whose acne-covered face showed she probably liked chocolate too much. Still, he smiled and told her, "You'll love this. It's my wife's favorite."

She thanked him and walked out to the patio, where she joined others her age at one of the metal tables fronting the store. Jenn and the kids had made this place so inviting for all ages. Chad didn't deserve it, but God had given him his dream.

After three months of freedom, he was finally beginning to feel free. He was a whiz at the register now, though he preferred to make drinks and deliver them. He could—usually—make eye contact. And finally, he was shedding the Pavlov's-dog prison syndrome, where he didn't make a move until a buzzer rang or until someone told him to go. At last, he was becoming independent again.

He looked out over the dining area as he whipped up a Chad's Choco-Latte for a customer. Jason was bussing tables that filled immediately upon cleaning. Every chair was occupied by content coffee and cocoa drinkers—though he never failed to remind Jenn that coffee sold much better.

Jenn . . . *His* Cocoa.

He spotted her at a table, taking a much-needed break, laughing with a customer and building that crucial community rapport. She looked his way and winked before returning to her conversation. During this past month, her true smile had returned. The stress he'd brought on her upon release was finally melting away, and as a couple, they were in sync again, like their before-prison days. She didn't have to boss him around anymore, making him feel like a child. He'd tease her, and she'd give it right back.

Sure, they had things to work out. She was still chauffeuring him around. Their bed was too soft. The world was too quiet. And judgmental. He'd forever be an ex-con in everyone's eyes but his family's and God's. That was something he had to live with, and unfortunately, his family had to live with it as well.

But they served a mighty God who was bigger than all their problems.

As he topped the Choco-Latte with whipped cream, a new order came through the system, keyed in by Elaine, who was working register.

Okay, there was another big issue he and God still had to work out. In prison, segregation meant survival, and gangs were separated along racial lines. Eight years of being wary of those whose skin color was different than his, whose facial features might be shaped differently, had ingrained unwanted bigotry in him. He was always polite to Elaine, but when he looked at her, all he could see was the Asian gang that tormented others. The Aryan gangs were often the worst, so his bias made no sense. But was racism ever logical?

All he could do was work with her, be polite, and pray that the Holy Spirit would do a work in his heart toward her.

He finished making the drink and called out the name on the cup, Rhonda. A sixty-something woman stepped to the counter.

"Enjoy." He handed her the drink, along with his trademark smile. "I guarantee it's the best latte you've ever had."

"That's a big guarantee. Do I get a refund if it's not?"

He laughed. Crossed his arms. "Try it."

She sipped, and he watched her expression. The hooded eyes, relaxed shoulders, the big sigh. Oh yeah, she liked it.

"Okay, you win." She pulled a bill out of her wallet and tucked it into the tip jar.

"I knew it." He grinned. "And thank you. Hope to see you again soon."

"I'll be back." She did a little finger wave before turning away. Joining a friend who already had her drink, she not so quietly said, "He's such a cutie."

"Isn't he?" The women chatted their way out of the shop.

"You schmoozer," Jenn whispered as she passed behind him.

"That's two more customers drawn to the dark-roast side." He smirked and drew two pretend hash marks in the air. "I'll get you there yet, Cocoa."

"Ha. Fat chance of that."

"That schmooze is how I caught you."

"True." She set something on the counter in front of him. "It's also how you keep me."

"Oh, it is?" He grinned.

She kissed him on his cheek.

Okay, maybe not professional, but who was he to complain? Humming, he began the next drink, a strawberry-lemonade with a dollop of ice cream. Like a root beer float, but better.

"By the way." Jenn passed him again and pointed out a note she'd placed on the counter in front of him. "Thomas is coming in shortly. He and Noelle are leaving town on Monday. I invited them over for s'mores tonight."

Hallelujah. He swore he heard the angels singing.

And there was one more little matter he was still working on, but that issue would be leaving town on Monday, taking the problem along with him. Chad was all for celebrating Thomas's departure.

Yeah, life at Chad's Choco-Latte was good.

He finished the float and turned. Bashed into Elaine. The drink splattered over him. The counter. The floor. Her.

"Why don't you watch where you're going, you . . ." A slur erupted past his lips.

He froze and silence screamed across the shop. He looked down at Elaine, whose head was bowed, but no doubt, tears formed in her eyes.

"I'm sorry. I'm so sorry, Elaine. I didn't mean that. I'm so sorry."

She backed away.

As did he, until the wall separating the shop from the breakroom stopped him.

Chairs scraped the hardwoods, overtaking the silence. The air turned blue with comments meant for him to hear.

"He should go back to prison."

"That's the last time I come in here."

"Racist."

Others called him words he'd only heard in prison. He deserved every one. His thumping heart should have drowned out their voices.

Jenn. Had she heard him? Where was she? He peered upward. Glanced around the shop. There she was, by the door, no doubt attempting to do damage control.

But what he'd done couldn't be fixed.

Jason walked toward the door, his arm around Elaine, caressing her back as he whispered something to her. Then he kissed her. On the lips.

They were a couple?

Jenn closed the door after Elaine left. Locked it. And Jason strode toward him, eyes red with rage, and his fists balled tighter than a prison door.

"How dare you." Jason shoved him, nailed him against the wall, and called him a word Chad had never heard his son use. Jason cocked his fist and drew back his arm.

Jenn grabbed it. "You don't want to do that," she said calmly, but there was an edge to her voice, and her milk chocolate eyes had turned dark. In prison, he'd learned what hate looked like, and this was it.

One irrational outburst, and he'd ruined everything. The shop. His son. And worst of all, Jenn. Would she ever forgive him?

Could he ever forgive himself?

Chapter Twenty-Two

Jenn kept her gaze nailed on Chad as she pulled Jason's arm away, though part of her wanted that fist to land on Chad's face. How could he spew something so vile toward Elaine, who was one of the kindest, most respectful young adults she'd had the pleasure of meeting?

"Didn't you hear what he said?" Jason shook off Jenn's grip, but didn't re-threaten to punch his father. Yet.

"I did." She kept her tone cool as she read Chad's face. Fear. Regret. "Will you excuse me and your father, please?"

"Fine." He withdrew. "I'll go walk Elaine home, if she wants anything to do with me anymore."

Jason and Elaine were dating. How had she not known?

She shook her head to return to the matter at hand. "Let's sit." She gestured to the private corner booth, and he obeyed, like he always did when given instruction. Maybe she wanted him to fight back for once.

To keep their conversation private, she pulled down the blinds on the windows and the door, then sat across from him, though it didn't feel far enough away. How had she gone from flirting to despising in a matter of minutes?

"I'm sorry, Cocoa." His gaze didn't lift to meet hers, just like in the early days of his release. He laid his hands on the table, palms up, their during-prison sign language asking her to reach across.

Nope. She would not take those hands. If she did, she'd likely squeeze the life from them.

"I'm sorry, too." She kept her voice at an even keel to prevent herself from crying or screaming. "How could you say such an awful thing?

There's no one sweeter or kinder than Elaine. And apparently, our son thinks so, too."

Chad's Adam's apple dipped down and up. "I know it's not an excuse. It just happened. It just came out, and I couldn't feel worse."

She vigorously shook her head. "You do realize that being unable to control your tongue has probably cost us our business? Every single person I talked to at the door said they're not returning as long as you're around."

He dipped his head and tugged his hands away. His arms fell to his sides as he whispered, "I know."

"And that our son's first relationship might be ruined?"

He said nothing but kept his head bowed.

And she had nothing left to say. The business had been going so well, but now?

Things between her and Chad had been going well, too.

Finally, he looked up, but still didn't meet her eyes. "I'll go pack."

"What? Why would you do that?"

"To save the business. You said yourself, they'd only come back if I was gone. Chloe's been volunteering at that homeless—"

"Whoa. Stop." She held up her hands, trying to wrap her brain around what he was saying. "Absolutely not. You think I would turn you out of our home?"

"Is it? *Our* home?"

Was it? She looked upward, picturing the apartment. The man cave. Then she glanced around the shop. While the apartment had been decorated for her, everything else had been designed with Chad in mind. Nothing had been designed for the two of them together.

"I need time, space," she finally said. "To think. I have no clue where any of us go from here."

"Understood." He looked toward the draped window that would normally frame in the bar across the street.

He got up, and she grabbed his arm. "Don't do anything stupid."

"Ha." He shook her off. "That's all I know how to do." He strode toward the front door, but then spun around and headed for the hallway.

"Don't worry. I'm just going upstairs. At least there I can't hurt anyone."

She should get up, go after him, but her limbs wouldn't allow her to move. A storm brewed in her stomach and zinged through her exhausted muscles. She folded her arms on the table in front of her, lowered her head, and allowed tears to leak out.

When Chad went to prison, she'd wept for him, but always had the goal of freeing him to spur her on. Now, she had no goal but to reassemble a marriage that had been fractured and pieced together, then suddenly burst apart again. Did she have the desire to keep mortaring a marriage that shattered quicker than she could mend it?

The doorbell dinged and the front door slammed open. "Mom, what's going on?" Chloe hurried toward her, with Thomas close behind. "Why are the shades pulled? Where is everyone?"

Jenn sighed. Good thing Chloe had been serving the Saturday meal at the homeless shelter and had missed the drama. She loved her dad so much, witnessing his vile behavior would have tainted their relationship for good. Telling her about it would be bad enough.

She motioned for Chloe and Thomas to sit across from her. To no one's surprise, Chloe cried as Jenn relayed the story.

Thomas shook his head. "This isn't good."

"Tell me about it." Jenn drummed her fingers on the table, running scenarios through her mind of how she could save the shop. Her marriage. Every option wore her out and made her want to run away.

"Where did Dad go?" Chloe looked around. "Is he upstairs?"

Like Chad, Jenn couldn't look her daughter in the eyes. "He is."

"And you let him go alone?" Chloe motioned toward Thomas that she wanted out of the booth, and she practically pushed him out of her way. "He's depressed. Who knows what he might be doing?"

Mired in her own despondence, Jenn hadn't considered that. Maybe it was the kids' turn to do the fighting. "Go find him. Tell him I love him." Which was true. She always would, but was love enough anymore? She glanced across the table. "Thomas and I need to talk."

"I will. Someone has to care for Dad." She stalked down the hallway.

Jenn heard the apartment door slam and sighed with her entire body.

"You don't want to check on him?" Thomas remained standing.

"Right now, Chloe is better for him. We both need some space, or we'll say more that we'll regret." She motioned to the seat across from her. "Please sit."

He obliged and folded his hands on the table. "What do *you* need, Jenn?"

What did she need? To not feel exhausted anymore. To not worry that she'd say or do the wrong thing that would make him explode. Even though Chad was around nearly all the time, she felt alone. She was lonely for equal companionship, not a mother-child relationship. And for a moment, they'd had that. But now?

Marriage wasn't easy for anyone, but couples separated by years in prison had it more difficult. One article she'd read cited statistics showing that eighty percent of marriages don't survive the first year in prison when the husband is incarcerated and nearly a hundred percent when the wife is jailed. The divorce percentage grew by thirty-two percent for every year after that.

Where did that leave her and Chad?

She stared at her hands clenched on the table, then at Thomas's folded hands, and mumbled, "I don't think I can do it anymore."

"Jennifer . . ."

She looked him in the eyes. "You can't deny that you're lonely."

"I am." He squirmed and broke eye contact, not something the controlled attorney normally did.

"I am too."

"You have Chad."

She shook her head. "He's not the man I married, and you know that."

"But he is still your husband." Thomas stood and with one hand kneading his neck, he paced the room.

She couldn't believe she was going to say this. It was a reality she'd fought, but after today, she had to acknowledge the truth, though it broke her heart. "I don't know for how much longer. After today . . ." She shook her head and stood, her arms spread out at her sides. "How can I live with a man who says such horrific things?"

"You've said he was getting better."

"I thought he was, but now I have my doubts." She rested a hand on his arm.

And he turned to her, looked down on her, but didn't back away.

That gave her the courage to speak. "Take me with you on Monday."

He stood there, staring at her, hiding his thoughts as he'd been trained to do for his profession. Then he grasped her arms, leveled his gaze at her as if he was about to examine a witness on the stand. "I have one question for you."

She gulped and nodded.

"Are you in love with me?"

Something clattered behind them, and they both jerked toward the hallway. A cup lay on the floor between the shop and hallway, its dark brown contents pooling on the floor like blood. She hurried away from Thomas, through the hallway, watched Chad's figure push past Chloe by the apartment entrance and out the back door.

Chloe glanced between Jenn and the door then at Jenn. "What did you do now?"

"I—"

"Never mind." Chloe waved her off. "He never could be good enough for you. You're just like Gran."

Then Chloe hurried after him, and slammed the door behind her.

"You should go." Thomas gestured toward the hallway.

"No." Not if Chloe was right, not if Jenn was following in her own mother's judgmental footsteps. "I'd only make things worse."

Although they couldn't get much worse than her throwing herself at Thomas. What had she been thinking?

"Then have a seat, I'll make you a drink." He aimed for the bar.

"You know how?"

"I've watched enough baristas at work. I'll figure it out."

No doubt he would.

Moments later, he returned with a strawberry lemonade for her and a plain old coffee for himself.

She sipped at her drink. It was okay, but couldn't compare to what Chad would make. Somehow, his beverages always tasted better than anyone else's. He'd spoiled her in his three months of freedom.

But had he really been free? With all the obstacles he had to overcome, with her hovering over him, making sure he did everything exactly the right way, had he really been free?

"I'm sorry." She breached the awkward silence between them.

"I'm sorry for the moment I considered your offer." He sipped at his coffee then placed it on the table. "The idea of not being alone is a very attractive one, but I refuse to satisfy my own wants at the expense of your marriage."

Always a man of integrity. Someday, he'd find someone to fill that loneliness. The right someone.

As for her and Chad's future, that chapter was yet to be written.

Speaking of Chad . . . She glanced toward the hallway. What was taking Chloe so long? Jenn had expected her to return quickly.

She heard the front doorknob wiggle, then Chloe entered, perspiring and breathing hard as if she'd run a marathon.

"Where's your father?" Jenn stood so quickly, her chair toppled, clattering to the floor.

"I don't know." Chloe went behind the bar and poured herself some water. "He took off running, and I couldn't keep up, and then I lost him." She checked her phone. "I tried calling him, but no answer."

She took a long sip of water, wiped her mouth, and glared at Jenn with a laser-like focus. "What happened? Why did Dad run away?"

Jenn swallowed, but it didn't rid her of the guilt. "Your father heard me say something irrational to Thomas."

Chloe looked between Jenn and Thomas, then her eyes widened. "No." She shook her head for what seemed like a minute. "The two of you? Have you been cheating on Dad?"

"What? No!" Jenn slammed her drink down and lemonade splashed from the cup. She felt a nudge at her elbow, and Thomas gave her a look that made her feel more guilty. It was a wonder he didn't compel everyone who took the stand to speak *the truth, the whole truth, and nothing but the truth.*

Oh, she hated having to admit her sins to her daughter, but maybe that was the first step in healing, if healing was still possible. "I, uh . . ." She looked at Thomas, and he nodded. "I . . . uh . . . asked Thomas if I could return with him to Boston."

What a fool she was. God had to be mightily disappointed in her.

"It was a moment of irrational weakness—"

"But Dad isn't allowed to say something wrong?"

Ouch. The truth smacked her in the heart.

"You're right, Chloe." She owed her husband and family a huge apology, once Chad was found. She prayed he wasn't at the bar across the street. If he was, it would be her fault.

Chloe downed her drink. "I'm heading out to find him. Jase is on his way home from Elaine's and is keeping his eye out for Dad."

"I'll come with you, Chloe." Thomas set aside his drink.

"And I'll wait here in case he returns." Jenn took out her phone. "Everyone, please keep in touch."

They nodded their assent.

Then something Chloe had said poked at Jenn. "Wait, you knew about Jason and Elaine?"

"Well, duh." She headed out the front door with Thomas.

Yeah, of course she knew. They were twins. They shared everything with each other.

They used to share everything with her.

How had she muddled everything up this past year, when she'd been working so hard to make everything right?

Rather than sit and feel sorry for herself, she could at least clean the shop. It wasn't going to open tomorrow—of that she was certain. But would it open Monday? A week from now? Ever?

Mom had dangled that kindergarten teacher opening a few days ago. Perhaps she was right. Perhaps they should close the shop, say they gave it a good try, and get on with their lives without the stress of running a small business.

Especially one in which they'd chased away all their customers. There was no way it could survive.

Jenn hand-washed the remaining dishes, covered all the containers and syrup pumps, mopped the floors. She cleaned the espresso machines and turned them off. She removed the remaining chocolates and placed them in boxes to be sold later, should the shop ever open again. Lastly, she counted and balanced the drawers. Even with Chad's blunder, it had been a good day.

She emptied the tip jar and placed it all in an envelope to give to Elaine. She'd been the only employee working, so she'd earned it all, but hopefully it wouldn't be seen as an attempt to buy her off.

What Jenn needed was to go outside in the fresh air, sit on the swing, watch the river flow over and around obstacles. Smooth out rough edges. Carve niches and detours around those obstacles. The river didn't stop flowing because it encountered roadblocks.

She wouldn't either. Regardless of what Chad did tonight, she had to keep fighting for their marriage. Her during-prison motto had been, Fight Until He's Freed. Maybe it should have been, Fight Until He's Home, because that was still a work in progress. It hadn't been a true home to him, not yet.

She locked the front door, but kept the lights on. She also turned on music, so the shop looked and sounded like someone was there. Then she stepped out the back door, locked it behind herself, and headed for the swing.

Someone was there already. She squinted. Chad?

She jogged toward the swing. Yes, it was him. Had he been here all along? She stopped and sent out a group text, letting them know she'd found him, thank God.

"Chad," she called out, giving him a heads-up that she was approaching.

He stood and held out his hands. "You really don't want to come any closer."

"Why n—" The stench of alcohol stung her nostrils. Oh, no. He'd been gone two hours at the most, yet he still managed to reek like a brewery.

This was entirely her fault. No, that was a lie. His choices weren't her fault, but she'd still do whatever she could to make it better. She wouldn't stop fighting until he found his way home.

Chapter Twenty-Three

Chad had been afraid this would happen. "It's not what it looks—or smells—like."

She stopped. Stood silent, as if measuring her words. Something he wished he'd learn to do. If he'd only kept silent, none of this would have happened. Their relationship would still be moving forward rather than retreating so far that he doubted they'd ever make up the distance between them.

"Then talk to me." She approached him slowly, gestured to the swings.

They both sat with the tumbling river within their sight.

"I went to the bar." Chad clung to the swing's chains. "Angry with God, with you, Thomas, planning to get plastered, but God intervened."

She studied him, opened her mouth as if wanting to refute what he'd said. He knew his odor contradicted his words.

"One of our customers from this afternoon recognized me, called me some names I deserved, then baptized me with his beer."

She closed her eyes, breathed in, and sat up straight, clearly relieved. "I'm sorry I doubted you."

"You had every reason to."

"But why didn't Chloe see you enter? She ran out after you."

"Do you think I wanted her to see me go into a bar?" He rocked on his swing, his toes anchoring him to the ground. "I ran. Hid. Doubled back. All part of a really idiotic plan."

"I'm sorry I led you to that."

Yeah. This was the part of the conversation he didn't want to have, but it was necessary. "I was . . ." What? Mad? No, not that. Not really sad either. Grieving, maybe, for what he was about to give up. "It hurt."

"I'm sorry."

"Don't be."

"But—"

He held up his hand. "One thing my counselor taught me is that when we do react strongly to something, there's a measure of truth in that reaction. When I insulted Elaine, it was because I learned in prison that people of other races aren't to be trusted. It's wrong. It's not true, but it's not easy to unlearn something. God and I are working on that."

He looked upward at a blue sky just beginning to surrender to dusk. "After I left the bar, I came out here to yell at God, but I couldn't, not when He's gifted us with this." He spread his arms out, framing in a fraction of nature. "God's creation shouldn't be—couldn't be—caged. People shouldn't be either."

He stood and walked to the river's edge. Jenn followed, as he'd expected.

"Chad. Don't." Worry embedded her voice as she gripped his arm, pulled him back.

"I'm not jumping." Though her reaction wasn't without merit. Ex-cons committed suicide eighteen times as often as the general population. He knew that from research in his early days in prison, when he'd believed death was the best way out for him and the family. "I'm releasing you." The words burned from his throat as if acid poured from it.

"What? No." She grabbed both his arms.

Reluctantly, he turned her way. Seeing Jenn's face could convince him to change his mind. Man, he loved her so much, it hurt.

"I don't know what you heard me say to Thomas—"

"Do you love him?"

"What?"

"I heard his question. Do you love Thomas?"

Jen cupped his cheeks, wiped them with her thumbs. "No, not like that."

He hadn't even realized he'd been crying, but how can you not when you're severing a limb? "Yet you asked to go home with him." That was what had stung.

She looked away, not denying what he'd heard.

"Truth?" she finally asked.

"Always."

She gestured to the swings, perhaps not trusting him so close to the river's edge. They sat, swung without their feet leaving the ground.

"The truth is." She sighed, and stilled her swing. "I'm tired, and yes, going home with Thomas, in that moment, was very appealing. It would mean no more struggle. No more heartbreak, because I could never love him like I love you."

For some reason, that didn't make him feel better. Perhaps it only encouraged his decision. "The fact is, I've caused you heartbreak."

"No. This situation has. We're doing the best we can."

"Yet even our best isn't good enough." Oh, he wanted it to be. He wanted the happily ever after that romance novels bragged about. But every time things got better, something would come along and derail their relationship. "I'm tired, too. Tired of not ever being good enough. Tired of these prison shackles I'll never be able to remove." He angled toward her, trailed a finger down the side of her face. "Tired of hurting you. I can't stick around and hurt you more."

"And I won't let you go." She took his hand and pressed his palm against her cheek.

"Cocoa." He wanted to kiss her, but that would weaken his resolve. "Until I deal with my demons, it's best for me to leave."

"And go where?" Tears fogged her eyes, trembled in her voice. "The homeless shelter? No way. And your dad's in Florida."

"Dad would take me in." Though the thought of having all those states separating him from his family sat in his gut like rotten meat.

"No." She shook her head, stood, and paced the backyard for several minutes. She returned to him, resolve written on her face. "Fine. If you think we need a separation, I'll go to Mom and Dad's. Apply for that kindergarten teaching job she's been telling me about. This place." She gestured toward the store. “It was always for you. Even if the store doesn’t open, it’s a place to live.”

He glanced at the shop, then at Jenn. “Are you sure?”

“About you staying here? Yes. About the separation, no. I’m not giving up on you. On us. That’s a promise.”

And then she kissed him. He shouldn’t have, but he couldn’t resist kissing her back, pouring out all his regrets and frustrations. Letting her know he still loved her.

Enough to let her go.

SURRENDER

And he said to all, "If anyone would come after me, let him deny himself and take up his cross daily and follow me. For whoever would save his life will lose it, but whoever loses his life for my sake will save it.

Luke 9:23-24

Chapter Twenty-Four

Jenn never imagined she'd be back in her old bedroom again. She surveyed the deep purple walls she'd loved as a teen and hadn't painted when she'd moved in after Chad had been found guilty. That stay wasn't meant to be permanent. Then she'd moved out over a year ago, filled with hope and excitement and a sense of freedom.

Freedom . . .

A word filled with promise and hope that came with painful cost.

She threw one of her suitcases on the bed and unzipped it. She unpacked into drawers Mom had been too eager to clean out for her. Jenn had told her it was temporary, but Mom was still hopeful.

Problem was, Jenn was at a loss for what to do now. She sat on the bed and covered her eyes, though they'd been drained dry.

When Chad was in prison, she'd enlisted Thomas's help, never giving up on searching for the truth and fighting for Chad's freedom. Even when he'd been freed, she'd worked hard at making his transition from prison as smooth as she could, though it had been much more difficult than she'd imagined. She'd fought to keep their marriage upright, to love him through his problems. Somehow, she'd failed dismally.

She had no more fight left in her.

Maybe a separation was for the best. Maybe not being tethered to him constantly would build her strength enough for the next battle, because there certainly would be one. Giving up was not an option.

She scooted against the headboard and pulled a blanket over her lap. What she needed was a book, but she hadn't packed one on this trip. Mom and Dad had books, but she had no desire to face them again tonight. She'd told them to eat supper without her. Guess she'd take a nap and deal with life tomorrow. She laid down and covered herself with the blanket. Closed her eyes. Imagined her and Chad at Cuppa Truth before tragedy turned their lives topsy-turvy.

Knock. Knock.

Jenn bolted upright and blinked. Checked the clock. A whole thirty minutes had passed since she'd come upstairs. What part of "leave me alone" didn't Mom understand? She wanted to tell her mother off, but her folks had taken her in when they didn't have to.

"Come in," she said, with only a hint of a growl.

The door opened, and Dad stood on the other side. So, Mom was sending him to do her dirty work.

"Mind if I come in, Petunia?"

Softening her with his pet name, huh?

Well, it worked, but she had no intention of showing him that. Instead, she shrugged and hugged herself, as she'd seen Chloe do. "It's your home."

"And your room. We've always respected your privacy." He gestured to the side of the bed. "May I sit?"

She scooted over, giving him space. Dad had never been the one who comforted her after hardship, though he hadn't been critical of her, like Mom had.

"You'll have to forgive your mother," he said, as if reading her mind. "She means well, but she's not good at showing empathy."

That was the understatement of the year.

"All your mother's wanted for you is to avoid the chaos she had with her own folks. She blames their poverty for their problems, when it was poverty of spirit that broke your grandparents' marriage. They didn't have your faith or the selflessness you and Chad share. They didn't have the desire to press through obstacles. Your mother wants to remove those obstacles for you. It pains her to see you hurting. When you and Chad work things out—"

"You really think we will?" She hugged a pillow against her chest. At this moment, she had her doubts about saving her marriage, but that didn't mean she'd stop fighting.

"*When* you do, your mother will see the truth."

She harumphed at that.

"She only wants the best for you, and that, my Petunia, is Chad."

"How do I convince him of that?"

"Ah, I see you still have your old Bible." Avoiding her question, he picked up the Bible Mom and Dad had given her for her confirmation when she was thirteen. One with her name engraved on the now well-worn leather. That book had gotten her through her high school years, through her first relationship, and then her engagement with Thomas. She'd treated herself to a new Bible when she started dating Chad, to symbolize, if only for herself, new beginnings.

He thumbed through the pages, stopping in Exodus. "The parting of the Red Sea. That's what I'm looking for." He handed the Bible, open to Exodus, chapter fourteen, over to her.

She scanned the chapter. Was he comparing her relationship with Chad to that of the Israelites' flight for freedom and being trapped between the Red Sea and Pharoah's army? Quite the stretch, if you asked her.

"Did you see it?"

"See what?"

"Sorry. Your mother is much better at this than I am." He took the Bible, read, then pointed out verse fourteen. "Your mother said you've been going to battle all the wrong ways. She hoped I'd be able to help."

Mom said that? Jenn read verse fourteen, one she'd highlighted years ago, to herself. *The Lord will fight for you, and you have only to be silent.* Then all Moses had to do was stretch his hand over the sea, and God parted it, allowing the Israelites to cross over to freedom.

"Do you see it now?"

"I'm sorry, Dad, I'm clueless. Maybe I'm too tired."

"Good. That's when God can really work through you, child. You've been fighting for Chad and your marriage, and you've worn yourself thin. Perhaps it's time to get on your knees and let God do the fighting for you. You only need to be silent." With that, Dad kissed her forehead. "Know that your mother and I love you, and even though she won't say it out loud, stubborn woman, she's rooting for you and Chad. He's been put through so much, yet still loves the Lord. Let me tell you, the devil isn't happy about that, and when you battle on your knees, you will defeat him. Freedom is all about surrender."

So, she didn't have to fight anymore?

"Sleep well, Petunia. We'll see you tomorrow." Her father left the room and quietly shut her door.

Sleep wasn't possible now that she'd been given a battle plan. And to think it had been in front of her eyes all this time. She got out of bed, spread her Bible open in front of her, and surrendered.

Chapter Twenty-Five

The empty shop was too quiet, even for a late Sunday afternoon which, when it had been open, had always been slow.

After another sleepless night on the bedroom floor, Chad had spent the morning doing church on his own, like he had in prison. He read the Bible, prayed, and did a whole bunch of complaining and then apologizing. Asked for wisdom concerning Jenn, though he already knew God wanted to kick him in the butt for sending her away. Perhaps that should have convinced him to get on the phone with Jenn and beg her to come home, but he couldn't shake the voice inside that reminded him she was better off without him.

That voice had grown loud in prison. Now it only whispered, which was almost worse. Another reason he hated silence.

He asked Zena to turn on music, Jenn's worship playlist. Maybe not his first choice in music anymore, but it was certainly better than the garbage he'd been filling his brain with. Could it be that the lyrics he'd been ingesting hadn't helped his transition to freedom? Few were honorable, pure, lovely, or any of those things mentioned in Philippians that God commanded him to focus on.

"Different music for you." Chloe came up to him from the hallway and kissed him on the cheek. She'd been putzing around in the kitchen, making more chocolates for the store. Why, if they weren't going to open?

"Yep. Something more uplifting."

"Not a bad choice." She'd insisted on staying with him and not following Jenn, though he'd tried his best to convince her otherwise.

Stubborn, like her mother. Jason had moved in with his friend Carlos. Getting away from both Chad and Jenn was probably very healthy. In turn, Chad had given Chloe free rein of the attic space. At least until they were kicked out for not being able to make the mortgage payment. If Jason ever talked with him again, he'd find out where the store stood financially. Whatever the case, he didn't plan to abandon it.

Like he'd abandoned Jenn?

No, he'd set her free. There was a difference. The coffee shop had never been her idea, but she'd gone along with the dream for him. She'd opened this store for him. Now he was finally able to free her from that obligation, even if his heart complained loudly.

"What do you think?" He rubbed his stubbly chin. "Should we open tomorrow?"

"I would have opened today. I wouldn't have given people the satisfaction of us being closed." She walked around the store, examining the commissioned artwork on the wall, the shelving filled with plates and cups salvaged from a secondhand shop. The free library. The food shelf. What was she thinking?

Finally, she turned to him. "Have you ever considered speaking to a newspaper?"

Say what? "Why would I want to do that?" He walked behind the bar and poured himself a plain coffee. With the shop closed, he didn't want to dirty all the equipment.

"You've got a story, Dad." She sat on a stool at the bar, directly across from him. "This town needs to hear it. They need to know how prison changes a person, how tough it is reintegrating into society—socially, mentally, and emotionally. That nothing is easy for the ex-con, the emphasis on *ex*. If our so-called justice system wants to reduce recidivism, then our society has to have a hand in that change. May as well start right here in Donaldson." She slammed a fist on the bar.

He stared at this young woman he was blessed to call "daughter." She'd always been spirited, but this was the next level. Still, what she was fighting for didn't apply to him. Did it? "I don't have a story, not like a lot of the guys I was in with. I've been lucky. I had a place to come home to, a job waiting for me." Though it had placed financial stress on Jenn, and he hadn't heard from the companies he'd applied at.

"I disagree. This is a good town, a caring town that needs to know your story. Mom's too. Even mine and Jase's. When someone goes to prison, their entire family loses their freedom. Once this town knows what you've . . . what we've all been through, they'll be more forgiving when we make a mistake."

"I don't know." He poured a coffee for Chloe and stirred in one of the chocolates remaining from yesterday. Airing his dirty laundry to the world didn't sit well with him. And Jenn certainly wouldn't go along with that invasion of privacy.

"Nope. You're not allowed to give in." She checked her watch, which was more like a miniature computer. That still blew his mind. "Tonight, you can test the waters with church."

"Church?"

"Well yeah. Your church meets here in about thirty minutes." She took a sip of the coffee drink. "Oh, this is good."

"I knew you'd like it." At least he hadn't lost his touch when it came to making coffee.

"And I know you'll appreciate having your church family support you."

"If they come."

"I'll facilitate tonight since Mom isn't here. Barbara has already said she'll bring treats. Caleb and Lissa offered to lead the Bible study. Jase said he'd bring—"

"Jason's coming?"

"Of course he is, and he's bringing his guitar."

"He plays guitar?"

"Yep. And he sings. With Elaine."

"I didn't know."

"He's always kept it private. Doesn't like attention. But he likes to play, and this small group is the perfect size for him"

What else didn't he know about his kids?

"Wow," he said more to himself than Chloe. "And you think this group would like to hear my story?"

"Mom always told me that's who the church is. I haven't always paid attention like I should. I've sort of been upset with God lately. But if you can't be open and honest with fellow believers, who can you be truthful with?"

He stared into his mug at the black coffee, as if he'd see a dark image of himself glaring back at him. He struggled enough with being open with Jenn and his counselor. There were many things he could never tell Jenn, so how would he be able to share with people who were really strangers to him?

"Can I think about it?" Asking for his daughter's permission felt strange, but in this instance, that was the right thing to do.

"Sure." She finished off her coffee. "You have exactly fifteen minutes to think about it, and your answer better be *yes*."

He laughed in spite of his unease. "You sound like your mother."

"I'll take that as a compliment."

It was. "Okay, here's the deal." He rested his arms on the bar top and leaned toward her. A conversation she'd had with him at Eastertime still weighed on his heart. "I'll share my story *if* you tell your mother what you told me at Easter."

Her shoulders sagged, and all her bluster seemed to disappear. She nibbled on her lower lip as she studied her empty cup. "She'll be disappointed in me."

"Hey, baby girl." He reached over and raised her chin until her eyes met his. "More so, she'll love you through this in a way I'm not able to."

"I suppose." Her focus remained downcast.

"It's a deal then? I talk tonight, and you go visit your mom, soon."

"I'll talk to her."

"That's my girl." He came around the counter and hugged his daughter, who'd suffered through her own ordeal lately. "Now if we're having church here tonight, I suppose we should get ready."

Right on time, Barbara, alongside her husband, knocked on the door of Chad's Choco-Latte Corner. She balanced one of those charcuterie boards with berries, grapes, nuts, carrots, meats, cheese, and crackers. It looked too fancy for their little gathering.

Chad opened the door and took the board from her, forced himself to greet the couple as if yesterday hadn't happened, though he struggled with looking them in the eye. "Thanks for coming, and for this." He raised the board slightly. "I don't know what anyone else is going to eat."

"That's what I told her." Her husband offered his hand in greeting.

Barbara laughed. "Jenn said you appreciate food."

"And I have the abs to prove it." He patted his stomach, which had lost its washboard shape. That was perfectly fine with him, as he'd been too thin. All muscle with no meat. But after surviving on prison food for years, he planned to appreciate freedom food. So what if he gained a little weight along the way.

He set the board beside the carafe of coffee and cups on the coffee table placed in the middle of a circle of chairs. The attendees could snack before, during, and after the service. Though their church didn't really hold a service in the formal sense of the word. They'd have fellowship time followed by music, then they'd dig into the Bible. And even that wasn't set in stone. They went with the flow. If someone needed extra care, this group gave it to them.

Jenn had done this for him, too, knowing that crowds would be intimidating for him.

Minutes later, Jenn's carpenter, Caleb, along with his wife and two daughters, showed up, followed shortly by Carlos, which took him by surprise. Why would a young Hispanic man show up at the shop of a bigot? Showed that the kid's character was far better than his own. No wonder Chloe and Jason had befriended him.

Speaking of Jason, would he really show up? And if he did, would his son speak to him?

He started perspiring just fretting over it, even though he knew the Bible said not to worry. Another spiritual growth item on his massive work-in-progress list.

"You sure Jason's coming?" He whispered to Chloe, seated beside him in the circle. Carlos sat next to her. An apology would never be enough for what Chad had done to Elaine, but that was all Chad had to give. That and getting better was all he could do. But would that be enough for his son? For Jenn?

Chad checked the time. He may not need the buzzer anymore to get anything done, but being timely was ingrained into him now. Prompt, like Jason and Jenn. If his son hadn't showed up by now, he likely wasn't coming, so Chad nudged Chloe to get things started. Before prison, he would have been the life of the party, wouldn't have worried about living by the clock, but doing time had sucked the extrovert out of him, and these events stressed him now instead. Especially since he'd promised Chloe he'd share his testimony.

"Okay," she whispered, then she sat up. Cleared her throat. "Hey everyone, thanks for coming. Jase is bringing his guitar, so maybe we'll sing after—"

A jingle announced the door opening again, and Jason stepped inside with his guitar.

And Elaine.

And a man walking with a prosthetic leg, someone who looked like he could be Elaine's father.

Chad gulped. The man wouldn't punch him in church, would he? Though Chad would certainly deserve it.

"Speaking of Jase, we now have music!" Chloe got up and hugged her brother and Elaine.

"Sorry I'm late." Jason sat and removed his guitar from its case.

"My fault." The man who came in with them sat beside Elaine, his gaze flitting past Chad's. "I got busy with housecleaning and the time got away from me."

"By the way, everyone, this is Mr. Kim, Elaine's dad." Jason made the introduction.

"Call me Patrick."

The guests took turns introducing themselves. Jason completely ignored his father, and Elaine dodged his gaze. The closer the intros came to Chad, the more he sweated. Beside him, Chloe stated her name, and said that she was Jason's twin, Chad's daughter.

Signaling that it was his turn.

He gulped, tried to look Patrick Kim in the eye, but failed. Instead, he looked beyond him, at the bar, the place where Chad's mistake had cost him everything.

"I'm Chad. Not Chadwick, not Nebu-Chad-Nezzer, just Chad," he spouted his before-prison introduction nervously. Somehow it no longer flowed from his tongue. Once upon a time, it had charmed Jenn and other women. Now it felt clunky. He cleared his throat and began again. "I'm the Chad of Chad's Choco-Latte Corner."

"Nice to meet you all," Patrick said and looked directly at Chad, whose mouth went completely dry. "If you don't mind, I'd love to have a word with you afterwards."

Chad nodded. Wiped his mouth. He could imagine what Patrick Kim would have to say, most likely communicating with his fist. Not that Chad didn't deserve what the man threw at him—if someone had spoken like that to Chloe, Chad wouldn't have been able to contain himself.

"Before we begin"—Chloe spoke with a confidence he hadn't heard before—"Dad was wondering if he could tell his story, for those of you not familiar with it."

No, he wasn't wondering that, and had hoped Chloe would forget. He studied his fidgeting, perspiring hands as he listened to several voices urge him to tell it. Jason's wasn't among them, no surprise.

Still, he robotically talked about their before-prison time, them being an average family. How Chad had stopped by Cuppa Truth, after hours, to request more hours because raising kids was expensive. How he'd found his mentor on the floor, lying in a pool of blood, a stapler the obvious weapon. If only he hadn't picked it up. If only he hadn't tried to revive Garrett, and had called 9-1-1 right away instead. Then his best friend wouldn't have found him holding the murder weapon, his fingerprints the only ones on it besides Garrett's.

He summarized the arrest, the jail time, the trial. Conviction, then eight years combined spent in jail and prison before the town gardener confessed his guilt in a suicide letter explaining where further evidence could be found. Not enough to erase Chad's conviction, so he'd forever be an ex-con.

Then he talked about coming home. About how wonderful Jenn and the kids had been through everything. But then he told them about the too-soft bedding, about not fitting in or finding a job. Panicking in crowds, overreacting to situations.

Which ultimately led to his abhorrent behavior yesterday that spelled The End, not only for the coffee shop, but also his marriage.

"As you can see." Chloe took his sweaty hand and didn't flinch. "Life after prison isn't easy. Dad is fortunate in that he has a home and family and even work, but few ex-convicts do. How can we expect people to get healthy if we don't provide opportunity?"

There was some mumbled assent, which he understood. Garrett had been the only person he'd known who gave potential troublemakers a chance. At one time, that had been Chad, before he met Jenn, who had introduced him to Jesus.

"Anyway. Not one of those people who walked out of the store yesterday was perfect, right? We've all made mistakes, some bigger than others." Chloe squeezed his hand, an acknowledgement of what she'd told him and sworn him to secrecy over. "That said, I believe we should open up the store again tomorrow."

Barbara clapped. "Good for you. I'm right with you."

"I also realize we'll have to do some damage control, maybe offer specials to entice customers to return."

"Ha." That from Barbara's husband. "The second they all need their coffee fix, they'll be back."

"I agree," Caleb's wife said, while bouncing a toddler on her lap.

"But that's easy for us to say." Barbara brought her mug to her lips, then lowered it. "We don't have money on the line, so weigh our opinions with that."

Chloe nodded. "We will. And we appreciate your encouragement. I guess that leads to a second question I had." Chloe gripped his hand for support. Or to support him? He wasn't certain. "Barbara, do you think the *Donaldson Herald* would be interested in interviewing Dad? I think it's important for him to share his side of the story with the town, not just our church."

"Hmm." Barbara tapped her chin. "I think that sounds like a brilliant story, and the *Herald* is always looking for human interest pieces. I happen to have an in with the editor, if you'd like me to contact her. Besides, she owes me." Barbara concluded with a smirk.

"We'd love that, wouldn't we, Dad?"

He felt Chloe's gaze on him, so he forced up his chin, and looked at her, then smiled. "It would be good." Not that he had a desire to bare his soul to an entire town who now hated him and would think he was whining. In prison, that would have landed him in the infirmary.

"Then that's settled. Almost." Barbara reached her hands to those beside her. "Let's not wait, let's begin in prayer."

She prayed as if Jesus sat right beside them, with an intimacy that was foreign to him. The whole group prayed for him, the store, Jenn, the kids. Hands rested on his shoulders as different people prayed over him. The Holy Spirit's presence filled his being with goose bumps. Only in prison, when his life had been threatened, had he known without a doubt that the Holy Spirit was in his presence.

Music—guitar strums—came from his left. His eyes still closed, he listened to Jason and Elaine sing a beautiful tenor-alto duet. Others joined in singing lyrics that spoke of God's goodness and the cross.

Then the chorus reached into his heart with words Chad had literally lived, and he couldn't sing along. Not these words speaking of once being a prisoner, but then being freed by the blood of Jesus. That was true freedom.

He looked to his son, who nodded and offered a smile—small, but it was a smile. Absolution. For the rest of the song, he listened, but mostly kept his eye on Jason, this young man Chad was blessed to call "son," who, in spite of the difficulties he'd faced over the years when Chad was absent, had turned into a responsible, caring, God-fearing young man.

The same went for Chloe.

Because of their mother, the family had not only held together in his absence, but they'd prospered.

Until he'd returned home, and their lives had shattered. Didn't Jenn deserve better? How could he believe that his getting back together with Jenn was the best thing for all of them, when their lives were in turmoil?

Caleb's wife had them all turn to Psalm 139 in their Bibles. Another Chloe-plan to lift him up? He practically knew the Psalm by heart. In prison, he'd wrestled with God knowing all his days and that he was fearfully and wonderfully made. For some reason, on the inside, he'd come to believe those words. There, he'd had purpose, but on the outside? Things had been improving until yesterday. Some days it seemed like he'd stepped out of one prison and into another.

None too soon, the discussion surrounding Psalm 139 ended with him having contributed nothing but a few nods. Honestly, right now, he was just confused.

Chloe closed in prayer that he heard little of, then guests slowly excused themselves.

"Thanks, everyone, for coming." Chloe hurried to the door and held it open, playing hostess to perfection. He took her side, standing there with a plied-on smile.

He waved as the young family left, followed by Carlos.

Barbara's husband offered his hand. "Hang in there, Chad. You've got all these people rooting for you, praying for you. Open these doors tomorrow, show this town you're not leaving with your tail between your legs. The townsfolk'll appreciate that."

"I agree," said Barbara. "And I plan to do a little coaxing on your behalf as well." She winked.

"You don't have to." The mayor could hurt her reputation by standing up for him.

"You're right. I don't. But I want to."

That should have encouraged him, but it only added to his confusion.

In the dining room, Jason sat with Elaine and her father. Fear inched up Chad's spine. He'd nearly forgotten that the man wanted a moment with him. Now that there were no witnesses, Chad would allow the man to take his best shot.

"Time for you to head upstairs." Chad kissed his daughter on the cheek. She didn't need to see her father get pummeled.

"Things are going to get better, Dad. Just watch." Chloe said goodbye to Jason and Elaine.

"Could we join you upstairs for a bit?" Jason looked from Mr. Kim to Chad to Chloe, his hand permanently connected to Elaine's, it seemed.

"Sure. Come on up."

The three kids scurried away, and Chad took in a slow breath. May as well get this over with now. Once the beating was done, he'd sooth it with ice packs. That was more than he'd had in prison.

He held up his chin as he approached Mr. Kim, who stood with his arms crossed. The man's facial expression didn't scream anger, but perhaps he was good at hiding his feelings.

Should he offer to get the man a coffee? Nope. Not a good idea. Chad could handle a fist to the face, but boiling coffee? He debated offering his hand along with an apology, but pocketed both hands instead. "Thanks for staying." The words felt forced out over gravel. "I know an apology won't cut it, but I deeply regret what I said to Elaine. It just came out, but that doesn't make it right. And I am sorry."

He steeled himself for the blow, but the man stood there, arms crossed, unmoving.

Then he gestured toward the chairs.

Okay . . .

Perplexed, Chad pulled a chair from the circle and positioned himself facing Patrick from a few feet away.

The man bowed his head. Praying? Then looked up. "Apology accepted."

Chad blinked and pressed back in his chair as if a fist actually had punched him. "I don't understand."

Elaine's father crossed an ankle over his other knee, the one attached to his prosthetic leg, and looked Chad in the eye. In prison, that would have been a challenge. Chad gulped and did his best not to be cowardly and look away.

"I served three years in Iran." Patrick nodded to his leg. "One step in the wrong direction ended my service."

"I'm sorry."

"My wife was too." He uncrossed his legs, placed both feet on the floor. "The leg didn't bother her, but my attitude did. Nightmares. Anxiety. Depression. Problems sleeping. Panic attacks." He looked down. "Lashing out at her or anyone over random triggers. The therapist calls it PTSD."

Chad stilled at the term and the too-familiar list of behaviors. He hadn't had nightmares, but the rest was him to a T. "How did you deal with it?"

The man laughed. "Alcohol was my first choice, which of course gets you nowhere."

"I second that."

"When my wife left me and Elaine for another man, well, that got my attention." His foot bounced on the floor. "I finally sought professional help. Spent more time in nature. Started going to church."

All of which Chad had done.

"But one of the most effective things was getting together with brothers and sisters who understood what I was going through. A place without judgement."

Exactly what Chad needed.

"I recognize symptoms of PTSD when I see it, so I'd like you to join us."

Chad blinked. "How did you know I . . . ?" He gulped. He'd never admitted this aloud, not even to his counselor, though she'd thrown the label his way. "That I have . . ." He sighed, hating to say the letters aloud, but he gulped and forced it out. "That I have PTSD?"

"Elaine." Patrick sat up straight. "For full disclosure, I didn't know for sure after she came home and told me what happened the other day. Let's just say, it was a good thing my car was in the shop. But the more I thought about it, having heard your prison story from my daughter, the more I comprehended why you'd reacted that way. I realized you were a brother in need. By the end of church this morning, God had completely softened my heart, and I knew that He was calling me to help you."

Chad looked upward, resisted the tears that too often wanted to flow.

Another prison by-product.

"There is one caveat, though."

Of course there was, because life never flowed smoothly.

"The last place we were meeting has new owners, and they use the space for something else. We've been meeting in homes, but if we could gather in this shop on an evening you're closed, we'd be grateful."

"That's your condition?"

"Not really a condition. You're welcome to join us, regardless. But if we could meet here, that would solve a lot of problems."

For the first time today, Chad felt a genuine smile. "It's yours. Name a night. Coffee and treats on the house." That was the least he could do for the man not bashing his face in.

"We appreciate it." Patrick stood and offered his hand.

Chad rose and accepted it. "Thank you for your grace."

He nodded, but then a scowl took over his face. "But don't do it again."

"I won't." He prayed that was a promise he could keep.

"One other thing." Patrick crossed his arms, looked Chad in the eyes. "Don't let that wife of yours get away. Biggest mistake of my life. Don't let your depression convince you she's better off without you. From what I've heard from Elaine, Jenn adores you, so you'd be believing a lie. Surrender those lies to the truth, and talk with the One who is the Truth. That's your first step in getting better."

Chapter Twenty-Six

Jenn's stomach growled as she submitted one more online application. She reclined in her desk chair and sighed. She'd begun applying late in the summer, nearly August, so many of the positions had been filled already.

Of course, there was that one offer already on the table that she'd been praying about without a firm answer. Two weeks of fasting, Bible reading, praise and prayer—fighting on her knees—and she still waited for answers to two life-changing questions.

Do I take the offered position?

But more importantly, *Can I return to Chad?*

Whatever the answers were, she was at peace for the first time in years. She'd always thought she'd allowed God to have control of her life, but these past two weeks had opened her eyes. Yes, she'd prayed for God to take control, but then she'd always stolen the reins back.

Praying and fasting had helped her surrender, but Mom wasn't happy with the fasting part.

Speaking of Mom, she was probably waiting impatiently for Jenn to come down for supper, though water was her meal of choice at the moment. She'd closed her laptop and was heading for the door when Chloe's ringtone went off, probably her daughter calling with her daily update. Mom would have to wait.

Jenn pulled her phone from her pocket and swiped Answer. "How's it going?"

Silence followed by a noise that sounded like a car door slamming shut. "Are you home?"

What did she mean by home? That was on the other side of the metro area. "I'm at your grandma's."

"Yeah, that's what I meant."

Jenn heard a horn honk through the phone and outside her window.

"Are you here?" She hurried to the window overlooking the driveway. Yep. There was Chloe, striding toward the front door with something clutched in her hand. A newspaper?

Oh, boy. That didn't bode well. She could imagine the headlines lambasting Chad and the coffee shop for being racist.

"We need to talk."

I'm sure you do.

"I'll be right there. Let yourself in. Grandma will be thrilled to see you." *Just don't show her the paper.* Jenn jabbed at the End Call button, grabbed her wallet and keys, and hurried downstairs. This talk needed to be handled away from this home.

By the time Jenn arrived in the kitchen, Mom already had Chloe seated at the table, naturally, the newspaper—the *Donaldson Herald*—open beside her plate. *Wonderful.* More ammunition for Mom to fire at Chad.

Jenn forced herself to look at the paper and did a double-take at the below-the-fold headline: Local Business Owner Fighting the Stigma of the Ex-Con.

Without saying anything, Jenn picked up the paper, sat, and read through the article. Then read it again.

No condemnation for his racial slur, but rather an explanation behind it along with Chad's repeated apology. Forgiveness from Elaine and Patrick Kim. And it shared a snippet of the difficulties he had adjusting to life on the outside, not just for him but for his family. It didn't make him out to be a victim, but offered sympathy.

"Quite the article, isn't it?" Mom set a plate with lasagna in front of Chloe.

All Jenn could do was nod. She barely heard her mother's blessing over the food.

"It's helped the town understand Dad." Chloe took a bite of the lasagna and moaned her satisfaction. "I forgot how good your lasagna is, Gran."

Jenn's mouth watered at that, and she glanced at the other filled plates around the table. The scent made her salivate more. To make it worse, her stomach joined in. But she couldn't break her fast yet, not without some answers to her prayers, though this article was pointing in the direction of reconciliation.

"Has it helped the business?" She'd prayed the incident would be forgotten, but people had long memories.

"It has." Chloe scooped a second helping of lasagna. "But it's not the same."

"What do you mean?"

Chloe shrugged. Chewed. Swallowed half a glass of water. "I guess that's something you and I need to talk about. The reason I came out."

"This isn't what brought you here?" Jenn gestured to the paper.

"Uh-uh," Chloe said while chewing. Mom didn't even reprimand her. "That's the cherry on top. Have to eat that first before you get to the rest."

Whatever that meant. Hopefully the ice cream analogy meant Chloe had good news.

Chloe finished her second helping, and Mom shooed them from the kitchen. Was she in on this?

Jenn fingered the keys in her pocket as she and Chloe stepped onto the home's front porch. "Want to walk around here or should I drive to the river?" The St. Croix was only about five miles away, and Jenn knew the perfect place for a private talk.

"The river." Chloe's expression didn't give anything away, but her silence did. That told Jenn her daughter had something serious to say. Was it just about the shop? Or Chad? Herself? Jason? All of the above?

Jenn's imagination wanted to shoot off in a million directions, but she banished the wayward thoughts. "The river it is." She aimed her remote at her pickup, unlocking it.

More silence filled the truck's cab on the short drive to the river. Jenn turned down a gravel driveway marked with a Private Property sign. She followed the bumpy road between old growth trees that created a dark but cooling canopy above them. Light shone ahead, and the trees spread apart, opening to a parklike area, also used for a boat launch. Friends of her family owned the place, but they had an open-door policy when it came to using the land. Jenn liked to come sit at the edge of the river, like at home. She'd pray and release her problems and imagine them being whisked away where the St. Croix merged with the Mississippi, then to the Gulf, never to be picked up and carried around again.

Whatever Chloe needed to talk about, hopefully the river would have the same effect on her.

Jenn parked and retrieved a basket from the rear seat. She took bug spray from the basket, and they sprayed each other down. It was always better to be proactive and eliminate the threat in this mosquito-rich area, rather than wait until they got bitten. That happened too much in life.

Then she led Chloe to her favorite spot overlooking the river. Beyond the sight of the boat launch, so that if the neighbors did show up, she and Chloe would have privacy. She took a blanket from her basket and spread it over the ground where insects flourished. Before sitting, she sprayed the blanket, too.

Rather than hounding Chloe for why she'd made the trip way out here without calling first—calling *Jenn* anyway—she sat silent, waiting for Chloe to begin when she was ready.

Chloe picked at the grass, threw it toward the river, and it blew back in their faces. They both laughed, though it was a nervous laugh born of avoidance and anticipation. Her daughter stood, walked closer to the river's edge, near enough to make Jenn nervous. She remained there, her arms crossed, head bowed.

Jenn couldn't remain silent anymore. She joined her daughter, hugged an arm around her shoulders. "What's wrong, Chloe?"

Her daughter sniffled, wiped a hand beneath her nose, inhaled a deep breath. "I lied to you about why Jerkface broke up with me."

Jenn involuntarily stiffened, her anger toward the man who'd used her daughter resurfacing. "You can talk to me."

More silence ensued, followed by a heavy sigh and whispered words. "I told him I was pregnant."

Pregnant . . .

Jenn blinked, trying to sort through the mess of thoughts and emotions swamping through her. Her daughter was pregnant. As Jenn had feared, Chloe had been sleeping with . . . with Jerkface, She clenched her fist at her side, wanting to call him a few names much worse than that. She should contact the college, let them know what their vaunted professor was up to.

And Chloe?

Jenn's arm grew stiff around her daughter's shoulder.

Chloe knew better. Jenn and Chad had raised the twins to wait until marriage. How could Chloe have been so foolish?

Stop it, Jenn.

She inhaled and slowly let out a breath and hugged her daughter closer. Anger and disappointment were exactly the reactions Chloe didn't need right now. Oh, Jenn was her mother's daughter.

Then reality hit, and she gasped. She was going to be a grandma, way too young. Was that why Chloe had been so difficult in that month following Easter? She glanced at Chloe's belly. Her T-shirt clung to her skin, and her belly was flat as ever. She forced the words as gently as she could, "How are you feeling?"

Chloe tugged away and formed an X with her arms over her stomach. "You don't need to worry. I had a miscarriage on Easter morning."

"Oh, baby girl." Jenn closed her eyes, holding in tears. She enveloped her daughter, who fought to be released, but Jenn had none of that. Chloe needed to be hugged, whether she knew it or not. "I am so, so sorry. Why didn't you tell me?"

She sniffled. "I told Dad."

But not me? "I don't understand." She drew her hand down the back of Chloe's head, combing her fingers through her blonde tresses like she used to do before all their lives turned inside out.

Chloe pulled away again, and this time Jenn allowed it and kept her gaze toward the river, her back to her daughter, hoping she'd open up more.

"You're so busy all the time, and I knew you'd be upset, and Dad knows what it's like to be wrongly judged, so I knew he wouldn't judge me."

Meaning, Chloe had believed Jenn would have.

Isn't that the truth?

"Jason has things he hadn't told anyone."

"Like him dating Elaine?"

"Uh-huh. And Dad has stuff too. Until he gets it out, he won't get better."

And they kept it from her because she was a harsh judge. *Okay, God, is this what You wanted to reveal to me during my fasting?* If so, all this felt like a hammer to her psyche. Had she been that poor of a listener that her family was afraid to talk to her? Like Mom had been to her when she'd chosen Chad over Thomas? Maybe they were all better off without her.

No, that last half was a lie, but the first?

She turned to her daughter, who remained a few feet behind her. "I'm sorry I've prioritized the store when I needed to be there for you and that you haven't felt you could come to me. It breaks my heart that I wasn't emotionally available for you. Can you forgive me? I promise to do better."

"It's not just you." Chloe kept her head lowered as her foot drew circle eights in the grass. "I knew you didn't like the jerk, didn't trust him, and that always made me mad. I did some things just to hurt you. I never did love him, but I loved feeling special. I found out how special I was when I told him I was pregnant, and he broke up with me."

Jenn kept silent, though she wanted to give the professor a sound tongue-lashing.

"When I had the miscarriage." Chloe sighed and her shoulders heaved up and down. "I had to blame someone, but I didn't want to blame myself." Chloe looked Jenn in the eyes. "The truth is, you've always listened, always been there for me and supported me. When Jerkface dumped me, he wasn't there to lash out at, so instead, I took my sadness, my anger at myself out on you. You were right not to like him. You were right to question my judgment. You were right to tell me not to sleep with him. I'm finally realizing how stupid I was."

"You're not—"

Chloe raised a hand, silencing Jenn. She sniffled and turned around. Tears washed over her cheeks and her chin quivered. "I held you responsible for a crime you didn't commit. I'm just as bad as that judge and jury that sent Dad to prison, and I am so sorry. Can you forgive me?"

Jenn pressed a hand to her mouth and closed to her eyes, but that didn't contain her own tears. She closed the distance between them and hugged Chloe tightly.

Chloe's tears turned to body-wracking sobs. "It hurts so bad."

"I know." Jenn rubbed her hands down Chloe's back. "I forgive you, baby girl, of course I forgive you."

Jenn shed tears for her daughter's pain, for lost time they could never make up, for the baby they'd never meet. But moving forward, she would change, make certain she was available for her family and prioritize them over the store.

"You'll come home?" Chloe stepped away yet kept her hands on Jenn's arms.

Was that an answer to Jenn's prayer? She looked upward but didn't feel that was the answer. Yet.

"Does your father want me home?" They talked every night, but he hadn't offered the invitation, not that she was waiting for one. Honestly, she didn't know what sign to look for.

Chloe threw her hands in the air as if the answer were obvious. "He's been moping around the apartment since you left."

"But the shop has been doing well, he says."

"Different, but well."

"Different?"

"Guess you'll have to come out and see, won't you?" Chloe wiped the remaining moisture from her cheeks and a grin peeked out on her face.

Now that was the spirit Jenn expected from her daughter. "I will, huh." And she would. Tomorrow even.

"Yep." Chloe pointed to the blanket. "There's something else I need to tell you." She sat cross legged on the blanket. A glow had overtaken her grief. Confession really was good for the soul.

Jenn joined her daughter, promising herself to be open and listen and not judge, no matter what.

"I have a new boyfriend." The shine on her face said she was smitten once again.

Jenn should have guessed. "Tell me about him."

"Well, he's cute."

Of course. Chloe wouldn't settle for less.

"And smart. He's studying to be an architect."

Both were positives.

"Kind."

That put him steps above other boyfriends. Oops, there she went again.

"And you already know him."

"I do?"

"Yep. From the shop. He likes to order *ex*presso." Somehow Chloe's smile grew bigger.

"Carlos?"

Chloe nodded. "Turns out, Jase had been trying to set us up for months, but I was dating the jerk—who Jase hated—and I was clueless. Last week, Carlos came to place his order but asked me out instead."

"I can already tell you I approve a hundred percent, even though he can't say 'espresso.'"

"Oh, but he did. Right after asking me out, he said he'd promise to say *espresso* correctly if I said *yes*."

"And your father approves?"

Chloe shrugged. "He wasn't there at the time, and I wanted to tell you first."

Jenn closed her eyes, absorbing that precious gift. "Thank you."

"You're gonna come out and see Dad?"

"I'll be there tomorrow. Let me surprise him."

"Yay! He's gonna be so happy to see you!"

Chad wiped down the countertop bar that had been occupied much of the day. He couldn't believe how much he'd grown since Jenn had left. Maybe because he'd been forced to interact with the customers, always measuring his responses when someone tried to yank his chain. His knee-jerk reaction to rudeness happened less frequently, and customers were slowly returning.

The mayor's husband had been right. People's memories were very short when they needed their coffee fix. Elaine had forgiven him and now worked beside him often, with her taking the register while he delivered the drinks along with a heavy dose of cockiness. He especially enjoyed the late afternoon shift when men would come in just to talk. He'd give them the ear of a bartender without the intoxication.

This was the life he'd dreamed of.

Well, if Jenn were here, it would be.

Elaine rang up an order, and he turned to create the cappuccino. He began to prep the espresso grounds and heard the bell jingle behind him.

"Welcome to Chad's Choco-Latte Corner." Elaine greeted the new guest. "What can we get started for you today?"

"I need to speak with him."

Chad froze. He recognized that deep timbre, even though he hadn't heard it since the trial. What was he doing here now?

His entire body stiff and fists ready to defend himself, he glanced at Elaine and smiled as friendly as was possible in this moment. "Could you finish this, please?" He gestured to the drink he'd barely begun creating.

"Sure."

Chad moved behind the register. Didn't even try to smile at his former best friend. As much as he wanted to tell Dajon to get his rear end out of the shop, in not such nice terms, he gave the usual spiel without any warmth. "Welcome to Chad's Choco-Latte Corner. What can I get started for you?"

"I'll take a coffee. Plain."

"Haven't changed, have you?" Chad rang up the drink as Dajon held up a five. "It's on the house."

"Thanks." He stuck the Lincoln into the tip jar instead. Elaine would appreciate that.

Chad poured the coffee and placed it on the countertop by where Dajon sat on a barstool, then he looked to Elaine. "Could you take over here for a bit?"

"No problem."

Yeah, for her it wouldn't be a problem. Even if the shop was busy, she could handle it. And to think he'd called her such a despicable name two weeks ago. That she even wanted to work here yet was a true miracle. Amazing what God could heal.

Chad made himself a double espresso and joined Dajon on the front side of the bar. "What brings you here?"

The man sipped at his coffee, then looked straight ahead. "I've been doing some soul searching."

Chad practically laughed, but schooled his expression. "What did you find?"

Dajon turned on his stool, facing Chad.

Chad forced himself to look his former friend in the eye, forced his fists to remain at his sides.

"God and I had it out after the hearing." Dajon took a long sip. "Rather, I did a bunch of smack talking."

Chad nodded. Been there, done that.

"Then after your release, He had me sit down and shut up while He did the talking." Dajon rubbed a hand over his slightly gray beard. "Opened my ears, my eyes." He pounded his chest. "My heart."

That commanded Chad's full attention, and he didn't like it. Not one bit.

"Brother," Dajon continued. "I know what I saw that night, and you looked guilty as sin, and I couldn't lie about that."

Chad started counting down from ten, a calming technique he'd learned from Jenn.

"But I now know you are innocent."

Chad blinked. He'd anticipated maybe an apology, but this? In spite of what he'd believed, what he'd told Jenn at one time, he was still angry at Dajon. He'd become used to carrying around the grudge and didn't want to release it. Without it, he'd feel naked.

"Is there any way . . ." Tears glistened in his friend's—was Dajon still a friend?—eyes. "You'll forgive me?"

Forgive someone for stealing years of his life? Of his family's lives?

How was that even possible?

He glanced upward to do some of his own smack talking with God, but instead heard, *"Forgive as I forgave you."*

Uh-oh. No can do.

"I need a moment." He hurried outside to the river and watched it flow over and around obstacles, never letting them slow or stop it. His jaw tight, he railed up at God, "How can I forgive this? He was my friend, and he stole my life."

Like Jesus' friends stole his. Peter denied Him. Judas betrayed Him. None of the disciples stood up for Him. Yet, Jesus was innocent of any wrongdoing. He was perfection.

Chad was far from perfect, but God had forgiven Him.

And Jenn . . . After what he'd done to her and the kids, she still fought for him. For their marriage.

Elaine had forgiven him. Her dad as well.

Actually, the entire town of Donaldson was in the process of forgiving him. The busy shop proved that.

So, how could he deny his friend?

He sniffled, dried his face, and forced his feet to carry him to the store.

Dajon remained on his stool, his head bowed. Praying?

Chad sat beside him, and Dajon looked over, his expression a mixture of hope and trepidation. Right or wrong, Chad didn't want to simply speak the words of forgiveness. Rather, he first wanted to spread out Dajon's sins on the bar for all to see and hear, but the accusations stuck in his throat.

Instead, he inhaled a deep breath, then extended his hand.

Dajon glanced at Chad's offering.

"I forgive you, man." Freeing the words enveloped Chad in a peace he hadn't anticipated.

Then Dajon's arms were around him, wrapping him in a hug.

Chad didn't care about the people watching, or if the hug was manly or not. He had his friend back, and that was what mattered.

Now, to make life perfect—well, maybe not perfect, but close—all he had to do was convince Jenn to come home to stay.

Chapter Twenty-Seven

Jenn entered through the back door of Chad's Choco-Latte Corner, hoping to surprise Chad. Praying he would be happy to see her, and that he wouldn't tell her he needed more time apart.

Regardless, whatever happened, she was leaving it in God's hands. This battle was His to fight, and He'd give her the words.

She remained in the shadowed hallway, enough so she could observe what was going on in the shop. Chloe was right in saying the shop was different. Physically, all was the same. What had changed was the clientele. In addition to the twenty- to thirty-somethings that had previously frequented the bar, more men with graying or no hair filled the seats. Not exactly the typical customer for a coffee shop. Business owners were always searching for ways to draw in more diverse clientele. Apparently, Chad had discovered it.

To tell the truth, it looked as if she'd stepped into an alcohol-serving bar.

Chad was yakking with three men who had bellied up to the right of the cash register. The register was being run by an older man who looked familiar somehow. Not as a customer, but . . .

She tapped her fingers on her thigh, trying to figure out where she'd seen him before, but nothing came. No matter right now. She'd figure it out. Instead, she focused on Chad.

A light had returned to his eyes, and he was actually looking at people directly, with little effort. Like the Chad she used to know.

Had her moving out been instrumental in his growth? If so, would her coming home stunt that growth?

No, that was more of the devil's whispers, which she'd listened to too often. *Lord, help me hear Your voice and not believe the devil's lies.*

She was praying more now, too. That Bible verse about "praying without ceasing"? She was doing her best to put that into action, something she'd failed to do after opening the shop. In that respect, Chad had put her to shame—he'd continuously sought the Lord without reminder, where she only did so upon witnessing Chad's faithfulness. She'd let her fighting get in the way, when what she should have done was surrender.

She shifted to the other side of the hallway to get a better view of the bar and its patrons. Was that Elaine's father? Jenn had only met him once, and was only seeing part of his profile. She had to be mistaken, because there was no way that man would step into this coffee shop after what Chad had said to Elaine.

Beside him was someone who didn't look familiar, but the man next to him? That couldn't be Dajon, could it?

Chad turned his back for a moment, and she stepped from the safety of the hallway to an empty table close to the bar but not within the normal sightlines. From here, she could hear what they were saying. Yes, she was eavesdropping and didn't feel one ounce of guilt for it.

"How'd you get your prison nickname?" the stranger asked when Chad handed him a paper cup of some beverage.

His prison nickname? Jenn hadn't heard about that.

"Well . . ." Chad refilled the other cups with black coffee. He leaned against the back counter, his focus downward. When he looked up, his expression had turned serious. "I'd only been there a couple weeks, but it seemed like forever. Prison scared the heck out of me. I was this scrawny guy living among men who'd murdered people. And bragged about it. I was the type that they'd . . ." Chad looked upward, likely lifting a prayer.

"Take your time," the man on the right said.

Chad lowered his head, cleared his throat, and spoke barely above a whisper, but she could read what his lips said. "They'd gang rape."

Jenn slapped a hand to her lips, and tears formed. She'd heard about that happening but hadn't wanted to believe it could happen to Chad. No wonder he was a broken man.

"I was cornered by three men, and I thought for sure that this was it, that I'd be meeting Jesus, but then . . ." He shook his head. "It had to be the Holy Spirit. I shouted out, 'I'm a child of God. You will not harm me.' And they stopped."

Dear God, thank You!

"You should have seen the look of terror on their faces as they turned and ran, saying, 'The dude's an angel.' Well, their language wasn't quite as clean." Chad finally smiled.

And Jenn breathed easier. Still, the terror he must have felt was unfathomable.

"You think they really saw an angel?" This from the man who really looked like Elaine's father, especially with the prosthetic leg.

"That's my only explanation. Happened one other time as well when I was in big trouble, so my nickname became Angel. One inmate tattooed the cross on my shoulder blade, signifying I'm part of God's gang. For the most part, after that, I was left alone. Cons gossip more than women at a knitting party."

All three men guffawed at that.

But she couldn't. How many other horror stories did Chad have that he hadn't felt free to share with her? That had to change, starting right now.

She stood, the chair scraping against the floor enough to draw attention from the bar area. She gasped. It was Dajon. And Elaine's dad. Seeing both men here, laughing and talking with Chad, was a true miracle, though her stomach knotted at the sight of Dajon.

Keeping her focus on her husband, she walked toward him, and his gaze ratcheted onto hers. She smiled, and he grinned.

The men peeled away from the counter, giving her space.

She looked up at the menu to see if anything else had changed. There were fewer non-coffee options, which wasn't a surprise.

"Welcome to Chad's Choco-Latte Corner." Chad bent toward her, a familiar twinkle in his eye. "What type of coffee beverage can I serve you today?"

"Hmm." She tapped her lip. "I'll have a hot cocoa."

He slapped a hand to his heart, feigning shock. "When it's ninety degrees outside, you want a hot cocoa?"

She studied the beverages on the counter, steam rising from all three. "You're drinking hot coffee. How is that different?"

"How is that different?" He planted both hands on the counter, looking much like the young man who'd flirted with her over twenty years ago. "Does hot cocoa wake you up in the morning, turn your grumps into grins? Does it clear your mind? Energize you? Make the sun look brighter? Coffee is a balm for your soul. And don't forget all the health benefits."

He held up a hand and raised a finger with each point. "It has antioxidants. It's good for your heart and your memory. Some folks say it'll cure cancer. And it keeps you regular, if you know what I mean," he said with a wink and a grin.

She chuckled, recalling a similar sales pitch when she'd first met the cute barista. He'd aged, but he was still adorable.

"See, I'm winning you over to the dark-roast side." He grinned. "Now tell me which coffee beverage you're going to try."

With as straight a face as she could muster, she said, "I'll have a hot cocoa with whipped cream on top. Please."

He released a dramatic sigh and shook his head. "You have no clue what you're missing."

"I think I do." Her expression turned serious and she rested her hands, palms up and open, on the bar top, hoping he'd accept them. "I'm missing this. I'm missing you."

The men who'd remained near the bar scattered, probably to be polite, but they could have stayed. She wouldn't mind their ear- and eyewitness.

"Me too." Chad's fingers closed around hers.

She blew out a relieved sigh and clung to him, never wanting to let go again. "Why didn't you ever tell me about Angel? About prison life?"

His gaze focused on defects in the bar top. "There's a lot I haven't told you—things you shouldn't have to know about."

"Things you shouldn't have to be burdened with on your own. That's what I'm here for."

"But—"

"No more buts. Only truth."

He nodded, but didn't look convinced.

Maybe this would convince him. "Speaking of the truth, I want to come home, but you should also know that I've been offered a job."

He loosened his grip on her. "I don't understand. By your folks' place?"

"Yes, I received an offer there, but I didn't accept it."

"Oh?" Light and hope shone on his face.

"I'm talking about a job offer much closer, here in Donaldson."

That fully restored his smile. "You want to teach?"

She nodded. "I really do. I miss it. And this?" She glanced around the shop. "It was always for you."

"Let me get this straight." He leaned back but didn't release her hands. "You want me to handle the shop while you teach."

She nodded, nibbled on her lower lip. "If that's okay with you. Looks like you have everything under control here."

Momentarily, he looked down, then scanned the shop. All eyes were on them, and that was okay. Good, even. Her husband was home.

Chad kept one of her hands in his while he gestured to the guests. "I'm finding a lot of people who need a listening ear. Veterans." He nodded to Patrick Kim. "Ex-cons." He gave a side nod to the man at the register.

She snapped her fingers at the recognition. Adam, the homeless man Chloe had helped shortly after the store opened. She shouldn't be surprised that Chad had hired him.

"Even old friends." Dajon came up beside her.

She gasped and shifted away from the man who had torn their lives apart.

"It's okay." Chad squeezed her hand. "The two of us battled it out with God. We're good now."

Jenn gulped, but still kept her distance. Maybe Chad and Dajon had worked it out, but Jenn wasn't ready for that. Yet. Thankfully, Dajon stepped way, and she breathed a sigh of relief, but her heart still pattered at a furious clip.

Chad shared a smile that told her he understood, then he glanced around the room. "So many here need a place that doesn't offer alcohol or drugs to chase your demons." Chad stood tall, shoulders squared. "I'm continuing Garrett's legacy."

"He would be proud of you."

Chad half smiled at Jenn. "What about you?"

"Am I proud of you?" So much so, she wanted to kiss him right here in front of everyone. "Immensely, but I need to apologize first."

"I'm the one who recommended separating." Chad averted his gaze. "There's no need for you to apologize."

"But there is." She raised his chin. "When you got out of prison, I could see your depression, felt you pushing away from me, and I kept fighting back until I had no more energy. The truth is, I'd stopped praying for us, even though, all along, you set the example. When you faced hardships, prayer was your first thought. It was my last. It *had* been my last, but I've spent the past two weeks fighting on my knees for us, and that's a fight I won't ever give up. You are too important to me to ever give up praying for you. For us."

"Jenn." He sighed and motioned with his head for her to come around the counter.

She held her breath as she made her way to the back of the bar, to Chad.

He held out his hands, and she grasped them. He rested his forehead against hers. "I've got baggage, Cocoa, issues I might spend the rest of my life working on."

"I know," she whispered. "And I need to be here to help you. I want to listen, to hear about those things that hurt you, that still grip you."

"Like my story about Angel?" He searched her eyes. "It's not pretty."

"Which is why you need to set it free. If it takes spending every night for the rest of our lives at the river, releasing our problems and letting the waters carry them away, that's what we'll do."

"You would do that for me?"

"I would." She pulled away a few inches. "But I have an important question to ask first."

"Oh yeah?" His lips quirked to the side in his familiar smirk, but worry still floated in his eyes. "Would that be, do you love me?"

She laughed. "That would be, do you know that I'm in love with you, Chad Taylor?"

"In love, eh?" The worry lines on his face vanished, and a flirty smirk took their place.

"And you?" She nibbled on her lower lip.

The adorable grin broke out on his face, and he inched closer, tempting her to narrow the gap and kiss him before he could answer. "Cocoa, I've been in love with you since that first time you stepped up to the counter at Cuppa Truth and asked for hot cocoa."

She could tease, too. "Oh really?" She drew closer yet, his lips a mere breath away.

"Would you kiss the woman already?" Dajon yelled out, and other patrons echoed the sentiment.

"Don't mind if I do." Chad released her hands, cupped her cheek with the slightest of touches. He closed the gap and kissed her.

Heaven help her, she wrapped her arms around him and kissed him until the room broke out into cheers.

"Geez, would you guys get a room?"

Jason? She broke off the kiss and spun toward her son.

No surprise, Chloe was by his side, not rolling her eyes, but grinning. "You'd think you guys were married or something."

"Hey, that's a good idea." Chad snapped his fingers, then he was down on a knee behind the bar. "Cocoa, would you marry me again—renew our vows?"

"Yes!" Chloe clapped.

And Jenn shot her a look that said, *be quiet*. Then she smiled at her husband. "Chad, not Chadwick, not Nebu-Chad-Nezzer, I'd be honored to marry you again, as long as I don't have to drink coffee." If they could survive these past eight years, they could survive anything. And if life threw more at them, she'd know which weapon worked best for fighting their battles.

He pouted, but then stood and kissed her again. Much too soon, he stepped back and grasped her hand. "Let's go."

"What? Where?" He practically dragged her around the bar.

"Chloe. Call Mayor Barbara, tell her we need her. Jason, lock the front door and grab your guitar."

Jenn tore her hand from Chad's. "What are you doing?"

"Going to say our vows again."

"Whoa. I thought you meant we'd plan something for a few months out. Dress nice. Have a party."

"Babe, seriously. I've been without you for two weeks. I don't think I can handle another night."

Chloe pulled the phone from her ear. "TMI, Dad."

All the rascal did was grin.

"You're serious." Jenn remained rooted in the dining room. "You want to renew our vows, right now, when I look like this." She motioned at her T-shirt and shorts. She hated to think what her hair and makeup looked like in this heat and humidity.

"You've never looked more beautiful. The guests are all here. Chloe's arranging for the mayor to preside."

"She's coming." Chloe tucked her phone into a pocket.

"And you're full of it." Jenn poked Chad in the chest, and he grinned. Oh, was she going to give it to him when they were alone.

"Goin' at it like an old married couple," one of the patrons hollered out, and the now locked-in customers laughed.

"Jenn." He touched her cheek. "I am serious. You couldn't be more beautiful to me than you are right now."

Jenn propped her hands on her hips. "I'd like to challenge that assertion."

"Me too." Chloe piped in a little too eagerly. "Dad, you've gotta give Mom time to freshen up, put on something . . ."

"Sexy?"

"Dad!" Chloe shook her head. "At least let Mom do her hair and makeup and put on something nice."

"And let me call my parents and your father." This spontaneous celebration suddenly excited Jenn too. It would be a perfect way to take that next step, to refresh their marriage. To remind Chad that she was with him, no matter the obstacles placed in their way.

"Fine." Chad raised his hands. "I'll call Dad."

"I talked with Gran." Even Jason got into the fun. "She and Pops are on their way."

"Any more excuses, Cocoa?" Chad grinned.

She wanted to kiss it right off his face. "I guess we're having a party, and you're all invited." She pointed to the clock. "See you out by the river in two hours."

Only two hours? Jenn sat on the end of her bed staring in the mirror on the dresser at her mess of hair. What had she been thinking to agree to such a ridiculous timeframe? At least it was going to be dark outside by the time the ceremony started, so no one would see how awful she looked.

Her hair. Nails. Makeup. Ugh.

The dress was a winner, though. She'd showered while Chloe picked out a sundress Jenn had recently purchased for a special occasion. If she'd only known what occasion that would be. The fabric had muted purple flowers. The neck draped in front, not enough to show cleavage, although it definitely hinted at it. Spaghetti straps crossed in the back, and a slit ran up the left leg, enough to entice. So, yeah, Chad would like it.

But now she had to do her hair while Chloe was off playing Miss Wedding Planner. The only hair skill she had was putting it up in a ponytail. Why had she agreed to this?

Someone knocked.

"If that's Chad, you need to stay out."

"It's your mother, dear."

Oh, yippee. Just in time to be warned once again that she was making a huge mistake. Still, Jenn welcomed her mother in.

The door opened slowly. Mom squeezed through a slim opening and shut the door. "You never know when the men might show up."

"It's not a wedding, Mom."

"Yes, but this is still important. It shows you're both dedicated to each other."

"You approve?"

Mom sighed. "I know I make a lot of noise, but that's only because I want the best for you. After you moped around our house for the past two weeks, I assured Chad that I am one hundred percent for this renewal."

A backhanded way of saying this was right, but Jenn would accept it.

"And now we have to solve this problem." Her mom stood over Jenn, eyeing her mess of hair.

"That bad?" Jenn wrinkled her nose.

"Nothing I can't fix. Direct me to your supplies."

Jenn pointed to the top dresser drawer. "It's all I have."

"Then it will be enough."

Thirty minutes later, Mom had done a miracle with Jenn's normally straight hair, now draping downward in luscious waves. Mom helped with her makeup, her nails, and then some alterations on the dress. Turned out, she'd lost some weight during her fast. If she said so herself, she looked pretty darn good.

Chloe burst into the bedroom, looking like she'd spent two hours sprucing up, when it had only been about fifteen minutes. "Mom, are you ready?" She handed Jenn a bouquet made of purple hyacinths and baby's breath, just like the one from her wedding.

"Fiona's Flowers?" Jenn breathed in their fragrance.

"Yep." She pointed to the door with the ribboned candle she held. "Everyone's waiting."

That time already?

Jenn inhaled a slow, cleansing breath, talking to God for the umpteenth time today, making sure this was the right thing to do. All she saw in her mind were hands applauding.

"I'm ready, except for one little detail." Her nose wrinkled as she glared at her feet covered in old, falling apart dress sandals. She hadn't purchased new ones yet, because there hadn't been a need. Today, there hadn't been time for shoe shopping.

Chloe shrugged. "Go barefoot. You'll be walking on grass, right?"

"Barefoot?" Jenn said simultaneously with her mom.

"Why not?" Chloe kicked off her sandals.

"Oh, why not?" Mom even kicked hers off.

"If you can't beat 'em." Jenn stepped out of the sandals. "It's a memory maker, right?"

"You know Dad'll like it."

"He'll tease me endlessly."

Chloe grinned and dramatically bowed toward the open door. "Shall we go?"

"Let's do this." Jenn led the way from the bedroom, aiming for the apartment door.

"Uh-uh. Gran and I go first. We have to time this right."

"Whatever you say. I'm only the bride."

Chloe smiled as she sent a text message. "It's time."

It's time.

Honestly, Jenn felt as giddy now as she had for their wedding. This was the right thing to do. Frightening, too, knowing how very broken they both were.

Chloe opened the apartment door, and Dad waited at the bottom, all decked out in a suit. A rare occasion for him, but he looked handsome.

The three women descended the stairs. Chloe and Mom slipped outside as Dad took her arm.

"You look as lovely as you did twenty-some years ago."

Her blush was her thank you.

She heard guitar chords being played, and two lovely voices began singing. Jason, she knew, but who else?

The door opened wide, and Jenn gasped. Strings of lights draped over posts spotlighting a path to the river. By the river, lights bedazzled trees, making it look as if the stars were meeting them below, not just blinking from above. Somehow her family and friends had recreated their wedding.

Oh great, she was already getting misty-eyed, and she hadn't even set foot on the grass. By the time she reached Chad, she'd look like a zombie.

Jason—and Elaine!—were set up behind the guests, singing. How very *Jason* of them to stay out of the spotlight. Together they sang "All Things New," one of her favorites from Big Daddy Weave. Weren't she and Chad proof that God made all things new?

Her dad led her over the path, past Jason and Elaine, and through the aisle between four rows of chairs.

Chad stood at the end in a suit that Chloe had dug up from somewhere. Maybe it was Jason's? In the dark, she couldn't read his expression, but she could imagine the half smirk, half smile he wore so well.

Barbara stood beside him. Neither had on shoes.

Jenn tried to contain it, but still laughed out loud.

"What's so funny?" Dad glanced around the yard.

"Nothing. Everything's beautiful."

And it was. No doubt, Chloe was behind all the personal invites. Even with the lights twinkling, she barely made out who the guests were as they passed the rows of chairs. There was Caleb and his wife. The shop's newest employee, whom she hadn't been formally introduced to. Dajon and his wife. Elaine's father.

At last, Chad's face came into view. Tears dripped over his cheeks.

Drats. Now, her eyes wanted to leak again, too.

Dad released her arm and shook Chad's hand. "I trust you'll take good care of my daughter."

"I promise," Chad said to Dad with his gaze not wavering from her. He took her arm, kissed her cheek, and whispered, "You take my breath away."

Her voice caught, and she couldn't reply. They turned to the front, facing Barbara.

Uh-oh. Now what? They hadn't rehearsed. Hadn't talked about what they wanted said. Did she need to say something other than "I do"? She lifted a prayer, asking for calm. It would all work out, even if she was clueless.

Barbara folded her hands and said a prayer over Jenn, Chad, and the guests, then she opened her Bible. "Jenn and Chad, I love your story. Twenty-four years ago, you met over coffee and cocoa. Three years later you promised to love, honor, and cherish each other through sickness and in health. Today you're renewing your vows at a coffee and cocoa shop. An outsider would say, 'How romantic' without knowing the strife you walked through in those years."

She flipped a page in her Bible. "But the point is, you've kept walking through. You didn't stop when life flung obstacles your way that few of us could imagine. I know it hasn't been easy, but the two of you are proof of what Solomon says in Ecclesiastes 4:12, that '. . . a cord of three strands is not easily broken.' Both Matthew and Mark tell us that, 'What therefore God has joined together, let not man separate.'"

She lowered her Bible, glanced from Jenn to Chad. "Most of the witnesses here today will affirm that the two of you have certainly had your share of circumstances doing their best to pull you apart, yet you remained strong."

Jenn shared a glance with Chad, both agreeing that Barbara was being generous.

"Ah, I saw that look you shared." Barbara wagged her finger. "Now, I know it hasn't been perfect for you, don't mistake what I said for that. The point is, you've endured. And not on your own strength, but by relying on the Lord. He's that third strand that's held you together when the world wanted to tear you apart. My husband and I have learned much from your battle, and I trust others have as well."

She closed her Bible and held it in front of herself. "Would either of you like to say anything?"

Jenn felt her eyes go as wide as one of the pinecones hanging from the trees surrounding them.

"I've got something." No surprise, Chad had a bit to say. She'd gladly let him speak for them both. He turned to her, took her hands in his. "Cocoa, I know life hasn't been easy for you and the kids. In prison, three things kept me going. God, you, and the kids." He grinned. "I guess that's four things."

The guests all chuckled.

"It was your constant encouragement, your letters, your prayers that lifted me up, that gave me a reason not to give up. Knowing I had you to come home to kept me alive. Now, I know that things haven't been easy since I got home. I've changed. You've grown. And blending all that together has been tough. But we serve a mighty God who isn't afraid of mixing the tough parts of our lives. I know it won't be easy going forward, I know we each will have to give and take, but with you, Cocoa, the fight will be worth it. And I'm so blessed that you love me, a very broken man."

Jenn couldn't refrain from hugging that broken man, whispering to him that she loved him, as God gave her words. "And I stand before you a broken woman. Too often when we're fighting for an important cause, we forget to weave in that third strand. I too often forgot that God would do the fighting for us. Yet I love how God has taken our broken pieces and bonded them together into this breathtaking mosaic. We are broken together, and that's something beautiful."

A guest sniffled, but she refrained from looking, afraid she'd join in.

Barbara opened her Bible again, squinted at a piece of paper she removed from it. "Chad Taylor, do you reaffirm your love for Jennifer? Do you promise to love her through sickness and health, for richer or poorer, through all life's challenges, and to be faithful to her as long as you both shall live?"

He looked Jenn square in the eye without difficulty. "Oh, I definitely do. I love you even more than coffee."

Jenn laughed, as did their guests.

"Jennifer Miller Taylor," Barbara continued, "do you reaffirm your love for Chad? Do you promise to love him through sickness and health, for richer or poorer, through all life's challenges, and to be faithful to him as long as you both shall live?"

To answer, Jenn kissed Chad, then said, "I do, too. I love you far more than hot cocoa."

"You cheated," he whispered.

She shrugged. "Couldn't help myself, and I promise a whole lot more than that."

"Geez, Mom, TMI," Chloe said from the front row, but there was definitely sunshine in her words.

"Well, then." Barbara closed the Bible and held her arms out to the side. "By the power vested in me as mayor of Donaldson and best friend to the bride, I verify your vows are renewed. *Now* you may kiss each other."

"Don't mind if I do." Chad took Jenn's hand, shook it. Gave her a too-quick hug. Kissed her on the cheek.

Her mouth fell open.

"What?" He shrugged. "That's how we did it in prison."

"This is how we do it on the outside." She wrapped her arms around his neck, then feathered her lips across his. Chad took it deeper and she gladly obliged, to the cheering of the guests and the groaning of their kids, until her legs felt wobbly, and she struggled for breath.

With a happy sigh, she pulled away and looked her husband in his glinting eyes.

"And that, my dear Cocoa." He kissed her one more time. "Is how we'll do it for the rest of our lives together."

"So if the Son sets you free, you will be free indeed."
John 8:36

Dear Reader,

Thank you for reading Broken Together. Years ago, I watched a late-night interview with a woman who'd fought to free her husband from prison, and she finally won that fight. Then the interviewer asked how she and her husband were doing now, and she replied that they were divorced. It shocked me that she'd fought so hard for him, but then couldn't hold their marriage together. I knew then that I needed to explore through fiction how that could happen, and Jenn and Chad's story was born.

The truth is that their marriage couldn't have survived without God holding them together. That's really true for all of us.

If you'd like to read about Jenn and Chad's romance, check out my short story, "Hot Cocoa Summers," which first appeared in the Before Summer's End Mosaic anthology. And if you'd like to know more about Thomas, you'll find his story, "Broken Noel," in The Heart of Christmas, A Mosaic Christmas Anthology III.

If you enjoyed Broken Together, please consider sharing a book review telling others why you liked the story. Your review doesn't have to be long or eloquent, just honest.

You'll find additional inspiration and encouragement at www.MosaicCollectionBooks.com and by reading other books in this uplifting series.

To be notified of all my upcoming releases, join my email list http://brendaandersonbooks.com/subscribe/. As a Thank You for subscribing, you will receive a Free copy of "Coming Home," a Coming Home Series short story.

Thank you for joining me on this writing journey.

God bless,

Brenda

Hot Cocoa Summers

a short story

To barista Chad Taylor, life is always better with a cup of coffee,
so when spunky Jennifer Miller walks in and orders hot cocoa—
in the middle of summer!—he's challenged to win her over
to the dark roast side!
His heart tells him that's not the only challenge Jennifer brings.

Purchase **Hot Cocoa Summers** separately,
or read it in The Mosaic Anthology, **Before Summer's End**.

ACKNOWLEDGEMENTS

This book, perhaps more than any other I've written, has taught me how true it is that writers do not tell a story on their own.

Applause to my daughter Sarah for helping me maneuver through the coffee shop world. Like Jenn, I'm a cocoa drinker and am clueless when it comes to coffee. With all the help Sarah provided on this book, it only made sense to give her second billing.

Thank you, Julie Jonas, Legal Director for The Great North Innocence Project, for answering my many questions and helping me understand the legalities involved in freeing the innocent. Any mistakes in this story are my own.

Thank you, Lesley Ann McDaniel and Sara Davison—editors extraordinaire!—for helping make this story so much better!

Book Boosters – Thank you for helping to spread the word about *Broken Together*. You help make every project a success!

Readers – You are why we write! Thank you for spending valuable time with my characters.

To Bryan and Brandon for your continued support and encouragement. I look forward to the day when I'm reading your work in a book!

Marvin, your support of this writing career of mine is what real love looks like. I've loved traveling this journey with you.

Whenever I've sat at the computer to write during these past couple of years, I've done so with a blank mind, and I've prayerfully sought help. Every time I sat and put my fingers to the keyboard, You supplied me with inspiration and words and taught me that obedience matters. Saying Thank You is never enough. It's my prayer that readers will see You through the words.

Also By

Brenda S. Anderson

A BEAUTIFUL MESS

"Anderson delivers an impactful story about the power of faith within flawed, complicated people. . . . Readers who enjoy the work of Karen Kingsbury should check this out."

—**Publishers Weekly**/Booklife

A BEAUTIFUL CHRIST-MESS

A Mosaic Collection Short Story

When prodigal son Zachary Belden returns home at Christmas to surprise his family with news, he's surprised with other news that turns his surprise into a big mess and challenges his newfound faith.

Books by Brenda S. Anderson

THE MOSAIC COLLECTION
Broken Together
Pieces of Granite
A Beautiful Mess

THE MOSAIC COLLECTION ANTHOLOGIES
Hope is Born: A Mosaic Christmas Anthology
Before Summer's End
A Star Will Rise: A Mosaic Christmas Anthology II
The Heart of Christmas: A Mosaic Christmas Anthology III

THE POTTER'S HOUSE BOOKS | One
Long Way Home
Place Called Home
Home Another Way

THE POTTER'S HOUSE BOOKS | TWO
Hands of Grace
Song of Mercy
Season of Hope

WHERE THE HEART IS SERIES
Risking Love
Capturing Beauty
Planting Hope

COMING HOME SERIES

Pieces of Granite

Chain of Mercy

Memory Box Secrets

Hungry for Home

Coming Home – A Short Story

www.BrendaAndersonBooks.com/books

Books in

THE MOSAIC COLLECTION

When Mountains Sing by Stacy Monson

Unbound by Eleanor Bertin

The Red Journal by Deb Elkink

A Beautiful Mess by Brenda S. Anderson

Hope is Born: A Mosaic Christmas Anthology

More Than Enough by Lorna Seilstad

The Road to Happenstance by Janice L. Dick

This Side of Yesterday by Angela D. Meyer

Lost Down Deep by Sara Davison

The Mischief Thief by Johnnie Alexander

Before Summer's End: Stories to Touch the Soul, A Mosaic Anthology

Tethered by Eleanor Bertin

Calm Before the Storm by Janice L. Dick

Heart Restoration by Regina Rudd Merrick
Watercolors by Lorna Seilstad
A Star Will Rise: A Mosaic Christmas Anthology II
Totally Booked: A Book Lover's Companion
Eye of the Storm by Janice L. Dick
Lifelines by Eleanor Bertin
The Third Grace by Deb Elkink
Crazy about Maisie by Janice L. Dick
Rebuilding Joy by Regina Rudd Merrick
Song of Grace: Stories to Amaze the Soul, A Mosaic Anthology
Out of the Storm by Janice L. Dick
Written in Ink by Sara Davison
Open Circle by Stacy Monson
The Heart of Christmas: A Mosaic Christmas Anthology III
Where Hope Starts by Angela D. Meyer
Flame of Mercy by Eleanor Bertin
Through the Lettered Veil by Candace West
Broken Together by Brenda S. Anderson

Learn more at www.MosaicCollectionBooks.com/Books

Coming soon to

THE MOSAIC COLLECTION

EVERY STAR IN THE SKY

By Sara Davison

She is willing to testify against her trafficker.
If she can stay alive that long.

"You're safe here, Starr."

How many times has Detective Cole Blacksky said that to her since helping her escape the life she'd been forced into eight years earlier?

Starr desperately wants to believe him, but she knows Brady Erickson, her former captor, too well. Although Cole has promised her protective custody on his family's remote ranch, no place on earth is safe enough. Brady will stop at nothing to permanently silence her before she ever reaches the witness stand.

And he is powerful enough to do it.

If Starr wants to help the other women, she has no choice but to put herself in God's hands. And Cole's. But the longer she and Cole stay hidden, the more her life is at risk. And her heart.

EVERY STAR IN THE SKY

By Sara Davison

Chapter One

"Desiree's pregnant."

The words, whispered from girl to girl and accompanied by furtive glances around to make sure no one else was nearby, turned the blood coursing through Starr ice cold. No. How could this have happened? Whenever Brady brought a new girl in, the first thing he did was call for the doctor to come examine her and insert an IUD. Brady prided himself on running a clean house and on ensuring that none of the girls contracted any diseases. Or got pregnant.

Starr had only known it to happen once in the eight years since she'd been forced into service for Brady. Charlotte. She shuddered. Within hours of Charlotte whispering her secret to Starr between bouts of weeping and plaintive wails to help her, Brady and one of his men had dragged Charlotte from her room in the dark of night. Starr never saw her again.

Grabbing a robe from her closet, she slipped into the hallway and crept toward Desiree's room. Somehow, they had to find a way to keep Brady from finding out before they could figure out what to do to help her.

Boots thudded along the hallway from the other direction. It was too late. Starr stopped a few yards from Desiree's room and pressed into a shadowy doorway. Her breath tangled in her throat. Brady and two of his men. They stopped outside Desiree's room and Brady jerked his head at the door. One of the men with him flung it open and the three of them disappeared into the room. Desiree cried out and Starr pressed her eyes shut tightly. Her heart thudded against her rib cage. Was there anything she could do?

Several other doors along the hall slid open a crack, but no one else dared to step out of their rooms.

"Starr!" Desiree's anguished cry as Brady's henchmen dragged her into the hallway spurred Starr into action.

She opened her eyes and pushed away from the doorway. "Brady." She made her way toward the group on trembling legs.

Brady stood with his back to her, arms crossed over his chest, as hard and unmoveable as an oak. "Stay out of this, Starr. It's none of your business." His voice held a steel-cold warning.

Normally she would have heeded that warning, knowing what would happen if she didn't. Tonight, she couldn't.

With her light brown skin—an inheritance from her Filipino mother—and piercing blue eyes from a Caucasian father she'd never known, Starr was in high demand among Brady's clients. And she earned him far more money than any of the other girls did. Sometimes that meant she had a little more leeway to talk back to him than the rest of them did.

Desiree yanked her arm from the grip of one of the men and reached out for her, the gold charm bracelet she always wore jangling against her wrist. The man grasped her arm again and twisted it behind her back. Desiree whimpered. Starr summoned up every ounce of courage she had in her. "Please don't do this, Brady. I'll take care of her, I promise."

"She was stupid enough to get pregnant; she deserves what she gets."

Anger flared, sending a rush of heat through Starr. "Stupid? Do you think she asked to have an endless line of disgusting men coming to her and . . . ?"

Even before he moved, she knew she'd gone too far. Brady uncrossed his arms and whirled around, his eyes hard as flint. "Stay with Desiree," he ordered the men over his shoulder as he started for Starr. Before she could get out of his way, he had wrapped his fingers around her elbow in an iron-tight grasp and hauled her along the hallway to the doorway of her room. Starr pressed her lips together to keep from crying out at the pain that shot up and down her arm. Brady stopped and spun her around to face him. He looked like something out of Greek mythology—tall, blond, and muscular with a close-trimmed gold beard. His good looks and the charm he could turn off and on at will had lured more than one woman into this house. Of course, they found out quickly that the gorgeous exterior masked a cold, cruel monster. By then it was too late.

"If you say one more word, I'll let the boys handle Desiree while you and I take a trip to the basement."

His face was so close to hers she could feel the heat of his breath as he spoke. The intense fury coursing through her was doused immediately. Brady did not allow drugs in his house. He preferred to use intimidation and fear to keep everyone in line, and he yielded both weapons with the deadly effectiveness of a Samurai warrior. Terror rose to take the place of anger, drying out Starr's mouth and throat so she couldn't have spoken if she wanted to.

Brady tightened his grip on her arm, his fingers digging into bone. "Is that what you want?"

Starr held out for three seconds, her eyes welded on his, before shaking her head, slightly.

"I didn't think so." Brady shoved her through the doorway. "Do not let me see you again tonight or that's exactly what will happen."

He slammed the door. Starr stared at the back of it for a moment before stalking over and grabbing the knob. Then Brady's threat hacked its way through her muddled thoughts and she stopped, paralyzed. The basement. Slowly, she let go of the knob and backed away from the door. When she reached the wall, she slid along it to the floor, wrapping her arms around her legs and lowering her head to her knees. Brady never made idle threats. If she opened the door to her room, he would take her to the basement. And after what had happened down there the last time, she doubted she would survive the trip. Even given her value to him, she had no illusions about her standing in this house—he wouldn't hesitate to kill her if she crossed another line with him, if only to make an example of her to the others.

Her elbow throbbed and wave after wave of cold chills shuddered through her. Jesus, help Desiree. I can't. Only you can. Her chest ached, but she didn't cry. She'd wept almost every night the first year she'd been brought to this house. After Charlotte was taken away, she stopped weeping. What good did tears do? Only got her in more trouble if she was caught shedding them.

"Starr."

The heart-rending cry drifted along the hallway to her. Starr let go of her legs and covered her face with her hands. If she lived to be a hundred years old—which, given the life she'd been dragged into against her will, wasn't likely—she would never forget the sound of Desiree calling out her name in the night before she disappeared forever.

About the Authors

Brenda S. Anderson writes authentic, gritty, life-affirming fiction that shows God at work in people's messy lives. She enjoys live music and theater, walking the shores of Lake Superior, and sharing hot cocoa with friends and family. She lives near Minneapolis with her newly retired husband. Together, they plan to travel across the United States, checking items off their bucket list, beginning with a bus trip to Niagara Falls.

A former barista, **Sarah S. Anderson** loves all things coffee, so when her mother asked her to help with a book set in a coffee shop, the answer was an enthusiastic "Yes!" When not creating imaginary coffee shops, Sarah spends much of her time at the theater, either on stage acting, singing, and dancing, or offstage as musical director. She lives near the heart of Minneapolis with her two cuddly kitties.

Let's Connect

Visit Brenda online at www.BrendaAndersonBooks.com and on Facebook, Goodreads, Instagram, and BookBub.

For news and encouragement about upcoming books, contests, giveaways, and other activities, sign up for Brenda's monthly newsletter at BrendaAndersonBooks.com/subscribe.

CPSIA information can be obtained
at www.ICGtesting.com
Printed in the USA
LVHW040728310523
748468LV00013B/48